Swan Music

SARAH HARRISON

Swan Music

HODDER &
STOUGHTON

Hodder & Stoughton

Copyright © 2005 by Sarah Harrison

First published in Great Britain in 2005 by Hodder and Stoughton
A division of Hodder Headline

The right of Sarah Harrison to be identified as the Author of the Work has been
asserted by her in accordance with the Copyright, Designs and Patents Act 1988

1 3 5 7 9 10 8 6 4 2

A CIP catalogue record for this title is available from the British Library

HB ISBN 0 340 82851 X
TPB ISBN 0 340 82852 8

Typeset in Plantin Light by Palimpsest Book Production Limited,
Polmont, Stirlingshire

Printed in Great Britain by
Clays Ltd, St Ives plc

Hodder Headline's policy is to use papers that are natural, renewable and
recyclable products and made from wood grown in sustainable forests. The
logging and manufacturing processes are expected to conform to the
environmental regulations of the country of origin

For Wizz, my dearest coz

I

The swans had their territory; the boys had theirs. From their respective river banks the two factions watched each other, ready for fight or flight. Of the two, the swans, under threat from the old enemy, were the more dangerous.

The boys sat on a wooden bench. Among the rest of the rubbish surrounding the bench was the plastic carrier bag containing the aerosol can they'd been sniffing. On this golden late summer's day one had a hat pulled down low over his brow, the other wore an outsize top with a hood that obscured his face. The civic environmental improvement scheme on the part of the river bank where they sat had been only partly successful. Graffiti-scribbled concrete and brick walls rose at their backs. Between the walls an alley scuttled away in the direction of the industrial estate and the edge-of-town retail park beyond. A litter bin overflowed, attended by dawdling, gluttonous wasps. A perky red dog-nuisance container had been largely ignored.

At this point in its journey the river was like a moat, separating the town from its surrounding countryside; so the swans' territory, by contrast, was unspoilt. The bank on their side was divided into a sequence of small islands and promontories where the river had pushed long fingers into the marshy ground. Sedge and spiky grasses gave way to reed beds and shocks of bullrushes. Behind them was a line of trees, and beyond that brown fields, already ploughed after a long spell of good weather, rose glinting in the sun.

'A rat!' The boy in the hood stood up, pointing, his sleeve dangling over his hand. 'A fucking rat!'

'Get it!'

The second boy picked up a scrunched Coke can and shied it inexpertly at the water vole, managing only to disturb its small wake; and the cob, who left his mate and lowered himself into the river, gliding towards the boys with his wings arched in discreet warning.

The first boy snatched up the plastic carrier bag and held the aerosol over his head.

'Watch this, I can get him, no sweat!'

He was a better shot than his friend, and the empty tin hit the side of the cob's neck and fell harmlessly into the water. Furious, his warning ignored and his territory invaded, the cob reared up on the surface, hissing, his wings spread, his head thrust forward like a cobra, before steaming forward on the attack. It was fortunate for the boys that he couldn't get out, the bank having been built up with grey brick which afforded no foothold.

Jeering nervously, they scrabbled around for more missiles, but they were befuddled and unsteady and by the time they'd found another can and a plastic bottle the swan was already returning to his mate, his wings at half-mast, signalling his disdain.

The boy in the hat sat down on the bench and took a packet of cigarettes from his pocket, offering one to his friend. The hooded boy helped himself and sat down at the river's edge, his legs dangling over.

'Watch it, he'll come after you!'

'I'll move then, won't I?' he mumbled. His hand shook as he lit the cigarette. 'Or give him a good kicking. Big stupid bastard . . .'

There followed a minute or two of seething silence as each side regained its composure. The hooded boy scrabbled for small stones and threw them into the water, not hard or far enough to antagonise the swan, but plopping them about a metre or so from his own legs, picking truculently at the truce.

A large, tangled floe of weed and sticks drifted round the

corner. A torn rag of white polythene had become attached to it. As it came closer, still on the far side, the boy threw one of the small stones a bit further in a desultory attempt to hit it, but missed, and he sat there watching as his target slid by between him and the swans' cold, sooty glare. Caught by some random current it turned, slowly, as it moved away. He saw, or thought he saw, something else white, which might have been another shred of polythene, or – blearily, he screwed his eyes up – what might have been— 'Oy!'

He gestured, the cigarette protruding from his enveloping sleeve.

'What?' said his friend, without much interest.

But the boy couldn't see anything now, and felt stupid. He must be tripping, big time.

'*What?*'

He got up. 'Forget it. Let's go.'

The angler was positioned about half a mile down river, on that section of the bank between the town and the private stretch belonging to the big new house, Eadenfield. Unlike the boys he was not skiving, but had used a day of his holiday entitlement to take advantage of the fine weather. There had been a little bit of hassle involved in getting here: a good deal more traffic than you'd normally expect in the middle of a weekday – some sort of do on at Eadenfield – but that made his present tranquillity all the more delightful. At this moment he was conscious of feeling as contented and serene as it was possible for a middle-aged man employed by the local environmental health department to be. His wife had made him sandwiches – egg mayonnaise, and ham and mustard – and a flask of tea, a picnic which he had supplemented with a kingsize Mars Bar. Also, much as he enjoyed the company of his colleagues from the angling club, it was very pleasant to be alone, with the sun gleaming on the water and the faint chuckle of the river's gentle current. He didn't much mind if he caught anything or not. It was the process, not the catch, that he savoured.

Not a cloud in the sky, he thought. Set for the day.

Every few minutes he re-cast, just for the pleasure of hearing the line hiss in the reel, float, whispering through the air, and land with the faintest spit on the sliding surface of the river. From where he was he could see the town in one direction, dominated by the church spire, the Bancroft building and the clock tower on the town hall; and in the other the graceful, low-lying gabled outline of Eadenfield, looking as if it had been there for ever. Some people didn't like it because of where it stood, dominating the bend in the river, but he thought it a positive enhancement to the landscape. The house was no less handsome for being new. More so in his opinion – good-looking and every mod con too. He wondered what the celebration was.

A snag on the line caught his attention. A big lump of rubbish had floated by during his reverie and he seemed to have hooked something at its edge. The line was subject to a moment's tension before freeing itself. Carried by the momentum of release, the mini-island of vegetation span round once, slowly, and continued on its way.

Paying it no attention, he wound the reel in. The line brought with it only a dripping hank of black weed. Tutting under his breath he began to pick it off. This proved more difficult than usual; there was some more resistant material twisted in with the weed, little short, fine threads as distinct as fishbones in the soft slime. Not surprising it had given the line a jerk and got him all excited. Tough stuff, hair.

It was fully half a minute later that he considered this thought, and his eyebrows drew together in a small frown.

The couple regularly walked their collie along the river path, but they were conscientious keepers of the country code and didn't allow her into the river, though she loved to swim. There were people trying to fish, and the wildlife to consider, especially the swans who could be very aggressive. They'd almost reached the stile when a big lump of rubbish came floating by on the far side and the dog started to bark excitedly and make little sallies at the water, her ears pricked and her tail wagging.

'Best put her on the lead,' said the man to his wife.

'What's getting her so agitated, I wonder?'

'I don't know. Daft as a brush.'

The woman grabbed the dog and clipped on her lead. 'She can smell something.'

'I'm not surprised,' said the man. 'This river's none too clean upstream.'

Undisturbed, the raft, with its shrouded burden, moved downstream, occasionally bumping the bank, or getting hooked by an overhanging branch, once almost running aground, tilting dangerously on a shingle ridge. But always, in the end, being freed by the gentle persistence of the river, and continuing on its way towards Eadenfield.

2

2003 – Bryn

Bryn Mancini had almost forgotten how pleasurable it was to entertain, especially where money was not an issue. He took a simple, almost childish delight in being able to do what he wanted without counting the cost. For many reasons he gloried in the giving of this party, and though he was very far from being a religious man, if it was also more blessed than to receive, then that added value not to be sniffed at.

But though it was delightful to be filling this house with people, and making them happy, he liked to escape, to relish the sense of the party achieving its own momentum, taking on independent life, as a building sometimes did when it was finished and no longer part of him. So he'd walked quietly away, with his cigar and his glass of champagne, in the direction of the river bank.

This last Friday in August was the occasion of a multiple celebration. First and foremost it was to warm Eadenfield, the house he'd built as fortress and sanctuary. And twenty-one years ago today he and Linda had got married, on a day as golden as this one. At the beginning of this week their son Nick, approaching his second year at Oxford, had returned from three months' travelling in South-East Asia, smelly and tanned, world-weary but no wiser. And tonight's dance would carry them through midnight into Sadie's eighteenth birthday. So many rites of passage, a day for the different generations, and strange to think that both his children were now – only nominally he considered in Nick's case – adults. Though she was more than two years her brother's junior, Bryn had no trouble seeing his daughter as grown-up. It had happened suddenly, as though she'd made a conscious decision to take control of her life after the recent upheavals that had shaken all of them. Lady boss material to her computer-literate finger-tips, bless her, working hard, and rapidly acquiring her mother's poise, even if the looks had gone Nick's way.

It was Sadie, his beloved neurotic Sadie, who had the capacity for graft, and it would stand her in good stead. Bryn understood its value. From the sheikh's vaunting desert tower to this, his perfect English family house, his business as an architect was the realisation of ideas and dreams, and that realisation had been achieved through effort and application. He had known the exhilaration of early success, and what it was like to lose it. Painstakingly, he had started again. It had taken nearly eight years of training and one admittedly lucky break to get on the first rung of the ladder. And now look. In all modesty he had achieved a success greater than the first, and more precious for being hard-won. As a parent he knew that he was probably seen by his children as a soft touch, indulgent and liberal to a fault. He just hoped that both – especially Nick – would learn something from his professional example: that hard work worked.

Now he continued right down to the riverside. The sound of the party, its music and laughter, was like the sun on his back. He was pretty sure that Linda, even if she missed him, would not come after him; though Sadie might. She was anxious and bossy and liked everything, and everyone, in its place.

He drew a deep breath and gazed about him with intense pleasure. *This* place, the little River Eaden, had been the starting point, the genesis, of the house. Bryn liked to be near water. He could understand the impulse of older people to retire by the coast; but for him, a river was better. Rivers were the veins and arteries of England, constant but changing, from source to sea. It fascinated him that with every second – every fraction of a second – different water slipped by, flexing its glossy muscles over the gravel banks, and combing through the rippling strands of weed. Canny brown trout hovered in

the current, facing upstream. Moorhens bustled about beneath
the overhang of the far bank. Sometimes he saw a kingfisher
here, plummeting like a fiery turquoise dart from branch to
water. And more often the swans, whose domain this was,
patrolled grandly back and forth, keeping an eye on things.
Today there was no sign of them. There had been only one
cygnet this year, and it had gone. Bryn feared the worst. The
lords of the river were subject to depredation from louts, and
fishing lines . . .

There was a seat on the bank, screened from the house by
a natural arbour of trees, and he sat down – an immensely
tall, heavy-set man, back straight, feet squarely apart, cigar
held before his face, eyes narrowed against the smoke. He was
no longer a habitual smoker but enjoyed the occasional
Havana. An unashamed sensualist, he felt no more guilt about
that than at leaving his family and friends to enjoy themselves;
they had everything they could possibly want, including each
other. He had a speech to make, and toasts to propose, but
it wasn't time for all that yet. The little stone nymph they'd
brought from London glanced over her shoulder at him from
beneath the weeping willow. Today she was serene, and he
smiled back at her.

That family, those friends, were his greatest treasure.
Especially his family: in Linda and the children, Bryn considered himself thrice blessed. Only an hour ago he had overheard the word 'Camelot' used in connection with them, and
their new life in this house. It had pleased him immeasurably,
and he warmed his vanity on it now. ·

He drew deeply on the cigar. An uneasy peace had followed
the real war, won back in the spring. But the peace he had
found was deep, and real. He thought: this is happiness. Yes,
I think I dare to call myself a happy man.

Linda Mancini dressed for men, and especially for her husband.
She was a man's woman, but one who was generally adored
by both sexes. To know Linda, people agreed, was to love her.

Contentment, generosity, *joie de vivre* and an expansive sweet-natured sexiness emanated from her in warm waves to the benefit of those around her. Rare carpers pointed out that she'd had a charmed life: a long and happy marriage, two delightful children, and everything her heart desired and that money could buy. The diamond and emerald choker Bryn had given her for their anniversary testified to his uxorious devotion. But those in the know pointed out that she knew about hard work. For years before she met Bryn Linda had held down a job for one of the most demanding bosses in the country. Once the children were grown up, though there was no longer any financial imperative, she had, entirely through her own efforts, developed a successful business designing the *mise en scène* for special parties – the flowers, the tables, the lighting, the decorations. Today's celebrations at Eadenfield were the perfect advertisement for her skills, with everything in shades of pink, white and green, soft and abundant but informal.

Sadie Mancini had long ago realised that while in some ways she was like her mother, her mother was beautiful and she was not. This was something she had come to accept over the years. The low, wide brow with thick hair springing from a widow's peak, the far-apart speckled eyes, the short upper lip and large mouth that were gorgeous in Linda were translated into something plainer and heavier in Sadie. And the square-shouldered, short-waisted figure that was voluptuous in her mother she herself regarded, unflinchingly, as stocky.

Recently Sadie had learned to compensate for this with an attention to turnout and detail which would have shamed a drum major in the Horse Guards. Not for her the fluctuating fashion allegiances of the high street: she favoured classics. For today's lunch party, which was chiefly her parents' occasion, she wore a sharply tailored cream linen shift and matching kitten-heels, with plain pearl earrings. Her hands – of which she was justifiably proud, and on which she lavished attention – were enhanced by a slim gold watch given to her by her father, a fine chain bracelet and two rings on her right-hand annular finger, a narrow band set with diamond chips and a round antique amethyst. Her only concession to youth style was the fan-shaped squirt of hair, like a bird's crest, that topped her otherwise impeccable chignon.

When she finally found her mother, who was subjecting the marquee to a swift last-minute inspection with a pair of seca-teurs and a plant-humidifier, the contrast between the two women could scarcely have been more marked. Linda wore a fitted, long-sleeved turquoise silk dress with a plunging neck-line and two diaphanous panels at the back that floated from her waist as she walked. At her throat and wrists diamonds sparkled; a purple silk flower adorned her auburn hair, which was worn in loose and abundant shoulder-length waves.

'OK. Where is he?'

Sadie stood in the entrance to the marquee. Her mother, scanning a table at its centre, waved the humidifier.

'Don't fret, darling, he'll be back.'

'Be back? But why isn't he here? Where's he gone?'

'I've no idea – do the McIntyres have an "a" before the "c"? I checked, but now I'm having a crisis of confidence . . .'

'I do hate the way he wanders off. It's rude.'

'No it's not, it's just him. No, of course there isn't an "a" . . . There's nothing he likes better than the house full of people, but he has to escape from time to time.'

'Escape from what?'

'Oh, you know . . . the whole thing.'

'Us, perhaps?'

'Don't be silly, he *loves* us.' Linda focused on her daughter and came over, beaming. 'It's all *for* us.' She shook her head affectionately. 'Look at you, worrying away.'

Sadie evaded an embrace. 'I'm not worried, but I am annoyed.'

'You mustn't be. Come on, let's you and me go back and do our stuff. We can't leave it all to Nick.'

Sadie puffed out her lips and rolled her eyes at the thought of her brother shouldering responsibility for anything. 'Dad doesn't seem to mind who he leaves it to.'

This time Linda managed to put her free arm round her daughter's shoulders and kiss her cheek. 'Enough, my darling. They need us in there.'

For occasions such as these Nick Mancini had perfected a veiled, amiable stillness, low on words but high, he considered, on charisma: hooded eyes, a slow hint of a smile, a voice that, when employed, required people to bend towards him a little in order to hear. He remained on the edge, in every sense, leaning on wall or door jamb, allowing the company to come to him. He declined utterly to cast himself in the role of co-host. This whole over-the-top thing was down to the rest of the family. He was prepared only to grace it with his travel-honed presence.

Unlike his mother and sister, Nick was not dressed up. But this was not to say he had made no effort. On the contrary, he had deliberated long and hard over what to wear and had settled on faded green combats, a black sleeveless T-shirt and threadbare moccasins. On his wrist, an elephant hair bracelet. In his left ear, a single microscopic diamond. In his dark hair, two beaded rat's-tail plaits.

If Sadie resembled her mother, Nick was like his father, but in his case the alchemy of looks had worked in his favour. Bryn was not a handsome man, but one on whom humour, strong feeling and the exigencies of life had bestowed a certain rugged glamour. Nick, on the other hand, was beautiful. Androgynously, universally so, like a saturnine angel, or a court favourite. And his beauty, if it hadn't actually made him lazy in the first place, contributed to his being even lazier than he already was. A former girlfriend (not realising that by doing so she was contributing to her own downfall) had once compared him to the actor Jude Law, a compliment he had never forgotten.

The pianist, a friend of Linda's co-opted for this stage of

the party, was playing 'Our Love is Here to Stay'. His father's sister, Aunt Alison, was all over him like a cheap suit. She was normally OK as relations went, but the drink had brought out a terrifying girlishness in her.

'. . . a really *lovely* family occasion! And tonight as well – our room at the Rosemullion is much more than we're used to, my LBD looks quite lost in the walk-in wardrobe . . .'

She rattled on. Nick braced himself for the moment when she would ask him what he planned to do, a question that seemed to have been coming his way from all quarters for years. It was a question that never bothered Sadie, because bloody Sadie always had a perfectly clear plan which could be briskly outlined before moving on. He'd assembled a collection of all-purpose fudges and deflections, but he was bored shitless with both them and the ceaseless bright-eyed interrogation. The day was fast approaching when it would all become too much and he'd tell whoever it was to fuck off and die.

Even Nick could appreciate that today was not the one. His maternal grandparents were present, and it would have them in bits.

'Two more years to go! So what's next?' enquired Alison, twinkling flirtatiously at him over her glass.

Two could play at that game. He placed a conspiratorial finger to his lips. 'I've got a few irons in the fire.'

'I'm *sure* you have! Any clues?'

'Let's put it this way,' said Nick. 'I shan't be asking Dad for a job.'

'Good for you. Do you think now you've seen the rest of the world that you might go abroad again?'

This hadn't occurred to Nick. 'It's a distinct possibility.'

'Wonderful! The world is your oyster. Europe? The States? The Far East?'

Nick gave a small, mysterious grunt of a laugh, to indicate there was much he could say, but would refrain at present. Alison, as he had predicted to himself, was absolutely enchanted to be fobbed off in this way.

'My lips are sealed. Good luck, anyway. If I were your age again I'd make a point of travelling more, but in those days there was this peculiar idea of a *career*, a job for life, that you were terrified to jeopardise in any way, it seems incredible now . . . And then of course there was *marriage*, God help us.' She cocked her head quizzically. 'Anyone special in your life, Nick?'

'No.' He said this in a way that indicated clearly how out of the question it was.

'No. And a word from the wise –' Alison placed her fingers on his wrist – 'you keep it that way.'

The pianist embarked on 'Love Changes Everything'. Jesus! Rescue came in the unlikely form of his sister.

'Nick – excuse me, Auntie – have you seen Dad?'

Nick shook his head and Alison, moving away, laughed gaily. 'Families, families! I'll leave you to it.'

'Jesus,' muttered Nick, 'she does bang on.'

'If you moved about a bit more,' Sadie pointed out, 'you wouldn't get cornered.'

'I'm going out for a fag.'

'You can smoke in here.'

'Not this one I can't.'

'Well, if you see Dad—'

'I'll leave him alone, right?'

A friend of Sadie's at work had once remarked that she had 'issues' with her brother. Though she vigorously refuted this, she could tell from the friend's expression that she was protesting too much, condemned out of her own mouth. When they were both little she had worshipped Nick. Part of the trouble, now that she envied and resented him much of the time, was that she mourned the loss of that innocent adoration. At four, five and six it had been so simple and right to look up to her older brother, to be his acolyte and handmaiden, to be bossed, protected, patronised and petted by him. She had observed with respect how readily life came to him and how easily he handled it. That, she thought, was what life became as you got older: a gift bestowed by maturity, that would in time be hers also.

The discovery that this wasn't necessarily the case came as a painful blow from which she was still recovering. The realisation had crept up on her over the course of a year, during which time she had chosen not to turn and confront it. Then one day it had leapt out in front of her and could no longer be ignored. The fact was, there were different rules for different people. Some, Nick among them, swanned through life for no better reason than that of the dog licking its bollocks – because they could. And the dog's bollocks is what they thought they were. They did nothing to deserve their easy ride, or the love and admiration that daily came their way. They were fortunate, conceited, and idle; none more so than her brother. With this realisation came its corollary, which was that she herself, not being like that, was going to have to work harder and expect less, while having more required of her.

The day when these harsh facts became inescapable occurred on a Mancini family holiday in Suffolk when she and Nick had been fourteen and seventeen respectively: his birthday was in May and hers at the end of August, so there was an annual window of a few months when he could claim to be three years older than her. At that time the Mancinis owned a house on the seafront at Aldeburgh to which they went for odd weekends during the year, and for the whole of August. Holidays had a pattern: January was snow, May was palm trees, autumn was France or Italy – but August was Suffolk. This was partly practical and partly due to a sentimental attachment of both Linda and Bryn to the notion of the British seaside family holiday. Linda in particular, having spent holidays on the south coast as a child, was a firm believer not only in the home-from-home aspect of such a holiday, but in the soothing and strengthening qualities of clean North Sea air, and pebbles, and rumbustious ocean swimming. A good dose of these things each year would keep their children clear-headed and bright-eyed and stop them from getting spoiled. Bryn had bought into this philosophy, and liked to think of his family benefiting from it, though when he stayed in Aldeburgh he tended to sleep late, listen to music and spend a lot of time discussing and selecting fresh fish from the fishermen on the prom.

They'd had a dog then, christened Flora but known as Flo, a golden retriever bitch of exceptional sweetness. Aldeburgh was the one holiday when Flo did not have to endure jankers at the local kennels but could accompany the family. When the weather was bad, which was quite often, the children in particular recognised that only Flo's unalloyed pleasure in being there, with them, kept them cheerful. It would become Flo's holiday, which relieved them of the responsibility of having to enjoy it themselves. In other words, she was a blessing.

On this particular holiday the weather had been good, by the standards of the East Anglian coast in August. They'd sailed, and swum, and been out with Mr Crane in his fishing boat, twice, and had several notable pub suppers and historic fish and chips. They'd been to the cinema to see *Sliding Doors*, and (under protest) to the local production of *HMS Pinafore* which Sadie had rather enjoyed, though she had been at pains to keep her face as stonily supercilious as her brother's.

Nick was no longer happy to be on holiday with his family, and Gilbert and Sullivan in the public hall was the last straw. The hormones had kicked in a good three years ago, and he was now nearly the same height as his father, with a deep voice and the body not of a tall youth, but a young man. There was even a faint smudge of black down along his upper lip. Val d'Isère, Martinique, Umbria and the Dordogne were to be tolerated, especially if a friend could be included, but Aldeburgh, this summer, was beyond the pale. He had managed to wangle a week's reciprocal holiday at a friend's villa near Bordeaux, and a week's work experience on a building site through the good offices of his father, but that still left a fortnight to be tolerated in this armpit of a town. Compensations had to be sought, and Nick found them in the denizens of the public bar at the Ship Inn. His father was strict about licensing laws and pubs generally, but his mother took the view that if a lot of young people wanted to have a good time in a place like Aldeburgh they might as well do so under the eye of a sensible landlord.

This tolerance did not, of course, extend to Sadie. She affected a mild air of rebellion, but wasn't too put out. Unlike her brother, she was not a party animal, and though Breezers, Hooches, Hotshots and Alcopops tasted nice enough she didn't like the attendant loss of control. Family holidays suited her, with their mix of organised activity and empty time. Nick experienced both as almost agonising tedium, but she could happily go along with the former and fill the latter. She went for walks, she kept a diary, she made plans. And she observed.

There was a particular girl Nick was shagging, called Leanne. She was a bit older than him, and a raging exhibitionist. Even if he hadn't told Sadie about the shagging she would have guessed. Leanne had bobbed hair that fell over one eye, a ring in her upper lip, and a bee tattooed on her hip (readily visible because her clothes didn't meet in the middle). She had 'easy' written all over her, but one never doubted for a moment that she was in charge. Sadie considered her absolutely gross, and it was clear that the feeling was reciprocated: Leanne certainly regarded her as a tight-arsed, up-herself (if the two weren't mutually exclusive) spoiled brat. Sadie's trump card was that their parents didn't know about Leanne, let alone about the shagging. She kept her powder dry.

None of this affected her feelings towards Nick – even if she didn't share his boredom she could sympathise with it and she felt a grudging, puzzled admiration for his ability to pull – but the day in question changed everything.

It was without doubt the worst thing that had ever happened in her life so far. And what made it even harder to bear was that it was Nick's fault. He had been told – they both had – that if they walked along the beach to Thorpness, Flo was always to be put on the lead well before they got back to the town because of her tendency to take off and head for home, tail waving and brain in neutral, in expectation of a hero's welcome.

On this particular occasion Sadie and Nick had gone out together, she because she'd wanted to, he because he had nothing better to do. His excuse was that he needed to buy fags, but the purchase having been made within ten minutes of leaving the house he kept walking in a meandering, half-hearted way, smoking and silent, exuding waves of dark hormonal boredom. Sadie could have done without all that, and him, but put up with it because she had no option. They walked some distance apart, and never parallel, but with one always ahead of the other. When they reached the path that went over the marshes, Nick broke his silence.

'Let's go that way.'

'You go. I want to go on the beach.'

'The dog'll like it up there.'

'She likes it on the beach. You don't need the dog. You didn't even *want* to walk the dog.'

Nick dropped his cigarette and trod on it. 'No, well, I'm here now. Come on.'

The next moment was to give Sadie pause for years to come – the moment when in the wee small hours she feared she might be implicated in the awful thing that subsequently happened. Peevishly, she held out the lead to her brother.

'There you are then.'

He hesitated for a nanosecond but it wasn't lost on Sadie, who was all the more determined that he take some responsibility, and gave the lead a little shake.

'Here!'

'OK.' He took it. 'Seeya.'

She supposed at first that he was going to meet up with the tart, but then remembered that Leanne had taken a job

working in the RNLI gift shop in the afternoons. And whatever his motives, Sadie did not intend to give them the oxygen
of her attention. Miffed at not having Flo, nose well and truly
cut off to spite her face, she headed for the beach and began
trudging along the lower shingle shelf, without looking back.
She was confused and hurt as well as irritated. Only last year,
given similar circumstances, she would have gone with her
brother as a matter of course, his unquestioning shadow and
sidekick. There would have been none of these self-inflicted
complications, or this small, mean pain.

She walked for about a mile, fast, hauling her feet in and
out of the pebbles, not looking either at the sea or the occasional other walkers. In her pockets her hands were balled into
fists. Her gradual distancing from Nick served also to remind
her of a world of which she was not part – one of parties and
shopping and bands and boyfriends in which she could not
summon a scintilla of interest. She did not despise this world,
or its adherents; on the contrary she longed for some sea
change in herself that would enable her to participate. But
though her body was undergoing that change, her mind and
heart remained resolutely unmoved. So it looked as if Nick,
along with her friends, along with almost everyone under
eighteen that she knew, would simply move away and be lost
to her.

When she turned back the wind was in her face and she
put her head down. She wore black, not because she was a
Goth or a Grebo but to show that she had no intention of
competing in the fashion stakes. Nick wore black too, but in
his case it was a statement of a different sort, to do with being
cool and clever. Her clothes, purchased from charity shops,
were the despair of Linda, who could tell the difference. She
wore an outsize black blazer with the badge removed, a black
T-shirt, baggy black needlecord jeans and thick-soled black
lace-ups. The giveaway was her pair of nice, expensive gold-
rimmed glasses. She couldn't see a thing without them and
had been told her eyes weren't yet ready for contact lenses.

She ploughed on. When she reached the steps that led back up to the gravel road between beach and marshes she plodded up them. A big estate car was approaching from the direction of the town, barrelling over the rough surface towards the marina. Sadie took in several things at once: the car itself; Nick, a couple of hundred yards away, standing with his back to the wind, and the road, lighting a cigarette; and Flo, galloping up the path towards her in full greeting mode. In two seconds Sadie had made a series of lightning judgements and was already moving forwards to implement them, but those two seconds were too many. She saw the driver's contorted face as the dog bounded over the rise and on to the road, heard the horrible, rasping crunch of the slewing tyres, the thump of the impact and Flo's yelp of agony.

The driver was first, out of the car and over to the dog's side, holding up his hand palm outwards to keep Sadie at bay.

'No, don't! Stay there, love – she's gone I'm afraid.'

Sadie had stood there, crying – wailing – while the man's wife made comforting noises and suggestions which she could not take in.

Nick of course was last, on his own, and she'd always remember how his face looked – pale but with a telltale flush of panic on his cheeks.

'Shit!' he'd said. 'Shit! What happened?'

She had not said a word. Never grassed him up nor dobbed him in. She was too miserable to bother; when beautiful, soft, loving, playful Flo had gone. She half-heard his paltry excuses about the dog not coming when she was called, and not having seen any traffic and how he'd just looked away for a moment, but their mother was too sympathetic and too upset herself to do anything but tell him it wasn't his fault.

And perhaps it wasn't, *strictly* – but Sadie knew that she herself would not have allowed such a thing to happen. She would have been Flo's companion and carer, entirely focused on her, and would have made sure she was back on the lead long before the road. She was exhausted by remorse, anger and grief; and by resentment that their mother seemed to be expending more sympathy and attention on Nick, the culprit, than on her, who (though not, she admitted to herself, entirely blameless) had seen the accident at close quarters.

This emotional exhaustion led to her retreating into stony-faced impassivity, so that when their father joined them at the weekend and tried to comfort her she was unable to respond and heard her mother whispering that she 'just wanted to be left alone'.

It was horrible, horrible! But she would still in due course have forgiven Nick if she hadn't witnessed his final treachery – the one that proved beyond a shadow of a doubt that he had not cared about Flo, nor tried to keep her safe.

On the Monday morning after the accident the sun shone. Bryn had returned to London and Linda was playing tennis. Sadie, still in her Simpsons nightshirt and flip-flops, was eating cornflakes while watching Richard and Judy discuss get-rich-quick schemes. She heard Nick's footsteps on the stairs at the same time as the phone rang. He picked it up and said 'Hi . . .' as he carried it into the living room, but on seeing her he withdrew, and sat down on the stairs.

Sadie did not turn down the volume on the television, but she did listen to Nick. Over the course of this holiday, with Leanne on the scene, she had perfected the rather shameful ability to focus her hearing and blot out the competition.

'. . . fucking awful,' he said. 'Flo, our dog, remember, she got killed . . . yeah, yeah . . . I know. She just ran out on the road . . . I know, she was a really cool dog, we're all in bits about it . . . No, I'll be OK, but I saw it happen, you know? I couldn't get there in time. Yeah, thanks, Lee . . . thanks. The thing is, it was my fault . . .'

He lowered his voice at the moment when Sadie's attention was most keenly engaged. Quietly she got up and went to stand near the door. Nick's tone was broken and husky; he sounded almost in tears. Sadie pursed her lips.

'. . . you know, maybe if I'd noticed a bit sooner, or been able to catch up with her, but she's always been bad about coming when she's called . . . I know, but . . . yeah. OK. I know I shouldn't, but I can't help it, it was me that was with her at the time, shit, I saw it happen . . . It's going to be something I'll carry with me to my grave. Would you? I'd really appreciate that . . . tonight. Yeah, yeah . . . thanks, Lee. I know it's only a dog but this has really done my head in . . .'

His voice dropped even more, and Sadie opened the door as he replaced the phone. For her that instant was to define for ever the phrase 'moment of truth'. Her brother's face was, if not actually smiling, then at least bright with satisfaction at a job well done. He had lied to get in Leanne's knickers, and he was proud of it.

And there was no point in letting him know her feelings, because he didn't give a stuff what she thought.

Taking his mobile phone out of his pocket, Nick crossed the hall and went into the games room. He closed the door behind him and leaned on the pool table while he picked up his text messages. There were two. The one from Darius read: 'Trvler rtns – any gd tales? Lts lge it snest.' The other was from a girl called Ruth whom he'd met in Darnang, not a beauty but with the softest, slipperiest mouth he'd ever encountered. 'Hi bg boy, b in tch, pty tim ok.'

This evidence of the real world cheered him up somewhat and he replaced the phone and came out of the games room to find bloody Sadie hovering in the hall. As far as he was aware she had never snitched on him, but she had a snitch's mentality.

'What's your problem?' he asked coldly.

'Nothing, what's yours?'

'How long have you got.'

'Couldn't you snap out of it, Nick, just for today?'

In the past Nick had sometimes wondered why his sister didn't have a boyfriend, but since returning from travelling he knew exactly why – she was a prudish, sanctimonious bitch without a sexy bone in her body. Unless she was gay, of course, a possibility that he found repellent and titillating in equal parts. He viewed with misgivings the party tonight, which would highlight her shortcomings in the social arena and perhaps infect him by association. Though he had to admit she had one or two fit friends who might repay a bit of effort.

'Find Dad?' he asked. 'Checked he's not snorting coke in the greenhouse?'

She actually reddened – result! 'No, that's your idea of a good time, remember?'

'Chance'd be a fine thing.'

She whispered something brief and fierce, scarcely more than a hiss, and disappeared along the hall and out of the front door. Nick realised with a mixture of satisfaction and something deliciously approaching fear that his sister actually hated him.

Linda was on song: effortlessly overflowing with charm and *joie de vivre* and affection for her fellow man. She was rarely less than buoyant, but today she knew, without vanity, that she was radiant. She could see that radiance reflected back from the people she spoke to, and even in the faces of others, not close to her, who were watching from across the room. She understood the expression 'walking on air'. Floating – she was floating. Everything that made her life so good had come together on this one day and in this one place, and she was the presiding deity, the good fairy at the feast. She put her hand to the diamond and emerald choker in a small caressing gesture not wasted on her guests. They envied her – not the choker itself, but the warm, enduring marriage of which it was a symbol. It was good to have Nick back, no less amusing, but more grown-up and thoughtful after three months away, and to see Sadie looking so lovely on the eve of her birthday. Someone had mentioned 'your elegant daughter' and that was immensely pleasing. Sadie was growing into herself. She might not be a beauty, nor ever be glamorous, but she was evolving, slowly, into an attractive young woman. Linda like the idea of having a daughter with never a hair out of place. That all fitted in. They would complement each other as the years went by.

It was a quarter past one: fifteen minutes until the start of lunch. She wondered whether she should, in fact, go and prise out Bryn from wherever he was dreaming, but decided it wasn't necessary; from their earlier exchange it seemed likely that Sadie would do that for her, indeed might already have done so.

The final medley of this set was *My Fair Lady*. The best and most romantic musical ever produced, Bryn said, as well as the most literate, and today she felt inclined to agree. Appropriately enough, it was 'On the Street Where You Live' which accompanied her encounter with an admirer in the very centre of the drawing room, beneath the Waterford chandelier. He put his hands on her shoulders. They smiled, and kissed – two amiable, social animals.

He glanced up at the chandelier, then down at her. 'Here we are, you see. The still point of a turning universe.'

'I'm so glad you're here.'

'There's certainly nowhere else on earth that *I'd* rather be . . .' he murmured cajolingly. 'You know that.'

Linda's smile became if anything even more brilliant as her voice dropped. 'You will dance with me tonight, won't you?'

'Any other partners will be the purest duty.'

The next people Linda spoke to did not have her full attention. They weren't aware of this. She was effervescent as ever, but she was on autopilot. She needed saving from herself. She needed Bryn.

'. . . so sorry,' said her voice. 'You'll have to excuse me.'

To say that Sadie was dreading the evening's festivities was an understatement. She had not actually pleaded with her parents – she no longer did pleading – but she had indicated to them that as far as she was concerned it would be a wasted expense. She should have known better; expense was not an issue. The marquee would be in place, it was to be a celebration for the whole family – a housewarming, an anniversary, the traveller's return – as well as her birthday, so she mustn't give it another thought. She had found herself, as so often, in the position of indulging her mother and father, of acceding to their bubbling enthusiasm without being able to match it. As far as she was concerned the 'bash' as they insisted on calling it would be something to be got through. The one concession she had wrung from them was that there should be a fixed time for departures and no leeway given. She had tried for midnight but it was hopeless.

'Surely the thing will barely have started,' said Bryn, baffled. 'We can't simply throw people out.'

Sadie pressed on. 'No, but the band can stop playing and we can begin putting the chairs on the tables.'

Linda, emollient as ever, had laughed at this. 'She's right, Bryn! I suggest carriages at one a.m. How about that, darling, then we stand a chance of getting all your gang out of the door by two!'

This had had to do. Linda liked to think of the younger guests as Sadie's 'gang', but they weren't. She had no gang, and didn't want one. She was a loner who craved an ordered, restrained grown-up world which she sometimes suspected no longer existed. By far her favourite relation had been Jocelyn, an elderly cousin of her father's occasionally referred to jokingly as a 'maiden aunt' and regarded as something of an eccentric, who had worked all her life in the civil service, never married, and lived alone in a large flat in Swiss Cottage with two Yorkshire terriers and a housekeeper, Phyllis. On the few occasions when Sadie had met Jocelyn she had thought her not in the least eccentric, and enjoyed her company. Even then Sadie had been able to appreciate this woman's keen, clear mind, uncluttered by the perceived need for emotional games-playing or social dissimulation. And there had been something else: an underlying kindness born of understanding, the recognition, across an age difference of more than half a century, of a kindred spirit. When Bryn described his cousin, however affectionately, as 'a funny old girl', Sadie was incensed on her behalf. Jocelyn did not seem to her to be particularly old, she was never unintentionally funny, either peculiar or ha-ha; and as for girlishness she seemed miles more grown-up than any other adult of Sadie's acquaintance.

She also overheard her mother musing from time to time, not apparently with any malice, as to the exact nature of Phyllis's housekeeping duties. In response to her own question Linda had explained that Phyllis was more of a 'paid companion' – an apparent contradiction in terms which left Sadie no wiser as to Jocelyn's situation, but which rather appealed to her as an idea. To have someone living in one's house to help with the day to day business of life and be nice to you (which Sadie presumed also meant going away when not needed) seemed like a brilliant idea, and one which she still considered had much to recommend it.

Jocelyn had died only the previous year, quietly at home after a short illness, and left almost everything to Phyllis, with the exception of a few individual items. One of these, a gold brooch in the form of a tiny pair of scissors, with diamonds set into the handles, she bequeathed to Sadie. Linda pointed out that it was a coat or hat-brooch, the pin was far too thick for use on finer materials, and therefore Sadie might want to have it altered, but she declined: she wanted the brooch exactly as it was. To this day she hadn't worn it, but she often admired it in its velvet box: bright, angular, sharp and distinctive as its owner who, she felt sure, had understood her.

Phyllis, herself in her late sixties, took off to the west of Ireland with her very considerable haul which included the proceeds from the Swiss Cottage flat. No one said a word against her. She was a nice woman and had made herself indispensable to Jocelyn, so good luck to her, seemed to be the verdict. Some day Sadie intended to go to Ireland, look Phyllis up and ask her some pertinent questions.

Today she found herself thinking of Jocelyn with envy, admiration and respect. And of her brother with something perilously close to loathing.

Bryn looked at his watch: a gold Rolex engraved on the back with 'from Linda', which she had given him on his fiftieth. Not long till lunch; it was time he returned to the party. But not only the time factor concerned him. There was also that patch of worry, the dark cloud no bigger than a man's hand, that appeared on the edge of his mind's eye if he was on his own for too long. A cloud for which, if it assumed storm proportions, he would have no one to blame but himself.

Bryn stood, stiffly – feeling his age. He paused for a moment to gather himself, gazing up river, his shadow a black dwarf crouched at his feet.

'It's only for now,' said Linda, defending her seating plan to Nick. 'Tonight I don't care where anyone goes.'

'I'm not with Alison, am I?'

'No, you're with Jim and Victoria, and a nice colleague of your father's, Bob Savil and his wife, and Rosemary.'

'What, Rosie Savil? I didn't know she was here.'

'You won't have recognised her.' Linda stroked his cheek with her finger. 'Trust me.'

'I wish I could.'

Linda gazed fondly after her son as he slouched towards the designated table.

'Sharper than a serpent's tooth?' murmured her admirer *en passant*.

'Don't worry, I've seen him right.'

Sadie was happy with her table. Here was the sort of well-regulated and predictable social situation at which she excelled. She understood, and had no trouble complying with, the rules of engagement. She did not in the least mind how often she was quizzed about her first job and future plans, and she had learned to deflect roguish enquiries about her love life with a calm 'too busy'. She knew exactly what was appropriate and was content to deliver it. Glancing across at Nick, taking his place between Mrs Savil and the nubile Rosemary while reserving his judgement on both, she experienced the vengeful sweetness of pitying him.

Alison leaned across as wine was poured.

'Sadie – how are things at Markham Routledge?' She was referring to the North London estate agents where Sadie was the most junior employee.

'Very good, thanks.'

'What a time for a smart girl to get into the property business!' commented Alison's husband, Uncle Malcolm. 'Will you soon be a whizz-kid, tearing about in a sports car?'

His wife nudged him, while smiling at Sadie. 'Don't be silly, she already *is* a whizz kid.'

'I don't know about that,' said Sadie. 'I've got a second-hand Mini, does that count?'

Alison raised her glass. 'More than. Every girl should have a Mini at some time in her life. A Mini is a car you form a relationship with. It's the first boyfriend of cars, you never forget it.'

'But actually,' said Sadie, with the pleasure that accompanies the announcement of a sudden, damascene conversion, 'I don't know that estate agency's my thing. I'm going to pack it in and go to Ireland.'

With the arrival of the smoked trout roulade Linda could no longer ignore the failure of Bryn to reappear. She also observed approvingly that Sadie was very much the centre of attention at her table, so she could scarcely carp at her for not having hunted down her father to his lair.

She said, both to her neighbour, and across the space on

her other side: 'Don't wait for me, I'm going to see where he's got to.'

They were enjoying themselves too much to be concerned, but one friend did catch her arm as she passed.

'Is everything all right, Linda?'

'Oh, *fine*,' she replied. 'He goes AWOL occasionally, and then loses track of the time.'

Unusually it was Nick's eyes, not Sadie's, that she felt following her as she went out of the marquee.

The afternoon's clear brilliance came as a shock. The trees, the house, the distant hills, all seemed enormous, and etched so sharply against the piercing clarity of the sky that she blinked, and shielded her eyes with her hand as she looked around. The great sweep of park down to the river was empty and silent, like a post-apocalypse landscape left with nothing but its pointless beauty. Linda had a sudden sense of the people she had just left in the marquee as ignorant, innocent, survivors by default, laughing and talking on borrowed time.

'Silly . . .' she murmured to herself, partly to hear her own voice in the stillness.

Without having made a conscious decision to do so she began to walk down the slope of lawn in the direction of the Eaden. In spite of the sunshine the ground beneath the grass seemed cold, and sent a chill through the thin soles of her Jimmy Choos.

The floating mat of vegetation which had caught for a moment on the opposite bank freed itself and moved downriver. As it did so it rotated slowly on the uneven current. In the centre of the river was a blackened branch, its curves and angles breaking the surface like the skeleton of a giant water snake, culminating in a rearing head and neck. The floating island clipped the first hump of the branch and continued its slow-motion spin at a more acute angle, towards that part of the bank where Bryn stood.

Half hypnotised he watched its approach; stared in disbelief as bit by bit the true nature of the thing revealed itself to him.

The silver-grey fabric beneath the tangled greenery . . . the long, listless fingers combing the water . . . and now, gazing up at him, calmly, sightlessly through the lattice of leaves, the face. A face pale and impassive as that of an ancient queen on a cathedral tomb, but etched with minute detail: fine turquoise veins on the eyelids; freckles, grey as raindrops across the nose and cheeks; thin lilac-tinted lips; neat, lobe-less ears like those of an elf.

A face that the final peace of death had made lovely.

Linda could hear something now – her own quick breathing. She was unaccountably agitated. She felt compelled to move faster and broke into a run, tottering awkwardly in her spindly heels, the fine straps cutting her ankles. She was about twenty metres from the river bank when she stumbled and fell. When she got to her feet she was trembling. Her knees and hands were streaked with green and the hand she had thrust in front of her to break her fall was grazed where it had skated across the ground. Minute beads of blood oozed through the torn skin, and tears, not of pain but of fear, welled in her eyes.

'Bryn!' she called, her voice tremulous and childish.

Careless of his bespoke suit, Bryn sank to his knees on the grass and leaned down to catch the hoops of willow in his hand, and draw in the raft and its burden to hold it against the bank. The face below him rocked and shifted with the river's movement. He himself was shuddering, chilled with shock.

She was dead: but in death she had set out to find him.

Linda could see him now, between the trees, kneeling on the river bank looking down at something in the water.

'Bryn!' This time her call was stronger, closer, but still he did not look up. He got heavily, awkwardly to his feet like an old man. She knew then that she was right to feel afraid.

Moaning in pain and frustration, hopping and stumbling, she pulled off her shoes and ran more quickly, but still awkwardly with her unathletic middle-aged gait. When she reached her husband's side she was gasping for breath, and clutched his arm for support. She saw that the same clammy mud clinging to the soles of her feet was all over his beautiful new suit, and his hands, masking their wedding ring.

'Bryn! What is it?'

He didn't answer. As if she weren't there, the arm she was holding moved to point at the thing in the water.

She looked, and through her rising sickness she heard him say:

'God forgive her.'

3

1989 – Api

Of all the children born to Xanthe Durrance, Api was the one she worried about least. This wasn't saying much, because she'd trained herself not to worry a great deal about anything. In the big house on the edge of the fens she cultivated an atmosphere of healthy neglect. What she had long ago decided *not* to do was reproduce her own fraught upbringing and inflict it on her family. 'Let them be free' was a motto which chimed nicely with her laissez-faire attitude towards all matters maternal and matrimonial.

And Apollonia was the living proof of the efficacy of this approach – at nine she was independent-minded, resourceful, self-possessed and, most importantly, no trouble. In her youngest child Xanthe saw herself and her child-rearing methods entirely vindicated.

'Do you want to come and have tea?' asked Api.

'What,' replied Lisa. 'At yours?'

Api made a 'stupid!' face. 'No . . . What d'you think?'

'OK.'

'You'd better go and ask,' said Api with a hint of weary superiority that was wasted on her friend.

They were in the school playground. Lisa ran over to her mother; Api stayed put. Cheryl was a neat, smart woman with sharp edges. By comparison Api's mother Xanthe had no edges at all – her curly unkempt hair drifted about, her strangely colourless clothes floated and flopped, even her features had a soft, blurry quality. Not that Api remarked any of these things until she saw a woman like Cheryl who was coiffed, clad, manicured and made up so that every detail was visible at a distance of some twenty metres.

Api watched as Lisa asked her question. Cheryl leaned over indulgently as though Lisa were much smaller than was in fact the case. Then she glanced up. She gave a little wave, winking her hand at Api, and then beckoning in the same childish way. Api began walking over. In the split second before the wave she had caught the familiar look of hard, unfriendly suspicion.

Cheryl was all smiles now, though. 'Api, is that right, your mum's invited Lisa back for tea?'

Weasel words; she must know Xanthe had had nothing to do with it. But Api was an old hand. 'Yes.'

'Is she here?' Cheryl glanced round.

'No.'

'I see . . . How were you going to get there?'

'Walk,' said Api. 'It's OK.'

'It's a long way. Tell you what, I'll give you a lift,' said Cheryl, continuing before Api could demur: 'Then I can have a word about what time to collect Lisa.'

The girls trooped after her to the white Shogun, which blinked brightly at their approach. 'Do you want to go in the front?' asked Lisa. 'It's great, it feels really high up.'

'No thanks.'

Cheryl took charge. 'Hop in then, girls, and do those belts up.'

Cheryl's slim wrist jangled with gold bangles and a dainty watch worn loose as though it were itself a bracelet. A gold Celtic cross hung at the neck of her cerise cashmere polo shirt. Api had heard her mother (a self-confessed atheist) say that crucifixes, no matter how tasteful, worn by the ungodly as a fashion accessory, were common. Though of course none of them had any idea whether or not Cheryl was a church-goer. There was a swingeingly judgemental side to Xanthe's otherwise indolent nature, and in the case of Cheryl Api tended to agree with her. She and Lisa got on OK, but she wasn't going to be obligingly thrilled by the immaculate Shogun or anything that went with it. This lift wasn't being offered out of kindness but because Cheryl wanted to sniff out the lie of the land.

She sat poker-faced in the back, staring at her shoes, in a way that she was aware could only confirm Cheryl's misgivings.

The drive out of the village was a good deal longer than the walk the girls would have taken, and it was a full fifteen minutes before the house came in sight.

'So lovely to be really out in the country,' sighed Cheryl, but Api wasn't fooled. She could see their house through an outsider's eyes: square, bleak, untidy, even somewhat desolate, with its straggly hedge, and unkempt grass on which were a broken bike, two ramshackle hutches, a run made of chicken wire, a pushchair with a bald, blind teddy under a mildewed cover (hers, it had been there for years), the tattered remnants of a badminton net and a scattering of smaller debris. Alongside this dereliction her father's car, a bright blue Japanese convertible, fresh from its service while he was on tour in Frankfurt, looked conspicuously well maintained. Poised, as it were, for flight.

The freedom which Xanthe extended to their children was something of which her husband also took full advantage. Charles Durrance had long ago realised that the domestic zoo, while it might not be his scene, was nonetheless a milieu in which his presence would, happily, not be missed. Xanthe presided, but she did not supervise, at least not closely. Family life flowed around and beneath her: she floated on it, bobbing unconcernedly on its ups and downs. From the very moment the first tiny, sticky, effort-reddened head had pushed its way out of his wife's body, Charles had felt himself sidelined, except for the purposes of reproduction. That purpose had been fulfilled a further four times, with only occasional extra-curricular forays in between, a situation which they had both quickly come to recognise suited them fine. Theirs had never been a union based on passion or romance. It was an outwardly chaotic but wholly practical partnership which provided them both with an orthodox context in which to operate in their separate ways. The normal duties of husband and father were not required of Charles, only that he not be a nuisance nor make unreasonable demands, both activities that he was happy to forswear. When not blending into the background at home he was resident satyr of the Capital Symphonia – 'the Sin' – working his way through the female members of the orchestra with a smile on his lips and a bulge in his trousers. It was an almost perfect life for a man of Charles's temperament and proclivities, and he was the first to recognise his good fortune.

He said as much to his current squeeze, the Sin's chief tympanist, Rhona Sinclair, at present enlivening his lonely hotel room in Frankfurt.

'I'm such a lucky bastard.'

Rhona, a spirited advocate of the empowerment of women, felt obliged even while in bed with Charles to protest.

'Why don't you just get out of the marriage?'

'Why should I?'

'Because you're betraying your wife on a daily basis.'

'I wish!' Charles fingered Rhona's fanny affectionately.

'Often enough, then.'

'She's not bothered. A, she doesn't know or choose to know and B, if she did she wouldn't care.'

'How can you say that?' Rhona brushed his hand away and pulled herself up, adjusting the pillows behind her back.

'I know Xanthe extremely well.'

'You patronising bastard!' exclaimed Rhona, but there was a laugh in her voice as she reached for her toothglass of minibar Riesling.

'It works both ways,' explained Charles affably. 'I don't imagine for a moment that she thinks I should make do with what's available at home. Especially when I'm so often away, and in the company of some of the best-looking and most vibrant women to be found on the international concert circuit.'

Rhona, sipping, ignored this, but her brows drew together censoriously as she considered the situation.

'Anyway,' said Charles. 'I'm jolly glad you haven't allowed your feminist scruples to stand in the way of good old unregenerate fun.'

This got a rise as he intended it should. 'It's not my problem,' snapped Rhona. 'What you and your wife do or don't do is your business entirely. She's a grown woman and I presume an intelligent one –' here she flashed Charles a sour look – 'not a charity case.'

'Hmm . . .' Charles mused, thinking of Xanthe, whose precise nature it would be almost impossible to convey to Rhona, or for Rhona to understand. 'No. Certainly not *that*.'

'This is sex, Charles,' continued Rhona, 'pure and simple.'

'Absolutely.'

'It has nothing to do with emotional involvement.'

'I certainly hope not.'

'Let alone "commitment".' She placed audible inverted commas around the last word.

'Thank God for that.'

'Just as long as we understand each other.'

Charles took Rhona's glass and stretched over her to place it on the table on her side. Being in just the right place as a result of this manoeuvre he latched enthusiastically on to her breast, and was rewarded by the sound of her small, throaty sigh, and the sensuous touch of her fingers on the back of his neck.

'You're a good woman, Rhona,' he growled, around the hard stub of her nipple.

'Is that a compliment?'

'I'll leave you to decide . . .' He gave her a small nip and she sighed and surged obligingly against him. God, but it was easy.

★

Once away from the embarrassing exchanges between the
two mothers – Cheryl asking things like 'When shall I
collect?', adding 'Well, when do you eat?', and Xanthe saying
she really didn't know and it made no odds – Api enjoyed
having Lisa there. They were best friends, and it was satisfying to be the one with something genuinely different to
offer: freedom. At Lisa's, there was loads of new stuff and
things to do, and always a 'tea' that included chips and a
bought frozen dessert of great elaborateness with meringue,
crème chantilly, chocolate flakes or glazed fruit of Technicolor
brightness. At Api's there was a breadbin and fridge (whose
contents were far from guaranteed) and a general latitude
stopping just short of neglect which she, being used to
nothing else, took for granted but which she could tell was
quite thrilling to Lisa.

The house – oddly, Number 7, Eastleigh End, though there
was no other in sight – backed on to farmland. There was no
rear garden; the cultivated land washed against the back wall,
and in summer, if the farmer had planted barley or wheat
rather than sugar beet, the ears tapped against the bottom of
the ground-floor windows along with the nettles and goose
grass that sprouted fiercely at the base of the wall. The year
of the oil seed rape, the back downstairs rooms had been
flooded throughout the month of May with an eerie yellow
glow and in the evenings with an almost overpowering scent,
thick and sweet. To walkers on the footpath that crossed the
fields a quarter of a mile away the house appeared like the
superstructure of an ark, floating calmly on the flat, arable
swell.

Now, in late September, the deserted footpath was invisible among the gleaming cords of plough that streamed and
looped over the horizon. Lisa asked:

'Isn't it creepy here at night?'

Api was too shrewd to deny it. 'Sometimes.'

Lisa shuddered obligingly. 'Don't you think someone might
just walk over there and stare in at the window?'

'Someone did once. He broke in.' This was true, though the intruder had been only a local kid. 'But my dad was at home.'

'Was there a fight?' This was asked in the tone of incredulous relish reserved for horrors one was unlikely to experience oneself.

Api shook her head. 'No such luck. He ran off.'

'God! Did they catch him?'

'No,' said Api, and glancing sombrely out of the window added: 'So he's still out there somewhere.'

'God . . .' breathed Lisa again, almost reverentially. 'How awful.'

They were in a room referred to by Xanthe, and therefore everyone else, as the drawing room. Only Charles – a lounge or living-room man by upbringing – perceived this as an affectation. Api and her siblings, knowing no different, assumed the phrase merely meant this farrago of dog-eared magazines, books and music, mixed with battered toys and ravelled tapes; misshapen lumps of furniture draped with old blankets and shawls; a fireplace overflowing with pine cones and waste paper; a hearth on which dozens of half-used candles rose from islands of their own grubby wax. The floor-length umber brocade curtains had once been imposing but now the linings were stained and threadbare, and the pleated tops sagged like hammocks where hooks and runners had gone missing. Years ago, in a fit of enthusiasm, Xanthe had had the carpet ripped up, but had not got round to having the exposed floorboards stripped and polished, so an assortment of rugs, one genuine Turkish, the rest ranging from acrylic sheep to threadbare dhurris, had been placed here and there to cover the scabs of old underlay and adhesive. Around the chipped skirting board balls of slut's wool drifted like tumbleweed. Spiders had built fantastic structures in the far-off corners of the ceiling.

The two girls sat on the floor near the one shiny, new, state-of-the-art object in the room: the Japanese sound centre. Charles had rigged up speakers in every room, so that now Kylie

Minogue's remix of 'The Locomotion' blasted cheerfully throughout the ground floor of the house. Lisa was awed.

'My mum'd go spare!' she exclaimed.

'It's not the noise she complains about, it's the music,' Api said. 'They like classical.' Lisa pulled a face, but Api, who liked to confound expectation, added: 'So do I, it depends.'

'On what?'

'On what sort of mood I'm in.'

'They don't mind you using this?' Lisa nodded at the sound centre.

'There isn't another one.'

'Haven't you got one?'

'No. This is Dad's but everyone can use it as long as they're careful.'

Lisa looked around a touch nervously. 'Where is your dad?'

'In Germany,' said Api. When the tape ended, she asked: 'Want a sandwich?'

'OK.'

Lisa followed her friend to the kitchen, where Xanthe was sitting at the table with a slew of paper in front of her, the phone to her ear and a pencil between her lips – she had recently given up smoking and still missed a cigarette's oral gratification. She widened her eyes at the girls as they entered but her attention was elsewhere.

'What do you want in it?' asked Api, ignoring her mother and opening a cupboard in which the smeary bottles and jars were huddled like commuters in an overcrowded lift.

'Um . . .' Lisa was embarrassed both by the openness of the question and by the presence of Mrs Durrance, who had now removed the pencil and begun to speak loudly to the person on the other end of the phone.

'. . . I'd just like to know what you want me to do about it. There's no need for a lecture, I've chastised myself about it quite enough already.' Her tone was not plaintive but dry and uninterested; her free hand stirred the sheets of paper absently, lifting and dropping them as if sifting flour.

'Cheese spread or peanut butter.' Api reached down a battered tube and a jar.

'OK, I'll do that then, it's not as if we're exactly destitute, we've got this house, and . . .'

'Peanut butter,' whispered Lisa.

She watched as Api took a sliced white loaf out of the bread bin, and low-fat spread from the fridge, and began to assemble sandwiches on the not-particularly-clean work surface.

'. . . hope it goes well tonight, what are you playing, remind me?'

Api handed Lisa a sandwich on a square of paper kitchen towel. 'There you go.'

'Thanks.'

''Bye. Yup. 'Bye.' Xanthe put the phone down with a sigh, and tapped the pencil against her front teeth with an exaggerated narrowing of the eyes. 'Are you girls all right?'

They assured her that they were.

'Jolly good.'

They went back into the drawing room and Api tuned in to the local music radio station while they ate their sandwiches. Lisa was keenly aware of the ramshackle spaces of the house all around them. Anyone might be here, and anything might happen! It was thrilling as long as she knew her mother was coming at six to collect her.

'Where are all the others?' she asked.

Api shrugged. 'God knows.' Her siblings held precious little interest for her, let alone any danger or excitement, but she had come to recognise their novelty value for others. Her eldest sister, Gilda, was lead singer in an electric folk band, Solstice, currently playing local pubs and halls, but destined, so they'd been told, for great things, of which Glastonbury was the Holy Grail. At eighteen, Gilda was nearly six foot tall, with a shock of bleached white-blonde hair as dry as a doll's, and a doll's pale, spiky-lashed eyes. She smoked roll-ups, holding them between her long, stub-ended fingers in the proletarian manner like a dart, and wore immense, elaborate footwear – thigh boots, DMs or Roman sandals – and exiguous black clothes from which her pneumatic waxen curves seemed always about to burst forth. She strode the world armed in jewellery made up of teeth, daggers, rocks and chains. Api, who had known Gilda since she was a gawky middle-school misfit, was unimpressed by all this, but could see that to the outsider her sister presented an arresting spectacle.

Then there was Martin, who was a hermit. Api had heard her parents describe him in this way, though he didn't have the wispy beard and tattered robe associated with such people in books. As well as rarely going out, Martin was an elective (and selective) mute. When dealing with anyone outside the family he would communicate only through his younger brother, Saul, and avoided conversation with his parents and siblings as much as possible. Privately Api thought that this was no bad thing in a household where most of the occupants had far too much to say for themselves, but she could see it was a disadvantage in other ways. Because of these idiosyncracies Martin was home-educated. He had a computer in his room to which he applied himself obsessively ('Martin and that bloody pc are joined at the hip' as Charles put it), though these days there was some vague concern about what would happen next year when Martin was sixteen and due to take GCSEs.

Saul was thirteen and doing perfectly well at the local secondary school which Gilda had but rarely graced with her disturbing presence. Of the Durrance children he was the most easy going, because like his father he was not one of nature's boat-rockers, but essentially a fitter-in, able but idle, with Charles's puckish, sensual looks which made him the darling of the older girls.

Between Saul and Api was eleven-year-old Judith, who had learning difficulties and so attended a special school near Ely, begun by a group of radical free-thinkers in the 1930s. There was a small bus paid for by the parents which ran pupils from this area back and forth, but it meant leaving earlier and returning later than the others. Like everyone else in this (to Lisa) rather alarming family, Judith's life was distinct, separate, and curiously unregulated. Lisa had a younger brother, Brett, but the relationship between the two of them was dictated by their parents' view of what that relationship should be, and certainly bore no resemblance to anything here.

'Want to come up to the loft?' enquired Api, getting up, silencing the radio and putting her plate on the crowded mantelpiece. 'Just leave that there.'

'Should we take them back to the kitchen?' asked Lisa with trepidation.

'Don't worry about it.' Api was already halfway to the hall. Lisa followed.

They went up two flights of stairs. The first had a run of green carpet up the middle, so threadbare that it looked more like moss, or a particularly virulent mould. The landing was wide, with a window that overlooked the front garden. Glancing out, Lisa saw the bus dropping Judith off at the gate, and Judith beginning to wander in the general direction of the house, holding her arms away from her sides and swaying slightly as if moving to music only she could hear. Weird . . . Realising she was being left behind Lisa turned and saw that she was herself being watched from a doorway, by a boy with bare feet and a bad complexion. She blushed hotly but he at once withdrew into the bedroom beyond, closing the door after him, and she scurried after her friend.

The second flight of stairs had no carpet and Lisa was conscious of their two sets of trainered feet slapping on the bare boards, advertising their whereabouts to whatever other weirdos were in the house. As if reading her mind, when they reached the landing Api said: 'This is where Gilda lives, but she's not here at the moment.'

The loft was closed, but Api got a pole with a metal knob on the end from the corner of the landing, pushed the knob into its corresponding hole, turned it, and hey presto! the lid came down and with it a folding ladder. The space above them was dark except for a few thin threads of daylight where the rooftiles were coming adrift.

'Is it OK up there?'

'What do you mean?'

'There aren't any rats? My dad says you're never more than six feet from a rat.'

'No, no rats . . .' Api started up the ladder, adding insouciantly, 'We've got bats, but they're protected.'

Lisa felt that *qua* bats, she was the one who should be protected, but Api's confidence was infectious and she went up the ladder after her. As she climbed in, Api pressed a switch and a single sixty-watt bulb dangling from one of the rafters shed a pale, dusty light on an area in the middle of the loft. The mysterious darkness of the outer reaches made the place seem enormous, and creepy. Neither was it completely silent. Apart from the creak of their tentative footsteps the musty air seemed to seethe with small, resentful life. Lisa couldn't help thinking of the bats – and the spiders and woodlice, probably hundreds of them – every one objecting to this intrusion and gathering its leathery limbs for the onslaught.

Api said: 'Look at all this stuff. All these old records, they belonged to my grandmother.' She sat down on a trunk with initials stencilled on it in white, and began pulling big, heavy black shellac records out of their paper sleeves. She patted the trunk next to her. 'Come on.'

Lisa sat down. The records were by people she'd never heard of: Larry Adler, Noël Coward, Danny Kaye, Richard Tauber, Jessie Matthews. Api seemed to know something about them. She said: 'The Harry Lime Theme – this is good.'

It meant nothing to Lisa. She was awed by Api's casual familiarity with all things strange – bats, darkness, dirt, madness, ancient records – and was prepared to take her word for anything. Now Api stretched out and pulled over, by its handle, a square black box which she opened to reveal a felt-covered turntable.

'You wind it up,' she said, putting the record on the turntable, 'and I'll put in a new needle.'

There was a handle at the side of the gramophone and Lisa turned it a few times.

'More than that,' ordered Api. 'Till it stops.'

She continued until the handle grew stiff and finally, as predicted, could go no further. Api inserted the needle and lowered it with a sound like a spit on to the swimming, shiny edge of the record. After a few hissing seconds, plangent music issued forth. Lisa had never heard the zither, and it was unlike anything she had listened to before: she couldn't really say whether she liked it or not. In another place with other people she might have dismissed it as uncool but here, in the crepuscular attic, with Api next to her, the house with its inmates below and the bats above, it made her shiver, and the hairs on her arms rise, each from its separate goose pimple.

They listened to the whole record in silence. When it finished, Api removed the needle and said: 'It's from a film. *The Third Man*. Have you seen it?' Lisa shook her head. She hadn't even heard of it. 'It's black and white,' Api told her, 'really really old, but you can get it on video. It's my mum's favourite film.'

'What's it about?'

'A man called Harry Lime, who lives in the sewers.'

'Where?'

'Somewhere . . . Paris, somewhere like that.'

'Why?'

'Because he's a drug dealer.'

This Lisa could relate to. 'Cool.'

'He's *really* cool,' agreed Api. 'He's good and bad, if you know what I mean. He's doing the drugs, but he wears this hat, and he's got a kind of smile that gets to people.'

'So what happens?'

'I can't remember all of it, but in the end he gets shot, actually *in* the sewer. And there's a bit on a big wheel where he's talking to his old friend, explaining what he does. Anyway, this is the music, that's why it's called the Harry Lime Theme.'

Lisa was framing another interested question when Api remembered something.

'There's this good bit with a kitten, when it knows he's there, but he's standing in a doorway in the dark, so you can't see him. And then the kitten comes up and makes a fuss and he sort of half appears, half in the dark and half in the light. He's a man of mystery . . .' She made this last observation to herself rather than to Lisa, and then added more briskly: 'Do you want to hear it again?'

'Yes.'

Once more they listened. Api's outline of the film and its alluring anti-hero had the desired effect. Now, Lisa could almost see the wet city streets, the dank sewers beneath, the shadowy doorway and the sardonic smile of the half-seen Harry Lime, dark and light, good and bad . . .

The music finished, and in the ensuing silence they heard the creak of the ladder. Judith's head appeared in the aperture.

'What's going on? Can I come up?'

'No,' said Api. 'It's private.'

Judith took another step up. 'Who's that?'

'Me,' said Lisa. 'Lisa.'

'What are you doing?'

'I told you,' said Api. 'Nothing.'

'You were playing that record.' Judith's tone was insinuating and accusing. Lisa was nervous of her, and wished she'd go away. 'That ancient thing.'

'*So?*'

There was a moment when it might have gone either way. Judith's large, expressionless face with its halo of fuzzy hair seemed to be trained on them like a spotlight. For the first time Lisa sensed that Api was as profoundly uncomfortable as she was. *Go away,* she prayed fervently. *Go. Away.*

Her prayer was answered. Judith made a disparaging snorting sound. 'Have fun.' It was like a curse being cast. She creaked back down the ladder, but they didn't move until they heard her clumpy footsteps on the stairs.

'Phew,' said Api. 'She's such a pain.'

In this instance comment seemed superfluous, so Lisa made none. Way below they heard voices, Xanthe and Judith in discussion. This evidence that the focus was finally off them emboldened Lisa to ask:

'So what else is up here?'

'Loads. They don't even know about most of it. I'm the only one who ever comes up here. There's piles of stuff that belonged to my grandparents.'

'Which ones?'

'My mum's lot. But they're dead, so she got to keep masses of stuff that she didn't want to throw away, but she doesn't use it either. Look, I'll show you.'

There was a home apothecary with its own key and its compartments lined with green baize, full of dusty glass bottles with chunky stoppers; a black and white casket made – so Api said – of porcupine quills, and containing among other things a preserved alligator's egg with the infant alligator protruding from it; a cardboard suitcase full of brown photographs; a family Bible speckled with mould; boxes and bags of old clothes, damp to the touch, from which earwigs scuttled when disturbed; crates of china and glass buried in newspaper and woodshavings like a lucky dip; walking sticks, golf clubs, a sword, a pistol in a case . . . and still there were things, black secretive ramparts of things, way beyond the arena of light, that Lisa could only guess at.

'Hey, look at this.'

Api pulled back a motheaten rug to reveal a packing case containing several large framed pictures. She took hold of the biggest one, its massive gilt frame standing a good six inches proud of the others, and tried to lift it out.

'Give us a hand, Lees – but don't look yet! This is brilliant.'

Between the two of them they hauled it out, and on Api's instructions leaned it face forwards against the packing case, while she returned to the gramophone, wound it up and put the Harry Lime record on again.

'You'll see why. OK, turn it round.'

It was so heavy they had to turn it by walking in a half-circle so that they changed places. Api stood back, arms folded.

'Ta-ra!'

The picture was a portrait in oils; the subject, a black-haired man who might have been any age between thirty and sixty. He wore a plain dark suit, white shirt, and tie, but every part of the picture except the face had been allowed by the artist to recede into a mysterious darkness. Also, and here was the 'brilliant' touch which made the music so apposite, half of his face was in shadow. The visible half was at once compelling and frightening: a face with the harsh impassivity of an Indian chief, with a long nose, deep grooves between the nostrils and the corners of a thin, sensuous mouth, and opaque eyes, like those of the shark in *Jaws*, that stared intently at the onlooker while giving nothing away. Such a face, even in repose exerted a powerful and disturbing magnetism.

To escape the man's black stare Lisa turned to Api. 'Who is he?'

'John Ashe,' said Api, with pride. 'My great-grandfather. He died Before the War.' Here Api was quoting her mother. All she knew of the far-off war in question was that it was the only really big one, the one that mattered, so that the phrase 'before the war' denoted a time and place – another world – when things were done differently. She was unclear whether the change was for better or worse, but looking at the portrait of her ancestor she was sure that if he was typical, people then had been bigger, wilder, more exotic, and that the war had somehow stunted ensuing generations.

The music finished, and she went to silence the rasping breath of the needle.

'So what do you think?'

Lisa deflected this question by asking another. 'Was he someone important?'

'He was a millionaire.'

That was enough for Lisa. 'Oh wow.'

'But no one knows why the picture's like that, half and half. Except it's very dramatic. Like Harry Lime.'

'Why don't your parents have it hanging up in the house?'

'They used to. It used to be on the stairs. But he made Judith cry, so they stuck him up here. My dad calls him the surly old bugger.'

The picture's humiliating effect on Judith caused Lisa to regard it in a more favourable light. She peered closely to show how unperturbed she herself was.

'It might just be dirty,' she suggested.

'No,' said Api firmly. 'It's meant to be like that.'

This, as intended, was the last word on the subject, and soon after that they heard Cheryl being admitted (half an hour early, she'd been passing so she thought she would). In response to Xanthe's plaintive howl of 'Girls! Gi-i-irls! Where a-a-are you?' they abandoned the picture where it was, and left the attic. Api went last, because of turning out the light. As she was about to do so, and Lisa's foot was already on the top rung, she tapped her on the shoulder.

'Look!'

In the darkness, at this distance, the grubby gilt frame was barely visible, but John Ashe's half-face stood out as if lit from within, staring after them as they went.

'Cool,' muttered Lisa, her skin creeping as she fled.

Seconds later, Api followed.

4

1979–81 – Bryn

Bryn Mancini and Linda Reynolds met in the buffet car of a snowbound train somewhere to the north of Preston in January '79. He ordered a pint of Guinness and a cheese and chutney sandwich. She, just after him in the queue, asked straight-faced for a Bellini.

'You what?' The steward squinted at her.

'It's champagne and peach juice.'

'Sorry, madam.' His apology was heavily ironic, the next phrase perfectly timed: 'All out of peach juice.'

'Oh no, what a shame!'

Bryn noticed with amusement that she seemed oblivious of the restless queue, the steward's irritation, or the blizzard that screamed and scribbled furiously on the black windows of the stationary carriage.

'So what'll it be?'

'I'll have to make do with champagne, won't I?'

'We only sell it by the bottle, madam.'

'The only way to drink it,' was her spirited reply. The queue shuffled and sucked its teeth.

'Could we share one?' Bryn suggested.

She threw him a glance. 'You've already got a drink.'

'Yes, but not champagne.' The glance hardened into a stare. He inclined his head, smiling. 'Please. Indulge me.'

'OK.' She nodded to the steward. Then to him: 'Thanks.'

Linda, returning to her flat in London on a high after extended New Year's celebrations with friends in the Lake District, noticed that Bryn was quite simply the biggest man she had ever encountered, a man whose great height, width, girth and voice seemed to fill what space remained at the end of the crowded buffet car. Linda was more used to over-whelming others, but on this occasion she accepted his offer because she herself was overwhelmed.

They split the extortionate price tag. Bryn would have picked it up, but sensed a youthful touchiness on her part that might make such obvious gallantry unwelcome. They found a couple of recently vacated seats in the corner, and she put the bottle and two paper cups down on the sticky surface amid a debris of wrappers and crumbs.

'Not exactly the Orient Express,' she said, with a wry look.

'No,' he agreed. 'Except for the snow.'

She smiled a broad, Leslie Caron smile that put crescent-shaped dimples in either cheek. An hourglass redhead, early twenties, timelessly pretty. You could, he thought, have put her in a painting from almost any period and she would not have looked out of place. Adorable.

'I'm Bryn Mancini,' he said.

'Linda Reynolds, how do you do. Thank you for the gallant gesture.'

'My pleasure. Bellini!' He shook his head. 'You've got a nerve.'

'I certainly hope so.'

'And by the way,' he added, 'it was no gallant gesture, it was a pass.'

'Really? How lovely.' She raised her cup. 'Cheers!'

'Chin-chin.' Bryn laughed, partly at himself. He had been outmanoeuvred by an expert. She had finessed his bluntness into a bouquet and received it with the effusive grace of a prima ballerina.

This was a familiar scenario to Linda, but for one thing. In her experience even the most blatant chat-up came thinly disguised as something else. Both parties knew it for what it was, but the masquerade was in the rules of engagement. This giant with the squashed nose and curly black hair was either very confident or very crass, or both. Maybe, she thought, his *chutzpah* went with his enormous size – perhaps he was so used to dominating whatever environment and company he was in that he'd ceased to care about token niceties. Linda, sipping her champagne – *her* half of the champagne, she reminded herself – reserved judgement.

'I'm going to sound like a customer questionnaire,' he said, 'and ask you the purpose of your trip. A. Business B. Holiday C. Other.'

'Let's see. A. With B and C connections.'

'You're going to have to expand on that.' He rummaged in his pockets. 'Mind if I smoke?'

'Not at all, I'll join you.'

He offered first his cigarette case, then his lighter. She had all the moves – the take, the tap, the pose, the raised hand that stopped just short of touching his as she guarded the small flame between them . . . The deep intake of breath and long, languid exhalation, head tilted away, eyes slanted towards him beneath (no doubt ginger) lashes coated to the consistency of flue brushes. A long-forgotten American phrase popped into his mind. She was a piece of work.

'I've been staying with friends in Cumbria,' she told him. 'Now it's back to the Smoke – which is home and business. So, you see what I mean.'

'Cumbria's wonderful,' he said. 'All that scenery and fresh air.'

'Yes – it's enough to drive a person to drunkenness and debauch.' She gave a cute, tobacco-roughened chuckle. 'Kensington will be a health cure. How about you?'

'A and C,' he said. 'I've been putting a bit of butter on my crust in Manchester, and now I'm heading home, which means getting off at Watford, if we ever get there.'

'Is that where you live, Watford?' He caught the naive snobbishness behind the polite enquiry, the first hint of a genuinely unguarded reaction.

'Not far,' he said.

Linda tried hard not to stare at his hands, but her eyes kept being drawn back to them: their size, and their unusual shape. She was sure that like the composer Brahms, one of those hands could span an octave comfortably. The fingers were long, the tips sensuously padded and slightly spatulate. When he held his cigarette to his lips they formed an elegant, sculpted curve. It was impossible not to speculate on how those finger-tips would feel lightly brushing one's nipple, and she did so with some pleasure.

'What do you do?' she asked, to take her mind off this.

'I'm an architect.' Bryn spared her having to make a show of interest by continuing briskly, 'And you?'

'A secretary.' No 'only' for her, he noticed.

'Whose?'

'Sir Harry Frankel's.'

'Oh, my.'

'He owns Delancey Hotels.'

'I know who he is. Is he as formidable as they say?'

She shook her head. 'He's a pussy cat.'

Bryn sighed. 'That's something only very pretty girls can say about ferocious old bastards.'

'No, no,' she insisted. 'On a personal level he's a gentleman always, with everyone. On the other hand you don't get where he is by suffering fools gladly.'

'Of course not. And you, not being a fool, have made your-self indispensable to the great man.'

'We understand each other.' If she hoped her minute hesitation had passed unnoticed, she was wrong.

It spoke volumes. Bryn called to mind when he'd last seen Harry Frankel on the box – a small, sleek, savvy man of about sixty, with the controlling high-octane charm of the extremely rich and successful. There was not a scintilla of doubt in his mind that the understanding between the magnate and his PA extended well beyond her knowing the date of his wife's birthday.

'So are there perks?' he asked. 'A discount at the hotels?'

As she told this man about her job Linda thought of Harry. If sharing secrets was a measure of intimacy, then they could scarcely be closer.

'So that's me,' she said. 'Now it's your turn.'

He told her about his glory days on the rugby pitch. He didn't need to talk them up; they had indeed been glorious, and she knew a little about the game and was an appreciative audience. But he glossed over the grey despair that had gripped him when all that was over and he was left at twenty-three with nothing but a second-class degree and a job in insurance to which he'd never paid much attention in the past and which seemed to hold no future.

'So I packed it in,' he said easily, 'and trained as an architect.'

She studied him, frowning slightly. 'You make it sound simple, but it must have been hard to change careers like that.'

'Not really, because I was doing what I wanted.'

'Like the rugger.'

'Precisely. And then along the way, while I was training, I was lucky enough to win a prize – nothing world-shaking, but enough to raise my profile above the parapet, and get me a reputation so it started to be fun.'

She pushed forward her cup for a refill. 'Thank you. So, tell me, what have you designed? That I'd have heard of.'

'Let's see. The Marlin Building in Docklands? It's a seriously flashy skyscraper,' he added in response to her blank look.

She pulled an apologetic face. 'Sorry – aren't I hopeless?'

'Not at all. In the main people, especially Brits, don't notice architecture unless it has some direct bearing on their day-to-day lives. I bet you know Kensington Town Hall and the Brompton Oratory? The National Theatre?'

'Yes, but not who designed them.'

'OK, fair point. Anyway, that's what I do.'

'What competition did you win?'

'It was for a memorial garden.'

'Where?'

He considered, briefly but carefully, how much to tell her. 'Somewhere where terrible things happened.'

She picked up on his reticence, saying only: 'That must have been difficult.'

'It was. More a question of concept than design, which is why it was possible for a rank outsider to win. It's still the thing I'm most proud of.'

'Congratulations.' She lifted her glass, and then leaned forward confidentially. 'I'm so glad I met you.'

'Likewise,' he said. He suspected that, unlike him, she was displaying a charming insincerity.

Problems with delays further down the line meant the train didn't stop at Watford. Bryn managed, with difficulty, to conceal his delight.

They arrived at Euston in the small hours. Passengers who were asleep were allowed to stay on the train till six a.m. but the two of them disembarked. He helped her with the larger of her two matching suitcases. In the middle of the main forecourt he put the case down.

'Where to?'

'Taxi,' she said.

'Will you be able to manage?'

She gave him a look. 'It's very gentlemanly of you, but yes.'

'Well—' He held out his hand. 'It's been fun.'

She gave the hand a brisk shake. 'Hasn't it?'

'Good luck.'

'Always a help. 'Bye.'

They made off in their separate directions. By the pessimistic departures board it was Bryn who weakened and looked back, but she had already disappeared. More than two years would pass before he met her again.

From time to time during the decade when his fortunes began to prosper, Bryn reflected on the strangeness of a success built, literally, on so many dark and secret deaths.

The place he had designed on the spot where the killing-house had stood was calm, circular, sequestered; oriental in feel, English in content: white stone, scented herbs, a sundial commissioned from a local artist, the whole thing surrounded by high arched panels of plate glass, here and there etched with fine, wavering downward lines like raindrops, or tears. The idea he had – the 'concept' he had mentioned to his companion on the stranded train – was of peaceful closure combined with continuity. When he thought of those lost children, it was as though their agony and terror had conferred a nobility on them. He knew this was a spurious notion, its spuriousness confirmed by his meetings with some of their families, who were prosaic, vulgar and even occasionally repellent in their public grief. He blamed television, which had turned mourning into a semi-professional activity. Still the notion persisted. No one could endure what those children had, over weeks and months, and *not* have been changed. While trying to avoid the Victorian sentimentality of little angels or new stars in the firmament, he nonetheless took a few selfish crumbs of comfort from the thought of some good coming of their suffering. Martyrdom rather than murder. Innocent deaths that had not been in vain because we had been made to examine ourselves . . .

All meretricious shite, he would generally conclude. Better robustly to acknowledge the truth, that the only good to come of it all was to himself, in the shape of the prize money, and the boost to his work prospects.

The lost children had been good to him, no doubt of it.

He had a flat in north Hertfordshire, part of an old brewery conversion which he suspected irritated the long-term locals, fringed as it was by brash, middle-range convertibles and Japanese four-by-fours, but which was perfect for a single man in his situation. He liked, both personally and professionally, the spare, light functionality of the flat. It was a space that made itself available rather than imposed its own ideas. Given this freedom he left it pretty much alone. The items of furniture he did have were big – a bed like a prairie, a four-seater leather sofa, a custom-made slate refectory table and chairs, a twenty-four-inch television and a sleek, Scandinavian sound system. He wasn't by nature tidy, and counteracted this by keeping his possessions to a minimum, except for books, which stood in piles against the pale-grey walls: he preferred that to the looming presence of shelves. His few clothes hung on a rail purchased from a closing-down dry cleaner's. As many windows as he could, he kept uncovered. The kitchen, which looked across to apartments on the other wing of the brewery development, had a parchment blind, and the master bedroom dark blue curtains, made by his sister Alison, with some kind of fancy pleated top which she had recommended. None of it felt like home, nor was it intended to, except the room he worked in. This was a large gallery space beneath a south-facing sloping roof with four skylights. It was the reason he'd chosen a top-floor flat, notwithstanding the smaller living area and lack of a balcony. When he was in his atelier he was, in every sense, in his element.

By nature gregarious, he nonetheless avoided contact with his neighbours. It wasn't hard; this was not a neighbourly building. His social life centred mainly around various old rugby and university friends in London, some married, some still riotously single, and Sally, his girlfriend of two years' standing. She was a squeak older than him, divorced with a brace of teenage daughters. There was no doubt that the girls – Mary and Amy – were a large factor in the relationship. Not only were they extremely pretty, but he felt at home in all-female households. He had been raised in one. His father, in spite of distant Italian forbears, was a cold, brisk, hypercritical man with a waspish temper. He had succumbed to prostate cancer in middle age and Bryn, secretly glad to see him go, had been happy thenceforth to be cherished by his mother and sister. In this rich mulch of female devotion he flourished as the green bay tree, and not only emotionally. Neither his parents nor Alison were above average height and yet Bryn grew, and went on growing. High, wide and handsome, pre-eminent at sports and popular with both sexes, he acquired the shiny air of a young man leading a charmed life.

While he was a star with Harlequins nothing else much mattered. But the accident had entered and changed his life with the force of a meteorite: blinding speed, colossal impact, an explosion of pain and turmoil that ruptured the fragile caul of his youthful success and left him stranded, gasping for air in a new and hostile element.

He lost a week. A week when he was lying in intensive care, the barely sentient hub of a spaghetti junction of tubes. When he came round it was to a world in which the tectonic plates, like those of his skull, had shifted. He knew within minutes of regaining full consciousness that he would be 'all right' – that is, he had suffered no brain damage and would be able to walk, talk and continue to lead a full life. But during the ensuing weeks of painful recovery the realisation dawned on him that 'all right' was a weasel word, and that the glory days were over. Like the discovery of a partner's infidelity he, whom it most closely involved, was the last to know that he wouldn't play rugger again. His team-mates, the rest of the club, the board, his mother and sister, the doctors (especially the doctors) seemed to have formed a conspiracy of quiet, philo-sophical understanding – as if they could possibly understand! – beneath which he raged helplessly like a lion caught in a net.

Bryn wasn't neurotic, and he was physically strong; he got

over it. Got over all of it, though the depression took a lot longer than the head injuries. To feel well, and strong, to be one's old self but not given full rein, was pure purgatory.

Some years later when he was contemplating the children's memorial he remembered this self-pity, and reproached, then forgave himself for it. It had been a young man's bitter disappointment at having the cup of public success and admiration dashed from his lips. He had missed, no one knew how badly, the roar of approbation, the singing, the adrenalin-hit of beating the defence to an open try, the long, missed heartbeat of a goal kick . . . It had all come so easily and naturally to him. Now he was trying to do something slower, for which he might with a following wind discover an aptitude but which would not carry that instant gratification, the exhilarating tidal wave of approval from the stands crashing over his head as he breached the opposition line.

He had met Sally at the thirtieth birthday party of an ex-girlfriend in a room over a pub in Chiswick. He'd been unattached, she'd been accompanied by a man in an Aran sweater. They had observed the proprieties on the night, but he'd called her afterwards.

'You beat me to it,' was what she'd said, and he'd liked that.

'So I'm right – we have a thing?'

She laughed. 'Potentially.'

'Could we test the proposition over dinner?'

'Why not. Yes, I think we should.'

The proposition was duly proved: they had a thing. But it was a thing of a particular kind, unprecedented in his relationships with women. Sally was a mate, in both senses of the word. Their sex life was enjoyable and energetic, but what held them together was friendship, not the electricity of difference but the glue of mutuality. Bryn was well aware that in Sally's house – not just her bedroom but her big, untidy kitchen and comfortably relaxed sitting room – he was re-creating the past, the home where he'd been brought up as the apple of two women's eyes, and where everything had seemed possible and within his grasp. In her matter-of-fact way Sally spoiled him. She cooked things that he liked, she treated him as one of the family, gave him the run of the house, unlimited hot water and sofa space. Her manner implied, without in any way compromising her independence, that he was the man of the house, entitled to certain privileges, a status and a situation to which Bryn rapidly became accustomed. Notwithstanding an air of engaging slummockiness, Sally was more than competent, a dab hand both at her job as a doctor's receptionist ('the only halfway human one in the annals of the NHS' Bryn posited), putting up shelves, growing veg, and getting tough with her daughters without fear or favour. She was the opposite of ingratiating: straightforward and sensible, always giving of her best but not in order to court popularity. Once she came out with the old saying: 'If you can't have what you want, you must want what you have', and Bryn had laughed; they'd roughhoused, he hadn't been sure how to take it. She hadn't helped him out.

Life with Sally was so comfortable and content that it was almost like being married. Except in this one vital respect: he could leave at any time. There was a song, some country thing, that summed it up: Sally's door was open, and her path free to go. So he stayed.

Mary and Amy, fifteen and thirteen respectively at the time their relationship began, took him in their stride. The divorce had been eight years ago and they were on good terms with their errant father, an officer in the Signals, now remarried and currently at Catterick. Bryn hadn't met him, neither did he know how many boyfriends Sally had had since the divorce. Her manner with the Aran sweater had spoken of a sort of practised non-commitment. Though he couldn't be sure, he liked to think that he was the first since Chris (the husband) to be admitted so completely to hearth and home. It was certainly impossible to deduce anything from the girls' reaction. To begin with they were no more than flitting background figures, fey creatures caught in his peripheral vision darting across the hall, whisking into the bathroom or up the stairs, shyly grazing in the kitchen, faces shielded by curtains of fine hair, acknowledging him with a 'Hi', and gone in a flash.

It was Amy, the younger and marginally less aloof of the two girls, with whom he first established some sort of rapport, on an evening when he had turned up to find both Mary and her mother out.

'Mum's at the supermarket, she said to tell you she'll be back in a few minutes,' said Amy, and was already turning to go up to her room when Bryn asked:

'Do you think there's something useful I could do?'

She stopped and half turned back, not actually looking at him, her face blank with embarrassment and slightly flushed.

'What sort of thing?'

'I don't know . . . supper?'

'That's what she's shopping for.'

'Shall we lay the table?'

'OK,' she murmured and still without looking led the way to the kitchen. She opened a drawer and began taking out handfuls of cutlery. He got glasses out of the cupboard and clean plates from the dishwasher.

'So how is it?' he asked. 'Life, the universe and everything?'

'I don't know.' He caught a tiny sniffing sound, a sort of phonetic punctuation mark indicative of suppressed amusement: either at or with him, it didn't matter. 'OK.'

'That's good,' he said, adding as if she'd enquired: 'It's pretty good for me, too. Your mother's fantastic, isn't she?'

'I suppose so.' She tore three squares of kitchen towel off the roll and placed one square beneath each fork.

'I'm gobsmacked with admiration,' he continued affably. 'I've never been sure about this ability to do many things at once that women are supposed to be famous for, but your mum's the living proof if proof were needed. And I suppose you'll be the same.'

'I doubt it,' murmured Amy, which he took to be concurrence at one level.

The table was laid, but he was loath to relinquish his hard-won advantage. 'I might have a beer. Can I get you anything?'

'I'll have a juice – I'll help myself.'

She got to the fridge before him and took out the carton of orange juice; almost closed the door, opened it again, and fished out a bottle of French lager.

'That all right?'

'More than. Thanks.'

She sat down at the table and looked at him doubtfully. 'Do you want a glass?'

'I believe it's trendy to drink out of the bottle.'

She didn't dignify this with a comment. But there they were, sitting at the table together. All kinds of half-forgotten advice about how to approach animals – non-aggressively, without eye contact, and so on, came to his aid. He gazed out of the kitchen window reflectively.

'The Edwardians knew what they were doing when they built these houses, didn't they? The scale, the proportions, the layout . . . just about the perfect living space.'

There was such a long silence that he was about to continue. Then she said in a flat, I'm-not-arguing voice, 'But this house isn't how it was originally – is it?'

'Good point. This is an extension, yes?'

'We didn't do it,' she pointed out. 'It was here already.'

'No, but you're quite right.'

'The bathroom's bigger, too. And Mum put in the extra loo.'

'Very wise. We have no truck with single-loo establishments.'

He was rewarded with a reluctant smile as the front door rattled open.

'I'm back! Sorry, it was like the seventh circle of hell in that place this evening – hello, you're both here!'

Sally dumped four straining carrier bags on the side, then greeted first her daughter with a hand touched lightly to the back of her head, then him, with a kiss on the cheek. For an instant he felt not like her lover but like her other child, one of Sally's gang. Amy pushed her chair back.

'Give us a shout when it's ready.'

'I will.'

Amy paused in the doorway. 'Can I have it in front of *Top of the Pops*?'

'No.'

'But we do when Bryn's not here, often.'

'Never mind, he is here and we're going to be civilised.'

'That's really hypocritical,' said Amy, but without rancour.

'It is,' said Bryn. 'But I appreciate the sacrifice.'

He got up and began to help Sally take things out of the bags. When Amy's footsteps reached the landing, he left that and put his arms round her.

'What a woman!'

She laughed into his shoulder. 'It's only shopping.'

'Call it what you like.'

'Mm . . .' She squeezed him amorously. 'Nice.'

It *was* nice, and still remained so. Bryn had heard people draw a distinction between relationships that were passionate and those – not passionate, it was implied – that were merely comfortable. But as far as he was concerned this was a distinction without a difference. With Sally he felt as if he had been presented with a relationship complete in every respect, physical, emotional, material, even: a sort of marriage-without-baggage that could scarcely be improved upon. He knew he was a lucky sod, the luckiest, and said as much when his friend Jim chided him for laziness.

'You're getting sucked in, mate.'

'OK, hands up, I admit it. It's fantastic.'

'It's not good for you.'

Bryn barked with laughter. 'I'll be the judge of that!'

'Pardon my saying so but you have the judgement of a goldfish.'

'Thanks.'

'It's true!'

'I've certainly chosen poorly in my friends.'

Jim pushed his chair back. 'My round.'

This was a familiar type of exchange between them. They had been at school together, where Jim had been a reasonably bright hard worker and Bryn cleverer but too good at games to have to try. 'A bad case of "to them that hath",' as Jim said. To add insult to injury – had they not been firm enough friends to ride it out – Bryn's misfortune on the rugby field had led indirectly to his outstripping Jim, who was becalmed in a dull, low-grade academic post in a provincial polytechnic. The delicate calibration of their relationship required that they often fell into their old roles in relation to one another – Jim as the sensible, grounded realist and Bryn the buccaneer, gifted but unwise. Neither persona was entirely accurate and both knew it, but the game eased them through awkward patches.

Waiting for his friend to return from the bar, Bryn reminded himself to tread warily. Jim was married to a fiercely brainy, somewhat unsociable girl called Victoria, in line to be one of the nation's top epidemiologists. Her tendency to treat Jim as a kind of on-tap support system had always struck Bryn as outrageous. Now he asked himself, is that what he was doing with Sally? With her open-door, open-arms policy was she simply too easy to use? Justifiable jealousy apart, was Jim in fact right?

He returned with the drinks. 'There you go.'

'Whisky chasers, you shouldn't have.'

'Well.' Jim sat down heavily and raised his glass. 'Jammy bugger.'

Mary took longer to come round. Bryn could see why; could feel it himself. She was a young woman in all but law, taller than her mother and with that louche hauteur that is the special property of the young and lovely. For she was lovely, and at that quintessential moment when loveliness can be left to go hang. She stuck metal into her ears, nose and lips, she wore clunking boots and hideous, graceless clothes, did awful things to her hair and nails. But whatever she did in the way of brutal trappings, her beauty still shone through. The full sense of Keats's 'Beauty is truth, truth, beauty' was borne in on Bryn when he regarded Mary: like truth, beauty would out.

Her manner towards him was one of arctic breeziness. Any remark directed his way – in response to something of his, she never initiated conversation – always tailed off as she put distance between herself and this disobliging evidence of her mother's carnality. Mary was a girl in a hurry.

The breakthrough came on Sally's birthday, her thirty-eighth. Bryn had bought her some black pearl earrings. They were beautiful, he was sure of his taste, and they had cost more than he could afford, but on encountering Mary in the living room while Sally was getting ready to go out to dinner with him, he had the presence of mind to ask her opinion.

He raised his voice above the music. 'Mary.'

Her glance flicked briefly from her book and back. 'Yes?'

'I wonder if you'd give me the benefit of your advice.'

She leaned across to lower the volume and looked at the small blue box in his hands. 'Mum's present?'

'How did you guess?'

'Isn't it a bit late for that? My advice I mean. She'll be down in a tick.'

'Just the same. It's not so much your advice as your opinion. You know her better than anyone, and if you told me in all honesty that they're not her kind of thing, I'd change them, even at this stage.'

'Oh, *right*.' Her voice dripped with exaggerated incredulity.

'Really.'

'Let's see then.'

He sat down on the sofa next to her and handed her the box, watching her face as she opened it. The change of expression was so slight – a barely perceptible softening of the mouth – that only he would have noticed it. Then she closed the box and passed it back to him.

'They're nice.'

'But do you think she'll like them? Honestly, Mary.'

'Trust me, she'll like them.'

'I'm so glad.' He got up. 'Thanks for dispelling my small crisis of confidence.'

'No worries.'

She restored the volume, but just as he was going out of the door, added: 'They must have cost a fortune.'

'Well . . .' He was surprised to find her looking directly at him. It felt like a challenge; he chose his words carefully. 'Let's put it this way. Your mum's worth it.'

'Sure.' The single syllable floated to him like a petal on the wind as Mary redirected her attention at the page but used as he was to interpreting the minute nuances of such exchanges, he knew he'd done the right thing.

That was the night he very nearly asked Sally to marry him. Something about the kindly glamour of the river room at the Savoy, the intimate-sounding band, the sheen of the Thames beyond the window, the presentation of the tiny blue box, the rainbow of delight that was so unlike her daughter's response but which nonetheless showed the resemblance between them . . . It would have been so lovely, so fitting, so *nice* to crown the occasion with a proposal – the words were on his lips. Almost. But at the last moment a propitious uncertainty about his motives and her answer stopped him, and instead he allowed himself simply to bask in her gratitude.

'They're absolutely *gorgeous*. How did you know how much I love black pearls?' As she spoke she was removing her earrings, replacing them with the new ones. 'Not that I've ever had any, till now.'

'I didn't. I just saw them and thought of you. I found them in the British Museum. They're copies of ones owned by Anne Boleyn.'

'Oh God!' She laughed. 'How can I possibly live up to that?'

He said: 'You're just as beautiful.'

'It's sweet of you to say so.'

'I mean it.'

He did. He could imagine no woman lovelier than Sally at that moment. Just then it was as if the sum of her parts, her looks, her kindness, her energy, her exuberance, amounted to far more than the nice, vital middle-aged woman she was. That evening she had a glow, a radiance that turned heads. He was indeed a lucky bastard. A huge gratitude, to and for her, surged through him. But inherent in that gratitude, though he didn't recognise it at the time, was an acceptance of what it was that had stifled his proposal: that this would not be for ever.

Still, Bryn knew when he was well off. He was not looking around, far from it. He adored Sally, and now that his relationship with the girls was improving all the time, he revelled in being sole male in her household. He began to pitch in, to make more of a contribution, doing jobs around the place, giving the girls lifts, and the occasional handout, when it was in his power to do so; he helped Sally to buy a new car. In other words he assumed a certain status, without undue responsibility. It was hard to imagine the woman or the situation that would lure him away from all this.

Afterwards, he could never say whether he fell in love with Linda at their first meeting. What he felt had more to do with him than with her. In her presence he had experienced for the first time in years a vivid sense of his *self*. It was as if he had been suspended in amniotic fluid, nourished, cradled and protected. Meeting Linda was an emotional rebirth, a startling recognition of where his edges ended and those of the rest of the world began.

Their second meeting was on the face of it as much a matter of pure chance as their first, but Bryn did not take long to decide that it was one of those chances dictated by fate. Becalmed as he was by comfort, at that meeting a warm, wild wind got up, and he began to race towards the horizon, and uncharted waters.

He was taking Mary out to lunch. It was her gap year and she was working as an assistant in what he considered to be a rather dodgy small, cheap clothes shop in Oxford Street. The owner, Mrs Govinda, was a painted amazon who looked as if she might eat gently reared teenagers for breakfast, and the tacky, highly coloured outfits came in in unpredictable waves that probably, Bryn thought, coincided with the accessibility of a manufacturer's lorry in the car park of Scratchwood services. Outside Motown Modes there was always a wide boy with an open suitcase full of vibrating clockwork guardsmen or Big Ben snowstorms, and inside, just Mary and the 'manager', Duane, a young person who seemed to hover in some inter-gender dimension of his own, and whose trappist demeanour can have done nothing to inspire confidence in the customer. Every time he went to visit Mary at Motown Modes – which was fairly regularly, Sally having begged him to maintain a watching brief – Bryn expected to find that Duane had taken the plunge and gone one way or the other, but it never happened.

Lunch hours were a strict hour and fifteen minutes, which had to be taken at a time to fit in with Duane's own lunching arrangements. Fortunately, eating wasn't high on his agenda, and most days he only went out to collect deep-fried nuggets and a large cola, thereafter being happy to sit by the till, eating, and turning the pages of a bondage magazine with greasy fingers.

In his role as quasi-godfather, neither relation nor, exactly, friend, Bryn saw it as his pleasant duty to introduce Mary to the finer things in life. Which he had to admit wasn't hard if you were taking Motown Modes as the starting point. It was his custom to pick her up at twelve forty-five, and walk her the couple of hundred yards or so to any one of a handful of sympathetic eateries near Soho Square. On this occasion it was Rico's in Dean Street, a cheap and cheerful Italian café, the size of whose pepper-grinders never disappointed.

They sat at their preferred table for two in the window alcove. Bryn's declared reason was that it was amusing to watch the world go by, but it also appealed to his vanity to be seen with this graceful, unusual teenage girl, and to imagine that passers-by might say to one another, 'Interesting combination, did you notice?' as he, in their place, might have done. He hoped very much that he did not look old enough to be her father. This little indulgence was no secret, he'd mentioned it to Sally and they'd laughed about it: he was keenly aware of what was appropriate in the circumstances, and the space between him and Mary was as solid and uncrossable as Rico's chequered table top.

Perhaps it was this ambivalence, this need for suitability, that made his second encounter with Linda such a jolt. In a split second it returned him to his other, sexually free self. They had ordered – American hot pizza for her, spaghetti carbonara for him and a bottle of house red – and Mary had gone to the ladies'. As he gazed out of the window Linda just appeared, suddenly, and so close that he flinched in surprise as she tapped the glass with her nails and mouthed: 'Hello!'

As he was still taking in the shiny swag of red hair, the cream tailored suit, the skyscraper heels, she was there – perched on the chair opposite, enveloping him in a wave of scent and all the polished playfulness he remembered from that marvellous snowbound train.

'Well, *hello* again, I was just whizzing by and I thought, *I* know that face, but where from? And then it came back to me – you were kind enough to help me out with that British Rail champagne on the journey from hell! How the devil are you?'

'Very well, extremely well—' He'd half risen to greet her but now he saw Mary returning and remained standing. Linda's arrival had thrown him off social balance. She glanced in the same direction and at once got to her feet.

'I'm so sorry, I'm sitting in your friend's place.'

'Not at all – well,' he waffled, 'you are, but why don't you join us for a drink? We could move, or it's the easiest thing in the world to get another chair.'

'Sweet,' her smile was almost too big and shiny for the split-second it occupied, 'but no thank you, I'm on my way to a lunch of my own, not nearly as nice as yours, I'm sure. Hello,' she addressed Mary. 'Don't worry, I'm off in a minute.'

'This is a young friend of mine, Mary.' He hoped the 'young friend' conveyed the precise weight and warmth of the relationship, but Linda seemed oblivious to any possible embarrassment as they shook hands.

'Mary, nice to meet you. Linda. Look.' She took a business card from the outer pocket of her handbag and handed it to Bryn. 'If you're in town and you'd like to have that drink, give me a buzz.'

He pocketed the card without looking at it, aware of Mary's watchful eye upon him. 'Thanks, who knows . . . Can't remember offhand what the diary holds for the next—'

But she was already leaving, holding up a hand in farewell as she went. ''Bye, enjoy!'

'Well, well.' They sat down opposite one another again as the wine arrived. He declined to taste it, waving a hand over Mary's glass. 'Fill 'em up.'

'Who was that?' she asked with an air of polite interest. 'Linda?'

'I hardly know myself, to be honest,' he explained. 'We met in the buffet car of a stranded train some years ago and cheered ourselves up with a bottle of bubbly. Nice woman. I'm amazed she remembered me.'

'You're quite easy to remember.' Mary snapped off a segment of breadstick. 'You must have made an impression.'

He laughed, finding it a relief to do so. 'I bought the damn champagne!'

Mary allowed a telltale beat to elapse before commenting: 'She's very attractive.'

'Yes,' he agreed. Useless to deny it. But he still added, cravenly: 'In an obvious sort of way. Ah, food!'

They let it go there, but for reasons he didn't choose to examine their lunch that day had an edge of self-consciousness.

Outside Motown Modes they touched cheeks, and he said: 'OK then. See you soon. Like this evening, probably.'

'I'm out.'

'Whenever. Better get in, you've got a customer, Duane's at full stretch.'

She turned towards the shop and with head averted asked: 'Are you going to call her, then?'

'Who?' There was no reply. 'Linda? I seriously doubt it.'

After his meeting he rang Sally and told her he wouldn't be round that night. 'Overtaken by events' was what he told her – a bland, portmanteau excuse which, as always, she didn't question. Their relationship was entirely free of games-playing. The unwritten contract stated that everything should be taken at face value: if something complicated or important needed to be said then it was the responsibility of the person concerned to say it.

Until now, this grown-up arrangement had worked well.

Linda's recorded voice was warm and silky, conveying an entirely spurious intimacy, like that of an American receptionist.

'*Hi there, this is Linda. Can't come to the phone right now, but please say who you are and what it's about and I'll get back to you as soon as I*— Yes, hello?' The real voice was louder and altogether brisker.

'Is that Linda?'

'Yes.'

'It's Bryn Mancini here. We bumped into each other earlier.'

She chuckled fruitily, the briskness gone. 'You mean I barged in on your lunch date.'

'Not at all. And anyway, I'm so glad you did.'

'I hope you apologised to – Mary, was it? – for me.'

'No need for that.' He smothered a small prick of conscience. 'In fact I wondered if you'd care to have that drink some time?'

'Do you know, I would. Hang on a moment.'

While she checked, Bryn recalled that in deference to Mary he had made some fatuous reference to the state of his own diary and yet here he was ringing that very evening, putting himself in her hands, allowing himself to be subject to her more pressing arrangements.

'Not this week,' she said. 'But Tuesday, Wednesday, Thursday the week after.'

'Sounds fine.'

'Which?'

'Wednesday?'

'Fine. Do you know Vlad's champagne bar in Frampton Street off Piccadilly?'

'No, but I'll find it.'

'You're on. Six thirty suit you?'

'Perfectly.'

'See you then.'

The phone her end went down at once. Another arrangement made, was the impression given. He had to remind himself that it was she who had seen him first, who had come into the restaurant, made herself known, given him her card, suggested he ring . . . He was slightly dazed by the speed with which everything had happened. It occurred to him, not without a perverse vanity, that he had been bounced by an expert.

On checking his diary he found that he did in fact have an appointment on the Wednesday in question, but one that he could reschedule without too much difficulty for the following day.

There remained Sally. Sally, who asked no questions and made no claims; to whom he had never declared love and who had not declared it to him, but who nonetheless commanded his loyalty and respect.

He put off seeing her until the weekend. He had never avoided her before and it made him uncomfortable to do so now in spite or because of the fact that he knew she would not question him directly or by implication. He could find nowhere to park near her house, but as he drove slowly past he looked in and saw her, sitting outside the living room French window, reading a book with her glasses on. The calmness of this image haunted him as he himself became hot and bothered, backing into a space in the next street.

This part of North London comprised broad avenues lined with red-brick semi-detached Edwardian villas two to five storeys high. The occupants of these houses shopped at the supermarket in the high road or, if short of something needed urgently, in the small parade of shops near the park: video store, chemist, mini-mart, greengrocer and newsagent. Bryn liked the neighbourhood's unruffled solidity, its air of modest prosperity, honestly worked for. At regular intervals along the pavements plane trees stood like a guard of honour. On every third corner a letter box was set in a wall or clipped like a nesting box to the trunk of a street lamp. Beyond the broadly similar facades of the houses were, Bryn knew from his social life with Sally, wonders of imaginative refurbishment and reconstruction: palaces of polished wood and sleek chrome; snug period interiors for which every detail had been painstakingly researched and tirelessly hunted down in salvage yards and junkshops; high urban chic and artful faux rustic. It never failed to astonish him how much time, trouble and expense people put into customising their homes. It was a tribute to the domestic architecture of the period that it could accommodate so many different styles without ever losing its particular character. True, there were a few double-glazed porches, and the odd unsympathetic loft conversion, but in the main the streets looked as they must always have done.

The decor of Sally's house, which he was now approaching, was not high-concept. It was evolved and eclectic, and displayed the confident carelessness of its owner, a woman who could display the china donkey brought back by her daughter from a school trip to Barcelona alongside a Clarice Cliff vase, using the two as bookends for a sheaf of bills and invitations. It saddened Bryn to think he would not be seeing so much of it in the future.

He went up the alley at the side of the house, and through the tall wooden gate. At once he was aware of that air of seclusion which is the special property of the town garden. The side door stood open but the kitchen was empty, so he threaded his way between the dustbins, the watering can and hose, the leaning towers of flowerpots and the bicycle and came to the back of the house.

Sally was no longer there, but her book – the much-trumpeted biography of a famous explorer – lay face down on the seat of the wooden garden chair, with her spectacles, arms wide, on top of it. As he approached he heard voices; she was in the living room talking to someone. The garden on this midsummer's evening was bright, casting the interior of the house into shadow. He could make out the two figures, and then the pale, accusing oval of Mary's face looking over Sally's shoulder. As Sally turned towards him, her daughter disappeared.

'Sorry to creep up on you,' he said. 'When I drove by a few minutes ago you were in the garden.'

'Dirty rotten spy.' She came over and lifted up her face to kiss him, but he managed to escape into a hug, and she put her arms round his neck. 'Lovely to see you.'

They stood like that for a second or two and then she said, from within his embrace, 'I bought Pimm's, would you like one?'

'Sounds wonderful.'

'Sit yourself down, it won't take a second.'

He took off his jacket and tie and slung them over the arm of the sofa, loosening his tie as he went out and sat heavily on the swing seat, setting it rocking. Sally's cat, Jonah, lay on his side on the hot patio tiles. The faint, insistent squeak of the swing seat made him lift his head and cast a slumbrous, slitty-eyed look in Bryn's direction. Their gazes met with a perfect mutual lack of interest before Jonah's head sank back down.

A small sound, a movement from above, advertised Mary's presence in her bedroom, which overlooked the garden. A thin arm pushed the window open, and pulled a blind down; there ensued the muffled chirrup, twang and nasal harmonies of pop on commercial radio.

Sally came out with the Pimm's on a tray, which she set on the ground. She handed him his glass and lifted hers.

'Good health.'

'This looks great,' he said. She smiled, agreeing.

Silence, but for the yammering of the distant music, now with a wailing falsetto descant. Sally dropped her head back and closed her eyes, the shadow of a smile still on her face. Her focused tranquillity was, as he was sure she intended, a barrier between them.

In an attempt to breach it, he asked: 'Where's Amy?'

'Umm . . . Gone to a friend's for the night.'

'Mary off out too?'

'Yup.' She nodded. 'Friends to consult, lads to spurn.' She looked his way, shielding her eyes with one arm. 'So we shall have the place to ourselves.'

There was another intense silence. Jonah got up, stretched and stalked inside. Streets away, the urgent yelp of a police siren emphasised the uneasy peace where they were. Or perhaps – Bryn stole a look at Sally, her familiar body softly slumped in the garden chair, her glass held loosely on her lap between linked hands – the uneasiness was his alone.

Sally said, in an inconsequential tone: 'By the way, she enjoyed her lunch with you the other day.'

'Good. I certainly did.'

'It's kind of you to bother, Bryn.'

'It's a pleasure.'

Sally's voice became almost dreamy. 'She said you met an old friend . . .'

Now, thought Bryn, I can do it now.

'Not exactly a friend, someone I happen to have met before.'

'And she's thrown you into confusion.'

'Yes.'

Sally straightened herself, took a sip of her Pimm's. 'It's all right, you know.'

'Is it?' He felt hope, anxiety, sorrow. Most of all, hope.

'Of course. You're a free agent. I'm a free agent.'

'In theory,' he agreed. 'But we've meant so much to each other over this past couple of years.'

'We have,' she said, and he couldn't fail to miss the echo of his own past tense.

'I haven't *felt* free,' he explained. 'I've felt – free to be with you.'

'But now you're attracted to someone else. It's OK.' Her voice was soft. She turned to look at him and her face was the same.

'For one thing, it's allowed,' she said. 'And for another, the sad truth is that your happiness is important to me. I had no idea I was so selfless . . .' She gave a little laugh and stretched out her hand. He took it, and she squeezed his and gave it a little shake before releasing it. 'She knew right away, Bryn. My daughter's not daft.'

'I see.' No wonder Mary had gone so quickly, without so much as a 'hello'. He felt a prickle of annoyance. 'What can she have said?'

'Nothing loaded. She didn't snitch on you—'

'There was nothing to snitch on.'

'No. No, of course not.' Sally held her glass against her closed lips for a moment. 'She did mention how attractive Linda was.'

'Look.' He felt some emollient gesture was required of him. 'I'm going to meet her for a drink, that's all.'

'Of course. And you don't want to feel guilty about that, why should you? This isn't a big deal, Bryn, just something to be got out of the way.'

The music was switched off. Seconds later a door slammed.

'Do you think she's been listening?' he asked *sotto voce*.

'Well, wouldn't you?'

'It's not her business.'

'Yes it is!' Sally's voice remained quiet but her cheeks showed a pink flare of anger. 'You made it her business. She thinks you're great.'

'I can't imagine why.'

'Maybe,' said Sally, 'she takes after me.'

Now the nearer, heavier bang of the front door punctuated their bruised silence.

'I'm so sorry,' said Bryn.

'Don't be. You've done nothing wrong.'

Shortly after that he left. It was clear to him that Sally would have continued with the evening, not exactly as if nothing had happened, but as if what had happened was of no consequence. That, he reflected, was the difference between them: she said that it didn't matter, and by saying it hoped to ease the pain; he knew that it did, and that by pretending they hurt each other more. It was more awful than he had imagined. He had always perceived Sally as someone whose calm good sense far outweighed his own. For the first time he now saw that she was vulnerable, capable of jealousy and self-deceit – that perhaps she had cared for him far more than he had known. That he was being a rat.

They said goodbye in the darkening hall and, also for the first time, the house in which he had so often been so happy seemed a sad and unsettled place. He tried not to think of the mats, napkins, cutlery and candlestick he'd seen in the centre of the kitchen table where she'd put them when she fetched the Pimm's, ready to be laid out if he'd chosen to stay. He had always come and gone here accepted and unchallenged, but he wanted his departure to be clearer, more defined than that.

'Please give my love to Mary and Amy,' he said, 'and wish them all the luck in the world.'

'I will.'

'And you—'

'I'll look after myself.' She said this as if supplying the cliché he might have used.

'Please.'

'Right.' She leaned forward, arms folded, and kissed him on the cheek. ''Bye then.'

'Goodbye, Sally.'

Afterwards, he couldn't remember returning to the car because, though his heart was heavy, he was walking on air.

5

1981 – Linda

Linda liked visiting Aylmer House. It meant a day out of London, it was generally undemanding, and she enjoyed the sense of importance that it gave her.

Also, it was a beautiful place. This part of Essex was a fantasy rural England within easy reach of town, as different by nature and design from its estuarine counterpart as it was possible to be, the rich, rolling farmland interrupted at regular and pleasing intervals by charming villages and pretty cottages clad with white clapboard and topped by mossy red tiles, with here and there a gracious Tudor or Georgian manor, of which Aylmer House was one.

Arriving as she did in her forest-green MG convertible with its cream leather seats (the journey here and back took her in the opposite direction from the stream of commuters) Linda felt herself well up to her surroundings. She considered it vital to make an extra effort on these occasions; she saw herself less as an agent, than an ambassador, and as such she aspired to nothing short of an immaculate *soignée* elegance.

Once she'd turned off the road, given her name over the discreet intercom and passed between the filigree wrought-iron gates she pulled over for a moment to brush her hair and refresh her lipstick. She'd been driving with the top down, and now that the engine was switched off the grassy slopes and massive shade trees of Aylmer Park seemed in contrast so quiet that it was a while before she could hear the birds singing and the distant, desultory barking of a dog. In the middle distance a group of fallow deer were grazing. The parked car attracted their nervous attention as the moving one had not, and she could make out their raised heads and twitching leaf-shaped ears turned her way, alert to possible danger.

In a moment she moved off again, well within the required fifteen miles per hour. She was in no hurry. On the contrary, she liked to savour these moments of approaching up the drive – a young woman in a smart car on important business. She had always thought she would have made a good friend, or even girlfriend, of royalty – reliably glamorous and couth, the soul of integrity and copper-bottomed discretion. Sir Harry was, she told herself, the next best thing, royalty of a sort. He was right to put such trust in her, to place this burden of responsibility on her young shoulders. He discerned in Linda a steeliness that matched his own, a desire to do what was required and behave in the right way for reasons of pride rather than morality. He was flattering her by placing tremendous personal power in her hands, but both of them were shrewd enough to know that the greatest power of all lay in restraint.

After the half-mile or so of gently meandering drive you came upon the house suddenly, round a wooded bend, its broad Georgian curve at a slight angle to the visitor in order that it could command a view of the valley, complete with gazebo and artificial lake. A handsome building, Pevsner-recognised and glacially formal; immaculate but no longer cherished as before. Those to whom it was home these days were not discriminating.

She parked in the marked area at the back of the house, walked the thirty metres to the main door and rang and entered as instructed. The instant she stepped over the threshold Gordon Follayne appeared.

'Linda, good day to you. Are you well? I scarcely need to ask, you look wonderful as ever.'

'Gordon . . .' She smiled as she took his outstretched hand and held it for a second longer than necessary. 'It's a lovely day out there.'

'Makes one glad to be alive,' he agreed. They set off together along the corridor. 'Good run?'

'Perfect.'

Gordon turned left up the broad staircase. 'All sunny here too, I'm happy to report. I spoke to Sir Harry this morning.' He chuckled. 'Crack of dawn as usual.'

'He gets up at five, at his desk by six thirty.'

'I know, I know, all that energy and at his age, how does he do it . . .'

The question was rhetorical, and anyway Linda, charged with carrying out duties of a highly personal nature for her employer, would never have pointed out that the real interest lay not in how, but why, Sir Harry contrived to spend most of his waking life at work.

Sunlight streamed in through the long windows. A towering arrangement of delphiniums, pink, blue and white, with fountains of trailing greenery, stood on a polished oak table on the landing. The Turkish carpet, once a rich red and blue, had faded to the colour of storm clouds. As always it was very peaceful here. The only sound was that of a Hoover in the far outer reaches of the house.

'Would you like some coffee while you're here?' asked Gordon.

'Yes please.'

'I'll get Simonetta to bring some up.' He paused outside a door. 'Let's just take a peep . . . All quiet on the Western Front. Bleep if there's anything.'

'Thank you.'

Gordon opened the door and held it for her. 'Visitor for you, Al.'

The door closed.

'Hello, Al.'

Linda always forgot, from one visit to the next, how handsome Harry's son was. The long, hard planes of his pale face and the darkness of his hair and eyes only failed to reach matinée-idol perfection because of that smudge of strangeness, the sealed and shuttered quality of high-functioning autism. That, and the too-neatly cut hair, the unexceptionable but style-free shirt and trousers, the clean, chainstore trainers purchased by staff. No clues revealed what he might have been doing before she arrived – no book, comic, cards or pencil and paper on the table, no music, radio or television on. The room, like its occupant, was quiet and neat.

'Hello,' he said.

'It's Linda.'

'I know.'

'I've asked for some coffee, is that all right?'

'I'd like a Coke.'

'I bet they bring one. If they don't, we'll ask.'

Al was standing by his chair as if waiting to be told to sit. She went over to him and, holding him by the shoulders, stretched up to kiss him on both cheeks. Like his mother, he was taller than Harry. On this warm summer's morning his face felt cold.

'Let's sit down, shall we?'

She sat down on one of the two round-backed leather armchairs and Al lowered himself on to his. Everything in the room was elegant and discreetly luxurious – from the furniture and the Persian rug to the wide-screen colour television and the bright, flat contemporary paintings on the wall. Harry had spared no expense, though he could without any loss of comfort to Al have spent a fraction of the amount.

She opened her Vuitton holdall. 'I brought you some things.'

'Presents, let's see.' He leaned forward, his face suddenly bright with interest. One at a time she took out the things she had bought on Harry's behalf, intent on making this easy period last. The Michael Jackson *Thriller* video; a kingsize Mars Bar; a bundle of superheroes comics; a box of three contemporary hits compilations; the latest Super Mario game; and the pièce de résistance – a digital watch.

'You've been wanting one of these, haven't you?'

She held it out to him, but he was absorbed in examining the comics, breathing juicily, his cheek bulging with chocolate.

'Al? Look.' She gave the watch a little shake. 'Your very own watch. And there's all kinds of things it can do – give you the time in other countries, and you can time yourself doing things, it's got an alarm . . .'

Now he glanced at it. She saw the words sink in, and being weighed up. But the instant gratification of sweets and the Incredible Hulk were too powerful, and his eyes wandered back to the page.

'I'll leave it there,' she said, 'and we'll look at it together in a little while.'

There was a tap on the door and the coffee arrived. Simonetta was a voluptuous middle-aged Calabrian with fuzzy armpits and a dusting of moustache. Along with the coffee she carried with her a musky whiff of bodily secretions. Just as well, Linda thought, that Simonetta looked strong as an ox and had a habitually forbidding expression: a more brutally direct sexual being would have been hard to imagine.

Next to the cafetiere on the tray was a bottle of Coke, still dewy from the fridge, a bottle opener and two candy-striped straws.

'I brought drink for you, Al,' said Simonetta, giving him her beetle-browed glare. 'Your usual. Coffee,' she added perfunctorily without looking at Linda, who nonetheless felt the unmistakable hot swirl of female jealousy.

'Thanks so much, Simonetta,' she said sweetly. 'I knew you'd bring his favourite.'

'Every day,' growled Simonetta. 'Never fail.' The door snapped shut behind her.

Linda opened the Coke bottle and slipped in a straw. 'There you go.'

'Thanks.'

She poured herself a black coffee and stirred in a spoonful of sugar. Al was still immersed in the comics, but he held out his hand to receive the bottle, and guided the angled straw to his lips without ever taking his eyes from the page. She got up and went to the window, putting her coffee cup on the sill.

'Do you mind if I open the window for a minute?'

'Sure . . .' He shook his head, answering in two ways at once.

The rooms were air-conditioned. The window, rarely opened, was stiff, but she managed it and breathed in the gush of fresh air and its accompanying sounds. They were only half a mile or so from the sea, and she could hear the repetitive keening of gulls. On the path below a couple walked, arm in arm. She wore a full-skirted pink dress and pink shoes, he was in shirtsleeves and tie, his jacket over his arm. They moved out of sight. From beyond the far end of the house a man appeared on a motor mower, slowed, turned, and disappeared again. Now she could see a handful of gulls in the valley, white sparks against the grey-green. With the motor mower gone there was no sign of anything that could have placed this house in the late twentieth century – no visible burglar alarm or security system, no aerials, outside lighting, telegraph poles, distant traffic or pylons. And within the house, so many separate and controlled environments, such careful comfort and discreet supervision. For the first time Linda found this faceless, timeless, sequestered isolation eerie. Her chest tightened and she forced herself to inhale deeply. It would be at least an hour before she could decently leave.

'Linda . . .'

It was unusual, and pleasant, for Al to address her directly by name. Happy to be reminded of her responsibility, she turned. He had dropped the comic and was sitting back in the chair. From the open fly of his trousers his cock rose, huge and red, dribbling. His big hands rested on either side of it. One of them, she noticed inconsequentially, had been scribbled on in biro. His face was blurred with lust and pride.

'Linda, look . . .'

'No, Al.'

She walked to the door, pressed the buzzer. Stood there with her forehead against the wall and her stomach heaving, as behind her his breath quickened and her name was repeated huskily, like a scarred record, over and over again.

All she wanted was to get away, but Gordon insisted she come to his office before she left.

'I am so sorry you've had this to contend with, Linda,' he said, giving her the glass of mineral water she'd accepted instead of white wine. 'And I realise it's no consolation to know that he'd be most unlikely to take it any further.'

'It was the shock.' She could still feel it, her knees quivered and there was a bad, metallic taste in her mouth. 'He's always been – not like that. So wrapped up in himself, not interested in other people.'

'He still is in many ways, which is why nothing would have happened. It's classic inappropriate behaviour. But he's nearly twenty now and there are these occasional embarrassing incidents.'

'It's happened before then?'

'Simonetta's been subjected to the same sort of thing once or twice.'

'And how has she dealt with it?'

'By ignoring it, I understand,' said Gordon.

But something, some nuance of expression that he could not disguise, caused Linda to understand something entirely different, and her skin shrank in disgust.

The small seaside village where Al's mother lived was no more than a half-hour's drive away, time enough for Linda to reflect on what she had got herself into. It was a measure of her closeness and loyalty to her employer that nowadays it took something like the incident in Al's room to remind her just how bizarre this situation was. She remembered only too well when she had first learned of it, and become an accomplice. Sir Harry, at his most urbane, had mentioned it almost casually.

'I have a couple of relatives in the country,' was what he said, 'whom I look after but am no longer in contact with. It would be a great help to me, Linda, if you could drive out and deliver a few things for me from time to time.'

'Of course,' she said. She was in awe of her boss in those days. But in any event she could scarcely have said no.

'The boy isn't well,' he continued, accompanying the last word with raised hands and a little frown that indicated the nature of the illness. 'Till now his mother has managed, he's been having an education of sorts, but now he's older . . . He has recently gone into a special home. I believe it's one of the best of its kind, but I'd like to know that everything is going to plan.'

Linda wondered how on earth *she* would know, but she was too flattered, and yes, enthralled, to demur.

'One takes responsibility for these things, one can scarcely just let them go when times become difficult,' he murmured.

'Absolutely not!'

He gave her a languid, complicit smile. 'None of this concerns Lady Frankel by the way. It's just a matter I chose to involve myself in some time ago; I don't want her to be worried with it.'

'No, I understand.'

'The boy's mother lives nearby.'

'Would you like me to call on her as well?'

'That would be excellent!' he exclaimed, as though the idea had not so much as occurred to him till then. 'Would you do that for me? I'm sure she'd appreciate it.'

It hadn't taken long, with the help of Al's mother Coralie, for the full picture to emerge, and once in possession of it Linda was bound to Sir Harry Frankel with hoops of steel.

The house was called Mizpah. This name (Coralie said) had been in place long before her occupancy and was Hebrew for 'God will watch over us when we are apart'. Linda had been sceptical that one word could mean so much and had even wondered whether the definition had been made up by Coralie as some sort of personal and defiant motto. But when she queried the definition with Harry he told her that no, it was genuine and its apparent aptness no more than coincidence.

The name was written in black on a whitewashed lifesaving ring that hung over the porticoed door. The house was separated from the pedestrian promenade by no more than a narrow strip of beach pebbles set like cobbles into the tarmac, and a low wall topped by white coping. Coralie had put window boxes on all four front windowsills, but they were always draggled and battered by the tundra-breath of the insistent offshore wind.

She opened the door wearing one of her characteristic quasi-oriental robes, straining leggings and Dr Scholl's. Her greying hair was in a loose bun dripping with grips. Her face, unmade-up, was pink with broken veins. She must have weighed twelve stone at least. Though she was still, just, a handsome woman Linda found herself thinking that it was just as well Coralie had not become Lady Frankel.

'Linda dear, come on in, how was our boy when you saw him?'

'Very well. Pleased with his presents, especially the comics.'

'He likes those . . .' Coralie clunked towards the kitchen at the back of the house. 'Tea? A drink? Have you eaten?'

Linda, who had learned to translate this menu as, respectively, stewed medicinal grasses, under-aged homebrew and glutinous concoctions of cold baked beans and wholewheat pasta, declined.

'Mind if I do? I'm gasping.'

'Please . . .'

She watched as Coralie made herself a khaki infusion of what looked like marijuana and hay. After the episode with Al, in this more predictable setting she felt her pulse slow

and her equilibrium return. At Mizpah, she was sure of her
ground. She was so practised in her role of threeway intermediary that it had become second nature. When she referred to
Al's presents, it was understood that she had bought them, at
Harry's suggestion, but that Coralie would take credit for the
ideas in the first place. Coralie never bought presents. She
was skint, dear, not a pot to piss in. By which she meant that
in spite of being catered for in every department at another's
expense she had no salaried employment.

'And how's himself, the lord and master?'

'Working a twenty-five-hour day as usual.'

'He'll kill himself,' said Coralie cheerfully. 'Come through.'

They went into the living room and sat at the gate-legged
table in the window. Beyond the broad path the shingle rose
gently, and far beyond that was the grey horizon. The inside
of Mizpah was comfortable and tidy but had a dejected feel
which Linda put down to its not being Coralie's own place.
Some women, if kept, might revel in their situation, and take
advantage of it in order to surround themselves with pretty,
well-chosen things, fresh flowers and sensual clothes; Coralie
vegetated contentedly in hers. She was the only person Linda
knew who did actually, literally, nothing. She had no job, Al
was taken care of, she seemed to pursue no hobbies or occu-
pations, not so much as an evening class in aromatherapy to
alleviate the gentle boredom of her days. As passivity went, it
amounted to a towering achievement. The twin peaks of
Coralie's weekly activity, as far as Linda could make out, were
her gentle strolls to the pub on a Friday night and a Sunday
lunchtime, where she engaged in the merest phatic communion
with other regulars before strolling even more gently, and rather
less steadily, back. She had a cleaner, and the house's maintenance was taken care of. Such an existence would have driven
Linda stark staring mad in no time. But such was the deal,
and perhaps it was as well. If Coralie had been a lean, mean,
driven woman things might have become a great deal more
awkward for all concerned.

'So you're well, Coralie?' she enquired, warmly and encouragingly, laying her perfectly French-manicured hands flat on the table before her as she did so.

'I'm always well, dear. It's a funny old life I lead, there's no escaping that, but I try not to dwell on it.'

'Have you been away at all since I saw you last?'

'I went to stay with my old school friend and her husband in France. They have one of these barns near Carcassonne to which they've retreated. I'm not sure it would suit me but they seem happy.'

'It sounds absolutely lovely. Did you have a good time?'

'I did. Ate and drank rather too much and read several indifferent novels. The time passed very pleasantly.'

This last sentence, Linda thought, should be on Coralie's gravestone.

'Speaking of which,' she said. 'Shall we go out to lunch? Harry was very insistent we enjoy ourselves, and I think we should do as we're told.'

'Oh, I don't know . . .' Coralie bit her lower lip in a gosh-must-we face. 'I'm not dressed for it.'

Linda refrained from suggesting she go and change. 'We can go to the Fisherman's Arms. And you look fine anyway.'

'No, I don't.'

The hard, sour tone shocked Linda.

'I'm sorry?'

'I look God-awful and we both know it. Don't bother, mere politeness never reaches the eyes.'

'Coralie, I assure you—'

'Do you want to know what I can't bear, dear? It's not that I'm fat and useless and bored and boring. Nor that out of the hundreds of men I slept with I fell in love with the one who didn't give a stuff. Nor even that I lack the pride to do anything about it and live out here sedated by his money. It's that other people think I don't *know*. Do you understand? I'll accept everything, take responsibility for everything, eat crow and like it but I *won't* be patronised.'

'That was the last thing I intended.'

'No of course not, nobody intends it, it's just *there*. It has to be pointed out. Except now, to you. We've known each other for a good few years.'

'Six.'

'Whatever. I'm awfully used to being on the list, somewhere about halfway down . . . I don't resent it.' She made a face that showed how resentful she was. 'I know my place and I don't need a hired hand to remind me of it.'

Linda had been about to say something spirited, subversive, encouraging, to galvanise Coralie out of her self-recrimination, but this stopped her. For she, too, knew her place. She knew what Sir Harry paid her so well for, and the successful execution of today's task formed a large part of it. She was good at this, he had told her and anyway she knew it. She was not going to be put off her stroke or tempted into indiscretion by a self-pitying, overweight woman who meant nothing to her.

'Come on,' she said, rising from the table. 'We could both do with a glass of wine. May I use the bathroom?'

The question was rhetorical, she didn't wait for an answer but left the room and went up the stairs. When she came out of the bathroom a couple of minutes later she could hear Coralie in the kitchen, running a tap, closing a cupboard. The bedroom door was open and she went in. The room overlooked the beach and from this angle you could see the sea and the brown hulls of a couple of overturned rowing boats, like cockroaches, on the pebbles. But Linda hadn't come in for the view from the window. She was drawn by a lascivious curiosity to the collection of photographs on the dressing table.

She'd seen them before. The first time she'd come here Coralie had given her a tour of the house and waved a hand in their direction. 'This is my life.'

There was Coralie in her prime: statuesque, broad-faced, high-cheekboned and wide-eyed, with long black hair that sprang from her brow as if growing while you watched. Then with Harry, holding the infant Al in her arms and laughing broadly into the camera as though the whole thing were the most enormous joke, on her. Harry's expression was one Linda knew well – eyebrows raised, one slightly higher than the other, the ghost of a small dry smile – an expression which said, without rancour, 'Heaven help us all.'

It had not helped. The next picture was of Coralie and the ten-year-old Al on their own, she seated, holding his hand, at arm's length as if displaying him to the camera. His face was shadowed and blank, his legs odd in some way as if not quite under his control. Linda had long since done her sums, and knew that this picture must have been taken at about the time of Jonathan Frankel's twenty-first birthday. It was one of the cruellest ironies in a story full of ironies that Coralie had conceived during the very last knockings of her relationship with Harry, when they had gone their separate, amicable ways and saw each other no more than once a year for old times' sake. When neither of them, certainly, could have expected this.

The young Coralie, that, to Harry, most dangerously bewitching of creatures, the dope-smoking, free-loving scion of a double-barrelled English family, had preceded the more conventional Elizabeth in his life by some five years. After that their increasingly intermittent affair had never threatened the marriage, if only because Coralie had continued to bestow her favours widely and freely. Whatever Harry's shortcomings, credit was due to him for never having questioned that the child was his, and to Coralie for being pragmatic – and phlegmatic – enough to take the money and sit tight. The hyphenated family had long since washed their hands of her, and she knew Harry well enough to realise that he would never allow anything as messy as her, her son, and their difficulties, to clutter his life, but would do whatever was necessary in monetary terms to keep the mess contained. Arrangements had been made, and honoured, which enabled Alan to remain at home for as long as possible, but shortly

before Linda came on the scene it had been deemed necessary for him to live elsewhere where he could receive the full-
time attention he required. That place was Aylmer House.

To Linda's knowledge, Sir Harry had not seen or spoken
to his son for over ten years. Much as Linda admired and
adored her employer, this was an aspect of his character with
which she found it hard to come to terms. It was the one area
in which she herself saw the ruthlessness for which he was
notorious.

'Find what you wanted?'

Linda turned slowly, with a smile that conveyed neither
shock nor guilt.

'I'm afraid I love people's photographs. I've seen these
before, but still . . .'

She said this to remind Coralie, gently, that this was not an
intrusion. She had not been caught out in an invasion of
privacy, but discovered in the act of admiring pictures with
which she was familiar.

'Mmm . . .' Coralie wandered over, and picked up the one
of herself with Harry and the baby. 'That was then, eh?'

Linda wanted to pinch her fat arm, to hiss at her: 'Don't
wallow, you lazy cow! Get out there and get a life!'

Instead, she said: 'He thinks the world of both of you. You
know the life he leads. You and Al probably have more of his
attention than most people.' She was careful not to be specific,
but she didn't have to be.

'Than the lady wife, you mean.'

'Yes. Probably.'

Coralie put the picture down and gazed at herself in the
mirror, holding a hand at either side of her face and pulling
the flesh back.

'God, the difference half an inch makes . . . What about
golden boy?'

By this she meant Harry's other son, Jonathan.

'He's in Sydney at the moment. Managing a hotel over
there.'

'Pretending to be poor,' commented Coralie.

'Gaining practical experience. He's not getting any help from his parents, if that's what you mean.'

'Yes, but they're hardly going to let him go to hell if he fouls up, are they, dear?'

'No,' agreed Linda. 'Any more than Harry would let you or Al suffer in a crisis.'

'The man's a perfect saint!' Suddenly Coralie was light-hearted, laughing at herself.

'Let's go and have that drink!'

In the event it was four o'clock before Linda began the drive home. In the intervening three hours she had drunk a glass of white wine and what seemed like pints of bottled water, and eaten a seafood salad. Coralie had followed her large gin and tonic with two glasses of the house red, and consumed cod, chips and mushy peas, and homemade pecan pie with ice cream. Linda was exhausted by the end of it; and disgusted, by Coralie and with herself. Self-disgust in particular was not something with which she was familiar. All she wanted was to get away and go home.

Driving out in the early morning sunshine, fresh, smart and confident, she had been looking forward to her day, but now it had left her feeling depressed. Things had been different this time. She had been wrong-footed, first by Al, then by his mother, though probably in neither case intentionally. That, she reflected, was the trouble. She had idiotically supposed that this situation, over which she had been given such a degree of responsibility, would remain always the same; that she herself would move back and forth between the points of the triangle doing what she did best – maintaining the equilibrium, spreading goodwill, contributing to understanding, smoothing things over. She had underestimated her charges and so, it appeared, had Harry. Al's innocence, always so much a part of him, was ended. No more holy fool. No more state of grace. He'd joined the rest of them in unregenerate darkness.

And Coralie? Was a rebellion at last going to happen? Was the worm of discontent and resentment finally about to turn? On this Linda was torn. Every feminist instinct in her knew Coralie should have risen up long ago, cast off sloth and asserted herself. But there were other more important considerations than those of Coralie's character. There was Harry, whose legendary toughness she had as yet only glimpsed. And the even more daunting collateral damage to Lady Frankel, and their son.

As she drove through the outskirts of London, heading for the sanctuary of her flat, the prospect of a first date had lost its power to charm. She sensed a wild animal at her back, distant as yet, but gaining on her.

Bryn was enchanted to find her waiting for him, and bewitched all over again by her luscious prettiness, sheathed in minutely tailored black, a silken leg dangling a spindly heel from the bar stool, her hair in a Holly Golightly chignon embellished with a small black velvet bow.

'My apologies,' he said. 'I thought I was on time.'

'You are, but I was early . . .' They touched cheeks; he was ravished by her scent. 'And I've ordered a bottle of the Widow in memory of our first meeting. You'll join me?'

'Of course, how delightful.'

'I owe it to you.'

As they clinked glasses he felt conscious as he had once before of being very slightly on the back foot. It was a not unpleasant sensation. He decided to relax and enjoy it.

'You look gorgeous,' he said. 'I must be the envy of every man here.'

She glanced round, eyebrows raised in amusement. 'Wouldn't *that* be nice. The competition is always quite fierce in this place.'

'You leave the rest for dead, believe me.'

'Well,' she said, turning back to him, 'do you know, apart from all the other reasons for wanting to look my best tonight,

I've had a long and trying day and really needed to lift myself out of it.'

'Tell me about it.' It was a pleasure to him just to hear her talk, but in case he had sounded too eager, he added: 'If you'd like to. Nothing like a dose of other people's troubles to cheer a bloke up.'

'Oh, it was nothing dramatic. Out-of-town meetings, but sort of –' she frowned, glass held aloft – 'vaguely unsatisfactory, you know? One of those days that raised more questions than it answered.'

'Yes,' he said, 'I do know. Sir Harry's a hard taskmaster, I take it.'

'I wouldn't say that. He gives me a great deal of freedom and autonomy. And trusts me to get on with it. It doesn't follow that if I have a difficult or unsuccessful day I'm going to get a hard time from him.'

'Because he knows you'll give yourself one.'

'Precisely. Now then.' Her manner changed, her tone became teasing. 'Tell me about the lovely girl you were lunching with. Mary.'

'She was the daughter of an old friend.'

She laughed. 'And still is, presumably.'

'Yes – you know what I mean.'

'That perhaps the father's no longer a friend?'

'The mother.' He corrected her assumption instinctively.

'What a shame.'

He played for time. 'I'm sorry?'

'It's always sad when a friendship goes to the wall.'

'No, I didn't mean to imply that. Sally and I go way back, we'll never be shot of each other.' He realised that almost everything he'd just said or implied fell short of the truth, but it didn't bother him.

'That's so interesting,' she said musingly. 'I don't have a best friend. In fact I don't have any close friends. Masses of acquaintances, colleagues . . . But that's it.'

'I find that impossible to believe.'

'I never said I regretted it.' Her eyelids were lowered as she retrieved a packet of Disque Bleu from her bag. The barman beat him to it with a lighter.

'You're enviably self-sufficient.'

'Not really.' She blew smoke over her shoulder. 'I'm a romantic. I don't want to be dishing the dirt with lots of other people, them knowing all about me and me knowing far more than I want to about them. It really doesn't appeal to me. You know, hearing myself say that I realise that that's the way most men are. Whereas you have this close woman friend. I've got it – you and I are in the wrong bodies!'

He laughed, looking her up and down. 'I wouldn't say that. I'd much rather you were occupying that one.'

'But you take my point?'

'I suppose so. I'm not sure I go for all this gender-differentiation. It's like horoscopes, it's too easy and you can make anything fit.'

'No!' She shook her head, eyes closed. When she opened them again they were bright and predatory. 'I've decided. We're the exception that proves the rule.'

Once more he laughed, but this time it was because of her implication, or his inference, that they were already in some way linked.

All that evening, vampire-like, she drank him in. Fed on him. Sunned herself. Preened. And, gradually, relaxed.

She noted a difference in Bryn Mancini. He was almost imperceptibly less assured. This was partly due to her having taken the intitiative. The openness of his response surprised and charmed her – he was not too experienced a player to express delight. Or perhaps it was a measure of his sophistication, that he did not have to fence, that he knew nothing succeeded like handsome, straightforward admiration. Still, there was something . . . a softness, a wound. She suspected, despite his protestations, the demise of the old female friend.

Following the bottle of champagne they left Vlad's and went

to an old-fashioned Greek restaurant of his choosing, where all the waiters looked like bouncers and a cheerful and delicious feast washed down with retsina could be had 'for twopence halfpenny' as he put it.

'I can't tell you,' he'd said to her, 'the simple blokey pleasure I take in coming to an establishment like this with quite simply the most beautiful and elegant woman in the place. Very possibly in London.'

'Good!' she replied. 'Flattery and stuffed aubergines, the perfect dish.'

Over dinner she'd asked him about his work and he'd painted a picture of solid achievement by which he affected to be slightly surprised. She suspected that he was rather cleverer than he let on and, knowing nothing about his field, reminded herself to ask around. He told her that he was now living in Camden Town.

'What happened to Watford?'

'It was never really Watford.'

'I'll believe you . . .'

'It was the country, really. I did the opposite of what most people do and moved into London as things got better for me. And I have to say I don't regret it. Whereabouts are you?'

'Still Kensington. I out-city you by a long way.'

'Conceded. And work?'

'The head office is in Piccadilly. Sometimes I go to one of the hotels, or the Frankels' house in Tite Street.'

'Which do you prefer?'

'The house. For a start it's absolutely lovely, you can imagine, and for another it's a proper home. Lady Frankel is an absolute gem. She nags me about my weight and then serves chocolate cake with the coffee.'

'She's probably earmarked you for a daughter-in-law.'

She laughed. 'If she were a Jewish mother, which she isn't, she wouldn't want her darling boy to marry out. And since she's not, she doesn't think like that.'

'What you're saying is that Sir Harry married out himself?'

'He's a pragmatist – she was the right woman for the job.'

'Are there Frankel daughters?' he asked. 'An array of little princesses with Daddy eating out of their hands?'

'Actually no,' she said.

'Perhaps that's where you come in.'

'The daughter they never had?' She shook her head. 'I think not. Lady Frankel indulges me, but as far as he's concerned I'm just a good PA.'

'And an exceptionally decorative one.'

'There are women who'd handbag you for that remark.'

'Do you know, I can't bring myself to apologise.'

'That's OK,' she said. 'I'm not one of them.'

Unusually for her, she found herself thinking: if, one day, it all comes out about Al, I wonder how this man will react? Because he will be the only person I shall regret having lied to.

Bryn's garden was long, narrow and enclosed: a neglected bower. Roses, honeysuckle, clematis, passionflower and ivy had romped unchecked under the previous occupant, a hard-pressed single mother, and had become mixed and mingled into a heterogeneous mass. Over the two summers that he'd been there these walls of foliage had thickened, and the space between them shrunk. Sally had teased him about it, said that one sunny day he'd fall asleep and wake to find himself immured in greenery like the sleeping beauty.

'And don't expect me to hack through and give you the kiss of life,' she said. 'It'll be Shamus from down the road with the big chopper and the halitosis.'

He knew he should be firm with the garden, bring it under control. Apart from anything else the climbers themselves were in danger from the insidious depredations of bindweed, whose deceptively elegant pink and white trumpets were beginning to push through everywhere. In the autumn, he told himself, he would do it, so that next summer all would be in order and the plants have space to breathe. But for now the sequestered greenness was too seductive. In the tangle of growth, birds nested and rustled, spiders spun, and bees buzzed. When, as now, he went out into the garden at night, he was sure that the eyes of contented small animals watched him, their space and his existing harmoniously side by side. He had no outside lighting, and the polluted orange glow of London was like the atmosphere of some distant planet.

The garden comprised three sections, divided by shallow steps. Nearest the kitchen door was a small flagstoned patio on which stood his cast-iron table and chairs; beyond that a gravel area with an unpruned central rose bed, its fragrant, prickly tentacles shedding waxy petals. Through an ever-narrowing arch was a tiny pond, home to a small migrating population of toads and entirely covered in lily pads. On one side of the pond stood a mossy stone bench, on the other a statue of a nymph. The nymph was his own addition; he had fallen under her spell in a garden centre off the North Circular. She looked as if she were made of pale greenish stone but was actually some sort of resin, with a stabilising weight set into the plinth beneath her feet. She stood three feet tall, her hair cascading over one shoulder, one hand holding in place the drapery which just covered her breasts but which hung to expose the full length of her back and the top of the cleft between her buttocks. Her head was averted; she looked down to her left at the foot which peeped from beneath her hem. In the manner of her kind her expression was demure, but tonight she reminded Bryn of Linda, pretty and playful, a sophisticate aware of her power.

He sat down on the stone bench and regarded the nymph. So casually lifelike was her attitude that it would not have surprised him to see her move, to raise her head, smile and turn away so that her hair swung across her back and the drapery floated as she went, revealing a tantalising glimpse of bottom . . .

In a guilty reflex his thoughts turned to Sally, but in his mind's eye her face had already slipped out of focus and her voice become an indistinct echo.

He sat in a trance, until the lights in neighbouring houses had gone out. Two toads crept and hopped across the stones and plopped into the water without him noticing. A few drops splashed on to the nymph's foot, but she didn't move.

Linda's flat was on the top floor of a mansion block, and she had access to the roof. Tonight, because it was warm, she stripped and went up there in her short silk nightdress. On hot summer days she had been known to sunbathe naked up here, like something out of Dennis Wheatley, a human sacrifice spread out on the hard stone between the brick ramparts and the tall columns of the chimneys. She found it extraordinarily sexy, as though she were being fucked by the sun, by Phoebus himself. There were several newer, taller buildings in the neighbourhood; she found the notion of an anonymous peeping Tom quite titillating. The buildings were far enough away that anyone watching would never be able to identify their cheap thrill with one smartly dressed young woman among thousands on the streets below. Let them look, and weep.

Her nightdress was the slippery white of a wet seashell, or of moonlight on water. She felt she belonged up here on these strange, half-lit heights, a creature of the night, and as she stretched, on tiptoe, arms wide, head tilted back, it was as if she might actually take off and fly like a pale and silent bird over the shining city. She turned to face north and thought of Bryn Mancini. A good man – contented, at ease, prosperous, and without secrets. Time, perhaps, for a change.

6

1996 – Api

By the time Api was sixteen she was giving her mother cause for concern.

'She's fine,' said Charles. 'I don't know what you're worrying about.'

'No, well, you wouldn't,' replied Xanthe.

'What's that supposed to mean?'

'You don't know her. Any more than you've ever known any of them.'

Charles assumed an injured expression. 'I'm wounded, Zannie, I really am. I do my best. I may not be a model father but I am out there providing—'

'Huh!' said Xanthe.

'As I say, providing more than adequately for everyone. I don't know why you're suddenly being so touchy.'

'Hm.'

'Anyway, what's the matter with Api? As you see it.'

It was seven forty-five on a thundery evening in mid-July and they were upstairs preparing to go to a dinner party. It was sufficiently unusual for them to be in the bedroom together, and awake, to give their exchange an urgency and a sense of occasion. Charles, in a grey shirt and black linen suit, admired himself in the mirror. Xanthe, abandoning the struggle with awkward earrings, sat down heavily on the edge of the bed.

'She's seriously weird.'

'She's sixteen. Weird's in the job description. Surely it's nothing we – you – haven't seen before.'

'This is different. It's not that she's making a statement like

Gilda used to, or that she has specific, identifiable problems like Martin or Judith . . .'

'And she's not a model citizen like Saul,' suggested Charles, referring to his younger son, now a giro-happy performance poet currently living with a lady horse-dealer near Diss.

'It's pointless making comparisons. Comparisons are odious.'

Charles opened his mouth to say she'd started it, but Xanthe flapped his thought aside.

'I know I did, but it's pointless! The thing is she's become completely unreachable. I can't, you *certainly* can't, and the school are on the phone day and night whingeing about what they refer to as her lack of motivation.'

Charles pushed up the sleeves of his unstructured jacket. 'I'm mildly astonished that a state secondary school in this day and age should find that worthy of note.'

'They say she's withdrawn, and when she's not withdrawn she's hostile.'

'To whom?'

'Everyone, presumably. Them, the teachers, mainly.'

'That doesn't matter so much, it's when she starts alien- ating her own kind that you want to worry.'

'I don't want to worry at all!' Xanthe began on the earrings again, fiddling and grimacing, in what Charles recognised gloomily was one of her extremely rare takings. Her general lack of temperament was one of his wife's chief charms. When he saw what friends and colleagues had to put up with in the way of PMT, excessive demands, depressions, issues with this and that and the rest of it, he realised he had got off lightly. The occasional upheaval was only to be expected.

'And to be perfectly honest I don't give a monkey's what she does at school, but in this instance I can see it too – bugger and fuck!'

'Do you want a hand with those?'

'No, because I'm not bloody well bothering with them!'

Xanthe cast the earrings aside. 'She's a lost soul – lost to them, lost to us, not that that particularly matters, most of all lost to herself.'

'Zannie.' Charles trod gently. 'I don't see what grounds you have for saying that.'

'I know it. I *feel* it. I don't expect you to understand,' she added dismissively.

Charles affected hurt at this gratuitous shaft. 'That's not fair. *I* have feelings.'

'I mean,' said Xanthe, 'about your children. We'd better go.'

She rose, and pushed her long, bony feet into embroidered sandals. Charles wished she'd paint her toenails, but it was never going to happen.

As they turned out into the lane they happened to see Apollonia walking towards the house from the opposite direction. She wore a long purple dress, against which her pale amber hair and white skin made a striking contrast.

'There she is,' said Charles. 'Want to stop?'

'No, of course not.'

He peered in the rearview mirror. 'She seems OK to me.'

'That's a ludicrous remark. What do you mean? How could you tell?'

'She looks rather attractive. Arresting in fact.'

'Looks,' said Xanthe frostily, 'aren't everything. And appearances can be deceptive.'

'Go on, make it three.'

'Three what?'

'Clichés,' said Charles.

The dinner party for six, over which the hostess Jayne had slaved for a day and a half, was not accounted a success, either by herself, her husband Mark or their guests. Charles Durrance got sloshed and behaved goatishly, to an extent that soon ceased to be amusing. And even the early stages had failed to amuse his wife so the evening's atmosphere had been

polluted by the acrid whiff of a domestic. The storm outside
had added to the atmosphere of mounting drama.

During the post-coital debrief Jayne and Mark agreed that
it had not been at all like the Durrances. Whatever the strange
nature of their marriage and the bohemian style of the household over which Xanthe presided, they were always good as
gold socially. Charles, though a ladies' man, could always be
counted on to be charming and entertaining and Xanthe, if
a bit of an old hippy, was agreeably laid-back and well –
different – and they were the most appreciative guests. You
didn't expect to be asked back, but given the state of the house
you didn't much want to be, either, so that was all right. Jayne
was blowed if she knew what could have been eating them
this evening. Of course they'd had much to contend with over
the years in the shape of those fearful children, and now one
of the relatively normal ones was playing up, so maybe that
was it.

Api liked it when she was on her own in the house. The place
seemed to settle round her and mould itself to her shape. She
was sure she was the one who suited it best; that secretly it
was more hers than anyone's.

This sense of belonging was an increasingly unusual one.
At school she felt out of place. She wasn't disliked so much
as left alone. Her peers had given up on her and gave her a
wide berth, which was in a way what she intended. She
couldn't be bothered – with them, their preoccupations, the
way they talked. Her aloofness may not have won her affection, but it did command respect. What the others didn't know
– and what she hugged fiercely to herself so that they never
would – was how much she wanted it all to be otherwise. Api
had her dreams, and those dreams would have surprised those
who thought they had her number.

When she saw her parents' car pull out of the drive her
heart sank. She knew they were going out and had timed her
return home so as to follow their departure. The car turned

the other way, but braked momentarily; for one awful moment she thought they were going to stop. If she, too, stopped, they would know she had noticed them, so she kept her eyes firmly on the ground. They'd begun to behave out of character recently, to be curious – solicitous even. Api didn't appreciate it. Why, with all the crap they'd tolerated over the years from her brothers and sisters, had they chosen this moment, and her case, to become concerned, interventionist parents?

To her intense relief they drove on, and she went over the grass and into the house.

Perhaps, she pondered morosely as she surveyed the contents of the fridge, it was because she'd kept her head down for too long. It wasn't constant crap that got people going, it was crap that hadn't been there before. Her big mistake had lain in being no trouble for too long. Not that she was much now, leaving aside school, which didn't count. She just hadn't made her mind up about things, so she remained silent. That, she concluded, was what got up their noses. They couldn't stand not knowing. Well, neither could she.

She picked up various items and studied their use-by dates. The low-fat spread was down to the wire. Cheese and milk were OK. Yoghurts were long past, but then yoghurt was a strange substance so normal rules didn't apply. The economy-sized tub of hummus had been removed from its packaging, so there was no way of knowing, but neither could she see any visible mould. The salad drawer held half a litre bottle of flat Coke; some wrinkly tomatoes; desiccated but trimmable spring onions; a cucumber in good shape; and two bags of ready-made rocket salad in which the stagnant green liquid was already forming. These she threw away. She made herself a hummus and tomato sandwich and a vodka and Coke and went into the drawing room.

She switched on the music centre. It was set to CD and the Elgar cello concerto began playing. It suited her mood. She turned up the volume so that the low notes created an answering vibration in her stomach. She did not associate the disc with her father, who had doubtless put it there. It felt as though the house were talking to her – or perhaps playing its own music, that only she could hear.

The storm was gathering itself, but she did not switch on the lights. She liked the way the reality of things, their true nature, gradually seeped through in the deepening twilight. If you switched on a light you drove things away, or made them freeze and stand to attention. She preferred this, to blend in with the darkness, at one with it.

Outside the back window the dead-of-summer stubble lay bleached and unrelenting, as far as the eye could see. If she turned on a light, this large, lone house would be visible for miles around; anyone watching would know that she was here.

She had always had this sense of watchers, quite unrelated to their single unpleasant experience with the boy intruder. She sensed them both inside and outside the house. It wasn't always unpleasant. Sometimes, as now, it was companionable. The spirits of Eastleigh End, the gods of hearth and home, kept her company as she ate her sandwich sitting on the floor. The notes of the cello tumbled, growled and keened with a soulful resonance, echoing the thunder which was beginning to rattle threateningly around the horizon. Was this, she wondered, what it meant to have one's heartstrings plucked? No, it was more like having them stroked, pressed, *urged* to feel what was being communicated, a strong and thoughtful melancholy. As with the house, the unseen watchers, she was in tune. She could hear what was being said. The edges of her self opened and floated like the fronds of a sea anemone. She became both less distinct and bigger than her self, a part of her surroundings.

She didn't wish to move. The house became darker, but the prowling storm seemed to be moving away again. When the CD ended she was suddenly aware of the red beady eye of the music centre, its insatiable demand for more, and she got up and switched it off. The machine must have given off some white sound of its own, an undetectable breath, because now the silence was absolute.

Api slipped off her thick-soled black shoes. She wanted not to disturb the hush as she went across the hall and up the stairs. The untidiness, glimpsed spilling from cupboards, peeping from the doors of rooms and huddling in corners, took on a homogenous appearance like ivy, or bindweed, a life-form in its own right with diverse roots but driven by a strong, united impulse: as if, when her back was turned, it might creep forward and advance with her, grandmother's-footsteps style, in her wake.

Her footsteps carried her softly to the top of the house. Her long dress whispered about her bare ankles. As she reached the second-floor landing there was a sudden burst of thunder, closer again. As it faded she thought she heard the tail-end of a single plangent chord. It didn't startle her – she had heard it before and half expected it – but it did send a Mexican wave of goose bumps over her arms and scalp.

With a dull roar the rain began to fall.

The loft door hung open by a few inches. Because of the ever-widening gaps between the roof tiles it seemed lighter up there than here. She took the pole and pulled down the door. The ladder creaked down towards her like the neck of a submissive dinosaur. She climbed up.

She now knew exactly where he was. Years ago she had moved him and arranged his surroundings so that she could come up here and visit him without having to disturb anything. Again without turning on the light she stepped carefully across the hidden joists to her left, then stepped forward and sat, gingerly, on the old brown suitcase. She could feel the curling scabs of old labels through her cotton dress. Now she looked up and met his gaze.

She had read somewhere that every face has a kind eye and a cold eye, but if this were true she was never sure which he was showing her. If this were the kind eye then the other one must be truly terrifying. His stare was merciless, all-knowing. She did not know who had painted the picture, nor whose idea it had been to cast half of it in deep shadow, but the effect was to intensify the whole, as if, by concealing so much, energy was channelled into what was shown. Once she had gone very close to the canvas and minutely inspected the aggregation of streaks and flakes of paint combed by the brush, and the whorls and dollops left by the palette knife. They were only paint, and didn't give up their secrets. Yet when she looked over her shoulder from only two paces away the alchemy of artist and subject made the material jump and re-form so that there he was, staring back at her.

Neither did the picture always look the same. It often seemed that some minute change had occurred, as if he had moved at some time during her absence and had succeeded in resuming his pose, but not quite perfectly. They were locked in a kind of silent struggle, in which he was in the ascendancy.

'I think,' said Charles, 'that you should be a lot more direct with her.'

'Me?' said Xanthe. 'Sorry – *I* should be?'

'Since you're the one who's concerned.'

'And what form should this directness take?'

'I don't know, do I? Tell her you're worried.'

'I'm not that worried.'

'Very well then,' said Charles, as if that proved his point.

The atmosphere in the car was acrimonious. In the case of the Durrances continual absence, if not actually making the heart grow fonder, at least ensured there was precious little opportunity for hostilities to break out. It may have been this which prompted Xanthe to blurt:

'Perhaps it's time we separated!'

To her, the mere uttering of the suggestion was a bomb-shell, but one that the moment it had been dropped seemed inevitable. The idea had been a heavy, undiagnosed weight inside her which had suddenly fallen away. But the weight had been an anchor, too, so that in an instant she was caught up in a swirl of panic.

'But Zannie,' said Charles, 'what would be the point?'

She had been driving, but now she stopped. The road was not wide here, and Charles leaned across and turned on the hazard lights. She tried to smack his hand but missed, and only succeeded in hitting hers on the handbrake.

'Bugger!'

'Why not let me drive?'

'Because you're drunk.'

'It's only another mile or so and when did you last see the rozzers round here?'

Xanthe, still rubbing her hand, let out a little sob.

'We could leave it here and walk, for Christ's sake.'

'It's raining. Ah!' She put her arms either side of her head. 'What on earth are we talking about this for?'

'Because we're pulled up in a country lane at one in the morning?' offered Charles.

'What did you mean, "what would be the point"?'

'I'd have thought it was obvious. We hardly see each other as it is. It's kind of, how we do things.'

Xanthe couldn't deny this. It *was* how they did things and it had always suited them. What she was experiencing now was a long-delayed wave of guilt. The two of them had allowed their marriage to atrophy through neglect and selfishness and she suddenly wanted nothing more than to jettison its corpse.

'And anyway,' added Charles, 'what brought all this on? We were talking about Api.'

She'd been in bed for about two hours when she heard her parents come in. She wouldn't normally have noticed, but the raised voices woke her up. It was sufficiently unusual for them to be talking at all, let alone arguing. She lay there, frozen with surprise, listening as they walked about downstairs in that pointless way they had. Music came on, not the cello concerto but one of the eerie, dissonant modern things her father liked to show off with. Her mother was in the kitchen. They were in different rooms, shouting at each other. You couldn't really call it an argument because there was no attempt to communicate. That figured; why change the habit of a lifetime? She caught odd words, flung like missiles across the twanging and moaning of the music.

'. . . bizarre idea . . . !'

'. . . never . . . the least . . . so why all of a sudden?'

'Don't be . . .'

'. . . *ridiculous*, and you know it . . .'

'. . . nothing of the sort!'

'– Api –'

'Ssh!'

It was the mention of her name, and the vigorous shushing, that made her go cold all over. So it was *her* they were arguing about. If she had been dismayed by their sudden and unchar- acteristic interest, she was even more dismayed to discover she was a bone of contention. Not one of them, not Gilda at her most excessive nor Martin at his most reclusive, not even Judith at her food-throwing worst, had been the cause of fights between her parents. It simply wasn't something they did. Their benign, absentee father took things as he found them when he was around. Their mother coped, after a fashion. Api and her brothers and sisters had few of the boundaries and rules which are said to make children – even rebellious ones – feel safe: the one absolute certainty, on which they could always rely, was their parents' self-centred idleness. And now it seemed that she'd been the one to test it beyond endurance.

'. . . going to bed!'

There was no reply to this announcement of Xanthe's. The music became more muffled as a door was closed. Api heard her mother's footsteps trudge up the stairs, take two steps on to the creaky board – and then, to her horror, creep more slowly in the direction of her own bedroom. She was lying on her back to leave both ears free for listening, and she didn't dare roll over in case the small sound alerted her mother to the fact that she was awake, so she lay still as a graven image, her nose pointing at the ceiling. As the door began to open she closed her eyes.

Xanthe stepped inside the door and paused, barely putting her foot down until she'd satisfied herself that her daughter was asleep. She had to creep in, and peer. The bedroom was not simply dark, but blacked out with all the drapes and wall-hangings Api had pinned up – they'd always allowed their children to do what they liked with their bedrooms, a respect for personal space was both perfectly proper, and expedient in a household where cleanliness and order had low priority – but the long mirror propped against the wall opposite afforded a good view of the bed and its occupant, half lit by the light from the door. Xanthe saw the pale, pointed profile, the stern set of the mouth, the rounded, light-lashed lids lying like seashells in their sockets; the ungroomed hanks of long hair runkled carelessly on the pillow. This side of Api's face was white, the other in shadow. The perfect privacy of sleep – its secrecy – shut Xanthe out.

She stepped back and closed the door.

Api breathed again.

She wanted out. Something was holding her back here, something she couldn't fight because it controlled all of them. It was the man in the attic, at the top of the house, Cyclops-eyed and motionless in his lair; his influence filtered down through the boards and joists, the bricks, the plaster, the paper and carpet . . . But she knew him better than anyone, and knowledge could be power. He was the puppet-master, but she didn't have to be his puppet.

★

The next day she got up early, took some money from the slew of notes and change her father always left lying around in the kitchen, walked five miles to the station and took the train to London.

She arrived at the photographic studio where Gilda worked at mid-morning. It was an uninspiring shed on a small industrial estate in Willesden. Gilda was an assistant. She no longer wore black, but khaki, with trainers. Only her hair was black these days, and tied up in a scrunchy. Because it was coarse, and the ends were ragged, it gave the term ponytail a fresh aptness. She still managed to look like a warrior queen, but one rather down on her luck.

'What on earth are you doing here?' she asked in a tone neither unfriendly nor specially surprised.

'I want a job,' said Api.

'Oh, is that all? One that involves neither talent, training nor too much work, yeah? And a flat and a car and three square meals a day.'

Api gazed at her. 'I've got to start somewhere.'

Gilda glanced over her shoulder at the photographer, Lawrence, who was eating a bacon roll and consulting his organiser.

'We're busy.'

'Can I sleep at yours tonight?'

'Sofa.'

'I don't mind.'

'You've got nothing with you.'

'I don't need anything.'

'We shan't be in, but the bloke on the ground floor's got a key.'

'Cool.'

Gilda shrugged. The negotiation was completed. But as Api turned to leave, she called, 'Hey!'

'What?'

'Do they know you're up here?'

'No.'

Gilda sucked her teeth and gave a heavy-lidded grimace to indicate she might have known.

By the time Api arrived at the flat in Kilburn that evening she had acquired not one job but two: one stacking shelves in Metrofoods on the Tottenham Court Road, and another (she lied about her age) behind the bar in the Ironmonger's Arms near Covent Garden. She had no idea whether the two sets of shifts were compatible but had decided that, like the squares on a Rubik's Cube, they could probably be shuffled around to fit. She sat in the dingy, peeling hallway for an hour and a half before the man in the ground-floor flat came back and let her in, with no questions asked. She was relieved that his neighbourliness didn't extend to demanding proof of identity.

Gilda got in at two a.m. with her companion, an Appalachian fiddle player named Carson, and shook her sister awake. 'What about somewhere to live?' she asked.

'I'll be out of here tomorrow.'

'Did you ring home?'

'No.'

'Well, someone better had. This isn't my responsibility.'

'In the morning.'

The Sin was leaving for Prague in twenty-four hours. Never had Charles looked forward so much to the company of that big, boozy, louche, talented, bed-hopping extended family. They were to have a guest conductor, Nodja Barenskaya, said to be the sexiest thing on the circuit, and he wanted to be there. Charles was a self-confessed star-fucker with several notable notches on his gun. And then Rhona was still available in spite of her feminist principles, and there was also Jenny, a wonderfully fat, creamy young oboist like something out of a Renoir painting . . .

So he didn't appreciate his youngest daughter's upping the ante in this way. He was reasonably sure she was fine, but even he could see that it would be unwise to make that assumption and bugger off to Prague without checking. In fact he would have been in favour of ringing the police earlier, passing the buck in the nicest possible way, but Xanthe had an antipathy to the police that dated back to an unfortunate drugs bust in her misspent youth.

When it got to the following morning, with his check-in at Gatwick at four p.m., he put his foot down.

'Look, it's been twenty-four hours. I'm ringing them.'

Xanthe threw her hands in the air, and at precisely that moment the phone rang. They were in the kitchen, and Charles walked with measured strides to pick it up. With that urgent sound he was suddenly reminded of what the possibilities were, and what they were dealing with here. His mouth became dry and the first time he tried to speak no sound came out. The second time, effort made it too loud.

'O-five-three?'

'It's me.'

'Hello, you,' he said, his heartbeat thrumming in his ears, waving an upturned thumb at Xanthe. 'About time.'

'I'm at Gilda's.'

'How long for? Only your mother has catering to consider.' This was a joke, albeit a feeble one. In any event Api ignored it.

'I'm going to look for a place today, and then I'll come back to collect my stuff.'

'I see. Is that place as in position, or as in pad?'

'Sorry?'

'How do you mean, look for a place?'

'Well, I've found some work, and now I need somewhere to live.'

'Couldn't you just stay at Gilda's?' Charles asked. 'It would be a lot easier for everyone.'

'She doesn't want me.'

This was said without self-pity, and actually Charles's sympathies were with his eldest.

'Of course you could always come home. Do your A levels, all that.'

This was met with a disdainful silence.

'No, right you are,' said Charles. 'Anyway, your mother would like a word.' He held out the receiver with a little shake, and Xanthe took it.

He left the room with a springy stride and only just prevented himself taking the steps two at a time as he went upstairs to pack.

Xanthe tucked the receiver under her bushy wing of hair and closed her eyes in order to focus on her daughter.

'Right, so what exactly is going on?'

'I told Dad,' replied Api. 'I've got a job and today I'm going to find a flat.'

'Just like that.'

'How hard can it be? There's loads of ads.'

'And what about school?'

'They won't mind. I don't want to be there and they'll be pleased to be rid of me.'

Xanthe didn't argue with this. How could she, when it was the plain unvarnished truth and she didn't have much time for schools anyway? It was left that Api could stay in London with the usual provisos that she keep in touch, contact her older sister in case of emergency, and remain alert to dangers from unpleasant people.

Api accepted these admonitions as something parents had to do, even parents like hers who didn't much care either way. They had to say it, she had to agree, then the token formalities had been got out of the way and everyone could proceed.

'I'll see you anyway,' she said, 'because I'll have to come back and get my stuff.'

'How will you get it all to London?' asked Xanthe, in whom the maternal-assistance gene was missing.

Api fully understood this. 'Dad could give me a lift.'

'He's in Prague till the end of the week.'

'Next weekend then.'

'You might not have anywhere by then.'

'I will.'

'I'll mention it to him.'

'Can't I ask him?'

'He's upstairs packing.' There was a grim silence. 'Hang on, I'll see if he's . . . Charles! CHARLES!'

Charles came on to the landing. 'Jesus wept, there's no need to shout, what is it?'

Xanthe lowered her voice exaggeratedly, to show that she had only been shouting because he was slow in responding. 'Api wants to know if you'll help her take her things up to London next weekend.'

He grimaced. 'I'll only just have got back, and it's the BBC Bristol thing next Monday.'

'Why don't you have a word?'

'No, no, don't have time . . . Tell her yes. If I can I will.'

Api addressed the phone. 'Did you hear that?'

'He will if he can.'

'He can't say fairer than that.'

'All right,' said Api, 'I'll be back Friday night.'

In spite of her brave words and her iron determination, Api found the intervening week horribly hard, as well as just plain horrible. Gilda was ruthless: one more night to allow for a day's flat-hunting, and that was it. Carson, however, was a gentler soul, and not in regular employment – his demo tape was lying on the desk of some jaded executive at Blue Moon Records at the time – and he contacted associates of his in Paddington to see if they could fit someone else in, in the short term. They indicated that it was not impossible, so Carson walked Api the mile and a half to Farnsworth Buildings off Praed Street (handy for St Mary's Hospital and various curry houses) and introduced her to Mina, Dodge, Giles and Kath – plus Dodge's ill-favoured brindle dog, China – all of whom were apparently in the sort of jobs that enabled them to pay the rent while allowing them to lie around at home at midday in a malodorous torpor. Api quickly realised that the flatmates' ability to fit her in was due to inertia on their part rather than any considered assessment of the situation. It was Carson who showed her round, and China followed them, curling his lip in a what-are-you-looking-at way whenever she glanced at him. The small living room was terribly hot, the windows filmy, the kitchen greasy and etched with black. In the bathroom the window was cracked and the tiles were coming off the wall revealing the sturdy Victorian brickwork beneath. The grouting was dark grey nearest the bath, white near the ceiling. Several spiders had colonised this more hygienic zone; the red lino was coming away in the corners like a scab that had been picked at. Collars of grubby limescale surrounded the taps and plugholes, and the bath, basin and toilet bowl carried evidence of a variety of past usages.

'Where will I sleep?' she asked. Afraid her voice would come out small and timid she sounded sharp.

'Settle down,' said Carson reasonably. 'We'll find somewhere.'

There were two double-bedded rooms with crumpled, stained sheets. One, to her horror, had a chamber pot beneath the bed. In both there were cases and boxes with clothes, in one a length of plastic washing line hung across one corner with hangers depending from it. The floor in each case was littered with shoes, cigarette packets, used mugs and dishes and a substratum of unidentifiable small rubbish and breakages. The rooms made you think of all the flakes of human skin, the strands of hair, the thousands of living parasites, the dead insects and rioting bacteria that flourished in even the cleanest domestic environment. It was enough to render Eastleigh End a shining example of domestic management. This level of dark, dangerous disorder scared Api. And these were rooms for couples, surely even these people—

'Looks like the living room,' said Carson, to her unutterable relief.

He took her back to the others. 'OK if she sleeps in here?' he asked. No one demurred. China, his duty done, joined Dodge on a chair whose ruptured entrails brushed the floor.

'Thanks,' she said in her loud, unconfident voice. 'How much do I owe you?'

Mina, who was making tea, looked over her shoulder as if seeing Api for the first time. Her eyes were dark and angry and tired.

'Have you got any money?'

'Not yet, but I start—'

'Then don't worry about it.'

'As soon as I—'

'Forget it,' said Mina. 'Want a brew?'

Api accepted, but couldn't bring herself to put her lips to the mug. She and Carson sat down on the floor and he made himself a roll-up with his thin, trembling, stub-ended fingers.

'So you're Api, right?' asked Giles, who was good-looking and well-spoken in a slightly sheepish way that reminded her of some of the musicians she'd met who worked with her father. Posh and privileged but trying not to be.

'Yes,' she said. And then, trying it on for size in this extraordinary setting: 'Apollonia.'

'Great name.'

'Gilda's sister,' explained Carson.

'Do you know Gilda then?' she asked.

'Everybody knows Gilda.'

Kath, who was fat, but whose little beaky, budgerigar face showed the thin person trying to get out, laughed bitchily.

'It's not hard.'

Api was not sufficiently sure of her ground to take issue with this. Whatever inside knowledge entitled this stranger to make what sounded like a very disparaging comment about her sister also prevented her from making any kind of defence. There were things she had intuited about Gilda from a very early age – that she was sexy, and wild and insecure – but she hadn't yet decided whether they were reprehensible or not, and the Durrances were strangers to the notion of family solidarity.

Dodge had been silent till then. He was sitting with China draped over his knees, scratching the dog beneath his studded collar with one finger. Dodge was thin – far more horribly, shockingly thin than Kath was fat, with a pallid face marked with grey scoops and gouges and greasy dark hair pulled back tight into a plait. He had a narrow beard and moustache that ran in a heart shape around his thin mouth, accentuating a rather cruel look. But his voice was soft and American, as alluringly foreign yet familiar as a voice in a Hollywood film, and when he spoke it was as though his were the only words that mattered, the words that everything else had been leading up to.

'So . . . where you from, little Apollonia?'

In a way, they knew already. That she was Gilda's sister, that Carson had brought here from Gilda's place. But that wasn't what he meant, and she knew it. And her intuition emboldened her to say in a voice that was no longer sharp and nervous but strong and sure:

'I'm not from anywhere. This is where I'm starting.'

'Sure,' said Dodge gently, nodding, sealing their understanding. 'I get it.'

Charles returned a chastened man from his trip to London with Api. He had gone there buoyant and burnished from several days of creative and sexual activity, his eyes and ears widened by the streets of Prague, the concert hall and the music, his muscles relaxed, his whole body cleansed by the ceaseless hot water and spotless linen of the hotel room. He had found himself all too willing to escape the considerably less shiny texture of the marital home and take on the role of solicitous father for a few hours. But exposure to 63 Farnsworth Buildings and a representative sample of its occupants – only Dodge and China were at home – shook him to the core.

'Api,' he said to her urgently as she attempted to show him out of the door. 'I've got to tell you I'm not happy with this.'

'Dad – it's fine.'

'No, it's not. Take my word for it. I'm quite sure if I speak to Gilda—'

'I'm not going back there.'

'Only till you find something else.'

'I *have* found something else.'

Charles glanced around, his face an agonised mask of ineffectual worry. 'I'm not even sure it's *safe.*'

'It's perfectly safe. Just because it's a bit messy—'

'A BIT?' Charles realised he was shouting and lowered his voice to a vehement hiss. 'A *bit* messy? Believe me, I'm not fussy, but this borders on the psychotic.'

She shrugged. The door was open. She was waiting.

'And that bloke,' Charles leaned towards her, widening his eyes for emphasis, 'looks like a walking health hazard. I'd ask what he was on, only I suspect it would be more realistic to ask what he's *not* on.'

'They smoke a bit of dope,' conceded Api, 'like you and Mum.'

'And the rest,' said Charles grimly, choosing to ignore this very palpable hit. 'I'm awfully glad your mother didn't come with us, she'd have a seizure.'

'No she wouldn't.' It was clear Api recognised this for what it was, a little tangential buck-passing intended to cast him in the role of the more stoical parent and his wife as the more sensitive and emotional one. Both crap.

The outcome was the same, whatever. In the end his desire for escape from this fourth-floor hell-hole was greater than his concern on his daughter's behalf.

'I want you to ring every evening, reverse the charges, and we'll expect to hear you're moving somewhere better very, very soon.'

Another shrug. 'OK.'

★

Never one to spare his wife's feelings, and hoping against hope that his perturbation would be halved by sharing it, he told her almost at once: 'It's nasty. Actually, properly nasty.'

She stared at him, lips pursed, gauging the degree of nastiness. 'Worse than Malahyde Road?'

'Oh, Jesus!' Charles waved a hand to indicate how infinitely worse this was than his own first flat in Kensal Rise. 'This makes Malahyde Road look like Trumpton.'

'Well,' said Xanthe, peeling the furry green layer off an onion, 'hygiene's overrated anyway and no one cares about it at that age. As long as she's happy she'll develop a good set of antibodies.'

'No, no, let's be quite clear about this.' Charles poured himself a large Scotch. 'Squalor's one thing. Sharing the squalor with some sort of barely sentient underclass is another.'

'You met them?'

'One of them. A bloke. And his junkyard-style dog, which I bet isn't allowed under the terms of the lease, and probably never gets walked.'

'You don't know that.'

'The fuckwit of an owner had a skin that hadn't seen daylight in months. Years.'

'So,' said Xanthe, opening a can of tomatoes. 'Why did you leave her there?'

'I tried to dissuade her, but she wasn't having any, you know what she is. And she did assure me that she was going to find something else a.s.a.p.'

'She said that before.'

'I had to take her word for it.'

'No you didn't, she's only sixteen.'

'Only? She could marry the bugger if she wanted to!'

'She's not the marrying kind,' said Xanthe.

Api soon realised – and it came as a revelation – that dirt, like pain, was less hard to bear if you gave in to it. It was the fighting of it that made it bad, the making comparisons and wondering about what it was. She told herself that in fact conditions at Farnsworth Buildings were not so different from those at home; the flat simply housed a greater concentration of people in a smaller space. She would keep herself, her own clothes and sleeping bag clean, always use the same plate, mug and fork, and learn to live with the rest.

As she got to know more about the others they became less weird and threatening. They had jobs, of a sort. Giles was a hospital porter at St Mary's. Mina worked at a women's refuge in Notting Hill and was often away for days at a time. Kath worked shifts in Boots to fund her real career as a children's storyteller. And Dodge was a musician, even less successful than Carson, who had a busking pitch in the Museum underpass at South Kensington and played an assortment of his own compositions and lesser-known Bob Dylan numbers. China went with him on these sessions, though whether in this case the dog proved an incentive to potential donors was doubtful. If she hadn't known better Api might have filed Dodge under 'loser' but he succeeded triumphantly, and not just in her eyes, in transcending his disadvantages. He was, she told herself with a thrill of awe and longing, charismatic.

She didn't see him very often. None of them had what could properly be termed day jobs, and all worked shifts or unsocial hours. At Metrofoods she worked on autopilot, putting in the hours and counting up the peanuts due to her. The Ironmonger's Arms was slightly different. She began to appreciate that at Farnsworth Buildings she was with people who did not regard 'fun' as something one had to have, an activity to be engaged in. Fun was an entirely foreign concept, as it was to her. The clientele at the Tintack, as it was known by regulars, were hell-bent on fun, with a pretty funny way of having it. Api had been helping herself to drink at home for some years, and had been to the more easy-going local pubs with school friends, but here she stood every night separated from people whose mission was to neck as much booze as they could before becoming first loud and obnoxious, then either aggressive, melancholy or ill, and finally – in the worst cases – insensible. Everyone had money to swill, and exuded a 'try-me' manic bravado. The young women in particular astounded and appalled her – so smart, so assured, so swaggering and swigging and chain-smoking and in charge. Api saw that here in London different tribes existed, and this one was not hers. But she kept her face straight and her head down and worked hard. She wasn't a born tapster but the landlady told her she was a good girl and that she was pleased.

Api thought, in ten years' time I shall come back here, dressed all in black, and light a cheroot and order champagne and sit on my own. And everyone can just drop dead.

Little by little she and Dodge became close. She knew there was something between them, something elemental like Cathy and Heathcliff. She longed for him to touch her but her longing was outweighed by the fear that physical closeness would change and spoil their special union of souls. She had no sexual experience, and the nakedness not just of body but of mind that such a thing would involve would rob her of whatever mystery she had in his eyes.

Nobody else was aware of this connection between them, she was sure of that. How could they be? It was too subtle and implicit. On those rare occasions when they were alone in the flat, if he was sitting there listening to music or reading, with China on his knee, he would intermittently look up at her and make little comments that fell somewhere in between an observation and a question.

'You like that,' he'd say, or: 'You're wearing the blue shirt today.' Sometimes just: 'Uh-huh . . .' as though he'd been thinking about her and was pleased to find her there in the flesh.

She felt these remarks settle on her like butterflies, or petals. He adorned her with his attention. When Dodge was

around the squalid flat became a bower, humming with in-
expressible mystery and sweetness. It would have astonished
her father to know how safe she felt with him. The possibility that he might seem dangerous to others only enhanced
this feeling.

He slept with Mina in one of the double rooms, Giles and
Kath in the other. Api drew no inference from these arrangements. She didn't care to think of Dodge and Mina together,
and the others were quite simply so ill-matched that the possibility of congress stretched the imagination to breaking point.
She had a mattress and a sleeping bag in a corner of the living
room, behind the sofa. She had begun by sleeping *on* the sofa,
but because of everyone's strange hours she often found
herself turfed off in the middle of the night, or hemmed in
by bodies, so it was easier to be out of harm's way. She'd
become accustomed, dog-like, to curling up, closing her eyes
and shutting down her senses so that she could sleep through
most things.

But she must have slept only lightly during those weeks,
because she dreamed a lot. Intense and vivid dreams of the
ark-house floating on its sea of fields; of music and voices,
her mother dancing in an empty room, her father in the corner
laughing, the faces of her brothers and sisters pressed like
stained-glass images to the outside of the windows. And most
of all of the man in the portrait, no longer a dusty half-hidden
canvas in the attic, but whole, and real, standing at the top of
the stairs. In her dream she could see only his feet in shiny
black shoes, because there was no light on the landing and
the top half of his body was obscured; but she knew that he
was looking back at her, and about to take his first step down
into the house. This last part became the *leitmotif* of her
dreams, the recurring factor, the moment at which she knew
she would soon wake, her eyes flicking open suddenly and
her skin creeping with apprehension.

Once, when she woke in this way, it was to a foetid smell
and the intimate touch of something damp. It was never

entirely dark in here and the first thing she saw was the head of the dog, China, who had lain down next to her. He was asleep, his eyes not fully closed but showing two thin slivers of white. His broad jaws were open, exposing perfect white killing-teeth. His blood-red tongue lolled, and as he dreamed and twitched the thick swatch of flaccid muscle touched her breast.

'Aah! Get away! Go!'

She pushed at the dog's barrel chest with both hands, frantic with revulsion. Startled by the scream and understandably outraged by the push, he exploded, snarling into life, and began barking manically, front legs braced, the short hairs along his back standing up in a bristling ridge.

'Help! Stop it!' Api buried her face in her knees and covered her head with her arms. In seconds the barking stopped. She looked up to see Dodge, crouching opposite, holding the dog's collar. China's ears and hackles were down, his fearsome jaws now relaxed in a benign, panting grin.

'Hey,' said Dodge in his soft voice. 'You're OK.'

It wasn't a question, but she whispered: 'Yes.'

'Come on, sit down for a moment.'

Her knees were shaking as she got to her feet and crept round to sit on the sofa. It felt warm; he must have been lying there. Now he sat down next to her.

'Sorry he bothered you.'

'No, no,' she protested, 'it wasn't his fault. I woke up and he gave me a fright.'

'So you gave him one.'

'I didn't mean to.'

'Here, boy,' said Dodge, 'make up with the lady.'

She patted China's broad, grooved head. His eyes closed in happiness; he was a simple soul.

'He likes you,' said Dodge. 'That's the problem.'

'I like him too,' she mumbled weakly.

'But not so close, huh.'

'No . . .'

There was a silence, during which Api felt him looking at her in that way he had, as if he recognised her and was working out why. She was not, nor ever had been, uncomfortable under his scrutiny, nor with silence. The only light came from the street outside. She remembered her last night at home, how she had sat in the drawing room as the summer storm rumbled round the house, and felt as she had then that she was dissolving . . .

'Why don't you tell me about your dreams,' said Dodge. He had known what she was thinking.

'I dream about the house where I lived with my parents.' She was careful not to say 'home'.

'The place you come from,' he reminded her.

'Yes, but—'

'You're starting over. I know that. Go on with the dreams.'

'The house is very lonely, it's in the middle of these huge fields.'

'It's a big house, right?'

'Yes. In my dreams it's always empty – I mean no furniture, no pictures –' she hesitated – 'no stuff. As if we'd moved out.'

'Any people?'

'My parents, sometimes, but they're kind of wandering about, not living there. Like ghosts. And my brothers and sisters are looking in through the window. Or not there at all. And then . . .' She paused again, this time deliberately, for effect, wanting him to tease it out of her. Flirting with him, in a way. He let the pause extend, expanding between them so they could both feel its weight and tension.

'There's someone else?'

'Sort of. There used to be a picture of a man up in the attic.'

'Old guy?'

She considered. 'Old-fashioned. A bit older than my parents.'

'Bet your dad looked really young.'

She didn't understand, and went on: 'It was a portrait of my mother's grandfather. It was painted so that he was half in shadow.'

'Which side was he showing you . . .' said Dodge, not asking her but wondering himself.

'It was a bit creepy, but I liked it. I've always liked it, I used to go and sit up there and look at it and play music.'

'What music?'

'The Harry Lime theme. There was a wind-up gramophone and some of those old records in paper covers. Have you seen the film?'

'Sure. Orson Welles, black and white, moody.'

'The picture reminded me of the film. I just used to sit there and dream.'

'And you still dream of him.'

'Yes.'

'He must be quite a guy.'

'He is.'

'Dead all this time but we're talking about him in the present tense,' mused Dodge.

'Oh, he's *there*,' she said fiercely. 'He is there.'

'Hey . . .' Dodge raised his hand in a gesture of peaceful acceptance. 'I know.'

She knew that he did. He was only the second person in the whole of her short life who she felt had truly understood her and the first was long-dead. When she was younger she had hidden behind the front of being her parents' 'easy' child; they and her siblings, her teachers and friends, had been all too ready to accept what she chose to give them. When she'd grown uncomfortable with that it had discomforted them, too, and their discomfiture had felt like her fault, as if she'd deliberately set out to wind them up. And it was not even as if they cared all that much. She preferred it when they didn't care, and that was the accepted deal. Api had regarded with astonishment the attitude of, for instance, Lisa's mother, Cheryl, who seemed to spend every other waking moment thinking about Lisa. What must it have been like to be the object of such obsessive attention? The mere thought gave her shortness of breath. Charles and Xanthe didn't want any harm to come to any of their children, and Xanthe had always put in place such measures as were necessary to meet the particular needs of Judith, say, and Martin – but for the most part they remained mercifully uninvolved. All of them in that house had moved around in their own spaces, on their own levels, like aeroplanes on flight paths. Api felt as if she had recently experienced a near-miss, and had taken herself out of the system. She'd spoken to her parents a few times on the phone and her father in particular had gone on at her about the flat, and moving, in that slightly whiney way he had as if the whole thing were more about him than about her. But in the end, since she was still there, still apparently in one piece and in work, he'd accepted it. He was too lazy not to. That was something she'd always been able to depend on, her parents' apathy. If you stuck with something for long enough, provided it was not causing them any immediate problems, they gave up.

Of the two it was Xanthe who was the more suspicious.

'Where do you sleep?' she asked in her deep, drawling voice. 'Your father said there were only the two bedrooms.'

'In the living room,' said Api. 'On the floor.'

'How can you work if you're not sleeping properly?'

'I am sleeping properly.'

She heard her mother light a cigarette (the pencils had been no substitute). She knew the moves exactly, and how long it took. One – two – three – four, and –

'Api.'

'Yes?'

'These men who are there—'

'Giles and Dodge.'

'Whoever they are, it's of no interest to me. So long as you remember that what's yours is yours. You don't have to do anything you don't want to.'

The wording of this implied that it was an oft-repeated maternal warning, but such was far from the case. Apart from what she had picked up from girls at school, Api was almost completely ignorant about sex, and had never even been kissed, nor wanted to be. Her looks were not of the kind to attract boys of her own age, and her air of focused detachment had been a deterrent.

'I do know that,' she said, 'I'm not a complete idiot.'

'No, but you're inexperienced.'

This struck Api as another strange choice of words, as if sexual sophistication were like an Equity card – you needed it to get experience, but you needed to have had experience to get it.

'Don't worry,' she said. 'I can look after myself.'

She heard her mother's little hoot of disbelief. Right, she thought, that's it.

It was Giles she slept with. She'd deduced that if there was anything at all between him and Kath it was nothing that couldn't tolerate a minor intrusion, and the ease with which she persuaded Giles to deflower her confirmed her in this opinion. Afterwards she was grateful, but unmoved. In the warm, stale, slightly crunchy cocoon of the double bed his muscly-looking arms were smooth and soft, his mid-morning breath smelt of coffee and the crumpled weight of his private parts leaked confidingly against her hip.

'Mmm . . .' he said, snuggling. 'That was sweet of you. I'm honoured.'

She wanted to say 'somebody had to be first' but that would have sounded a bit too pragmatic.

'It was nice,' she agreed. 'Thanks.'

He stretched behind him awkwardly to pick up a packet off the floor. 'Smoke, in the time-honoured manner?'

'No thanks.'

'Mind if I do?' he said round the cigarette as he lit it. She shook her head, astonished at how polite they were being in all the circumstances. A little conversation seemed not just in order but positively desirable.

'Why do you work as a hospital porter?'

'Why do I . . .' He reached again and brought up an ashtray which he placed on the pillow above their heads. 'Don't make any sudden movements. Because it's undemanding, amusing and useful. The money's shit but you can't have everything.'

'What did you do before?'

'I helped with kids' summer camps in the States. And before that I was a really, really unsuccessful student at Sheffield, and before that I was a public schoolboy who wanted to do as little as possible. So you could say I've achieved my ambition.'

She had to laugh at this unflinching self-appraisal.

'Bloody hell, was that a giggle?' He pulled his head back to look at her. 'I didn't know you did those.'

'But,' she pointed out, 'you must work quite hard at the hospital.'

'No decisions though, that's the thing.' He reached up to tap his ash. 'Pushing the poor sods around and being nice to them's easy. No initiative called for, no responsibility.'

You couldn't argue with the sweet reasonableness of this.

'And how did you meet Kath?' She thought she might as well ask the leading question so as to clear it out of the way.

'When I moved in here. I met Mina in a pub, she said there was a room but she'd told Kath the same thing, and she rocked up at the same time so we kind of sorted out an arrangement. Don't worry,' he added, squeezing her. 'It's cool. If she walked in now she'd say sorry and fuck off out again.'

Fortunately for Api, the episode didn't light a flame of undying passion in either her or Giles, but it did set the seal on an easy friendship, fraternal in a way her relationship with Martin and Saul had never been. From time to time thereafter they repeated the experience and as she got more used to it so she enjoyed it more, and began to get an inkling of what all the fuss was about.

This prompted her to ask about Dodge.

'He's all right,' said Giles. 'What I know of him, which isn't much. But let's just say I wouldn't go sharing any bodily fluids with him.'

She didn't intend to. Now she had the card, she understood the power.

7

1982 – Bryn

'Wife': Bryn had always considered it an unsexy word, even without its domestic connotations. It was short, and closed, and brought the teeth down over the lower lip in an emphatic and negative way. 'Mistress' was sibilant and secretive, and 'lover' left the mouth invitingly half-open, greedy for kisses. 'Wife' was a word without juice: a word of containment, control and lost opportunity.

He didn't think that now. He longed, yearned to use it. It was the word 'fiancée' that grated on him and which he refused to employ. A namby-pamby label for an outdated formality, a no man's land like Victorian mourning. Whereas the firmness, the sexy, solid closure of 'wife' . . .

He couldn't wait.

But Linda could, indefinitely. She teased him, invoking the joys of deferred gratification.

'It would be,' he said, 'if we were a couple of 1950s twentysomethings, dying to get licensed for sex. But we're not, so why wait?'

'Because I have a wedding to organise.'

'Why not get married now, today, and just have a big party later? You can spend all the time you like organising it *and* be Mrs Mancini.'

They were sitting on the river bank near Marlow. Linda was in shorts and sandals, a pink shirt tied at the waist, a white scarf round her hair, aviator shades. It occurred to Bryn that she did in fact look like a 1950s twenty-something. She had the knack of dressing for each occasion as if dressing up, as if she were in a scene from a film. He could not get enough of her; his desire was unquenchable, there were times when he thought he might lose himself altogether.

'I adore you,' he said ardently.

She turned her big black seal's eyes towards him. They were unreadable but her mouth curved in a luscious smile, bracketed by crescent-shaped dimples.

'I know.'

They'd set the wedding for the last Friday in August, the turn of the year. 'Everybody likes that time,' said Linda. 'And the garden will be beautiful.'

They were getting married in a country church outside Henley, near to where they were sitting this afternoon, with the reception in a marquee at her parents' house afterwards. The Frankels had offered them free use of the facilities at any of the Delancey hotels as a wedding present, but she turned it down. Bryn was appalled.

'You can't do that!'

'Why ever not? If there's one thing Harry understands it's plain speaking.'

'In business, yes, but this is different. It's as if you're bargaining with him.'

'Not at all. I explained to him that I wanted to be traditional, to be married from home, and he perfectly understands that. Lady Frank even more so, she positively applauded it. They approve of family values.'

Bryn had no option but to take her word for it. He was too embarrassed to express his fear that any alternative present couldn't possibly match the original offer, and in the event the fear proved groundless. The Frankels' cheque was staggeringly generous. Linda raised a mocking eyebrow.

'Happy, now we've come out ahead?'

'That's grossly unfair,' he protested.

She waggled the cheque in his face. 'O ye of little faith.'

He sometimes wondered how Mr and Mrs Reynolds viewed their daughter's other, surrogate parents with their shamefully open-handed, unabashed new wealth, but he could never have asked, and the Reynolds were far too well mannered to betray even a trace of negative feeling. They had the perfect in-bred dignity and restraint of the true, rooted English upper middle class. Bryn recognised in them a kind of courage, the grace under pressure which enabled people not just to be brave in wartime but every day: never to indulge unsightly emotion in public; never to complain about lack of money, or illness, or feeling depressed; to look after house, garden and possessions meticulously, not out of competitiveness but out of self-respect. Theirs was a combination of pride, industry and humility which he found completely admirable.

Barbara Reynolds was a woman whose silvery prettiness stopped short of beauty only because the habit of under-statement was so ingrained that she could not ever (unlike her daughter) have *behaved* like a beauty. She was like a pearl, thought Bryn, to Linda's fiery emerald. And just as pearls drew their lustre from contact with the skin, so she was at her most luminous when with her husband, whose love for her was undimmed by more than forty years of marriage. Andrew was a courteous, amusing man who had been an RAF rear-gunner during the war and done something in the City with scrupulous punctiliousness from then until his retirement ten years ago.

Bryn was surprised to learn that they had had a son, Robin, seven years older than Linda, killed by a petrol bomb while off duty in Belfast.

'You never mentioned him,' he said gently to Linda after their first visit to her parents. 'Why didn't you tell me?'

'It didn't arise.'

'Well, but surely – something like that doesn't need to, it's the kind of thing—'

'What?' She turned a cold stare on him. 'I don't know what you're saying.'

'Just that it was a facer.' He put his arm round her but her shoulders seemed to shrink with disfavour. 'I'm so sorry.'

'He was at boarding school, and then in the army. I hardly knew him. If you really want to know, it didn't affect me that much. Not as much as it should have done, perhaps.'

He smothered his shock. 'There's no should about it. People have different ways of coping.'

'I wasn't *coping*. I didn't need to. I wasn't that sad.' Each sentence was like a mean, hard little pinch.

'You were numb,' he suggested.

She looked away; said, with a cold, glassy brightness: 'If you say so.'

Defeated by her sudden hostility, he'd left it there. But the next day she'd phoned him at work.

'Can you be free?'

'Not really.'

'Please. I've told a lie myself, and you don't even have to do that.'

'Where?'

'I'll come round.'

The bell rang after two minutes, and she was on the doorstep, sleek and composed in her work clothes, a forest-green jacket and black skirt. His work didn't require him to be either sleek or composed and he was dressed for comfort in sweatpants and a check shirt.

'Wow,' he said. 'That's what I call translocation.'

'I was calling from the corner. Can we have a drink?' Some freelance's guarded instinct made him glance at his watch, and she cried, 'Don't do that!'

'I'm sorry. Of course we can.'

She swept into the kitchen and poured herself a vodka tonic, hammering the ice tray on the side of the sink with a sound like rifle fire. He got a lager out of the fridge and followed her into the living room. The air seemed to quake around her like heat on a summer road.

'Linda,' he said. 'Darling, what—'

'I'm sorry!' She turned and he was dismayed to see her face collapse in tears. 'I'm so fucking sorry, why can't I rewind the tape? Oh fuck!' She put her hands to her face, careless of the drink which poured down her jacket, ice cubes plopping on to the parquet. He rushed forward, rescued the glass, dipped to put it on a table, put his arms round her and kissed her warm neck, her cool, curled ear, her damp hair where it stuck to her cheek with tears. He was completely overwhelmed, would have taken her right inside himself and kept her there forever if he could.

'Linda, Linda, I love you so much, you have absolutely nothing to be sorry for, I promise you. You've transformed my life.'

She shook her head against his chest, sobbing helplessly.

After a moment he guided her, still in his embrace, to the sofa and they sat down. In summer the sofa faced the window, and they were on the first floor. The tall trees at the end of the garden masked the harsh sixties council block beyond with clouds of leaves, dry and breathless in the midday heat. In his arms, Linda's weeping gradually slowed.

At last she pulled away from him and got up, saying 'Damn!' in a fierce, broken voice, searching for her bag, half-running to the bathroom. He heard the tap gushing. When she came back she'd splashed her eyes and face, and her hair was brushed. He thought how sweet she looked, scrubbed and childlike, a different Linda.

'I should never blub,' she said. 'I look like hell.'

He held out his hand. 'You don't,' he said. 'And you can do it whenever you like, but please tell me why.'

She didn't take his hand, but sat down again on the sofa, legs crossed, hands on lap, keeping a little distance between them in her mortification.

'It was nothing,' she said. 'The way I behaved yesterday. About Robin.'

'Oh that,' he said, as if it really had been nothing. 'I'd forgotten.'

'Liar.' She didn't look at him.

'And anyway, families are complicated and I don't know yours yet, not really. It's not my business.'

'Robin was a wonderful son,' she said quietly, 'and a

wonderful brother. A real boy's own bloke; he didn't have a mean bone in his body. He wasn't their favourite or anything, I knew my parents loved me just as much, but it was understood that he was something special. If he was still here, you'd have adored him.'

'I bet I would have done, but then I'd have liked him anyway, for being your brother.'

She shook her head; he didn't get it.

'It's very hard . . .' Her voice broke, and she took another run at it. 'I don't know if you've ever tried, but it's very hard living with a truly good person. They're innocent, they have no idea, which makes it worse. It throws all your own shortcomings into sharp relief.'

'I can see that.' Bryn found himself wondering if Robin had not been an insufferable prig.

'And then,' she said, 'he was killed.' She glanced at him and pulled a face. 'Sainted, officially. Can you imagine what the funeral was like? A military funeral, with the flag and everything, a piper?'

'Ghastly,' he agreed. 'And you were only young.'

'I was fifteen, and I'd lost my whole family.'

He wouldn't allow her this. 'I understand what you're saying, how it must have felt, but one of the nicest and most obvious things about your parents is their love for each other, and for you.'

'But I'm *not* good,' she said in a tight, dry voice.

'Thank God for that. Nor are most people. Welcome to the common herd.'

She gave him a rueful, grateful smile. 'I behaved appallingly yesterday. I was hateful.'

He said quickly: 'It was obvious you had strong feelings, and I was blundering about on them.'

She shook her head, her eyes brimming dangerously again. 'Oh Bryn, darling . . . I don't deserve you.'

'Sod deserving.' He put his hand on her cheek. 'Let me refill that glass for you.'

They had the drink, and made love, tenderly and searchingly, with care and a sense of each other's secrets. And soon after that she went back to work. Bryn was pleased to see her buoyed up once more, her amour propre shining as it should. But when she'd gone he went into the bathroom and saw traces of black mascara-tears in the basin, and stood staring at them, feeling unaccountably bleak.

It was necessary to meet the Frankels, too, but in the event this happened informally. He showed up at the offices in Piccadilly to collect Linda on an evening when Lady Frankel was meeting her husband for pre-theatre champagne and sandwiches. Sir Harry was absolutely insistent that they join them.

The refreshments were laid on in a private reception room adjoining the great man's office. The style of the room was rich and jewel-coloured, like a Venetian palace. Even if Linda had not already told him, Bryn would have guessed that everything was genuine, from the vast, romantic landscapes to the cluster of minute enamelled patch-boxes.

Harry Frankel was smaller than he appeared on television, immaculately turned out in dark bespoke tailoring, a Turnbull and Asser shirt of blue-whiteness (Linda said he often changed his shirt twice a day), monogrammed cufflinks, handmade black leather shoes and a silk foulard tie with a very slightly over-large knot. The knot, the microscopic diamond that glittered below it, and the luxuriant well-groomed hair were dandyish. In certain kinds of company they would have betrayed Sir Harry as a man in whom natural exuberance and acquired good taste fought a constant battle.

'Lady Frank' – Elizabeth – was taller than her husband, a sleek elective blonde in cream trousers, a cream silk shirt shot through with gold thread, and an eye-popping array of diamonds. Bryn sensed that she was equally instinctive, but less cunning – a natural diplomat.

'To the happy couple!' she cried. 'We are so, so delighted!'

Harry lifted his glass. 'Linda and Bryn.' He stepped across to Bryn and laid a finger on his chest. 'You have any trouble, come to me. I know things . . .' He laughed, a flat, fruity 'Heh-heh-heh' like a cartoon character.

Elizabeth put her arm round Linda. 'Don't listen to him, she's a complete angel – she must be to put up with him, God knows.'

Linda's face was brilliant with pleasure. And Bryn shared in that pleasure, glad that here, at least, with these delightful, successful, expansive people, his soon-to-be wife was considered an angel and could bring herself now and then to believe it.

Harry leaned his scented head in a little, man to man. 'Do you think she'll stay with me for a while longer? Nobody's irreplaceable, but I shall miss her when she goes.'

Bryn's role seemed to have gone in an instant from that of lucky dog to agent. 'It's not down to me, sir. I know she loves her work for you.'

'Best I've ever had. We understand each other. There doesn't need to be a lot of fuss. Where will you live?'

'I have a house in Camden; we'll be there for the time being.'

'Till the babies come along.' Another touch with the finger. Bryn was beginning to see how this crafty old man maintained control of a conversation – by subtly changing its basis every now and then. Shifting between keeping you on your toes and slightly off balance.

'Who knows?' he said guardedly.

Harry gripped his shoulder and looked him up and down. 'You're a big fellow, but then she's a strong girl.'

'Harry,' reprimanded his wife, 'that will do!'

The 'sandwiches' – an array of tiny, exquisite food like trays of jewellery – were brought by the in-house caterer. There was far more of it than two people could possibly have eaten. Harry spread his hands in dismay.

'Betsy, what were you thinking?'

'No, no,' cried Elizabeth, 'I hate waste, Linda knows, you've seen the inside of my refrigerator, there's enough Tupperware in there . . . One night a week Lucia makes fridge pizza for us while we watch *Inspector Morse*. No, Jonathan is coming.' She checked her watch. 'He should be here, does he know which theatre in case he has to go straight there?'

'I don't know, I'm not in charge of the arrangements, I do as I'm told. Eat, eat! It's his bad luck if he can't be on time.'

'Our son, back from his travels,' said Elizabeth. 'Still in another time zone, probably.'

'Jet-lag – the modern excuse,' grumbled her husband amiably.

They all helped themselves, except Harry, who ate nothing, and who had changed to whisky. Linda said: 'It's a family party, anyway. We ought to be going.'

'Painting the town?' asked Harry. 'Where are you taking her?'

'Supper with friends at Bertorelli's,' said Bryn. 'What about you?'

'Some rude play.' His wife supplied the name. 'That's the one.'

'Goodness,' said Linda, 'the hottest ticket in town. And all that nudity.'

'Jonathan's request,' said Elizabeth. 'Just so long as it's a good story. I'm broad-minded, but I want to be entertained. He'll fall asleep,' she added, nodding at Harry. 'He doesn't like the theatre, do you?'

'No, but I live in hope of a pleasant surprise one of these days.'

Bryn smiled. 'This may be the night.'

As they left the son, Jonathan, arrived. Age hard to judge, fleshy and smooth. A widow's peak with early male-pattern baldness. Black T-shirt, grey suit, loafers without socks. As cool and dismissive as the parents had been welcoming. His manner signalled clearly that Linda was a favoured employee and Bryn a hanger-on.

As they went down in the lift Bryn reflected that if he had been wary of the old man, he positively disliked the young one.

'What did you think?' asked Linda. 'They're great, aren't they?'

'They think *you're* great,' he replied, kissing her, 'and that's good enough for me.'

They got rather drunk that night with Jim and Victoria. This may have been because they'd already had champagne, or because it was nice no longer to be on parade. Victoria, not usually a great socialiser, was dry and funny, and Jim was happy because she was happy. Bryn, well disposed towards everyone at the moment, felt that his disapproval of his friend's wife might have been misplaced: the marriage worked, who cared how?

It was a good evening, without edges. They'd downed about a bottle apiece and the grappa was ordered when the two men went to the gents'. Jim zipped up and shook his head in wonderment.

'You really *are* a jammy bugger.'

'I don't deny it.'

'I reckoned you were in clover with that other woman – that Suzie.'

'Sally.'

'But I underestimated you. With a single bound you were free, and now you're marrying a sumptuous redhead who works for one of the richest men in the land.'

'I love her, Jim. I worship her. This is It.'

'Ah, but can she sew a seam and bake a cake like the indomitable Sally?'

'Haven't a clue. But you know what?'

'No!' Jim raised both hands. 'No, don't tell me, I don't want to know.'

As they went out of the door, he added lugubriously: 'I can imagine.'

★

140

Sarah Harrison

Not long after that Bryn drove north to see the new clients in Yorkshire, hammering up the A1 in pouring rain, accelerating through the lorry spray with wipers going double-speed, headlights all the way.

To his southerner's ears, Yorkshire had a romantic ring. But the town was as unlike anything out of the Brontës or James Herriot as it was possible to imagine. Naively, he had pictured rolling moors and dales, tumbling streams, grey stone houses and pubs bursting with real ale and gravy dinners. What a mug, he thought now, what a sucker! The reality was a bleak sprawl, population down to twenty thousand and that mostly ageing, a place with the guts ripped out of it.

But not, it transpired, the heart. He was bought lunch in a mock-Tudor roadhouse by the local councillor in charge of the project, Sam Percival, a big, hawkishly handsome man in his sixties with wild white hair and overhanging brows. The choice consisted of an array of roasts under lights with saturated veg, leathery nuggets of mass-produced Yorkshire pudding and roast potatoes in a carapace of hardened fat; or, mysteriously, listed on a blackboard to the side of the bar, Thai curries.

'Landlord's wife,' explained Sam. 'Best day's work he ever did. I recommend the green prawn with coconut rice.'

Sam was a man of few words who did not believe it was his social duty to fill a silence, and this was, after all, a business lunch. What up till now Bryn had taken to be a poor telephone manner proved to be a bred-in-the-bone reserve. By the time Bryn had got the measure of this and was confining himself to questions about the project, the meal was nearly over and he was feeling frustrated. While respecting the other man's position, he would have liked to get to know him better before proceeding to the next stage. It made the exchange of ideas easier when the time came if each knew where the other was coming from. As it was he was able to fill in the usual mental questionnaire, the answers to some of which he knew, or could have guessed, already: the approximate budget which, while representing years of dedicated doorstepping and toil to the town council, was not enormous; the nature and provenance of the site, which Sam was going to show him that afternoon; the make-up of the steering group to whom Bryn would be answerable; and why – most importantly in his view – it was felt the project was something needed by the town.

This last was clearly a sensitive issue. Sam's fierce, high cheekbones grew slighly pink.

'We owe it to those lads,' he said. 'It's long overdue.'

Bryn persisted in his devil's advocate role. 'You're throwing a lot of money at it, and in any town there are those who feel money should be spent in a strictly utilitarian way for the good of the community.'

Sam snorted. 'You sound like the ruddy local paper.'

'This doesn't get a good press?'

'They blather on about "the community". But it's not what the community thinks.'

'And what does it think?'

Sam gave him a hard look. 'Do you want this job?'

'Very much.' He wanted to add that he did not have to take it, that he had choices, but would not give this stroppy old man the satisfaction of an argument.

'Good.'

They left Bryn's car outside the pub, and drove out to the site in the councillor's handsome Japanese four-wheel drive. Sam, alive perhaps to potential criticism, remarked defensively:

'Gas-gobbler this, but you need one of these buggers round here come winter, or leastways I do.'

'It's a good car.'

'I live out of town,' went on the other as though he hadn't spoken. 'I don't want to be stopped going where I want and doing my business because of a bit of weather.'

'Very sensible.'

They followed the ring road for about a mile and a half, and then turned right into what Bryn reckoned was the north-eastern quadrant of the town. This was an area that seemed, to his southerner's eye anyway, to have remained largely unchanged in a hundred years, in appearance if not in use. Narrow roads flanked by sturdy grey terraces marched up and down the slopes; there were a few corner shops and small newsagents, a betting shop, off-licence, tanning and massage parlours, a couple of well-maintained chapels, a primary school and a British Legion Hall. At the point where this neighbourhood began to give way to the next, and you could see the rest of the town spread out below, stretched an area of waste ground covering two or three acres, flanked at one end by unprepossessing sixties council blocks and at the other by some large shed units occupied by, among other things, a tyre and exhaust centre.

Sam pulled off the road on to the waste ground, the tyres crunching over stones and rubbish.

'This is it. Take a look.'

He got out and marched away, standing feet apart and hands in pockets surveying the view. His air was that of a man who had come here often, and was so familiar with the place he no longer needed to see it. His thinking was done; his decisions made.

For his part Bryn had seen a photograph of the area (though he'd brought his own camera anyway), from what angle he couldn't at present be sure. And received, in the same envelope, a plan of its situation and dimensions, the topography and soil components. But neither picture nor plan, though informative in the most literal sense, could have conveyed the atmosphere of this bleak shoulder of ground, standing as it did between the dour certainties of the old and the mess and make-do of the new. In the distance, beyond the town, rose the low ridges of what had once been the South Yorkshire coalfield.

Up here, autumn had arrived early and a terrier-like wind dashed, nipping, across the open ground sending bits of rubbish scuttling before it. Bryn got his parka and boots out of the boot and hauled them on, but for the time being left his notebook and camera in the pocket, and set out to walk the perimeter of the site. He knew it had been the old tram and bus terminal, left for so long it had become a hazardous eyesore before being pulled down last year. Remnants of the outlines of brick walls remained here and there, and he noticed quite a lot of broken glass, though whether from old windows or Saturday night's beer bottles he couldn't tell. As always, the hardy flowering weeds had pushed their way through this unpromising terrain and were hanging on, nodding their tatty heads, yellow and pink, in the wind.

It may have been fanciful but he could have sworn it was warmer on the side by the road, with the Victorian terraces wriggling away down the hill. He walked from there west, towards the small industrial estate. This was at least re-assuringly busy, with forklift trucks going about their busi-ness, the sound of canned rock from the tyre and exhaust centre, a smell of hot rubber and oil. From there he cut back across the centre of the ground to the eastern side near the tower blocks. There was a token playground area, sadly vandalised, between the blocks and here a group of youths in woolly hats were hanging around with the slightly menacing apathy of their kind – bored, disenchanted and hostile. One of them was sitting on a swing, plugged into a walkman. They were probably, Bryn realised, no younger than some of the boys who had lied about their age to join the local regiment in 1914.

He rejoined Sam, eager now to express his genuine enthu-siasm for the project.

'This is a wonderful site. Really exciting.'

'You reckon.'

'I do. There are so many references, so many resonances . . .'
What a poncey poof, he thought, hearing with Sam's ears, and would have added something less pretentious, except the other man said:

'You're not wrong.' He glared briefly in the direction of the tower blocks. 'Vandals could be a problem.'

'Perhaps we could do something to preclude that. Incorporate something into the design, I don't know—'

'We don't want compromise. There's too much half-cock nonsense has gone on in this town in the last twenty years. It's got to be proper.'

'I understand that.'

As if that concluded the business of the day Sam turned and began walking back to the car. He had a short, flat-footed stride: a stomp, thought Bryn.

When they were back in the car, Sam asked: 'You in a rush to get back?'

'Certainly not. This is what I'm doing today.'

'I'll show you something.'

He drove them back into the maze of terraces, cruising slowly between the parked cars until he found what he was looking for. He stopped with the engine running, hazard lights ticking. The electric window on Bryn's side hummed down.

'Thirty-two Lucknow Street. Where I was brought up.'

Bryn gazed out at the narrow house, indistinguishable in any material way from its neighbours. 'What would be different now?'

'From when I was a boy, what you'd expect – electricity, bathroom, inside lav, heating but we were snug enough. I didn't bring you here to give you a lecture on my deprived childhood.'

'So why did you?'

'My dad was in the Pals.'

'A regiment of local lads?'

'That's right.'

'And did he come back?'

'He did. For a while. But he was shell-shocked. One of the first things I remember was him sitting in his chair, shaking – shaking –' he demonstrated, crossing his arms over his chest, clasping his shoulders – 'with the sweat running off him and his eyes staring.'

'Poor man.'

'I didn't think so then. You know what kids are like. I ran out of the room and wouldn't come back in till my mother'd moved him. It disgusted me. Now I disgust meself thinking about it.'

Bryn was conscious of a moment which it would be unwise to disturb with comment. He kept his eyes on the house as Sam rummaged for something in his pocket. After less than a minute the hazard lights were switched off and the car moved forward again.

They did a slow patrol of the streets and as they did so Sam intoned a roll-call of names.

'Horton . . . Jephson . . . Halliwell . . . Cook . . . Rogers . . . Saxby . . . King – only fifteen, King, mother said . . . Larter . . . Dorkins . . .'

As they emerged once more on to the main road, Bryn asked: 'Do you know if any of those got through it?'

Sam made a chopping movement with his hand on the steering wheel. 'They're all on the list.'

They went back to the pub to pick up Bryn's car through what passed for the centre of town, though Bryn wouldn't have known if his driver hadn't pointed out the modern town hall.

'My place of work,' he said. 'Where we'll meet up next time when you bring the drawings.'

'It looks brand new.' Bryn allowed his voice no taint of opinion.

'Ten years.'

'And the old one?'

'Pulled down before it fell down. We've got a nice pedestrianised precinct instead. Cobbles and street lamps just like the old days, except you can't buy a bag of sugar. Kids roam around here on a Friday and Saturday night, half undressed, dead drunk, looking for trouble, great tribes of them like Red Indians. Nobody else about.'

Bryn looked in the wing mirror at the town hall as it receded. A group of men in suits, with briefcases, stood talking on the steps. Younger men than Sam, he deduced: careerists, movers-on, workers of the system. Not bad, but different.

Just his luck to be dealing with a dinosaur. A grand old dinosaur, but a dinosaur nonetheless.

They stood in the car park of the Tudor Rose and shook hands.

'I hope it's been helpful.'

'More than that. Invaluable. I think we can do something really good here.'

'Let's hope so.'

Sam stood as he unlocked the BMW, opened the door, threw his parka on to the back seat and changed out of his boots. 'Business all right then . . . Ever have the top down?'

'As often as I can.'

'Did I tell you I saw that other thing you did. Place where that bastard got up to his tricks. Didn't envy you.'

'It was a challenge.'

'You'll do it for us then.' For the first time Bryn detected a concessionary note, and acknowledgement that he had something they – this man – needed.

'Yes, Sam,' he said. 'I will.'

Two days before the wedding Bryn met Mary in Regent's Park. He was walking along the path that bordered the zoo. They'd had a hot spell; the dry grass was pale, an archipelago of green where it had been shaded, and the trees were just beginning to turn; the sky was a pure, penetrating blue, deeper than it ever was in June or July, aching with imminent change, autumn waiting to be born.

With the early-afternoon sun on his face and his heart full to bursting, he didn't recognise just one more skinny stunner in jeans and a sweatshirt. And only realised her brief 'Hi' had been for him when he was several paces past her.

He stopped and glanced over his shoulder. 'Hello . . .' Even now he wasn't quite sure.

'Mary,' she prompted drily.

'Mary!'

'Remember?' There was no attempt to disguise the sarcasm.

'Don't be silly . . . of course.' He moved forward to give her a kiss on the cheek, but saw at once that it wasn't going to happen and pushed his hands into his pockets to show nothing had been further from his thoughts. 'How are you?'

'Fine. Congratulations.'

'Thank you.' He tried to winch his smile up a notch, but it already felt like a vice gripping his face. 'You mean – me getting married.'

Her eyes were cold and hurt. 'Unless there's anything else we ought to know about.'

He noted the 'we'. 'No, absolutely not.'

'We read it in the paper.' The *Telegraph* announcement had been a concession to Barbara and Andrew. Damn, he should have known.

'So when is it?' she asked.

'On Saturday actually.'

'Let's hope it's a nice day then.' There was something faintly threatening in the wording of this.

'The forecast is set fair, not that it matters, everyone will . . .' He rubbed his face, erasing the crap, wanting to start again. 'Look, would you like a coffee, or a drink or something?'

'No thanks.'

'How were the As?'

'Good enough. I'm at UC.' They were standing a couple of metres apart, other walkers were separating to avoid them, or diving between them with shoulders hunched in apology. She closed the gap and stared into his face. He could see the student sleepy-dust in the corner of her eyes, and smell a piquant mixture of last night's wine and smoke, overlaid with some simple high-street-chemist fragrance . . .

'She was terribly upset, you know – Mum.'

'I can't tell you how sorry I was about that.'

'No.' Her voice was twisted with disdain. 'You bloody can't, because you weren't. You couldn't wait to sneak off with your younger model.'

'Now hang on,' he said, and thought, what am I saying? I never say 'now hang on', it's not an expression of mine, I'm being trapped by this teenager, this child, into behaving like a blustering old fart.

But having made him say it, she hung on: cocking her hip, tightening her mouth, angling her head to show just how patient she was being. He was absolutely determined not to say 'your mother and I'.

'Sally and I were – are – two adults who understood one another. We'd never discussed the future. We had a wonderful relationship, but it ended.'

'*You* ended it.'

He'd had enough. 'Somebody has to, Mary.'

She gave a bitter little smile as though she'd scored a point. 'Right.'

'Anyway. I hope the course goes well. And do—' He thought he'd swallowed the words in time, but she'd heard them.

'Give Mum your love?'

'Yes. Please.'

She turned, closing her eyes as she did so, blanking him. Her tall thin figure seemed to tremble with anger and injury as she walked away. And a moment later he found that he too was a bit shaky, and needed to sit down and gather himself.

He had never talked about Sally to Linda, but that evening – their last together before the wedding – he did.

'Do you remember that girl I was having lunch with on the day you spotted me?'

'The daughter of your then girlfriend.'

'Correct. Well . . . it was no particular secret,' he lied. 'I bumped into her today.'

'Oh yes?' said Linda. She had the air of someone readying herself for the inevitable, waiting to get it over with.

'She's started at UC, she got her A levels.'

'Good.'

'They – she and her mother – had seen the notice in the paper about us getting married.'

She turned down the music that was playing, the Cole Porter songbook. 'You win some, you lose some. I hope that wasn't awkward.'

'Worse than awkward. She was absolutely furious. Incandescent.'

'Bryn, I hate to sound harsh – but it's not your problem.'

'No, I know. But she's very young, she doesn't understand, and I felt like a shit.'

'She's probably got a crush on you.'

'I'm sure not . . .' He shook his head. 'It didn't feel like that. There was nothing remotely flattering about our little scene.'

Linda pulled back a little to see him better. 'Why are you telling me?'

'I don't know.'

'Cold feet?'

'Christ, no!' He threw his head back. 'No! How can you even think such a thing?'

'Then forget it. I've no intention of telling you everything about my past relationships, and I've no interest in hearing about yours.'

'You're absolutely right,' he said. He knew she was. That confession did not equal absolution, and that this particular trouble shared might well fester and double.

'Hey . . .' She put her arms round him and laid her head on his shoulder. 'Unknit the threatening brow. You didn't do a bad thing. And if you want to make peace with anyone, you go ahead. I don't have to know. I'm not interested.'

He could have wept, and was silent. She lifted her face and kissed his cheek. 'Mm?'

He nodded.

He took the next day off, and went to visit his mother. His brother-in-law Malcolm was there. Malcolm was a perfectly nice chap but Bryn was still disappointed when he almost tripped over him in the kitchen with a screwdriver in his hand, doing something to the back of the washing machine.

'Wha-hey, it's the groom, greetings! Come round for your last square meal for the forseeable future?'

'Hello, Malcolm. Is Alison with you?'

'You jest, she's having her hair done and I made the mistake of being at home today so she packed me off round here to make myself useful.'

Malcolm and Alison were childless but Bryn had no idea whether or not this was a secret source of sadness to either of them. They were both always cheerful, always busy, she as a maker of soft furnishings on a personal-recommendation basis, he as the roving representative of the British arm of an American soft-drinks company. They were more than comfortably off and Malcolm had already cut down to four days a week and planned to retire in a couple of years. They seemed to be happy, but it was a scenario that frightened the hell out of Bryn.

'Jean's just popped out,' Malcolm went on. 'Taken the dog to the kennels, but won't be long. Can I get you something – coffee? Something stronger?' He glanced at his watch. 'Sun's approaching the yardarm.'

'No thanks, I'll wait till she gets back.' Bryn leaned against the sink. 'Whatever you're doing to that machine, it makes me feel both guilty and inadequate.'

'It shouldn't, she was understandably alarmed because the drum was banging around like buggery, but it only needed a couple of new screws and I ran the rule over the whole thing while I was at it. Put on a new seal, checked the filters . . . All done, hang on.' He finished tightening the back of the machine, his hair falling forward from its neat parting. He wore a checked short-sleeved shirt and navy slacks. Alison probably called them 'trews'. Bryn knew that she bought all her husband's clothes for him and also packed his case when he went away. These arrangements were entirely up to them, of course, but they betrayed a lack of personal vanity on Malcolm's part that he found astonishing.

'*Le voilà.*' Malcolm straightened up and together they pushed the machine back into place. 'How's Linda?'

'Down with her parents, doing pretty much the same thing as Alison I imagine.'

Malcolm slapped his arm, and squeezed it briefly. 'You know we can't wait. We're so damn pleased. We couldn't get the silly smiles off our faces for days when you first told us. And she's such a lovely girl.'

They went to sit out on the patio. Or more properly on the low wall between that and the lawn, because the garden furniture had been put away.

'You know your mother, autumn begins at the end of August,' said Malcolm. He lit a cigarette and smoked it edgily and quickly, without flourishes, the legacy of his wife's disapproval.

'Building trade holding up?' he asked, dabbing ash into a tub of late-flowering fuchsia.

'Pretty good I'm happy to say.' Bryn always found himself falling into his brother-in-law's way of speaking. 'When we get back I'm starting on an interesting commission. It's a memorial, for one of those pals' regiments in the First World War.'

'Haven't they left it a bit late? What am I saying, it's never too late, but still . . .'

'They certainly don't think so. It's up north, rather a sad town in many ways, used to have coal mining but not any more. They've been fundraising for years for this; the best part of a generation of young men was wiped out.'

Malcolm frowned. Bryn knew what he was going to say. 'You'd have thought – and this has nothing to do with your involvement, you'll do a fantastic job as always – but you'd have thought an economically depressed place would find something more practical to spend its money on. I don't know – youth projects, small businesses, what you will – rather than harking back.'

Bryn thought of the town, stranded in its barren former

coalfield, its streets brutalised by unplanned 'modernisation', its once-grand station hotel run-down and seedy, its former courthouse a chain pub, the covered market full of cheap second-hand furniture and used 'white goods'. He chose his words carefully.

'I take your point. I agree in a way. But I think the city fathers feel that if they can do this right, honour the past in the best way possible, they'll restore a bit of civic pride and it could be some sort of turning point. It may seem quixotic, but the bloke I've dealt with up to now has got his head screwed on even if he is an old warhorse. I've got a lot of respect for them.'

'Fair do's,' said Malcolm. 'And if anyone can help them do it, you can. I saw that garden you did the other day – for the first time, I'm ashamed to admit. Never wanted to visit, thought it would be just too creepy, but I was in the area. Extraordinary.'

Bryn was touched. 'Thank you.'

They heard the sound of the car in the front drive, and then Jean's voice carolling from inside the house:

'Bryn? Is that my son out there?' She passed the kitchen window, waving madly, and came out, arms wide.

'What a gorgeous surprise – kiss kiss, and another – I needed cheering up after leaving Holly at that awful place. Well, it's not an awful place, they're nice people, but he does loathe it, he trembles like a leaf and gives me his best don't-beat-me look. Malcolm, bless you, have you fixed it, I thought it was going to blow up, I can't thank you enough. Isn't this lovely, what did I do to deserve all this attention, let's for goodness sake have a drink but I don't know if there are any beers, Bryn, does that matter, I've got some cheap fizz in the fridge—'

'Why don't I pour us all one of those,' said Malcolm. 'Might as well get in training for tomorrow. You stay put.'

'No, let's go in and sit in the warm, we'll all get piles perched on that cold stone. Malcolm, bless you, what a good idea, and there are some nuts in the cupboard over the bread bin.'

They went into the living room and sat on Jean's pink and grey Sanderson sofa. Holly's rug was folded on the seat of the smaller of the two armchairs and she sprang up again and removed it.

'I can't bear it, it's like a reproach, why do we have them, so darling, are you nervous? You don't look it.'

'Not in the least, I can't wait.'

'That's the spirit. Ooh!' She took his face between her hands and waggled it from side to side before kissing him with an enthusiastic 'mwah!' on the lips. 'It's so exciting, and Alison and I can't wait to see what Linda will wear.'

He smiled. 'Nor me.'

'You have absolutely no idea?'

'None.'

'Quite right, you should be the last to see her, it's traditional. She'll be nothing less than ravishing anyway.'

Malcolm came in with the Cava and glasses on a tray. When he uncorked the bottle Jean cried: 'Hooray! The wedding starts here!'

Every time he saw his mother Bryn was struck afresh by her capacity for delight. Not happiness, or contentment (though she certainly had those), but *joy*. People who knew her less well – even someone like Malcolm – may have thought it a sign of a slightly trivial nature, an impression which her garrulity did nothing to alleviate, but he remembered that she had always been like this, and it was a precious gift.

'Here's to you, my darling,' she said, lifting her glass. 'And to a great day tomorrow.'

'Hear, hear,' Malcolm agreed. 'To both of you.'

'I had a word with Barbara on the phone, because I didn't want to clash, I should really have rung earlier, but it's fine because she's going to be in grey and lavender, so my plum with the black will be a nice contrast. I've hired a hat, though frankly I could have bought one for the price. It's got a rose bang on the front, if I can't wear a fancy hat on my son's wedding day, when can I, I just hope it doesn't swamp me, I don't think it will, it may have the rose but the brim is quite small, so . . .'

Bryn put his hand on hers. 'It sounds great. You're going to look stunning.'

'Absolutely.' Malcolm quaffed his drink. 'Time I wasn't here, I'll leave you to it.'

'Malcolm, you've worked so hard – kiss kiss, drive safely – and you'll pick me up when?'

'Ten o'clock.'

'I shall be ready and waiting, and do give my love to Alison, tell her that colour is absolutely gorgeous on her, I know she feels it's too bright but I wouldn't lie to her, I love her too much, and anyway—'

'Will do. Au revoir, Jean, take care. Cheers, Bryn, see you in church.'

Bryn raised a hand. ''Bye.'

When Malcolm had gone, and before his mother could launch into another effusion, Bryn said:

'Mum, I want to say thank you.'

He had only thought of it at that moment, but when he saw how the expression in her eyes softened he realised how much he meant it.

'Sweet Bryn! There's nothing to thank me for. I've been your somewhat inadequate mother over the years, that's all.'

'I shall ignore that. And I know your views.' He took her hand, stroking its pale, soft, lightly freckled skin with his thumb. 'I know gratitude isn't necessarily part of the deal. But appreciation is. And far from being somewhat inadequate, as you put it, you've been my hero. You taught me all I know about love and generosity and how to be happy.' He brought her hand to his lips. It smelt as it always had, of Je Reviens and Fairy Liquid. 'So thanks.'

She squeezed his fingers and with her other hand made a little gesture as if brushing his hair out of his eyes. 'It's been my pleasure. Really truly.'

'I know.' He closed his eyes for a second, remembering; honouring. 'I know.'

On the drive back to town a word came into his head, a word he hadn't thought of, let alone used, in years: gallant. Surely it was no coincidence that the word sounded like a hybrid of glamorous and valiant. For that's what his mother was, gallant. If, as she got older, her manner caused people to think her silly, he would put them right. Her loquacious, emotional vivacity was like a bright pennant fluttering at the top of a mast. He had every reason to know that beneath the pennant was a tough, sound ship that had weathered the storms.

He drove down very early the next morning. Jim, who was best man, had wanted him to come the night before but he preferred to have this quiet, solitary journey, keeping company with the dawn. At this time of day the streets of North London became highways again, with a sweep and a perspective that recalled an earlier London where gentlemen rode out to hunt in the countryside around Hampstead, and stopped at an inn in Islington on the way back.

Out of town he drove past an airfield that was covered in birds. He had never seen so many in one place – gulls, crows, curlews, pigeons, more than he could name – a parliament of fowls, a peaceful, secret convocation gathered in the dawn light. He pulled over to gaze at them, and none flew away. If a lion had stalked soft-footed between the birds, not disturbing them, he would scarcely have been surprised. It was like some children's book illustration of a prelapsarian age.

By seven thirty he was on the motorway. There were still very few cars and virtually no HGVs. There was no hurry. He hummed down the middle lane, sticking to sixty-five, enjoying the non-competitiveness of the empty road.

It was just as well he wasn't speeding, or he might not have seen the swan in time as he came off a long bend. It was sitting, simply sitting, in the middle lane, its wings folded and its neck upright as if swimming on the smooth, hard river of tarmac. It was so startling and unexpected that he pulled out and was past it before the sickening implications hit him. And when he looked in the rearview mirror the only container lorry of the morning was thundering round the long curve of the motorway, its driver heading for breakfast at the next services.

Bryn fixed his eyes on the road ahead. He tried not to think about it; this was his wedding day. If the swan had a broken leg it was going to die anyway. But he was still haunted by its long agony of terror, and half an hour later as he approached his destination he tuned to the travel news. There was nothing about the swan, or a terrible crash. Perhaps – who knew – the lorry driver had been more on the ball and called the police.

He called them himself, just to make sure. He was passed around and finally spoke to a woman who checked the calls they'd logged that morning.

'No sir, we've had nothing. What time did you say this was?'

'About half past seven.'

'No . . . no. It seems as if the situation must have sorted itself out.'

They both knew what she meant. 'OK, thought I'd better just let you know in case. Thanks anyway.'

'No trouble, thank you sir.'

He and Linda were married at two thirty in the church near the river. Linda wore full-skirted white guipure lace over satin with the faintest blush of peach, and she carried flame-coloured roses. Her hair was up and her long veil was trimmed with the same lace. A bunch of former Harlequins formed an impromptu guard of honour like a line-out, and leapt into the air, shouting, as they left the church. There was a great deal of laughter. They were, Bryn noted, 'man and wife'. He was what he had always been, but Linda, in becoming his woman, had also become a wife, cleaving only unto him. The word he had once so disliked was now like his cloak, spread over and enfolding her.

When they were out in the churchyard in the sunshine, two swans and their young appeared, bobbing, near the bank, and everyone wanted photographs of them with the swans in the background. Because, as everyone knew, swans mated for life – so it was a good omen.

8

1996 – Api

'She looks terrible,' Gilda told her father. 'I mean it's her bed, she made it, she has to lie on it, but I think you ought to know. I've seen terrible in my time,' she added portentously in case he hadn't got the message, 'and she's right down there. You have been warned.'

They were having a drink at the Tintack. Api was not, as yet, behind the bar. It was Gilda's intention that they should catch her unawares so that Charles could appreciate the full extent of his youngest daughter's decline.

'She shouldn't be working in a place like this anyway,' said Charles in what even he could tell was rather a feeble manner.

'Forget it, Dad,' said Gilda. 'Take it from me, she's better off here.'

Charles groaned and downed what was left of his single malt as though it were castor oil. 'I was afraid of this – I told your mother the first time I came up.'

'The only time,' Gilda reminded him.

'I'm here now, aren't I?'

'Sure,' said Gilda. The 'you want a medal?' was left unspoken.

When did I become whiney? Charles thought. Breezy is my style, bright and breezy even. Cheerful, charming Charlie, the darling of the Sin. What the hell is happening to me?

Gilda, looking down as she fiddled with a beer mat, said: 'Judge for yourself. Here she is.'

He glanced fearfully over his shoulder, bracing himself for the unrecognisable foul and midnight hag that would turn out to be Api. But to his great relief he saw her at once, in jeans and a black T-shirt, lifting the bar-hatch to go through.

'She doesn't look too bad,' he said.

'Right,' said Gilda. 'Whatever.'

'I don't like this spying on her. I'll go over and say hello. Same again?'

'No thanks, I'm off.'

'What?' He was aghast. 'Gildie—'

'Don't call me that.'

'Don't go, sweetheart. Please.'

She got up and slung her small rucksack on to her back. 'Sorry, Dad, this is your gig. Call Mum if you want moral support.'

And she was gone, just like that. Charles was bereft. But his glass was empty and he felt pretty foolish just sitting there panicking, so he rose and went over to the bar. Of course it wasn't Api but the older woman who came along the bar in response to his raised fiver.

'Single malt, please, and – er – packet of Bombay Mix.'

'Sorry – peanuts, crisps or scratchings.'

'Packet of smoky bacon, then.'

The whole time she was fetching his order Api was up the far end serving other people. When his drink arrived, he asked:

'I wonder if you could let your other barmaid know I'd like a word with her?'

He realised at once, from the woman's expression, how extremely ill-judged was this request.

'Sorry, mate,' she said. 'You do your own dirty work.'

'I'm her father,' he explained.

'Fancy,' said the woman. 'She never mentioned.'

Charles was mortified. Only the knowledge that the truth would out, and very soon, prevented him from entering into an extremely warm exchange with the harridan.

Instead he picked up his glass and went down to Api's end of the bar. He forgot his crisps but was far too chagrined to go back for them. He found a stool right next to the bloke she was serving, and perched on it. Observing her at close quarters, he saw what Gilda meant. The *tout ensemble* was

neat, but the devil was in the detail: the greasiness of the tied-
back hair, the spots around the mouth, the general pallor and
a sense of dirt around the edges. And she was shockingly thin,
with sunken grooves down her upper arms and above her
collarbones. 'Terrible' might have been an exaggeration, but
she did look quite rough.

As soon as she'd finished it was plain she'd seen him all
along.

'Hello.'

'Api, darling . . .' He thought he should give her a kiss but
she was standing well back, and if he lunged over the bar he
risked acute embarrassment. 'Have you got a moment?'

'I'm working.'

'I know, but—'

'Why did you have to just turn up? Why didn't you ring?'

Her tone of complaint must have communicated itself to
her superior who hove alongside.

'Everything all right?'

'Yes, thanks.'

'He's your father, is he?'

'Yes.'

The woman addressed herself to Charles. 'Five minutes,
OK?'

'That,' he hissed in a splenetic undertone when she'd gone,
'is a prize bitch.'

'She's quite nice, actually.'

'Look, if we've got a few minutes, can we sit down?'

'I'm staying here.'

'Whatever. Look, your mother and I are worried about you.'

'Don't be, I'm fine.'

'No, you're not. You're far too thin, you don't look well at
all. And you're too young to be working in this place. I bet it
gets packed with undesirables later on – that woman didn't
even believe I was your father!'

'Why should she?' said Api. 'You ought to be grateful she's
looking out for me.'

'That's one way of looking at it.' He cut to the chase. 'Please come home, Api. We miss you.'

'Where are you off to tomorrow then?'

'Edinburgh,' he replied, before realising he'd been well and truly wrong-footed. 'That's not the point. The point is, you're not happy.'

'I'm perfectly happy, thank you.'

'Well, you don't look it.'

'It's a bit hard when you're sat there having a go at me.'

Charles, who wished to be on his way, was getting seriously annoyed by now. 'I'm not the only one who thinks so! It was Gilda who got me here.'

'Why doesn't that surprise me? I didn't think you'd have come of your own accord.'

This, finally, was all the excuse Charles needed to get up and walk out.

Xanthe had been having a somewhat trying afternoon mediating between Judith and her new employers (she was working at the local library as part of a youth opportunities scheme) and was consequently not receptive to Charles's complaints about Api.

'You were the one who said to be more direct,' she pointed out, pouring wine with her free hand.

'I could not have been more direct, I assure you. And nor could she.'

'So what do we do – wash our hands of the whole thing?'

'I wouldn't put it like that. Watch and pray, more like.'

Xanthe took a long mouthful. 'She'll be all right. She'll probably surprise us all.'

'Maybe.' There was the faint chime of a flight announcement in the background. 'Got to go. See you next week.'

''Bye . . .' He rang off, but Xanthe stood there for some seconds with the receiver in her hand, emitting its long, desolate tone. It was all such a trial!

★

Gilda had a conscience, and Carson was in the firing line.

'Why did you take her round there?'

His expression was injured. 'Because you wouldn't have her here, babe.'

'But that Dodge character. Dodgy more like. Worse than dodgy, he's creepy.'

'I don't really know him,' said Carson guardedly. 'He's gigged with us a couple of times, that's all, he's a good guitarist.'

'Great! Well, he makes my skin crawl.'

'Settle down, what's eating you all of a sudden?'

But Gilda couldn't tell him about the way Dodge had touched her when she went round there: casually but so intimately, pressing his long finger hard between her thighs, right up into her fanny so that her knees had almost given way. She'd been shaken, not just by the restrained violence of the intrusion, but by her body's response. She'd been turned on. The second he took his hand away the crotch of her pants was damp; she was afraid it might show through to her trousers. What's more the woman Mina, who she took to be Dodge's partner, had given her a cynical, complicit look as though she knew, though no one could possibly have seen. But Carson was old-fashioned in his way. He'd think she must have done something to provoke it. She thought it best to say nothing.

'He's manipulative,' she said.

'What,' said Carson, grinning affably. 'And your little sister isn't?'

Not long after her father's visit, Api gave up the pub job, but not because of anything he'd said. Dodge didn't like her working there, and when *he* said it it was different somehow. She respected him, for a start. His concern made her feel safe, and cared for, unlike her father's whingeings which always seemed more to do with him being able to enjoy a quiet life. Also, Dodge was cool and had credibility; he spoke with authority, whereas Charles knew diddly-squat about anything.

When she told Dodge she'd packed it in he didn't exactly praise her but she could see he was quietly pleased. And she wanted to please him, more than anything. She began to try harder, to anticipate things he might like. She bought some of the tobacco he used and left it on the arm of the settee. She did a bit of cleaning, and made the bed in his room, having taken the stinky sheets to the launderette. She made toast for him, and even walked the unwilling China on his chain lead in Hyde Park. She lived for Dodge's approval, which was never expressed but which she knew was there because there was this bond between them.

She was still sleeping with Giles a couple of times a week, but she stopped that because he would keep telling her not to get too involved with Dodge. Gilda came round once, and she hid in her place behind the settee. She heard Dodge say he didn't know where she was, but he did because the moment the door closed he sat down and said:

'She's gone.'

'Thanks,' she said, creeping out.

He was reading a book and he didn't look up. 'Don't be scared. These people don't own you.'

And he was right. No one owned her. Not Gilda, not Giles, not Mina with her funny looks . . . Certainly not her parents.

He began to ask her to do things, to run errands, to fetch things from another room, to take messages to a couple of friends of his who lived in Plaistow. The journey out there was long and the neighbourhood scared her. His friends lived in a block which made Farnsworth Buildings look cosy: it was covered in violent graffiti some of which looked as if it had been done in blood, and the staircase that she had to use, because the lift was broken, smelt bad. There were often spatterings of puke, and puddles, even turds in the corners. Once a man on one of the landings burst out of his door, shouting and screaming at her. The couple Dodge knew were at least quiet – quiet as ghosts and nearly as insubstantial. Their flat had almost nothing in it. Maybe they were ghosts. Certainly going there felt like a nightmare.

She started to stay near Dodge if he was in the house, sitting on the floor near his feet since the space next to him would be occupied by the dog. It wasn't long before he suggested she come along to his pitch in the underpass. She'd begin by standing by him, but since she had no instrument, and couldn't sing, she soon took to sitting on the blanket with China, saying thank you when people dropped coins in the guitar case. It was the end of summer and beginning to get colder; she often wore Dodge's old army jacket to keep warm. He liked her to have her hair loose, so she did that too. It made her feel warm and excited to think that he'd notice such a thing at all. She was often a bit late for her shift at Metrofoods, and too tired to work properly, and it wasn't long before they let her go, which was no bad thing because she preferred to be with Dodge anyway. She had been starting to pay a bit of rent, but now she had no money except what Dodge gave her out of the guitar case. She'd been taking a few small things from Metrofoods – packeted sandwiches, cheese, the odd apple and bar of chocolate – and now she began to do the same thing in the local Asian supermarket. Jamal, the man who ran it, came up to her once after she'd paid for some cornflakes – she made a point of buying something so as to keep him happy – and pressed a muesli bar into her hand.

'There,' he said. 'A present. I'm not a hard man, young lady, but I'm not blind either, so take this as a warning. Be good now, please.' He raised a long finger before her face. 'And have a bath, hmm?'

As she left the shop her heart was pounding and her legs were jellified. She never went back. Some time in the week after that, Mina left the flat.

Dodge said baths weren't necessary. China had never had one which was why his skin and coat were in perfect condition. You could see that was true. But having no money apart from the odd handful of change was worrying. She approached Giles one day when Dodge was still asleep, and asked what it would be worth to him to sleep with her again. The look he gave her was weird – angry and sad and almost as if he were a little frightened of her too.

'Have it,' he said, pressing three pound coins into her hand, 'and stay away from me, yeah?'

Not long after, Giles left too, and Kath the day after. Each of them slipped away, as if escaping, with no goodbyes and without taking all their possessions.

'Looks like you and me,' said Dodge. They'd got back from the underpass to an empty flat. It was a bit more echoey than before. He sat down in his usual place, and she curled up on the floor next to his legs. He pushed his finger and thumb into the back pocket of his jeans and produced a chocolate bar.

'Hey, look what I got . . . want some?'

She nodded. Watching him unwrap it she could almost taste it already, the delicious smoothness, the break between her teeth, the sweetness flooding her tongue. He broke off a square and put it in his mouth.

'Mm. Say, that's good.'

He broke off another and gave it to China, who swallowed it whole.

'And one. For you.'

He laid the square on the floor, on the filthy carpet. 'Wait now. It's better if you wait. O-K.'

She put out her hand and he caught it, and the other one, and held them behind her back quite easily and gently with one of his.

'Enjoy,' he said.

Slowly, she lowered her head and picked up the square of chocolate with her lips.

This time Gilda said nothing to Carson. She would keep it simple: go there, collect Api, bring her back, phone whoever was at home to come and pick her up. There had been too much messing about and consultation, and it had got them nowhere. Gilda was not in the habit of blaming, herself or anyone else. Let everyone get on with it and take responsibility for what they did, was her philosophy. She didn't blame and she didn't judge.

But she loathed Dodge with a visceral intensity. Indeed her desire to thwart and humiliate him was a far greater factor in her actions than the desire to rescue Api, who at the last count had appeared not to want rescuing.

She went to Farnsworth Buildings straight from the studio. She knew Dodge went out busking, but didn't know when; she was prepared to sit it out. When she arrived there was a woman just going in with handfuls of supermarket bags, so when she'd got the door open Gilda held it for her and nipped in afterwards. She trudged up the stairs and knocked on the door. There was no reply but she heard the dog's feet pattering across the floor, and his snuffles and warning growls. There was no light showing beneath the door, so she sat down in the shadowy angle at the corner of the stairs to wait.

She didn't have to wait long. After about ten minutes the main door opened and banged shut again and she heard the tap-tap of someone jogging lightly up the steps. She knew it was him even before he came into view, his head appearing close to where her shoulder leaned on the banister. She watched him go to the door and get his key. The moment he turned it in the lock she was up, and pushed past him as he entered.

If there was a flicker of surprise, she missed it.

'What's the rush?'

'I've come to collect Api.'

'Is that right?' He closed the door behind them and turned on the light in the small hallway. His movements were slow. Gilda felt as though he were slowing her down too, lowering her body temperature in some way so that she couldn't move fast. She really did feel cold – this place was cold. The dog, standing in the doorway to the living room, stared at them.

'Where are the others?' she asked.

'They left.'

'Where to?'

'No, they're gone. Outa here.'

'But Api's still here, is she?'

'Of course.' He nodded towards the living room but when she took a step in that direction the dog curled its lip and vibrated with a growl. 'China, come on, over here.'

Gilda was suddenly frightened. This was too weird. She'd expected crowded rooms, a shouting match – a scene. Instead of which she was alone in this small, ill-lit, foul-smelling place with this slow-moving, soft-spoken man who was mad as a snake, and his vicious dog. She wished she had brought Carson.

'Where's the light?' she asked.

His hand slid past her shoulder and pressed a switch. Her skin shrank, but he didn't touch her. She couldn't see Api.

'Her bed's over there. Behind the sofa.'

The room looked tidier, but she realised that was only because there were fewer things in it. It smelt if anything even sourer than before. If there had ever been anything homely about the place there wasn't now: it felt almost derelict. For a second Gilda thought, what if we are the only people in this whole building? And then she remembered the woman with the shopping. If she had to scream, someone would hear – surely.

'Api!' Because she was afraid, her voice sounded brittle, almost schoolmistressy. 'It's me. Come on, we're going.'

Api was curled up on the mattress, but her eyes were wide open. She was wrapped in a length of grubby printed material. She herself looked grey with dirt. She shook her head. 'No.'

'Come on, I haven't got all night.'

'No. I'm staying here.'

'Don't be ridiculous.'

Dodge sat down on the sofa and began rolling a cigarette.

The dog jumped up next to him. Without turning his head, Dodge said: 'Api – here.'

At once Api got up and went to him.

'Sit down.'

She sat down on the floor at his feet.

'Good.' Dodge glanced up at Gilda. 'She's not going anywhere,' he said, on a rising inflection, as though he'd made the point once already.

Gilda could see now that this was true. Api wasn't going to come with her voluntarily, not because she was being a stroppy little madam – that would have been welcome – but because she couldn't. She was an animal, lower than the dog: she'd do whatever Dodge told her.

'Right,' said Gilda. 'I get it. In that case I'll leave you to it.'

'That's my girl,' said Dodge.

Prickling with fear and outrage she walked to the front door and opened it. When she looked back her sister's head was leaning against Dodge's knees; her eyes, big and dull, stared at Gilda.

'You know where I am,' said Gilda, and closed the door.

She hadn't got a plan; she only knew that it was important Dodge thought she didn't care and had given up.

Api felt the air, that had been swirling and dangerous, settle back round the three of them. Peace returned. She was safe again.

But that night, in her dreams, the man from the picture was closer, and she could almost see his face. She woke up terrified and crying. She went to Dodge's room but he was fast asleep and China growled at her – bed-sharing wasn't in the deal. She stood in the middle of the flat, sobbing.

'Api! Api!'

The voice was scarcely more than a whisper; she thought at first she might have imagined it.

'Api, it's all right – open the door! Just *open* it!'

It was Gilda, on the landing. Api didn't want to go to her,

she knew Dodge wouldn't like it, but the need to escape her nightmare was overwhelming. While she was alone the man would continue his advance.

'Come on. I'm right here. Come *on!*'

Shaking, she went to the door and turned the knob on the latch. The minute it was open Gilda grabbed her wrist and yanked her through.

'Quiet!' Gilda pulled the door until the Yale lock clicked, with what seemed a deafening sound. Her face was white, but she was strong, tall as a giant, and her voice was a long, fierce hiss, like escaping steam.

'We're going. I'm taking you. You're doing nothing wrong, understand? I know you don't want to leave, but I'm not giving you any choice. Now come!'

Dodge never came after her. If he had, things might have been different. But because he didn't she realised that he didn't care about her, whatever he said. That their special bond wasn't a special bond at all. She wished she hadn't told him about the picture; she didn't want that man, with whom she did have a special bond, to be in someone else's head. But maybe he would forget.

She slept and cried for almost a week in Gilda's flat. Gilda refused to take time off work but Carson made himself useful with tinned soup and digestive biscuits. When she slept she slept like the dead, except for once when she dreamed of home, more as it really was, with untidy rooms and the portrait, her secret, in its place in the attic.

Now that Xanthe and Charles had decided to separate, the relationship between them had regained its equilibrium. The ructions caused by Api's late-flowering rebellion, they both conceded, had probably been waiting in the wings for years. All they were going to do, really, now that all the family but Judith had moved out, was formalise the existing situation.

It was a huge relief to both of them. They didn't say as

much, but there was an almost palpable lightening and warming of the atmosphere. Charles was renting a room in the spacious Hammersmith flat of a Symphonia colleague, and Xanthe would – in time, there was no hurry – sell Eastleigh End and get somewhere smaller, possibly by the sea. They realised, with pleased surprise, that they were at the very least old friends, with a shared past stretching back nearly three decades.

'We ought to get up in the loft some time,' Xanthe suggested. 'There's mountains of stuff up there. I've forgotten what half of it is, if I ever knew in the first place.'

'I'm game,' said Charles. 'Maybe we'll find a hitherto un-discovered art treasure that will keep us in the twilight of our years. Jude! Do you want to come and help us clear out the loft?'

'No thanks.' Judith had wandered into the kitchen, still in her checked pyjamas. She had her glasses on and was carrying an open book in one hand. With the other she took a bowl from the draining board and began pouring cornflakes into it.

'How's the job?' asked Charles heartily.

Judith glanced at her mother. 'It's all right now, isn't it?'

'Oh yes.'

'Glad to hear it. What are you reading?'

'This.' She held it up.

'*Dangerous to Know*,' read Charles. 'Sounds interesting, what's it about?'

'There's this woman who kills all these men she has sex with,' explained Judith, brightening visibly. 'And this man who's a police superintendent who's fallen in love with her, that's as far as I got.'

'Well,' chuckled Charles, 'I think we can see which way the wind's blowing. It sounds a right load of—'

'Judith has to read new stuff to keep pace with borrowing trends,' said Xanthe. 'She takes things at her pace, but you're doing OK, aren't you, Jude?'

Judith sat down at the table with the book open next to her. 'This is really good.'

'Going in today?' asked Charles.

She looked up. 'It's Saturday.'

'She does afternoons on Saturday,' explained Xanthe.

'Fine, I'll give you a lift.'

'OK.'

Charles and Xanthe exchanged a parental look. A sense of mutuality had not featured prominently in their marriage, but it played an increasingly large part in their impending separation. And now it prompted them to leave Judith to her bookish breakfast and go up to the top floor and thence to the attic.

It was rather more daunting than even Xanthe remembered. 'God almighty,' she wailed, 'where are we going to begin?'

'What I suggest,' said Charles, 'is that we get it down on to the landing where we can see it properly, and only put back what's definitely going to stay.'

'I'm not sure it'll all fit on the landing.'

'Then that'll be an incentive to get rid of it.'

This seemed sensible. Xanthe wondered if she had been getting the most out of her husband all these years. Maybe if she'd asked more of him . . . but never mind.

They began the operation with Xanthe in the attic and Charles at the bottom of the ladder. After half an hour Xanthe came down, her hair grey with dust, and went to make some coffee. When she returned, Charles was poking about at the top.

'Coffee up!'

'Cheers . . .' he replied vaguely, his attention clearly focused elsewhere. 'Zannie, come up here a second, can you?'

'I'm holding coffee.'

'Pass it up.'

He appeared in the aperture and she handed up the mugs and joined him. Stooping under the eaves he went and perched on an old school trunk and beckoned her to join him.

Sarah Harrison

'Look,' he said. 'Granddad.'

She sat down next to him. 'I thought we put him in the trunk with the other pictures.'

'I bet you kept him out. You always liked him. But remember how he used to make Jude cry?'

Remembering, Xanthe shook her head. 'I wonder what she'd make of him now . . .'

'Don't even think it.' Charles laid a mock-restraining hand on her arm. 'She's as happy as Larry these days with her little job and her junk novels. Why rock the boat? Besides, I'm with her on this one. He's a surly old bugger. Darth Vader meets Mr Brocklehurst.'

'But good-looking,' mused Xanthe. 'A handsome devil, that sort of man used to be known as.'

'You need a moustache for that, for twirling lasciviously as you pour Madeira down the neck of an innocent country maid.'

Xanthe peered at the portrait, squinting in the half-light. 'He was a millionaire when this was painted. Just think . . . And died a pauper, my mother said.'

'Who was the painter?'

'S R something. His name's down in the corner but it's impossible to read. I really ought to get it cleaned up and valued. Only out of interest, I wouldn't sell it. It's a family piece in every sense, one of the children might want it.'

'It's hard to imagine,' said Charles. 'But I suppose I agree. Back in the trunk?'

The portrait in its broad gilt frame was heavy, but together they swathed it in its wrapping and replaced it. Just before they closed the lid, Xanthe tweaked the cloth aside for a final look.

'I always wondered why he's half in darkness.'

'Obvious,' said Charles, 'it's a vanity portrait. He had a best side and the painter had the good sense to show it. Christ knows what the other one's like.'

★

The phone rang when Charles was out running Judith to the library. Xanthe was on the top-floor landing sifting through a cardboard box of tarnished, unmatched silver cutlery, and made it on the sixteenth ring.

'Where were you,' asked Gilda, 'on the roof?'

'Practically. We're sorting out the attic.'

'Find anything valuable?'

'Not yet. Or not that we want to sell. But it's interesting, you know, stuff you haven't seen for ages . . . Speaking of which, how are you?'

'Good, thanks. I've fronted Carson's band a couple of times recently and it's gone well. We got noticed.'

'Well done,' said Xanthe. 'So what happens next?'

'Not a recording contract, if that's what you're thinking, but some bigger gigs hopefully. If Dad's going to be in London, he could come to one.'

'I might even come myself,' said Xanthe spiritedly.

'That'd be good. Look – Api's here, she wants a word with you.'

'Gilda—'

'Mum?' It was Api's voice. 'It's me.'

Xanthe had never before noticed how much younger and lighter Api's voice was than those of her sisters – a childlike voice. She stifled a pang of remorse. They had done their best.

'Hello, you, how's it going?'

'All right. I left the flat.'

'You did? Thank heavens. So where are you now?'

'Here with Gilda and Carson.' A voice off made some comment. 'For the moment, it's only temporary. I've got another job.'

'Another? Three jobs?'

'No, a different one. I'm waitressing at this restaurant, Pastamento it's called, in Charlotte Street. It's really nice. I'm looking for a flat with one of the other girls there.'

'And is she really nice too?'

'Yes!' called Gilda. 'I checked!'

It was all so strange, but such an improvement – and one which Xanthe was aware she herself had done nothing to deserve – that she said: 'Your father and I are doing some sorting out in the attic; there might be some things you could use in the flat.'

'It'll be furnished,' Api pointed out.

'I know, but still – there are bits and piece of china, kitchen stuff and so on. Let me know when you get somewhere.' Charles came back and she pointed at the receiver and mouthed 'API!' He gaped obligingly and blew a kiss. 'Your father sends his love.'

'What are you going to do with the pictures?' asked Api. 'There's a whole trunkful of them up there.'

'There is, you're right.' Xanthe restrained herself from asking how her daughter knew. After all, why shouldn't she? It was just that the knowledge displayed a greater degree of interest in family matters than she would have credited Api with.

'We haven't quite decided,' she said. 'We haven't been through them all, but we won't part with anything the family want.'

'So you'll keep that one of my great-grandfather.'

Xanthe noted the 'my'. 'Yes, he's family.' There was no sound at the other end, and Xanthe added: 'Even if Jude wishes he wasn't . . . Api?'

'Yes?'

'You're there,' said Xanthe. 'I thought I'd lost you.'

Api didn't care what Metrofoods thought of her, but she did go back to the Tintack to apologise for disappearing. The woman there, Karen, heard her out stony-faced.

'I wasn't impressed,' she said. 'But it happens all the time, unfortunately; you're nothing special.'

Api inferred from this, correctly as it happened, that perhaps in a small way she had been. 'I'm sorry. I was having a bad time.'

'Shit happens, darling.'

'I know,' said Api. 'Sorry.'

She turned to go when Karen added: 'You're looking better. Got something else?'

'Yes, I'm a waitress.'

'That's hard work, waitressing, think you can stick it out?'

'Yes.'

'Even if you have another bad time?'

'I shan't. Not like that.'

Karen cracked a small smile. 'Drop in and see us when you're rich and famous.'

'Don't worry,' said Api. 'I intend to.'

She didn't talk about what had happened. Only Gilda knew, and the moment she'd got her back it was as if she wanted to pretend it simply wasn't there, as if she were so shocked, or disgusted, or embarrassed, or ashamed, that she refused to have any more to do with it. Api felt all those things too. The last thing she wanted was to go back over what had happened, but it would have been good to at least try and explain herself, to convey something of the spell she'd been under, its strange enervating power, its mixture of safety and threat. She and her friend watched the video of *The Godfather*, and it had left her white and sick. All those 'favours' expressed in soft voices reminded her of Dodge and the way he'd protected her and protected her until she was entirely unprotected, and his alone to. do with as he liked. As the weeks went by the episode became even more incredible and she lived with a fear like black smoke drifting in the back of her mind.

The fear was not of Dodge, but of herself – that part of herself which had sunk so easily, so *willingly* into squalor and slavery. Dodge had never hurt her, nor raised his voice to her. He had not ill-treated her, not really, he had inflicted no pain, had neither starved nor beaten her but simply bent her to his will by relieving her of hers. She who had taken her life into her own hands and run away, who had learned about sex so she could use it to her own advantage – she who had imagined she could control Dodge by withholding her body had wound up whimpering for the merest touch from him. A touch which never came. She had imagined Dodge understood her as no living person had done, and now she could see that wasn't the answer. Understanding was nothing on its own. It meant another person could see your weaknesses. For it to be any good you had to have love as well.

She cried when she thought of Giles – nice, straightforward, ever-ready Giles – and how in the end he'd paid her to get lost. Giles hadn't loved her any more than she'd loved him but they had at least been friends. And he had, like so many others, tried to warn her, to protect her from herself.

But in spite of the legacy of fear, positive things had come of the episode. She was on good terms with Gilda, and Carson. Her mother had sounded all right, quite calm and amiable in fact, and she knew that her father's relief would outweigh any residual resentment.

Most importantly there were her dreams, which she now understood. It was a revelation! Ashe had not been threatening, but warning her. As her darkness had drawn in he had begun emerging from his. And his warning, finally, had saved her – had woken her that last night so Gilda could hear her. It was to him, she was certain, that she owed her life.

Now her parents might be splitting up, but Ashe would remain immutable, she could rely on that, keeping his dark eye on her no matter what.

9

1983–1993 – Bryn, Linda

Linda would never have believed how much she liked motherhood. When she married Bryn she assumed she'd have children, in time, but she was in no hurry to give up work: one thing she had a healthy dread of was poverty. Not in its extreme form, as doing without comforts and necessities, but as the opposite of prosperity. She had witnessed times in her parents' married life, notably when her father had first come out of the air force, when things seemed to be falling apart for sheer lack of substance. Everything had been second-best, make-do and makeshift, and they had embraced this almost as a virtue in its own right, as if it were a sign of gentility to be a bit hard up. She remembered the extreme emphasis on cleanliness, as though to keep cheap or old things spotless were the next best thing to being able to afford new ones. The sense of standards kept up in the face of adversity, of plucky belt-tightening, she found unutterably depressing. She wanted her own life to be ample, to have plenty of room for the good things even if they weren't taken up. The assiduous maintenance of old stuff – clothes, gadgets, cars, kitchen equipment – seemed slightly pathetic, and pathetic was something Linda never, ever wished to be.

So it had been her intention to stay on at work, for three or four years at least. But the cluster of cells that turned out to be Nick was already clinging limpetlike to the inside of her uterus when she returned to the Delancey offices at the end of September. Even then she could have employed a nanny and continued, indeed that was her plan, but Sir Harry knew her better than she did herself.

'Wait and see, shall we?' he said. 'Just wait and see.'

She did, and the moment Nick was put in her arms she knew she couldn't leave him. He was a throwback to his paternal grandfather's side of the family, a Mediterranean baby with olive skin and dark hair, eyes like shiny black grapes. The Frankels paid for a nursery nurse for the six weeks after his birth, so Linda was eased into the broken nights to the point where she was longing to be alone with her son. He was a demanding baby – noisy, hungry and wakeful, but these things didn't get her down. Even her mother was astonished.

'I think you're doing wonderfully, darling,' she said on one visit when Nick was two months old. 'I thought I'd die of tiredness with Robin, and he was a placid child.'

'I don't really understand it myself,' Linda confessed. 'But it makes me happy.'

'And so it should, of course. But first-time motherhood is so – draining. And one's largely unprepared for it, or I was.'

'Nor I, not in the least,' said Linda. 'But all the surprises so far have been pleasant.'

Her mother kissed her cheek and touched the baby's head. 'Long, long, may that continue.'

What she could not have said to her mother, though she did to Bryn, who agreed, was that pregnancy and motherhood were sexy. The blooming and burgeoning, the rising of the juices, they both found profoundly pleasing and sensual, and she was astonished to discover that breastfeeding was not only satisfying but arousing. Her son's tugging on her nipple caused small orgasmic ripples and flutters. When she told Bryn about this his response was straightforward:

'I'm jealous. Can I have a suck?'

'When he's finished, and if I'm not sore . . .'

'It's me who's sore!'

When their second child was a daughter she had wondered at first if her feelings would be the same – was there something faintly suspect about the mother/son relationship? But her sense of kinship with Sadie swept these worries away.

Indeed, while Sadie was tiny she felt their similarities most keenly – another female body from her female body, part of her and her continuation.

Her gender wasn't the only thing that marked out Sadie from her brother. She was just as wakeful, but there the resemblance ended. Her eyes would stare back at Linda out of the dark oval of the bassinet at three in the morning when Linda would creep over to see if she was still alive. How could such a tiny baby be awake, and not cry? What was she thinking? What did she see? And what would she remember?

Now the children were ten and eight and Linda was in her element. Nick was at prep school in Hertfordshire and Sadie at the local fee-paying primary in North London. Linda enjoyed zooming up the A1 in the MG to attend plays, concerts and matches and to collect and deliver Nick at exeat weekends. There was the merest undertow of well-bred flirtation in her relationship with the head, and Nick's housemaster, and this amiable state of affairs was assisted by Nick's being a popular boy, good at games, bright but lazy, something of a favourite all round – Matron confided in Linda that in her opinion her son would turn out to be a heartbreaker, and Linda was bound to agree. If, years before, Linda had been asked to design her ideal son, she would have come up with something very like Nick.

But it would have been a dull world if one's children were all the same, and Linda was astonished that she and Bryn had produced two children so utterly different. In the case of Nick it was possible occasionally to glimpse flashes of themselves, his parents, but where had Sadie come from? From time to time they'd remark, only half-joking, that Sadie seemed the most grown-up of the lot of them. She was so serious, so conscientious, a perfectionist who wept quiet tears of self-reproach if her school work was untidy or if she left something at home (generally Linda's fault, not hers). The only thing that concerned Linda, if not Bryn, was their daughter's weight. She was a plump child, and approaching

the age when that would matter. Little girls not much older
than Sadie were becoming frighteningly fashion-conscious –
as often as not birthday parties were discos, and clothes at
such occasions were skimpy and colourful, hair adorned with
bright streaks, bows and slides. With Sadie it was impossible
to say which was cause and which effect, but she was having
none of it. She was happiest in her school uniform, which
required neither style-savvy nor decision-making. Linda daily
thanked God for the purple blazer, purple and white striped
dress with white collar (summer) and dark purple skirt with
white blouse (winter) decreed by St Margaret's. She tried to
keep Sadie's diet healthy without making her neurotic. The
trouble was exercise. Once again cause and effect were
blurred, but Sadie preferred to work, read, or watch television than do anything which involved getting her heart-rate
up. Linda maintained that her admirable studiousness masked
her unwillingness to ride a bike, take a walk, or engage in any
brisk physical activity. Bryn claimed that Sadie was naturally
bookish and thoughtful.

It was getting a dog that made the difference. They bought
Flo from some other parents at St Margaret's who advertised
golden retriever puppies in the school newsletter. They went
along *en famille* one weekend when Nick was home, and were
instantly lost. The puppies were simply the softest, sweetest
bundles of cream-coloured cuteness that any of them had ever
seen, and Flo the sweetest of all. From her melting dark eyes
with their slightly wistful downward droop to her adorable
nonsense of a tail she was perfection. And from the day they
brought her home she exercised a benign influence over the
household that the rigours of housetraining, chewed shoes and
clothing and dog hairs could not tarnish.

Nowhere was this influence more apparent than on Sadie.
Characteristically she took it upon herself to 'train' the puppy,
and spent hours patiently – and fruitlessly, for Flo was far too
young – exhorting her to sit, stay and come. When she could
be taken out for walks, Sadie wanted to be the one to lead

her, at first accompanied, and then only occasionally and under very tight conditions to take her round the block on her own, or with a friend. The friends were suddenly more numerous, too. Unlike Nick, Sadie had not been the sort of child to make friendships easily, but with Flo it was different. Linda soon became used to the delivery of small girls at the door, and a smiling, apologetic mother – 'I'm so sorry to do this to you again, it's that puppy of yours, do you mind awfully?'

Parenthood undoubtedly brought her closer to her own parents. As the years went by she came to understand that parental love was fluid, protean, endlessly expanding, able to take different forms, to mould itself to the individual child – that being different did not make it greater or less. She found herself scarcely able to imagine the pain of losing a child; the phrase 'crime against nature' took on a fresh meaning. For the first time, and not without difficulty, she spoke directly to her mother about Robin.

It was one Sunday in autumn when they had been down for lunch and Bryn, her father and the children had taken Flo for a walk by the river, leaving the two of them by the fire. Linda had kicked off her shoes and was curled up in the largest armchair; Barbara sat at the end of the sofa, legs elegantly crossed, gazing in wonderment at the colour supplement and about to muse aloud, Linda knew, who on earth actually *wore* these clothes . . .

'Mum, can I say something?'

Barbara laid aside the magazine. 'I'm all yours.'

'This is going to sound rather odd, after so long.'

'Try me.'

'I just wanted to say – how sorry I am about Robin.'

'Oh, darling . . .' Barbara's voice trembled, and there was a shine in her eyes.

'I mean *terribly* sorry. I don't think I've ever said it.'

'That's all right. You didn't have to. You were so young when it happened, you had your own life to get on with.'

'And I did. I have been, ever since.' Linda got up and went to sit next to her mother on the sofa. 'But I know now what you must have gone through. Still do, probably.'

'Well . . .' Barbara smoothed her skirt with firm, long strokes, as if ironing. 'There are times. His birthday, always . . .'

Linda realised to her shame that she could not remember the precise date. 'It's July, isn't it?'

'The fifteenth. We try to be on holiday then.'

'Oh Mum . . . It must be hell. I mean literally – like hell.'

'No, no, not any more. Life is sweet, after all. We have you, and Bryn and the children. We're very lucky.'

'But to lose your child, your son, I can't begin to imagine—'

'It happens all the time. It happened to thousands of people during the war. Rob was in the army, it was what he wanted to do.' She gave something close to a shrug. 'He died doing the job he loved.'

'God, Mum, you sound like a tabloid newspaper – ah!' she clapped her hands to her eyes, shaking her head in dismay. 'Sorry!'

'I didn't express myself very well. It's surprisingly hard not to fall into cliché.'

'No, you're right. But now we have our two, I've realised how unbearable it must be. And you and Dad were so brave. You never let any of it spill over on to me.'

'We tried not to. That wouldn't have been fair.' For the first time in the conversation Barbara turned to face her daughter. 'And don't worry about being jealous, it's the most natural thing in the world.'

'I wasn't,' Linda began, and then realised that of course jealousy was the nub of the matter, what she had most wanted to clear out of the way. 'Was it that obvious?'

'Only to us. Or to me, really, I don't think your father noticed anything at all. You behaved very well, we were so proud of you. But I could tell what you were feeling.'

'Not the right feelings, I'm afraid.'

Barbara shook her head. 'I'm not sure there is such a thing

as the right feeling. We're stuck with the ones we have.' She gave a tight smile. 'And most of them aren't very comfortable.'

'I feel as if I've been such a bitch all these years. Never saying anything, never mentioning it, feeling resentful . . . Resentful about someone who's dead! My brother – your son.'

'Darling. It's perfectly all right. You may have put yourself through all sorts of things, but you didn't put us through any of them. Truly.'

'I do hope not.' Linda knew this was the time to stop, but she had to get over one more thing. 'I didn't tell Bryn, you know. Not until after he'd met you.'

'There was no reason why you should.'

'I think there was, Mum. He was shocked when he found out.'

'He's a very nice man,' said Barbara.

'He is. I shouldn't have kept it from him. And I shouldn't have denied Robin.'

'You didn't *deny* him. Rob would never have thought that. It's taken you longer than any of us to come to terms with it, that's all.'

'Oh *Mum.*' The sweet good sense of this, and her mother's gentle generosity, became suddenly too much for Linda and she burst into tears. Barbara produced a scented tissue and sat with her arm round her until the brief storm subsided.

'I think,' said Barbara, patting her shoulder as she dabbed and blew and got a grip, 'that this was a very good conversation to have got out of the way. Well done, you.'

That evening after the children had gone to bed, Linda told Bryn about the conversation with her mother.

'She was wonderful. Simple yet sophisticated, like a little black dress by Givenchy.'

'It doesn't surprise me,' said Bryn. 'Our parents come from the pre-counselling generation. They dealt with things

Sarah Harrison

themselves, in their own way, and gave other people the space
to do the same.'

'Do you think I should tell the children about him?'

'Definitely. They should know about their uncle, he'll be a
hero to them. Where is he, anyway? We could go and pay a
visit.'

Linda's face grew hot. 'In the churchyard.'

'Where we got married?' She nodded. 'Fine, that's easy.
Next time we're down we'll walk that way.'

She was grateful to him for not missing a beat, for taking
that second small omission in his stride.

'There's somewhere I'd like to visit, too,' she said.

They went on their own to the peace garden, drove up there
on a day when Nick was at school and Sadie and Flo bestowed
with the tolerant family of a school friend.

The austere, unremarkable street on the outskirts of the
Midlands town had a queasy familiarity, legacy of a hundred
chilling news broadcasts. They parked in a side road and
walked in silence to the site.

If anything, the street was cleaner and more kempt than its
neighbours, as if the other residents had scrubbed up specially
hard to distance themselves from what had happened. Look,
said the whitewashed terraced houses, trimmed hedges and
spotless pavement – look, we live here, and are decent human
beings.

The garden lay at the end of the terrace, encircled by plain
black iron railings. They entered by an unlatched swing gate.
The area measured perhaps ten metres by six. A paved border,
then the glass panels with their fine downward streaks like the
trails left by waterdrops. Inside the panels was the Tudor-rose
knot garden with its tuffets and plumes of herbs – a faint
scent still lingered, even this late in the year – and the white
sundial monument with the children's Christian names
engraved around its upturned face so that each in turn had
its time in the sun. The sheltering shade moved round and

over the names; time moved on, and kept them safe.

Bryn sat on the stone bench in the outer garden while Linda went inside. He felt shaken, and humbled; he hadn't been back since the garden was completed and he was swept by a sort of wistful respect for his then-self. Not self-satisfaction, for he was by no means sure that given the same challenge now he would do it in the same way, but a recognition that this place was the creation of a young man, one only just moving from sullen bitterness to hope, and ambition. Not for the first time he thought: 'I used these children,' and told himself that that only mattered if he had failed to do them justice.

When Linda came out she sat down next to him with her hands thrust into her coat pockets; her collar was up around her face. She was silent, and he felt compelled to ask: 'Well?'

'You did a good job.'

'Thank you.'

She leaned her head briefly on his shoulder. 'I love you.'

As they left they encountered a pair of smartly dressed women, pausing to look at the garden. They exchanged 'good afternoons' and as they walked away they heard one say to the other:

'I wasn't sure at first, but now I think it works.'

'Absolutely,' replied her friend. 'The house had to go – who'd have wanted to live there?'

When Bryn glanced back a moment later the two women were getting into their car. So, not pilgrims, he thought: just passers-by.

But Linda hooked her arm through his. 'Did you hear that?' she said. 'It works. It really does.'

On his way up north for the Service of Remembrance, he collected Nick from school.

'I hope you don't mind doing this on your day out,' he said, over breakfast at the motorway services.

Nick, silenced by a mouthful of sausage, shook his head. After swallowing, he pointed out: 'We're having one of these at school, anyway.' By which Bryn knew he meant service rather than sausage.

'I certainly appreciate the company.'

'My pleasure. Anything for a decent roast.'

Having seen off the fry-up Nick repaired to the gents' with the sports bag Bryn had brought with him and changed out of uniform into his own clothes. He went in, his father noticed, as an individual, and emerged almost indistinguishable from a dozen other boys of his age in the cafeteria: sagging jeans, oversized plaid shirt worn loose over a black T-shirt, and ankle-high trainers with the laces undone.

'You might need your anorak the other end,' he warned as they walked back to the car in a freshening breeze.

'I'll be fine.'

'It's colder up there, and it's a very exposed spot.'

'Dad . . .'

'OK, OK but it's my duty to point out these things.' He handed him a poppy. 'And wear this, would you?'

Nick put it in his breast pocket. 'I will when we get there.'

When they had taken their places in the ranks of the heavily overcoated congregation, Bryn took no satisfaction in being proved right. It was bitter. The usual wind whipped across the hill, its North Sea breath carrying a thin icy rain off the moors, but Bryn betrayed nothing by word or look that could be interpreted as 'I told you so'. If ever there was an occasion when his son must freeze or fetch his coat from the boot, this was it. He checked – at least the poppy was in place.

There were, he surmised, about two hundred people present. Mostly his age or older, a few youngsters like Nick, dragged along to do their duty. A fair sprinkling of medals. Some bowler hats, plenty of flat caps. Donkey jackets, sturdy beige macs, several massive crombie overcoats. Bryn felt slightly out of place in his waxed jacket – at least it wasn't new but it marked him indelibly as a southerner.

The various contingents began to arrive, in strict order. The Boys' Brigade; the Scouts, Cubs and Brownies; some undersized sea cadets; a platoon from the local barracks who'd drawn the short straw. And finally the veterans, a couple of dozen of them, stars for a day, marching with chests thrown out and arms swinging as befitted the Real Thing, mouths set and eyes rheumy with cold and emotion.

Nick nudged him. 'How come they've got so many medals – did they all do that many brave deeds?'

Bryn couldn't work out whether the wording was ironic, or just the curious ragbag phrasing of the young.

'No, you get a medal for each campaign you've served in.'

'And for bravery too?'

'Yes. Ssh.'

The veterans took up their central position, flanked by the supporting cast. Now Bryn could see Sam in the back row: a true old soldier in the last big show, and in Malaya. There was one frighteningly old man, a frail scarecrow muffled up in rugs and shawls in his wheelchair: the last of the Pals. His head was tilted to one side, either because of rheumatic pain or because his neck muscles could no longer support it, but it created the effect of a man with one ear cocked, listening for a shout, a bugle call, the whine of a shell . . . The sounds of the distant past.

Sam stepped forward to do the honours. Bryn's neck prickled with pride, and a sort of embarrassment – Sam was so over-the-top, so vulnerable. His voice had the massive slightly threatening resonance of the union platform and the Labour rally. It was a voice which gave an imperious resonance to age not withering nor years condemning, and whose call to remember was not an invitation, but a command.

We will remember them.

The two minutes' silence opened, like a great space, around them.

The sound of cars passing carelessly on the road, and the wind thudding and whistling across the hill and round the tower, made Bryn aware that their silence was a created thing, made out of reflection and memory. That gave it its special, almost palpable quality. He glanced at Nick. No memory there, but some understanding, perhaps. He seriously wondered if all this was something a boy of his age should be concerning himself with.

The bugle call blared, a vivid flourish across the blank sheet of silence. The last long notes seemed to be caught by the wind, to swirl in the air long after the bugler had lowered his arm. The wreaths laid earlier fluttered; a poppy escaped and skittered across the open ground into oblivion.

Nick nudged him. 'How much longer does it go on for?'

'Not long.'

'Only I'm really, really cold.'

Bryn felt in his pocket for the car keys. 'Run and fetch it.'

'Thanks.' Nick took the keys but at that moment the town band struck up with 'For All the Saints'. 'Better not.'

'You can have mine,' mouthed Bryn, his hand showing willing on the zip.

'It's OK.' Nick would have died of hypothermia rather than wear his father's outsize Barbour. All through the many verses of the hymn he shivered convulsively. Bryn would have liked to put his arm round him but that was out too.

When the singing ended on a glorious final lung-busting 'A-a-a-leluja!' Bryn thrust the keys into his hand. 'Go.' Nick shot away. 'But come back! There's someone I want you to meet.'

Sam must have seen him, for they found each other easily in the mêlée. They shook hands, Bryn taking the older man's in both his.

'That was very well done, Sam. A very proper do.'

'Reckon we did them justice.'

'Certainly.'

'You want to come over to the pub and have something to warm us up?'

'Why not. I've got my son with me, though.'

'He'll be grand, we can sit at a table.'

'Fine, I'd like you to meet him.'

They threaded their way back towards the road. Bryn could see Nick shrugging on his anorak over by the car, looking round as he closed the boot. He waved to show where he was. A hand touched his arm.

'Hello there – good to see you.'

It was the mayor, Ron Chapman, a man of around forty with the silky skills of the natural facilitator. Bryn felt Sam bristling at his elbow; he didn't care for Chapman who as a modernising councillor had originally spoken against the project.

'Ron, greetings. Thanks for asking me along. Very moving.'

'It was Sam's idea,' Chapman pointed out, dissociating himself from it. Sam grunted ungraciously. 'What do you think of your handiwork now it's all on show, still satisfied? We are, I hasten to add.'

Bryn looked up at the tower, a smooth grey chimney of granite with slate-clad buttresses. Today someone had lit a flame on the round table inside and the arched entrance glowed like the open shutter of a lantern.

'I think,' he said, 'that it achieves the effect we were all after.'

'It's bloody fantastic is what we think, eh Sam?'

Another grunt. Nick, who'd seen the others with his father and dawdled to avoid polite conversation, finally arrived and Bryn was swift to play the advantage.

'This is my son, Nick. Nick, this is Mr Chapman and Mr Percival.'

'Ron,' said Chapman. 'Nice to meet you, Nick.'

'How do you do.'

Sam stuck to a curt, 'How do.'

'Well!' Chapman rubbed his hands together. 'The brass monkeys stayed at home. You know we've got some refreshments at the Town Hall, Bryn. Can you and Nick come along?'

'Thanks, but we'll pass,' said Bryn. 'He's out from school for the day and we've promised ourselves a roast.'

'Suit yourselves. 'Bye now, don't leave it too long. See you later, Sam.'

'Could do,' muttered Sam in a not-if-I-see-you-first tone as Chapman bustled away.

'We could have had the refreshments *and* the roast,' pointed out Nick.

'Now listen you,' said Sam, 'we're going to the pub. I'll get you a shandy and crisps, and after that you and your dad can stuff your faces with whatever you like.'

It turned out that there was roast beef and all the trimmings available at the pub, and Bryn persuaded Sam to stay and keep them company after they'd shared a pint. Like many blunt, reserved men he had an affinity with children: both sides knew where they were. He and Nick got along famously.

'So what do you think of your dad's handiwork then?' asked Sam.

Nick glanced at Bryn, who concentrated on his IPA. 'It's all right.' This was an 'all right' with a positive, upward inflection, constituting a good seven out of ten, an endorsement which pleased Bryn immeasurably.

Sam pressed on. 'He tell you what it was all about?'

'It's for the men from this town who died in the Great War.'

'That's right. Not even men a lot of them. Boys, they were, they lied about their age so as they could go and fight. Mad, weren't they?'

'Yes.'

Sam laughed. 'There speaks a child of the twentieth century. So do you think you'd do that, if there were a war on? Lie about your age?'

'It wouldn't work these days. There's information on everyone, they'd be able to check, and there's lie detectors.'

'Yes, yes,' said Sam, impatient with this nit-picking literalness, 'but would you try?'

Bryn studied his son as he thought about this. He realised that he could not begin to guess what the answer would be.

'No,' said Nick finally.

'Fair enough, and why's that?'

'Because I don't want to be in the army.'

'Trick answer,' said Bryn.

'No it's not. Anyway, I'm against war.'

'Aren't we all,' said Sam grimly. 'That hasn't stopped us.'

Nick, fortified by half a glass of shandy, paused for effect before saying: 'My uncle was in the Guards, and he was blown up in Belfast.'

'Oh dear, oh no.' Sam frowned. 'I'm sorry to hear that.'

'It was before I was born.'

Still frowning, Sam turned to Bryn. 'Your brother?'

He shook his head. 'My wife's. He was off-duty, in a pub when it went up.'

'Terrible. Bastards, pardon my French.' Sam turned back to Nick. 'That's not war though, that's terrorism.'

'*They* think it's a war.'

Bryn was agreeably surprised. 'A palpable hit, Sam.'

'It's not important what they think, they're a bunch of murdering so-and-so's.'

At this point Nick resorted to a shrug, but it was an eloquent one.

Bryn, who felt his son had played a blinder in the face of a fairly stern interrogation, said: 'Down with war. It's a counsel of perfection, Sam.'

'Perfection? Not likely!' Sam chortled; it was the most light-hearted Bryn had seen him. 'The lad's a pragmatist. A conchie, and good luck to him!'

Nick glanced at the blackboard by the bar. 'Is it OK if I have the Mississippi Mud Pie?'

When they emerged from the pub it had stopped raining but the sky was black and threatening and it already seemed to be getting dark. Nick, unleashed, and invigorated by a couple of thousand calories, tore away, coat flapping, across the grass in the direction of the tower.

'I don't like this,' said Sam, glaring about him. 'Since Avis died, going home to a dark house. It gets me down.'

Bryn could imagine. 'I feel for you. It must be tough.'

'Weekends are worst, Sundays worst of all.'

'Do you have family nearby?'

'No, no children, me and Avis. We were a team, and a good one though I say it as shouldn't.' He turned his sharp stare on Bryn. 'What about your wife, where's she today?'

'At home with our daughter. We thought we'd have a boys' day out.'

Sam's grunt denoted neither approval nor disapproval. He nodded in the direction of the memorial. 'He's flying.'

Nick came hurtling full pelt round the side of the tower, the sides of his coat stretched out like wings, weaving and swooping, completely off his guard – far enough away from them not to know he was being watched.

'Conchie,' said Sam, but his voice was warm. 'What's he playing at?'

As Nick ran towards them he slowed, and the coat-wings folded to his side.

The small orange light inside the tower went out.

10

1996–2000 – Api

That year, that terrible year of her utter debasement at Dodge's hands, was a defining one for Api. She had learned, in the cruellest way possible, that there was something about herself that she would never, could never, understand. That frightened her, more even than Dodge himself had done. None of it could have happened without her collusion. She had contributed, willingly, slavishly, to her humiliation. Long afterwards she could recall all too vividly the voluptuous quality to her enslavement and she would be sick with disgust.

She knew that it must never happen again, and that the only way to prevent it was to deny that other part of herself – that shocking, incomprehensible blackness that lay in wait and threatened to engulf her. She would not go there, would not let it encroach. She would turn her back on it, and walk in the light.

Api wasn't going to let John Ashe down. She took charge.

The clientele at Pastamento were a very different crowd from the punters at the Tintack. Because in the main she found them to be nice, and the manager thought the same of her, she blossomed. She was absolutely determined not to drift, but to do this one simple job so well that it would lead to something else. Her patience and industry were rewarded and she was put on reception, dealing with bookings and other front-of-house aspects of the restaurant.

Not long after, she moved on, and worked her socks off in a couple of other places, learning the business, keeping her mouth shut and her eyes open. In the second of these she took over as maître d'. She established, through a mixture of intuition, observation and experience, a special persona for herself so that the other staff shouldn't be miffed by her youth. She consulted them often, and presented herself in the light of a co-ordinator of their efforts and ideas rather than someone organising from above. But into this system she injected enough initiative and improved customer relations to show the owner that she meant business. She worked long hours and took a real interest in the restaurant from table settings and flowers to the condition of the cloakrooms and the menu, being careful always to show interest and enthusiasm and betray not a hint of criticism. It was of overriding importance to her to be liked. To stay in the light.

She wasn't sure, when she applied for a post as manager of Lowell's, whether her few years' apprenticeship had been long enough. The brasserie in Islington was a far smarter, cooler place than any she'd worked in before. But to her delight she got the job, and here she really went for it – became more proactive, more outspoken, spent more on her clothes, and succeeded within a few months in becoming the recognisable voice and face of Lowell's. She made a point of getting to know regulars, and treating new or casual customers with warmth and respect. She approached the staff in the same way. From the youngest commis (who was only a year younger than her) to the head waiter Paolo, the exhausted chef and the grumpy Greek cleaning lady she let them know that they had her admiration, loyalty and support. After all, they knew nothing about her. She had reinvented herself.

An act it may have been, but it was one that proved irresistible. Takings went up, morale was high, they got a starred review in *Metro* and Api herself an avuncular mention in the 'Winner's Dinners' column. She took out a mortgage on a little first-floor flat in West Hampstead; she passed her driving test and became the proud owner of an immaculate black Mini with red upholstery. She was in the driving seat, and on her way.

★

Meanwhile the fortunes of the other Durrances fluctuated. Xanthe eventually sold the ark at Eastleigh End and moved to the seaside at Aldeburgh. She had begun 'seeing', as she put it, a divorced, cricket-playing dermatological surgeon who owned a holiday house at the end of the prom.

Gilda still worked at Lawrence's photographic studio, but she and Carson split up when she joined another band and took up with the banjo player; fortunately Carson was an exemplary dumpee and bore no grudges. Judith was doing well at the library and had qualified for a council bungalow in the town where she lived with a nice, sensible older woman, Ruth.

Saul, no longer with the lady horse-dealer, was living in a minute, chaotic cottage the rent on which he paid for by writing (oddly for such a phlegmatic man) gags and short sketches for radio comedy shows. His name was regularly to be heard following the six thirty p.m. slot on Radio Four. To underline the creative course his life was taking, he had grown a beard.

Martin now spoke – in fact rarely stopped speaking – and sold IT systems to big business. He drove an Audi TT Quattro, lived in Manchester and had – currently, they didn't last long – a girlfriend who was a children's TV presenter with a huge smile and an exposed navel.

Only Charles trod water, still renting from his friend in Hammersmith, and finding the young ladies of the Sin – even the new ones – less receptive to his well-worn charm. His good looks, dependent as they were on a cute and cuddly boyishness, were not destined to age well and he was beginning to look puffy. As his naturally wavy hair started to thin, he made the fatal error of letting it grow longer at the back, and the effect was scruffy rather than romantic. The deterioration wasn't serious enough to warrant unsolicited comment but he gave Api an opening when they were having a pub lunch together one Sunday.

'Look at you,' he said. 'I can hardly believe you're the same grubby little waif I saw in that terrible boozer a few years ago.'

'Can we not talk about it, please?'

'Whereas I, sadly –' he patted his paunch – 'am giving out.'

'No you're not,' said Api sharply. 'It's only superficial.'

'Hm!' Charles pulled a face. 'You mean I haven't gone completely barking or doubly incontinent, I just *look* a wreck.'

Api didn't smile. 'Not a wreck. But you used to be so smart.'

'I'd have you know this is a Paul Smith jacket.'

She shrugged. 'I wouldn't know.'

'Well, it is.'

'It doesn't matter so much what you wear,' she said, 'but you ought to lose some weight and get a different haircut.'

'Get yer 'air cut! Hell's teeth, I wish I'd never asked. Hang on, I didn't ask – what is all this?'

'And get a place of your own.'

'What's that got to do with the price of fish?'

'Dad, you surely don't want still to be hanging around in someone's spare bedroom like some – I don't know, some student.'

'It's very comfortable and convenient and I flatter myself that Owen rather likes having me around.'

'Fine.' She glanced away dismissively; she knew how to press Charles's buttons. 'But you're not going to get together with a nice new woman while you're shacked up in that place.'

'Now that's where you're quite wrong, my girl,' said Charles, wagging a finger. 'It is no barrier whatsoever, I meet endless delightful ladies.'

'But you're not *with* any of them.'

His smile bordered on a leer. 'Depends what you mean . . .'

Api allowed a brief pause to speak volumes, and then asked pointedly: 'Have you seen Mum recently?'

'Now don't go invoking that damn acne-quack she's taken up with. Have you met him, incidentally?'

'No.'

'Neither have I. But she must be desperate.'

'I wouldn't know,' said Api, 'but she's looking wonderful.'

Charles was visibly deflated. 'Are you saying I'm getting old?'

'No, Dad. I'm saying you'll seem younger if you act your age.'

His shoulders drooped. 'Grow up, in other words.'

'I never said *that.*'

'You didn't have to.'

The rest of their lunch was rather subdued, but when they emerged into the mews half an hour later Charles put his arms round her and laid his face on her shoulder as though he were the child and she the parent.

'You're a stern judge, Api.'

'Sorry.' She stayed very still, shrinking inside his embrace, avoiding undue contact until he let her go.

'But you weren't always,' he said. There was a little flash of malice in his expression. 'Remember?'

She didn't answer. They walked in silence to the corner of the main road. Just before they parted company, she said, with quiet vehemence:

'I don't care what you do, Dad. I *don't care.*'

A few weeks later Api had a Saturday night and Sunday off, and went to visit her mother. The dermatologist, Derek, turned out to be nice – tall, thin, and engagingly enthusiastic about everything, especially Xanthe whom he continually referred to as 'this wonderful woman' or 'your estimable mother'. Api experienced a pang of jealous self-pity at all this eulogising of a woman who in her view had done nothing to deserve it. This was not to say that she was blind to the woman her mother was now, the one Derek could see and which he himself (though he didn't know it) had conjured into being. This Xanthe was slimmer, attractive, vivacious, still sufficiently unusual to be fascinating, a triumphant survivor *and* the mother of five grown-up children. Derek, childless himself, found this last bit, the bit that made Api's gorge rise, particularly admirable.

What Api found hard to take was her mother's unspoken invitation to collude in the earth-mother myth. Xanthe's warm embrace, her lively and interested questioning and tumbling laugh were all delivered irony-free and Api was expected to play along. She did her best, but it was hard work. The last thing she wanted to do was queer her mother's pitch with her new beau, but sometimes the urge to scream 'This is all crap! She wasn't ever interested, and she isn't now!' was overwhelming.

But taking a filial interest in her mother's new relationship was neither the only nor the primary reason for her visit. It was weird seeing things from the old house in the new one, pressed into service in different ways, keeping uneasy company with newly bought items, the products of Xanthe's awakening (and still uncertain) taste. But nowhere could she find the portrait of Ashe.

On Sunday morning when they were alone together at breakfast (Derek having sensitively returned to his own place at some point after supper), she enquired about it.

'Mum, I was wondering – you did keep all those pictures from the old attic, didn't you?'

'Yes, though I must say God knows why, I bet they're still lying around in that trunk when I pop my clogs.' It was noticeable that Xanthe was more like her old, pre-renaissance self when Derek wasn't there.

'But you do know why,' said Api. 'It was in case any of us wanted one of them.'

'You're right, that was the reasoning. But nobody will, surely.'

'I do. If it's just lying there I'd like the portrait of John Ashe.'

'*Ah,*' said Xanthe. 'Now he's with Derek at the moment.'

Api was shocked. 'Why? Where?'

'At his place.'

'But you haven't given it to him, have you?'

Xanthe looked uncomfortable. 'No, but he likes it much more than I do, and it is enormous so it seemed sensible to let him hang it in his house, which is much bigger than here.'

'But it's a family portrait – you said so yourself – it shouldn't go to anyone else.'

Xanthe refilled her coffee cup. 'If I marry Derek, he will be family.'

Api heard not what Xanthe intended, but her own conclusion. 'So you've given it to him!'

'No, no, I haven't *given* it to him,' said Xanthe as if trying to decide whether she had or not. 'Not in the way you mean. I've simply put it in his keeping for a while.'

'But why?' cried Api. She was almost choked with furious indignation. 'You knew I wanted it!' She sounded childish – she was a child again, first ignored, then misunderstood. Nothing that had happened, good or bad, meant as much as this.

'And I'm sure you can have it,' said Xanthe. 'You've met Derek, he's the kindest, most reasonable man imaginable.'

'In that case –' Api pushed her chair back – 'I'm going round there now.'

'Where?'

She rose. 'To his house. To see the picture, to talk to him about it.'

'But you can't. It's in London.'

'What?'

'In London. It's such a whacking great thing and he's got loads of space there, it'll look so much better on one of his big high walls—'

'But *I want it!*' shrieked Api. 'It's mine.'

Xanthe's voice dropped dangerously. 'I beg your pardon, it's *mine*. It may very well come your way when I'm dead and gone, but that won't be for quite a while yet, I assure you, and in the meantime I've chosen to let it live in the house of the man I'm going to marry. Whether you like it or not!'

It was impossible to tell whether this final shaft referred to the disposal of the picture or the intended union, but either way it was too much for Api, who felt she couldn't breathe and had to escape. Her chair hit the floor with a crash and she left the kitchen, and the house, and ran over the path on to the beach. As her footsteps smashed on the big wet pebbles she was aware of the front door being closed behind her. Her mother didn't come out, to call her back, or even to see where she was going. Yet again, no one cared.

It was March – the last bite of winter rather than the first brush of spring – and she had run out without a coat, wearing only jeans, baseball boots and a rugby top. It had rained in the night and would rain again, but for now it was simply bleak, with a cutting offshore wind and a sky piled high with dark clouds. There were huts at the top of the beach where you could buy fresh fish in the early morning but they were already closed. Beyond them, fishing boats lay at irregular intervals, and coils of wire and rope, lengths of thick hawser; here and there rough homemade wooden runways led down to the water's edge. Huge yellow-eyed gulls swooped and pecked at the litter of fishbones. The scummy tangle of sticks, weed and rubbish at the tideline stank. Gobbets of tar were spattered all over the stones.

Near to the water's edge the waves and wind were noisy, and Api found herself shouting: 'It's mine! My picture! Mine!' Her fragile shell of success and sophistication was blown apart, along with her willingness to cooperate in her mother's reinvention. She had never before hated her parents, but now she did: for their infantile selfishness, their laziness, their sheer lack of respect. Damn Xanthe, damn Charles, and damn the affable, deluded Derek with his loads of space in London. Only the knowledge of just how much damage she could do stopped her from going there and then to his front door and demanding what was hers; that, and the recognition that when all was said and done he was a nice man who had no idea what he had got himself into.

She must have trudged half a mile south along the beach, though it seemed further on the sliding pebbles, with the cold wet wind thrusting at her off the sea, when the girl ran down the beach in front of her. She was about fifteen, Api's height but plumper, and like Api wearing no coat despite the weather. Api instinctively recognised in this stranger a fellow sufferer, someone in flight from life's great conspiracy.

For a moment it looked as though the girl might run into the sea. She stumbled headlong to the water's edge and stood there with the edge of the white water rolling over her shoes. Api could hear her plaintive, childish sobs on the offshore wind. She hesitated.

The man, despite his size, was running so fast he almost crashed into Api as she stood there. He ran like someone accustomed to run, arms pumping, legs going like pistons, his big waterproof jacket, undone, billowing out behind him like a cape. As he crashed past on the stones he put out a restraining hand and shouted: 'Sorry!'

Temporarily distracted from her own misery she watched the little drama unfold. In her mind rose the awful possibility that she was witnessing some crime that – given the man's size – she would be powerless to stop.

But no, he ran straight into the water, beyond the girl, and turned to face her, his hands on her shoulders. He was not, Api saw, her tormentor but her rescuer. His legs were braced strongly against the incoming waves, he was like a rock between the girl and the sea. And then – the most amazing thing – he caught the sides of his coat, held them out like wings, and wrapped them round the girl, enfolding her completely, his head resting on hers. They stood like that for several seconds, melded together, his strength holding them steady in the wind and the rain, the surge of the waves.

Api stared, spellbound.

After a moment the two of them began to walk slowly back up the beach, not hurrying now, the crisis over. The man kept his coat around the girl, whom Api knew must be his daughter, and hugged her to his side. He was smiling now. Too late Api realised that she'd been caught staring, but incredibly his smile was for her as well. He squinted at her through the wind and rain, his black hair whipped across his forehead. The smile was warm and brilliant, a gift.

'Panic over!' he called. He seemed quite unperturbed that she'd been watching. 'What a morning!'

They drew closer. They were soaked, but the girl's eyes were closed, not just in weariness, but trust. She was safe – so *safe*. Api's envy was a stab through her heart.

The man paused as they drew level. 'Sensational weather though,' he said, 'don't you think? Wonderful sea, wonderful sky. Exhilarating!'

'Yes.'

'That said, I'm taking this young lady back to dry off. Enjoy your walk.'

'Thanks.'

They trudged on together up the beach. When they reached the final steep shingle ledge the man picked up his daughter and carried her. Api watched until they were out of sight. She felt lonelier than ever before in her life, caught on the cusp between girl- and womanhood: pierced by an agony of yearning for that sheltering embrace, the confident strength of those protective arms. Quite lost.

Bereft, she continued her hobbling progress along the stones, even more loath now to turn back, stumbling and choking through a drowning melancholy. In the man's face, his voice, his every strong and tender gesture, she had been vouchsafed a glimpse of what she had never had.

11

2000 – Bryn

When Bryn got back with Sadie, Linda had lit the fire in the living room and was sitting snug and catlike next to it, reading the paper. As Bryn appeared in the doorway, hopping to removed his thick socks, she smiled before looking up, and said:

'All well?'

'Oh yes.' He moved to one side. 'Here she is.'

A dripping Sadie presented herself sheepishly. 'Hi. Sorry.'

'All right, darling? Apart from being half drowned.'

'Yes.'

'Why don't you go and get in some nice hot water? Would you like tea, or hot chocolate or something?'

'Yes please, chocolate.'

'Go on then.' Linda got up. 'I'll bring it.'

Sadie glanced round warily. 'Where's Nick?'

'In his room. Don't worry, he knows he was out of order.'

'Right.' Sadie's voice had the feisty note of the totally vindicated.

Bryn gave her a gentle push in the direction of the stairs. 'Anyway, enough, bring the wet stuff with you when you come back down.' He made a sit-down gesture at Linda. 'Don't worry, I'll do the cocoa, I might even have one myself.'

'Coffee please.'

'You got it.'

Out in the kitchen he fell into a reverie and nearly let the milk boil over. He took Sadie's mug upstairs and banged on the door of the family bathroom.

'It's outside!'

As he turned to go back down the door of Nick's room opened.

'She OK?'

'Of course. A bit damp – we both are.'

'She gets on my nerves so badly sometimes.'

'Yes, but the difference is she doesn't mean to. Whereas you goad her.'

'I can't help it, she drives me insane.'

Bryn gave his son a look that conveyed understanding and mild censure in equal measure.

'Sorry, yeah?' said Nick, and closed the door.

Bryn fetched the coffee and took it in to Linda. He sat down by the fire, nursing his mug in both hands. She ran her hand over his hair. 'You're like a wet collie yourself. Shall I get a towel?'

'No.' He grabbed her hand and pressed his mouth to her fingers. 'I prefer to sit at your feet and steam gently.'

'It was a mistake,' she said thoughtfully, 'bringing them here this weekend. Trying to play happy families.'

'Sadly, I agree. Those days are gone.' He glanced at his watch. 'When can we decently take them back to school?'

She cuffed his shoulder. 'Six o'clock and not a moment before. I'm going to cook the ultimate roast.'

'He twits her, and she takes it so seriously.'

'She takes everything seriously, which is why she'll get straight As . . .' Linda glanced back at the paper; turned a page, her eyes drifting over the columns, not really concentrating. 'Anybody else out there enjoying the maelstrom?'

'Nobody we knew,' said Bryn. And then, to change the subject: 'Perhaps it's time we got rid of this place.'

She hadn't noticed. He had needed a split second to decide whether to tell her or not. And a split second after that, it became a secret: a secret shared with a complete stranger. He could not have conveyed to anyone, least of all Linda, the powerful, angry need in the girl's eyes, the shivering tension of her thin body, unprotected by a coat, the wild Medusa-locks of hair swirling round her white face . . . He closed his eyes.

A finger touched his cheek. 'Penny for them.'

'Nearly dropped off,' he said, scrambling to his feet. 'Maybe I'll go and jump in the bath.'

'Good idea,' said Linda. 'Then you can dream in peace.'

Immersed in the hot water, classical music swirling with the steam, Bryn did dream, but not peacefully. And though he lay there for half an hour he knew, when he finally emerged, that he was still marked.

Api returned to her mother's house two hours later to a somewhat tense truce. No more was said about the picture. Derek called round at one but stayed only for a drink because he wanted to get back to London in preparation for an early start next day. His manner was gracious and amiable as ever; it was clear that Xanthe had mentioned nothing to him, and Api was no longer inclined to upset the apple-cart. She took her mother out to lunch at the high street fish restaurant and afterwards they came back and watched *The African Queen*. All things considered, it was a peaceable afternoon.

Only at five o'clock when Api was leaving, did Xanthe say: 'Drive carefully. I do hope you're not still wound up about that picture?'

Api could think of no possible answer to this question which did not in some way misrepresent her state of mind.

She contented herself with saying, as they bumped cheeks: 'So long as it hasn't gone for good.'

Xanthe followed her to the car and stood on the pavement with her cardigan sleeves pulled over her hands and wrapped round her like a straitjacket.

'And I must ask – did you like Derek?'

'Yes. Yes, I did.'

'He's so good for me.'

'I can see that.' Api got into the Mini and wound down the window. ''Bye Mum – see you soon.'

As she drove down the road with the wipers cutting arcs on the wet windscreen, past the backs of the houses that faced on to the sea, she wondered which one of them belonged to the man she'd seen that morning.

Next day she rang the hospital where Derek worked and succeeded in leaving a message with his secretary, explaining that if he was able to call it would be best if he did so before eleven in the morning because of her unsocial work hours.

'I'll see what I can do,' said the secretary in a tone which implied that while moving mountains was her business, this particular one might take a bit of shifting. 'He is incredibly busy.'

'I know,' said Api, playing her privileged-insider card, 'he told me yesterday what a long list he had for today. Tomorrow's fine.'

'I'll tell him.'

He rang the following day at ten.

'Hello, it's Derek Powell here.'

'Thank you so much for calling back.'

'I hope I didn't wake you up – are you an actress by any chance?'

'No, I'm a restaurant manager.'

'Shall I be scragged if I say you don't look old enough?'

She laughed. 'Derek, I want to ask you something.'

'Anything at all.'

She chose her words carefully. 'I think you're looking after a picture for Mum – a big portrait of her grandfather?'

'Yes!' He sounded frankly delighted. 'He's gazing at me from the study wall as I speak, a very impressive fellow. Far more impressive than any of my forebears.'

'He's the business,' agreed Api. 'But he lived up in the loft at our old house. He was put away because he made my sister cry.'

'Well . . . I can see that he might seem somewhat forbidding.'

'Mr Brocklehurst meets Darth Vader.'

She'd never known who Mr Brocklehurst was, but it made Derek chuckle. 'I think that's a little harsh.'

'My father's description.' She liked Derek, but felt this attribution was appropriate in the circumstances.

'Very good . . .'

'The thing is, I've always liked the picture – I'm the only one who does, really – and it's probably going to come my way eventually.'

'Of course, of course – don't think for a moment that I regard it as mine, I'm a mere functionary, a caretaker. Although I must say,' he added, 'I think your mother's fond of it. The old boy is her grandfather after all.'

'My great-grandfather.'

'Indeed.'

For the first time Api sensed a hint of realignment on the other end of the line. Derek might be the nicest man imaginable but he was her mother's boyfriend, not her stepfather – or not yet – and his loyalties lay with Xanthe, not her.

'The thing is,' she said, 'I wondered if you might be able to discover who painted it. We've never known, and it would be interesting to find out.'

'Snap,' said Derek, his voice warming again. 'The first thing I did was peer through the magnifying glass. S R something was the best I could do. It needs cleaning.'

'Could we get that done?'

'We certainly *could*.' He implied that this was a path they might or might not choose to follow. 'It's a fairly expensive process, that would have to be up to Xanthe.'

'I'd like to do it,' said Api. 'I can afford it. It would be a surprise for her.'

'Look,' said Derek. 'I'm in your hands, I really have no say in this. You consult with your mama and get back to me. It shall be whatever you decide.'

Api realised she needed to be firmer. 'I have decided. It's going to be my treat.' There was a reflective silence on the

other end. 'And then we'll be able to find out something about
the artist, too.'

'That's true. I have a friend who does that sort of thing at
one of the big auction houses. Provenance, they call it, don't
they?'

Api pressed her advantage. 'Would your friend know where
to get it cleaned, as well?'

When Derek answered she could tell he was smiling, amused
by her pushiness. 'He might very well do. Would you like me
to make enquiries?'

'Could you?'

'Certainly.'

'As long as it's understood, the bill's mine.'

'Naturally. That, I lay no claim to.'

'And please don't tell my mother. It's a surprise.'

'Api – I confess I do feel a little awkward about that part
of it. This is a family heirloom after all.'

'Precisely. And no one's showed the least interest in it till
now.'

'Point taken. Look, I must go. I'll give you a ring when I've
spoken to Julian.'

'Thank you.'

Derek sat at his desk for a full minute after this conversation,
trying to work out what he made of it. Api was the first of
Xanthe's children he'd encountered, and she was a strange
one: a mixture of precocious competence and fey wilfulness.
The phrase 'whim of iron' sprang to mind. Perfect porcelain
skin, he'd observed, slightly freckled and none the worse for
that. Not pretty, she was too strange for prettiness with her
pointed features, pale cloud of hair and pixie ears. And those
odd, light eyes, with a glaring quality . . . He looked up at the
man in the picture. Yes . . . Genes would out.

12

2000 – Api

Having initially been unwilling to enter into this small conspiracy with Xanthe's daughter, Derek found himself rather enjoying it. His first marriage had been childless and (until the final showdown) placid, and he relished the sensation of dealing with these interesting and very different women.

He was captivated by Xanthe and was beginning to believe he was in love with her. He had never met anyone so *free* before (he was right to the extent that Xanthe herself had never felt so free), and the experience had a liberating effect on him. He felt lighter and looser, in mind and body. Every clichéd popular song lyric that mentioned walking on air, wings on heels, a spring in the step, seemed to Derek in his transformed state to be the apotheosis of aptness. He had caused jaws to drop at work by asking for Sinatra to be played in theatre instead of his usual Chopin or Puccini. His particular favourite was 'You Make Me Feel so Young', which caused the theatre nurses to exchange behind-the-fan glances over their masks.

Once persuaded that the cleaning and investigation of the family portrait was being undertaken as a surprise present for Xanthe, his conscience ceased to trouble him and he embarked on the enterprise with a will. Julian Royle at Creighton's was delighted to hear from him.

'Derek, you dog! It's been far too long – how's the world and its outer cortex?'

'Still in need of treatment I'm happy to say. And the collectors of fine art – as greedy as ever I hope?'

'Insatiable.'

'It was that I wanted to talk to you about, actually.'

'Hot damn, and there was me thinking you might have taken up with some *ER*-type totty with a heaving stethoscope.'

'Sorry to disappoint you. Although as a matter of fact . . .'

'Yes?'

'I do have a nice new lady friend,' admitted Derek, beaming into the receiver.

'Excellent! When do I get to meet her?'

'Not just yet. I'm looking after a picture of hers, and her daughter—'

'My God, you're going to be a stepfather!'

'Her daughter asked if I'd get it cleaned, see if anyone can tell us anything about it and so on. As a sort of present.'

Julian hummed playfully. 'It'll cost you.'

'The daughter's paying. It may not sound very gentlemanly, but it's her idea, her present. I'm merely the facilitator.'

'I'll charge her twopence-halfpenny, don't worry. But you, you sly fox, dinner at the Ivy and no holding back.'

Derek beamed some more. 'My pleasure.'

In fact deception was hardly necessary since Xanthe came to London only rarely and when occasion demanded. She made no bones about not being a townie, and besides, she had taken an agreeable small job at a shop specialising in the local amber. This arrangement suited Xanthe rather better than it did Derek, who would have liked her a little closer to hand, but for the time being he was content to make the two hours' drive to the coast every weekend. He considered himself so fortunate to have found someone like Xanthe when he'd almost resigned himself to singledom that he would have driven through hellfire to be with her, let alone up the A1.

He rang Api to let her know what was going on.

'My friend Julian Royle says the cleaning will take about a month, and he'll get his colleague Sarah Porter to run the rule over it as they go along so that when we collect they can tell us something about it.'

'Fantastic. Thanks, Derek, I really appreciate this.'

'I think,' he said, 'we both feel your mother deserves it.'

She made no comment on this, but asked: 'Can I come with you, when the picture's ready?'

'Of course. In fact you're very welcome to go on your own. My work's done.'

'No, I owe you. Let's go together.'

'Fine,' he said. 'I'll be in touch.'

For some time now, Api had felt the shadows closing in again. Not rapidly, but insidiously, a slow, nudging attrition on her nerves. They clustered on the periphery of her mind's eye, forming a patch of darkness, like the presence of a tumour on an X-ray. Except unlike a tumour they dissolved on inspection, only to creep back.

She could identify exactly the time when the shadows had reappeared. It was the night she returned to London after meeting the man on the beach. Meeting? It had scarcely been that. It was the merest encounter, almost certainly forgotten by him in an instant. But for her it had been like a lightning-strike: a shock, accompanied by a split-second illumination. She recalled the utter emptiness that had replaced her fury: an emptiness which slowly filled with the cold, sad realisation that for all her brave self-determination she did not, and might never, have what came so naturally to this splendid stranger.

For the first time in her life Api had not wanted to leave her mother, for no better reason than the simple, animal company she afforded: she did not wish to be alone. It troubled her that she could not picture the whereabouts of the portrait of John Ashe. She felt at a disadvantage, watched and powerless. When she got back to the empty flat she had turned on every light in the place and still could not banish the greedy shadows that clustered in her head and pressed blank, featureless faces to the window glass.

Though she'd taken some comfort from her conversation with Derek, and the setting in train of the picture's rehabilitation, the shadows had remained. Increasingly as the days went by she felt claimed by them as if reality was not out there, in the world she could see and in which she worked and conducted her daily life, but inside, in the dark at the back of her head. She dreamed of the picture as it now was – in the hands of strangers by day, in some vast storage space she could scarcely envisage by night – and hoped that Ashe would not hold this intrusion against her.

During this time her father was taken into hospital. Xanthe rang up to tell her, and to explain why she herself would not be coming up to London.

'A little warning shot, that's all. I'm sorry about it, of course, but the truth is it's not really my business any more.'

'You mean he's not.'

'Yes, that is what I mean,' said Xanthe a touch defiantly. 'But I imagine you and Gilda will want to pop in.'

'Don't worry,' said Api. 'I'll go.'

'And give him my best.'

As she put the phone down, Api wondered how Derek could believe, let alone suggest to her, that her mother deserved anything. It had to be love, surely, for it to be so blind! She wept jealous tears for the injustice of it.

She went to visit her father in the late afternoon before going to work. Though not exactly on her way, because it was in deepest South London in an area she didn't know. She was nervous on the journey, full of the foolish idea that she might not be able to get back, that she might lose her way or be mugged. It had been a beastly spring and at the end of April the wind still had icy rain on its breath. She had to walk for nearly a mile, her eyes watering and her feet freezing in smart black shoes. When she finally got there the main hospital entrance was wide and welcoming, the broad, bright spaces beyond like the Elysian Fields. Inside in the warm there was a bustling concourse with a coffee stall, a self-service restaurant, shops, and a florist. Api felt she shouldn't arrive empty-handed, but it was also to savour the comforting normality of shopping that she went into the mini-market and bought her father some chocolates. Then she followed the signs and went up three floors in the lift to Rathbone Ward.

The first thing she noticed was that he'd taken her advice and had his hair cut. The result made tears jump into her eyes – it did make him look younger, but more vulnerable, too, propped up on his pillows like a dissipated schoolboy.

'Hello, Dad.'

'Api – my first visitor.' He accepted her kiss. 'Possibly my only one.'

'Don't start that.'

'No, actually Owen's on his way. What's this, chocolates? You shouldn't have.'

'I know, but I wanted one.'

He handed them to her. 'Then you open them for us.'

She did so, took one herself and passed them back. As he sat gazing at the chart, she asked: 'How are you then?'

'Chastened. Facing an uncertain future. Praline, excellent . . .'

'What do you mean, an uncertain future?' she said testily. 'It wasn't a proper stroke. You're going to be fine, aren't you?'

Charles assumed an expression of Mr Toadish self-pity. 'It was the unexpectedness, you know? How am I ever going to feel safe again?'

'Because – I don't know – because these things happen!' she snapped. 'And it wasn't very serious, and you know exactly what to do to stop it happening again.'

'Not really. Contrary to what you seem to think my life's not one long round of unfettered debauchery.'

'You have to eat sensibly and drink less, and keep reason-able hours,' said Api, knowing she was hectoring but unable to prevent herself. 'And before you mention it, shagging's good exercise, but find someone your own age.'

Charles gave her a mournful, misunderstood smile. 'I'll do my best.'

She took another chocolate. 'It's up to you.'

'Seen anything of your mother?'

'Yes, I went out there a couple of weeks ago. She sends her love by the way.'

'Tell her thank you. And the boyfriend?'

'He was there. He's very nice. He thinks she's wonderful, and she says he's very good for her.'

'But you have other ideas.'

'Not really. I let them get on with it.'

Charles gave her one of his sudden sharp, sly looks. 'Like we did with you?'

She allowed this to pass, pretending keen interest in a nurse pushing a trolley down the centre of the ward.

'So when will they let you out?'

'Tomorrow as like as not.'

'Where will you go?'

'Back to the flat of course.'

'Doesn't someone need to be there?'

'Owen will be – at least part of the time. He's quite capable of bringing me a glass of water in the night.'

The bleakness of this made Api feel miserable and at the same time angry with her father who had brought it on himself and still had the cheek to be passive-aggressive.

'He won't like it.'

'Neither of us will. But for one thing I shall be perfectly all right, and for another who else is going to play the ministering angel if not him?'

'I don't know . . .' she muttered.

Charles needled on. 'Not you, I take it. Not Judith, who's safely shacked up with old sensible-shoes, and certainly not your brothers because men don't. That leaves Gilda who I suppose might, but frankly the thought of her rolling up her sleeves to administer a bed-bath is enough to bring on an instant relapse.' He looked suddenly tired. 'Anyway, I put the quacks in the picture. They're not going to send me out of here till I'm fully self-starting.'

'Of course not. Sorry, Dad.'

'Me too. It's all a bloody nuisance.' He ran his hand over his head. 'Notice the hair?'

'Yes.'

'Your idea – so what do you reckon?'

'It's good. It makes you look younger.'

'I hope so. I feel rather shorn and chilly. Ah – look, I told you, a crowd problem!'

Coming down the ward were Owen, large and bluff, whom Api had seen once or twice before, and a chiselled blonde in her thirties, dressed in a grey suit with a velvet collar and carrying a bouquet of yellow roses. Api half rose but Charles extended a restraining hand.

'Don't rush off, stay and say hello.' He broke into smiles as the couple hove alongside. 'Fee, my sweet, and flowers too!'

'Ssh, they're just a disguise . . .' The woman thrust her hand into the middle of the bouquet and produced a small bottle wrapped in white paper, which she put in the bedside locker. 'For nipping at in quiet moments.' She had an insinuating Scottish accent. Api was appalled, both by the present and the way her father's face lit up.

'Bless you, you know the way to an invalid's heart! Is this just a happy coincidence, Moore, or did you bring her?'

'We came together,' said Owen.

'A consummation devoutly to be wished,' responded Charles. It was all so corny and predictable they didn't even laugh at their own joke.

'Now,' he went on, 'this is my daughter, Api. I can't remember—'

'We've met,' said Api.

Owen clasped her hand more warmly than was necessary. 'Have we? I'll take your word for it, but I'm sure I would have remembered.'

Api turned to the woman. 'Hello.'

'Fiona Murray, nice to meet you.'

She noticed that Fiona wore a wedding ring. Not that that was any bar to her being Charles's latest.

'Are you in the orchestra too?' she asked.

'I don't play, I'm their press officer.'

'She is the sine qua non!' said Owen. 'The entire operation would crumble without her. Are we allowed to sit on the bed? When I was last in one of these places it was strictly *verboten*.'

Api got up and stood aside. 'Someone can sit here, I'm going.'

'Off to some nice, noisy bar?' asked Owen. 'Pardon me if I sound wistful.'

'Off to work, actually.'

'You've got her all wrong,' said Charles. 'She runs a posh eaterie.'

Amid their noises of polite admiration Api bent to kiss her father. ''Bye, Dad. Look after yourself. Let me know when you're coming out.'

'I will. Very soon, God willing.'

'It's up to you, not Him.' Rude or not, she couldn't resist adding, nodding pointedly at the locker. 'And go easy on that stuff.'

When she reached the door of the ward and looked back Fiona was in the chair, matchless legs elegantly crossed, and Owen was perched on the bed. All three were laughing like drains.

Outside, it was if anything even colder. As she turned the corner out of the hospital forecourt wet talons of wind slashed her face. The thought of her father and his friends sitting up there in the warmth, laughing at her, was nearly unbearable. She wished now that she had said immediately, as she had every right to do: 'I'm sorry, he can't have that. He's not allowed it and it might kill him.' She was his daughter, she took precedence. Instead of which she was out, literally, in the cold, while they made patronising jokes at her expense and congratulated themselves on their sophistication.

The tube station had no escalator; with a choice between the lift and spiral stairs, she picked the lift. Half a dozen passengers assembled before the doors closed, two of them men of her father's age. One wore a plaid jacket, workboots and a black woollen hat. The other looked like a businessman, or perhaps a doctor from the hospital, in a Burberry mac over a grey suit. Each of them seemed in his way a mature, solid individual with a grown-up attitude to life. Neither of them had Charles's febrile, Peter Pan quality. But, Api wondered, was that what kept him in women? That and his quite pathetic availability. She hadn't cared for Fiona with her cut-glass cheekbones and Miss-Brodieish twang, but she could see that she was smart and glamorous, the sort any man would like to show off. They came into the restaurant the whole time, these sharp, stylish, prosperous women who didn't need male approval but who got shedloads of it anyway and could afford to treat it as an accessory, like a Gucci handbag. If that one and her father were together, Api thought, it would have been Fiona who did the pulling, and who would do the dumping, too.

In the tube itself she found herself sitting almost opposite the Burberry man, who was a little like Derek. She assumed her default face, an expression of haughty introspection, but she still caught him looking at her a couple of times. Out of nowhere came the realisation – slightly to the detriment of the air of hauteur – that she had not slept with a man since Giles. Neither before nor since. Giles had been a good deed in the otherwise naughty world of Farnsworth Buildings, the only part she cared to remember. Even now she shivered slightly – she owed him. It was not so much that he had taught her all he knew, but that she had used him to learn on; in fact used him in every sense. She had actually imagined – it was almost incredible to her now –

that her small store of sexual experience would give her power over Dodge.

As she rose to get off at her station the man glanced up at her again, and this time she caught his eye and smiled briefly. It pleased her to think that though he would never see her again, he would almost certainly remember her – the girl young enough to be his daughter who had smiled at him on the tube.

It was a relief to be back in a neighbourhood she knew, but she still walked the half-mile to the restaurant fast, and set-faced. The tensions inherent in the visit to her father, and her anger at his siding against her, had kept more troubling shadows at bay. Now they were back, drifting and milling in the recesses of her mind, waiting to slip through a gap in her defences.

There was no table free, but Jonathan Frankel was a border-line case. In his own estimation, a special one. She expressed her usual devastation at the problem.

'I'm so sorry about this, Mr Frankel. Will you let me see if there's something we can do?'

'Of course.' His voice was smooth, and slightly sulky on the line. 'I'm sure there will be.'

'I'm going to put you on hold if that's all right.'

'I don't have long.'

'It won't take long, I promise.'

He was one of those customers with whom the 'do-you-know-who-I-am?' hovered just below the surface, unspoken but implied. Of course she did know who he was; she had made it her business to find out. He was heir apparent to the Delancey hotel empire which his father Sir Harry had built up over fifty years from a standing start; rather too conscious of his eligible-bachelor status, always came in with at least one other couple and a different young woman each time; fleshily handsome, expensively groomed, illegally parked (she noticed these things).

She spoke to the headwaiter, Paolo. 'What do you think, can I let the table for four go at nine p.m.?'

'Sure, we've still got the two twos if we need them.'

She returned to the phone. 'Mr Frankel? It's sorted. We'll be absolutely delighted to welcome you at nine.'

It was twenty past when he arrived accompanied by only two, male, companions, one of whom was wearing jeans. There was a no-jeans policy for dinner; most of the staff considered it stuffy and outdated but the proprietor felt it kept the tone up. Occasionally a new customer was unaware of the rule, but it was expected that those who knew the score, like Jonathan Frankel, would see that their friends weren't embarrassed. This was the sort of situation she didn't relish. It wasn't just diplomacy – Frankel had thrown down the gauntlet. He didn't expect his guest to be pulled up.

'I'm so sorry,' she said with her warmest, most *désolée* smile. 'We have a no-jeans rule in the evening.'

'Hey, you never said!' The man rounded amiably on Frankel. 'What's with this dumping me in it?'

'I didn't,' said Frankel. 'That's what you were wearing when I booked the table, I can't help it if you're a scruffy bastard.'

Api laughed, tried to draw the focus. She didn't want even a hint of this exchange permeating through to the other diners. These three had just enough drink inside them not to know how loudly they were speaking. Or in Frankel's case, if he did know, not to care.

'We'd hate to lose you, sir,' she said. 'We do keep a selection of plain black slacks in standard sizes.'

'There you are, Morgan,' said the third one. 'An offer you can't refuse, what are you waiting for? Get into the lady's plain black slacks.'

Morgan became slightly petulant. 'God, I don't believe this!'

'Nor me,' said Frankel ominously. 'Surely to goodness you're not going to insist on this charade at this stage in the evening. I mean look at the place, it's packed with people

off their faces on your overpriced wine, you think they're
going to notice?'

Api held the smile. She'd learned the technique: the greater
the outrage, the sweeter the smile.

'Probably not, sir, I agree, but it is a rule.' She turned back
to Morgan. 'I do apologise for the inconvenience, but the situation's easily put right, and we could have you at your table
in two minutes.'

'Yeah, yeah, lead me to your damn trousers.'

'Certainly, would you like to come with me.'

It was a formulaic phrase, but the second friend couldn't
resist saying, 'Like it? He'd like nothing better!'

When they returned, Api was irritated to find the other
two already seated. She considered this at the very least
slighting to Morgan, but as she delivered him to the table
it was clear that he was mollified by the smooth fit of the
house-Armanis.

'What do you think?'

'Great improvement,' said Frankel without raising his eyes
from the menu. 'Now sit down and order before we all die
of hunger.' He glanced about. 'Who do I have to sleep with
to get a drink around here?'

Api's smile positively sparkled. 'Not me, I'm afraid. I'll send
the wine waiter with the list.' Twats, she thought. Spoiled,
drunken twats.

A couple of hours later when they left, Morgan made a
show of clasping the trousers to his waist.

'No, no, don't make me take them off!'

The other man, whose name she gathered was Andy, chortled loudly. 'He wants you to do it with your teeth!'

She laughed obligingly. 'Your jeans are where you left
them. You may find they've been pressed, I hope you won't
mind.'

'What a woman!' sighed Morgan.

'Just get on with it, will you,' snapped Frankel.

'I have to see this sartorial sin-bin,' said Andy, following.

Api was determined not to allow room, or time, for Frankel to take a verbal swing. As they waited, she said: 'These rules may seem petty, but they make an indefinable difference. Quite an important one, we think. Thank you very much for being so accommodating.'

'I wasn't. In fact I wouldn't have been. It's up to others if they want to fall in with these ridiculous restrictions.'

'Well, it was very good of your friend.'

Frankel pulled a shrugging face that cast aspersions on both goodness and friendship.

She held the door for them: 'I do hope we'll see you again.'

Morgan placed a hand on her shoulder. 'You will – it's worth it for the trousers alone.'

Andy seconded that. Frankel was already out in the street, tossing his car keys in one hand. Once or twice he'd been brought by a driver, but she was sure he was over the limit now. She knew where he generally put the Jag, just round the corner on the edge of a residents' parking zone. Not that a fine of any size was a deterrent to someone with so much money, to whom such things were simply part of the normal expenses of motoring in London.

She called goodnight as she closed the door. Morgan, one arm round Andy's shoulders, lifted the other one in salute. Frankel was already out of sight.

Her head was splitting. After the last diners left, Paolo told her that Frankel had run up a bill of £275, and left no tip.

Three nights later she got back to the flat to find a message from Derek.

'Thought you'd like to know the portrait's ready for collection from Creighton's. Give me a ring when it's convenient and we'll arrange to go round and collect it.'

She called back there and then, and he must have had a phone by the bed because he answered straight away, in the slightly fuddled manner of someone still half asleep.

'Yup, hello?'

'Derek, it's me, Api.'

'Oh, hello, my dear . . . what time is it, good grief . . .'

'I know, I'm sorry, but what with my unsocial hours and your lists I thought no time like the present. I can do early mornings, late afternoons or Sundays.'

'Hang on, my brain . . . umm . . . Sundays are out, they'll be closed and I'll be in Suffolk, but I should think . . . ummm . . .' She could picture him rubbing his face. 'What about tomorrow afternoon as ever is?'

'Fine.'

'Shall we meet there at, what, four thirty?'

'See you then.'

When she put the phone down, her heart was beating so rapidly that she found it hard to catch her breath, and spots danced before her eyes. That night she hardly slept, and when she did it was to dream of running to catch up with a distant figure who, in spite of walking at a measured pace, remained always too far away. In each brief dream she would eventually stop, exhausted, and try with her failing breath to call out, and the figure would at last slow and seem about to turn – and that was when she woke, with a great gasp, staring around her in the dark, scarcely knowing where she was.

The next morning, oddly, she was up by ten, feeling bright and clearheaded. The restaurant was quiet at lunchtime and she was able to get away soon after four. The day had been brilliantly clear and spring, at last, was on the way.

Derek was waiting in Creighton's tastefully drab lobby off Bond Street. He wore a dilapidated anorak open over his suit, and a V-necked jumper beneath his jacket. It struck Api that one of the things she liked about him – which made her trust him, and worry about the thing with her mother – was his lack of vanity.

'Sign in,' he said, 'and get your little ID card, then we can go through.'

They went through a door supervised and opened by a uniformed porter, and along a corridor that was completely unadorned except for a narrow length of threadbare patterned carpet. At the fourth door on the left Derek stopped and knocked.

'Come!'

Julian Royle's office was large and functional. The roll-top desk was antique, but that was all. The floor was modishly stripped and polished, there were brilliantly coloured woven hangings on the walls, and a long table held a bank of state-of-the-art technology on which small lights winked and logos spiralled endlessly in black screen space.

Api took in all this in the second before she spotted the portrait, propped against the desk swathed in a grey blanket.

'Derek, greetings. And you must be?'

'Api Durrance.'

'Api, I'm Julian Royle and this is my colleague Sarah Porter.'

Julian was smooth, round and shiny as an apple. Sarah Porter was a little dark, hedgehoggy person in a waistcoat made of furnishing fabric and a dirndl skirt. Derek shook hands with both of them, but it was clear that he knew Julian well and Sarah not at all.

Julian indicated a group of spindly chrome and leather chairs. 'Sit down, do.'

Api sat, though she was bursting with impatience. To her great relief, Derek said: 'Best to tell you that we don't have unlimited time, so . . .'

Julian held up a hand. 'Understand perfectly. But we like to make a little presentation, don't we, so bear with us.' Api noticed that while he spoke, Sarah watched them with her boot-button eyes, as if gauging their reaction to every word.

'First of all,' he went on, 'you may be surprised that the cleaning of the picture hasn't made a very great difference to its appearance.'

'In point of fact,' added Sarah, 'none at all!'

'Now, now, not quite that, but very little. Anyway, rest

assured that it *has* been exhaustively cleaned so what you now see is what there is, if you follow me.'

'Thank you,' said Api. It seemed the only comment she could properly make at the moment, not having seen the picture.

Sarah took up the story. 'It's all in extremely good shape. The condition of the canvas and the frame is pretty well perfect considering, you say, it was in an attic for years?'

'Yes,' said Api, 'it was. Ten at least. It used to make my elder sister cry.'

'I'm not in the least surprised, he's a fearsome fellow in his way. It's also relevant—'

'Relevant?' asked Derek.

'Oh – to the value. Also relevant that the frame is the original one and really very fine. The old boy must have had plenty of money and no qualms about spending it on himself.'

'He was a millionaire,' said Api.

Julian arched his brows. 'You don't say? They were rarer in those days. Does history relate how he made his millions?'

'No. My mother used to say he was a dark horse.'

'Ah, perhaps she meant black sheep. They often do surprisingly well for themselves, to the chagrin of the rest of the family!'

Derek and Sarah Porter laughed at this, but Api could stand it no longer.

'May we have a look now?'

'Why don't we – no, don't move, we'll unveil it and bring it to you.'

She didn't so much as glance at Derek as they took off the blanket, carried the picture over and placed it on the easel. His reaction didn't matter. This was her moment: hers, and John Ashe's.

The first thing she thought was: *They were wrong that the cleaning made no difference.* The second thing was: *But no, because only I would notice.* And finally: *I shan't say anything; it's our secret.*

Derek spoke first. 'I must say you're quite wrong about the

cleaning not having made a difference. For a start, the frame looks marvellous. As good as new, literally.'

They agreed that it did, and sat down, turning their chairs towards the picture like people attending a lecture.

'Also,' went on Derek, 'the skin tone's brighter. More definition generally.'

'Yes, but, this area here . . .' Sarah got up again and stood by the picture, moving her hand over the right-hand side of the canvas. 'This area of intense darkness. We expected to find something there.'

'What?' asked Derek. Api felt him glance at her as if for endorsement, but she remained expressionless, concentrating on the picture.

'Well, a suggestion of the rest of the subject. It's very unusual for part of the figure to be simply blotted out – *negated* – like this.'

'If anything,' said Julian, 'the darkness is even deeper since cleaning. Almost black. One can only suppose that that was the original intention, and that over the decades dust had formed a sort of film and softened the effect.' He looked round at them. 'It is all very interesting. We like it tremendously, I must say.'

'Is it any good?' asked Derek. 'I mean, apart from being intriguing, the technique and so on.'

'It is,' replied Sarah. 'I mentioned value—'

'I'm not interested in that.' Api spoke for the first time.

'No,' said Derek gently, 'but your mother might be.'

'I told you, she won't be selling it.'

'But if it came to you, wouldn't you want to know?'

'No.'

Derek looked back at the others, neutrally. 'Fair enough.'

'Very well,' went on Sarah, 'value aside this is a very haveable picture. Very desirable. If it *were* to come up at auction I think you might be surprised at the number of people who'd want to own it, and would be prepared to pay quite a lot for it.'

'Tell us why,' said Derek. 'As far as you can in layman's terms.'

'Right. Apart from being technically accomplished, it has real presence. In almost any company it would draw the eye. What it isn't, is bland. As your sister discovered.' Sarah smiled at Api, who couldn't let this pass.

'And me. I've always liked it, and it never made me cry.'

'There you are. It's a portrait that provokes a reaction. You love him or loathe him, I suspect. Now – we did try to find out something about the man himself, but however he made his money he wasn't letting on. In that sense he was very private, but in another he was vain. He wanted his portrait painted.'

Derek asked: 'So you think he commissioned it rather than being invited to sit?'

'I do, for two reasons. One is the very unusual and idio-syncratic style of the painting, effectively showing only half the man. The other is that the artist was young, only just starting out.'

'And who was he?'

Julian raised a finger. 'This is the good bit.'

'It wasn't a he,' said Sarah. 'It was a woman.'

'You don't say? That does surprise me.'

Api thought: *But it doesn't surprise me. It makes perfect sense.*

She asked: 'What was her name?'

'Suzannah Rose Murchie. She was the wild child of her day. A perverse, almost quixotic choice for a rich man, but I think we can assume he was pretty unusual himself, so that wouldn't be out of character. She was an artist of great natural gifts, as you can see, but she did very few paintings, even fewer of which are in circulation, because she achieved that indispensable aid to market value, an early death.'

'In other words,' said Julian, 'your great-grandfather had an eye for a winner. She was regarded as eccentric, if not beyond the pale, in her day, but she'd be immensely collect-able now.'

Api never took her eyes from the painting. 'How old was she when she died?'

'Barely thirty.'

'And what did she die of?'

'That's unclear,' said Julian, 'like so much concerning this picture. "In obscurity" is the best we could come up with. There's no mention of a long and harrowing illness or anything like that. It was the twenties, she'd probably led a pretty louche life, wasn't making much money . . . who can say? But knowing you'd be interested we have made up a little file of information about her, copied from the various sources we used.'

He got up and took a folder from the desk. 'Who shall I give this to?'

Derek made a courtly gesture towards Api. 'My young friend.'

'Thank you.' She took the folder, with its elegant green marble-pattern cover, the Creighton's logo in gold in the lower right-hand corner.

'I've slipped our invoice in there as well,' added Julian in a discreet undertone. 'As instructed. Though I have to say the pleasure was all ours. Now,' he went on, resuming normal service, 'do you have time for a quick glass of champagne?'

The champagne was poured and Api took a glass, but while the others talked she stayed near the picture, studying it. The differences that she had seen in those first moments after it was unveiled became tinier the closer one got – she had noticed this before, the powerful influence of minute dabs of paint to change the whole. She wondered how it was possible that the others – the experts – hadn't observed them, but the next moment she thought: *Perhaps they didn't because it's only me who can.*

There was a light in his eye, now: a microscopic fleck of white. At first, it had seemed like a gleam of recognition but now she saw that it might be the shine of a tear, a glint of humour, or of desire, a sharp spark of anger . . . And on the right-hand side of his face, just before it was swallowed up in shadow, was now visible a fine, red line like the most delicate tracery of a mapping pen, emerging from the darkness and wandering down over the pale skin tone of his inner cheek to disappear again at the jaw.

Julian joined her. 'So intriguing, isn't he? An extremely compelling face, what we can see of it.'

'Yes.'

'The more so, somehow, now that we know about Suzannah Rose.' He tapped the folder that she held. 'There's not much, but it makes interesting reading.'

They arranged for the picture to be delivered and re-hung at Derek's house the following day, and left soon after. In the lobby, he asked: 'So all in all, are you pleased?'

'Very.'

'So am I – and I know Xanthe will be. Look, won't you let me sub up for half the cost? These chaps are charming but they don't come cheap.'

She shook her head. 'No, absolutely not. It's my—' She checked herself. 'It was my idea.'

'Will you circulate the Suzannah folder when you've read it?'

'Sure.'

'I'll look forward.' He made to go and then thought of something. 'Will you tell your mother about it? Say you pressed me into service, that sort of thing?'

'Of course. She's not going to mind, you know.' She wanted to say 'not going to care' but that, though truthful, would have seemed rude to him as well as slighting to Xanthe.

She declined his invitation to share a taxi at his expense, on the grounds that she needed to use the cloakroom, but really because she wanted to be alone with her thoughts on the journey to work. When she emerged once more into the lobby Jonathan Frankel was standing there, facing her way. After the events of a few nights ago mutual recognition was inevitable and avoidance impossible.

'Hello there,' he said.

'Good afternoon!' She kept moving towards the door, but he headed her off, getting there before her so that she had to step to one side to let others in. He wore a soft brown leather trenchcoat and smelt of some expensive aftershave, which seemed to Api like the sweet scent of wealth itself.

'Do I owe you an apology?' he asked, drawing his eyebrows together in a frown as if genuinely uncertain, or trying to remember.

'No, I'm quite sure you don't,' she replied.

The frown deepened slightly. 'I'm trying to decide if that's a professional or a genuine response.'

She felt trapped by this irritating distraction, at the very moment when she particularly wanted to be alone.

'A professional one.'

'I asked for that,' he said, and when she didn't reply, added: 'In that case I'll continue to be a customer and not offer one.'

'That seems fair,' she said. 'Now if you'll excuse me I must get to work.'

He stepped aside exaggeratedly. 'Don't let me stand in your way.'

'Goodbye.'

'See you soon.'

Api was all out of politeness, and pretended not to hear this.

In the taxi she sat back and closed her eyes in order to see again the image of John Ashe, with the gleam of recognition in his eye.

They were busy that night and she didn't get home until one thirty, but nothing could have prevented her from sitting down with the folder and studying its contents. There were about half a dozen Xeroxed sheets of text from various books. Two were no more than entries from catalogues of artists, listing Suzannah Murchie's name, with no letters after it, the dates of her birth and death, and describing her as a portrait painter usually working in oils whose milieu had been the London of the late 1920s and 1930s, the shortness of whose life and whose sporadic output meant there were few fully attributed pictures left. Only two were mentioned by name, as being her best-known: 'Woman at the Door', 1925; and 'The Lovers', c. 1929.

The other sheets comprised a more comprehensive biography from the catalogue of an exhibition of several artists under the title 'Jazz Age', held at the Morgensen Gallery in 1968, and included some illustrations. This Api began, voraciously, to read.

With all that had been going on, Xanthe hadn't thought much about the portrait, apart from handing it in to Derek's safe keeping. Her life had undergone such an unimaginable change, that the past – even if relatively recent – had taken on the air of 'old, unhappy, far-off things and battles long ago'. She would like simply to have sloughed and discarded it like an old skin, so as to go forward smooth and unmarked in her new one, but it wasn't as simple as that. The past left stains, like grease, which one could remove only temporarily and which came seeping back through the fabric of the present with horrible persistence.

A large part of the problem was Api. It was no good – Xanthe could fool a good many people much of the time, but her youngest daughter was not one of them. In Api were all her sins remembered, and it was very trying. The girl didn't even have to say anything: she simply knew too much. She appeared to get along with Derek, but she didn't buy the new improved Xanthe. Xanthe hoped and believed that there would not be some hideous outpouring of old grudges, but you never knew. She wasn't even able to sustain her new energy, good humour and *amour propre* when in Api's company; it was as though the fabric became brittle and transparent the moment she walked through the door, and within seconds had dissolved altogether. It was particularly uncomfortable when she, Derek and Api were together. She felt as if she were stretched taut over some awkward triangular frame and was in constant danger of a messy implosion.

The acrimonious exchange about the portrait had been a case in point. And though it had blown over by the time they parted it still, when she least expected it, snagged at her thoughts like a splinter. It was odd that some *thing*, a possession, could be so much part of one's life that one had no curiosity about it until it was too late and there was no one left who might be able to answer your questions. Old photographs, illegible names in books, ancient gadgets whose use is lost to history . . . And now this damn picture.

Xanthe cudgelled her brains to remember things her mother might have said about it. After all, this was her mother's *father*, and – Xanthe paused to consider fathers. A minute later she rang Charles's number.

Owen answered. 'Is that Xanthe? Ringing to welcome him home? He just got back this morning. And in true caring-friend fashion I'm off to Newcastle with the Sin in about ten seconds. He's sat on the sofa with a cup of sweet tea and the remote control. Stay there and I'll take you to him.'

While the phone was transferred – very silently, she noticed, Owen had his hand over the mouthpiece to protect her from Charles's unguarded reaction – Xanthe realised that she had entirely forgotten about Charles's hospitalisation.

'Here he is,' said Owen. 'I'll say cheerio.'

''Bye, Owen.'

'Zannie? What on earth brought this on?'

'I just thought I'd ring and see how you were.'

'Well.' She recognised an effortful pause as he adjusted his position on Owen's sofa. 'Much better obviously. It was something called a TIA, the teeniest blip. The boss has told me I can be back in harness in a couple of weeks. Till then I assure you I intend to make the most of it.'

'It's good to hear you sounding so cheerful. Api said you

were pretty good considering, but I wanted to find out for myself.'

'I must say it's very sweet of you,' said Charles. 'How did you know I got back today?'

Xanthe lied for the greater good. 'I rang the hospital. Charles—'

'I appreciate it.'

'Charles, since I've got you on the phone—'

'And there's precious little chance of my making a quick getaway, yes, go on.'

'Remember that picture, that portrait in the attic? The one we sat and looked at when we were clearing out?'

'Your gloomy granddad.'

'I was talking about it to Api recently, you know she's got a bit of a thing about it, doesn't want it going out of the family and so on.'

'Blimey, who'd have it?'

'Well, you never know . . . Anyway, it won't be, so that's . . . But I realised that I know absolutely nothing about it. About John Ashe. Only two generations back, but he's a complete mystery to me. And you know how very often an outsider notices things, pays more attention, and I wondered if *you* can remember my mother saying anything about it ever? Or about him?'

Charles gave a pensive groan. 'Ummm . . . These are pretty testing questions to lay on a chap the day he comes out of hospital. Besides, Zannie, it was a hell of a long time ago when the world was young.'

'Not that long. Thirty years?'

'And every one of them packed with incident. She didn't like it, that I do recall. Any more than she liked me. It used to hang at the end of that corridor that went front to back in that house in Parsloe Gardens.'

'That's right. You see, you *do* remember.'

'I think we only discussed it twice, ever,' said Charles. 'Once when I was still interested in making polite conversation, and we were carrying plates to the kitchen, so I asked who he was. She said it was her father, who she'd worshipped as a small child, but from whom she was estranged quite early on.'

'That must have been right, because I never met him at all. I didn't know if he was still alive, even. But I never knew she once *worshipped* him – that doesn't sound like Mother speaking, she was such a mouse.'

'No, that's my word, but she said something to that effect. Adored him, something like that. Then this rift.'

Xanthe was aggrieved. 'You never said anything!'

'Steady on,' said Charles, 'I'm not supposed to get overexcited. A, it was an exchange lasting about fifteen seconds that took place when we were both loaded down with gravy plates, B, I forgot about it more or less instantly and C, even if I hadn't forgotten I should have assumed you knew.'

'So what was the other conversation?'

'That was just before she moved to The Elms and I went to pick it up. I made various formulaic comments about how we'd look after it and so on, and she effectively said she didn't give a monkey's.' Xanthe gave a little bark of incredulous laughter and Charles played the advantage: 'Not a flying fart! Couldn't wait to see the back of it.'

'You make it sound like the black spot.'

'That was about the size of it.'

'Not terribly cheering, is it?' said Xanthe and then, her conscience nudged by references to polite conversation and formulaic comments, asked: 'So – are you seeing anyone at the moment?'

'I've been a bit out of circulation, haven't I?'

'I mean generally, before that.'

'No complaints. Owen's jammy though, he's taken up with our extremely sassy PR lady. Newly back on the market. He was lucky – I was about to make my move when I was struck down.'

As Xanthe put the phone down she was swept by the true

realisation of how fortunate she was; how little she deserved it; and how fervently she hoped that her good fortune would remain undisturbed.

At three a.m. Api set aside the sheets of paper, which she had read several times. At four o'clock she was still sitting there, and still awake, with the light on.

13

2000 – Linda, Api

When unmarried herself, Linda considered, with an outsider's ruthlessness, that the keeping of secrets between spouses was nothing short of treachery.

And yet there had been a secret between her and Bryn from the moment of their first meeting: a secret which marriage had, if anything, persuaded her to keep even closer. She tried to salve her conscience with the reminder that the secret was not hers, that she was merely its custodian.

In truth it was a part of her job she could not bear to let go. She prided herself that the discharging of this particular duty so reliably and discreetly over the years was of inestimable value to Sir Harry. It was quite simply unthinkable that anyone else, no matter how efficient, should take it over.

So three times a year she found some reason to be out for the day and drove out to Essex to visit Alan at Aylmer House, and Coralie at Mizpah; not hard with both the children away at boarding school, and Bryn often at meetings or visiting sites. It was in fact unlike him to be so wholly focused on work especially as everything seemed to be going well, and from time to time she wondered if he didn't need to take some kind of break, a sabbatical perhaps, to recharge his batteries. He had accepted a job for Harry, the designing of a boutique hotel in Bristol, and she sensed he wasn't happy with the commission. It differed from his usual sort of project, and he felt the weight of what was now virtually a family connection. His own family might have been neglected if not for her, but she made a point of visiting and asking them over as often as she did her own parents. She had taken on the roles of

wife, mother and daughter-in-law with the energy and application she had once brought to her job – indeed she looked
on them as a job, and one she was good at.

The visits to Essex had become no easier with time. Al's
occasional importunings meant she no longer saw him in his
room but in a public area where assistance was always at hand.
And Coralie with age was becoming more and more of a loose
cannon. While you could never have described her as proactive, she was querulous and forgetful, inclined to outbursts
of noisy complaint, not aimed at anyone specific but railing
against the unfairness of life generally. When Linda considered all the occasions on which she had been close to
screaming: 'Don't be so pathetic! Assert yourself! Get a life!'
it sent a chill up her spine. Assertiveness and initiative on
Coralie's part – though certainly what Linda would have exercised in her place – were the last things that were needed.

This particular day had been in mid-July, and eerily hot for
an English summer. The sky was grey-white and the surface
of the road trembled with mirages. Even wearing a hat, she
found it too scorching to have the car's top down, preferring
the air-conditioned shelter of the interior. She wondered if it
were true, as people were beginning to say, that the cycle of
seasons was shifting. Already she'd noticed the odd combine
harvester churning about its business, and some fields were
already cut, the bales standing at regimented intervals like the
pillars of a Roman hypercaust. The countryside had a tranced,
dry stillness and there was very little traffic about. Minutes
went by when, apart from the comforting drone of the MG,
she could have been passing through the landscape of any
period in the past two hundred years. In one tiny village,
almost deserted, its inhabitants paralysed by the heat, she was
obliged to stop in the road outside the church by a woman
in a long print dress, shepherding a crocodile of small children in boots and smocks over the road and through the lych-
gate. For a few seconds she felt a prickle of shock, until she
saw the teacher's clipboard, and a little girl's trainers and

realised that what she had seen was a re-enactment for a history project.

She saw no deer in the park of Aylmer House, and most of the building's doors and windows were open, like panting mouths. As she left the car she heard her name called and saw one of the male nurses waving to her from further down the terrace where seats overlooked the rose garden.

As she walked along he came to meet her.

'Good morning! We're out here today.'

'I hope there's some shade,' said Linda. 'I don't have the skin for sitting out in this.'

'Don't worry, we've had the parasols up for a few days. Just like abroad.'

Alan was sitting at a table on which lay a snakes and ladders board. Next to him, beneath the overarching canvas umbrella, was Coralie. Her presence at the same time as Linda's was unprecedented. She looked up as Linda approached.

'Bet you didn't expect to find me here.'

'No,' said Linda. 'But it's a very pleasant surprise.'

Coralie gave a sceptical little laugh as she rattled the dice.

'Anyone for a cold drink? Coffee?' enquired the nurse.

If only to ensure he came back, Linda said: 'A cold drink would be lovely. Anything at all.'

'Anyone else? Tell you what, I'll bring a jug.' Repulsed by the atmosphere, the nurse withdrew.

Linda sat down. 'Hello, Al.'

His eyes remained firmly on the board. 'I'm winning.'

'Clever you,' she said. 'Beating your mum, eh.'

Coralie propelled her counter up a ladder. 'Clever *me.* There you are.'

Alan took the dice and began shaking. Linda asked: 'How are you, Coralie?'

'Very low since you ask. Very blah.'

Oh God, thought Linda, I can deal with them one at a time but both together's too much.

'Me too,' she said. 'It's the weather, we're not used to it.'

'No, no, no!' bellowed Alan. 'A snake, do I have to?'

'Yes,' said Coralie, 'now who's winning?'

'All still to play for,' soothed Linda.

Coralie rattled and threw a two. 'Of course it's not the weather. As soon as we get a bit of sunshine in this country people moan about it.'

Linda gazed out over the lake. This was a beautiful place – architecture and landscape, artifice and nature, in perfect harmony, and she was sitting over a snakes and ladders board with these two crazies who didn't even notice their surroundings, let alone appreciate them. Their inconsequential bickering blended with the rattle of the dice. Sitting there Linda was vouchsafed a revelatory insight, a sort of out-of-body experience. What was she doing here, deceiving her husband because of her loyalty to an old man rich and powerful enough to do his own dirty work? And, she reminded herself, deceiving his wife who had shown her nothing but the utmost generosity? If her two companions were mad in their way, then so was she in hers. She thought: *Enough is enough. If she's going to be here from now on, I shall stop coming.*

But for today, she was here, and had only just arrived, so the best had better be made of a bad job. The nurse reappeared with a jug of fruit juice, three glasses and a plate of biscuits.

'There we go,' he said, sliding the tray carefully on to the table so as not to disturb the snakes and ladders board. 'I'll leave you to pour.'

Linda took this to mean her since neither of the others showed the slightest interest. She half-filled the glasses as one might for children, and picked hers up; just as well, because at that moment Alan passed the winning post and leapt to his feet, causing the table to rock dangerously and the tray and its contents to hit the ground with a crash. Fortunately the nurse was still close enough to have heard, and came hurrying back, oopsadaisy-ing away as he cleared up, as if they all needed reassuring that it wasn't their fault and didn't matter a bit. It was however pretty clear no one felt in the least guilty, let alone remorseful.

The nurse got all the debris back on the tray and set off to fetch replacements. Alan was sitting with his head between his knees peering at the gravel for the missing counters and dice. Coralie did something ineffectual to her sagging hair. It never, ever, looked as though it had been fixed properly in the first place. Why didn't she get it cut? wondered Linda. It would take years off her and be so much easier to manage.

What she said was: 'The people here are wonderful, aren't they – the staff? The patience of saints and the stamina of steeplechasers. I couldn't do it.'

'Oh, I could,' replied Coralie. 'You can do anything if it's your own.'

'Maybe that's true,' said Linda, adding: 'I've never had to put the theory to the test.'

If she hoped to make the point that neither had Coralie, she failed: Coralie's next remark stopped her in her tracks.

'He's coming home with me.'

'What?'

'I'm taking Al back to Mizpah with me, where he belongs.'

'But – why?'

'I just told you. It's his home.'

Linda glanced at Alan. All that could be seen of him was his rounded back, the shirt parting company with the waist-band of his jeans.

'No it's not, he's never lived there.'

'Then it's high time he did.'

Linda was aghast. It wasn't that she didn't believe Coralie, but her stolid announcement had released a swarm of disturbing implications.

'Coralie, have you really thought about this? He's so happy here. It's a beautiful place, he has the best possible care, the right medication—'

'Do you think I won't look after him?'

'Of course not, I know you will.'

'I did it before, when he was young.'

'But he's a grown man now with very severe difficulties.'

'I could get help at home if I need it. Harry would pay. It would be nothing compared to this.'

'Have you discussed it with him? I mean, with Harry?'

'Not yet.'

'And what about Al?' Linda lowered her voice as Al came up for air, triumphantly holding a yellow counter between finger and thumb. 'What does he want to do?'

'He won't mind as long as he's comfortable.'

'Are you sure? He's been here for what, twenty years? He's used to it, he knows the people.'

'They come and go,' said Coralie, as her son bent down again to resume his search.

Linda bit the bullet. 'Coralie, I hope you don't mind, I have to say this – he hasn't seen much of you over those years. Or his father, I concede that. If there's been a constant, the truth is it's been me.'

She was rewarded by a look of cold rage, the more shocking because she realised it had probably been bearing down on her for some time, freighted with years of accumulated resentment.

'What are you trying to say?'

'Only that. I'm not trying to make a point about myself, but about continuity. Aylmer House is what he's used to, the routine, the geography, the food, even. We've only ever been visitors.'

'Exactly,' said Coralie. 'It's high time all that changed. I don't know why I've left it so long.'

'Because it was easier,' pointed out Linda. 'For everyone.'

'It will be much easier for you if Alan's living with me. You won't need to visit any more. His father will know where he is.'

Linda watched as Al, now on all fours on the ground, began crawling about. The gravel must have been hard on his palms and knees, but the discomfort didn't dent his concentration. She was reminded of her own children between the ages of one and two, when the minutest pebble, flower petal or insect became the object of intense, effortful scrutiny. But Al wasn't a toddler, he was a thirteen-stone severely autistic man, the inside of whose head was a closed book which even the experts could barely prise open. She couldn't begin to imagine what went on in it, how it worked, what connections he made. Only minutes earlier she had been ready to leave this situation, to finally hand over responsibility to those most directly involved. Now she felt trapped. It wasn't going to be as easy as that.

'I think you should talk to Harry before you do anything,' she said. 'Why don't I get him to give you a call?'

'If I want to talk to him I can phone him myself.'

This was the sort of assertion Linda had feared might be coming, and she hastened to deflect it. 'He's so busy, it's so hard to pin him down, it would be easier—'

'Easier!' barked Coralie. 'Easier! You're obsessed with things being *easy*. Easier for who? If I want to speak to Alan's father then the *easiest* way for me to do so is to pick up the telephone and dial his number.'

'I appreciate that.' Linda kept her own voice low in an attempt to lower Coralie's. 'But for Al's sake the last thing we want is to create difficulties.'

'The last thing *you* want, you mean. It might queer your pitch with the great and wonderful Frankels. As far as I'm concerned it's high time Harry had a few difficulties to deal with, like the rest of us.'

Linda was granted a few moments' respite by the arrival of the replacement orange juice. Talk about hoist with one's own petard, she thought. At long last Coralie had rediscovered her spine and was sticking up for herself. But the timing could not have been worse.

Al came and sat down, this time with the red counter.

'Got it. Can I have a biscuit?'

'Of course.' Linda pushed the plate his way.

'Alan,' said Coralie, 'would you like to come and live with me, in my house?'

'I want to be at the house.' Though muffled by digestive crumbs the words were clearly audible.

'That would mean you were living with me all the time. Not living here.'

Al nodded enthusiastically. Coralie looked at Linda. 'You see?'

All the way home Linda cursed herself. Cursed herself for ever getting into this invidious situation, and for the vanity which had kept her in it long after she should have gone.

The situation rumbled on, unresolved, for over a year. Late the following autumn Linda went for a walk on Primrose Hill, to escape the pre-Christmas pressure with which she had a love-hate relationship. She still couldn't get used to this without Flo. People were engaged in peaceful pastimes – young mothers walking well-muffled toddlers, pram-pushers, dog-walkers, couples snogging, shivering tourists with maps pointing out landmarks to one another . . . All seemed care-free, none, Linda was sure, harboured secrets. But then how would she know? They probably thought the same about her. And *she* might be looking at the recently bereaved, the drug-dependent, the clinically depressed, or tomorrow's lottery winner, or first-time grandparent. You couldn't tell. People could cover things up. Everyone had an outside face.

She sat for a while on a bench in the chilly wind at the top of the hill. She wished she could have discussed this with Bryn, who was such an optimist, and who could always see a way through. 'Keep it simple' was his motto. 'Don't make complications.' As her own confused reactions gathered and settled, she tried to imagine what his advice would have been. After about half an hour a single thought had risen above the rest. She must tell Harry, and let him deal with it.

This, though simple and obvious, was not a course of action even Coralie could have called easy. Harry himself wasn't easy. Genial, energetic, mercurial, hard-headed, generous, single-minded, demanding, shrewd, manipulative and loyal were all adjectives which had been attached to his name in the press, but never 'easy'. Still, she told herself, all she had to do was say the words, get them out, in the right order, audibly and comprehensibly, and the problem would be his.

When her face began to ache with the cold, she moved. She was standing on the pavement waiting for the lights to change when she saw Jonathan Frankel. He was standing on the far side of the road, next to a young woman – a girl, actually. Linda noticed two things: the appearance of the girl, and the couple's body language. The girl was turned away, looking out for a taxi, perhaps, presenting the back of her head with its cloud of pale orange hair to Frankel; her sharp face in profile was pale and stern – almost fierce – and the brow rather high, like portraits Linda had seen of Elizabeth the First. She wore a short, tight black coat with a high neck, and her slender foal-like legs were in opaque black tights and long boots. Most crucially, Linda saw, she was in charge. Jonathan's expression was wheedling, he was leaning forward with folded arms as though his wrist had only that moment been slapped. When the girl's arm went up to hail a cab he had to jerk back to avoid being struck in the face. The taxi pulled up. When it moved away, the girl's hair filled the taxi window like vapour. Jonathan was left standing on the pavement, alone.

Linda realised she was directly opposite, and staring blatantly. But though he was facing her way she could tell he didn't see her. His mind was elsewhere, with the girl in the taxi.

Api had never been pursued before, and she liked it. This, she realised, was the control she had dreamed of when she learned about sex, with Giles. But with the control and the power went responsibility. To herself, mainly: decisions, although they could be placed on hold for as long as she chose, would eventually have to be made. And then there would be no going back. So for the moment she was keeping Jonathan at bay. Paolo, who took a close interest, said knowingly, 'Quite right – The Rules!' but she'd never heard of them. She was acting on instinct.

She certainly wasn't in love. She didn't know about it, had had no role models, though she had once glimpsed its possibilities. She had grown to understand Jonathan and to like him, to be fond of him, even, but now she had to make up her mind whether she could marry him.

Whether he was in love with her was in doubt, too. He never used the word. What he said was that he was 'mad about' her, that he 'adored her', that she was 'driving him crazy'. All this seemed a bit silly and over the top, and also showed that he didn't quite get it, or her. He didn't really *know* her. But that was OK, she didn't want him to – she liked to keep a large part of herself to herself. All those things which were hers alone, about which she would never confide in anyone: Dodge, the shadows, John Ashe . . . the man on the beach.

The truth was she didn't expect to feel love, or anyone to feel it for her. Perhaps neither she nor Jonathan was capable of it. But she didn't necessarily see this as an obstacle to their relationship, she simply had to decide. He made most sense when he said they'd 'make a great team'. That she could almost believe, and the possibility tempted her.

After their meeting at Creighton's, when his apology had been suggested, declared unnecessary, and withdrawn, Jonathan had moved in on her relentlessly. There was a juggernaut quality to his attentions. Like an HGV on the motorway he simply indicated that he was moving into her lane, expected to be accommodated and was astonished when she – a cheeky Mini – put her foot on the accelerator. He was not, she decided, a specially confident man, but he had the superficial self-assurance of the extremely rich. He was accustomed to getting what he wanted. Api was not so naive as to imagine herself the most glamorous or alluring woman he had ever encountered. He could take his pick; she had seen him with some of them in the restaurant. She knew that her looks were idiosyncratic and her social status lowly compared to what he was used to. What he didn't, couldn't, know was the strangeness of her life experience – but her own sense of that strangeness and its mysterious influence gave her a poise beyond her years. In the restaurant she wore her professionalism like a perfect, concealing *maquillage*. It was part of her attraction, but what lured Jonathan Frankel was the part that it concealed.

He had conducted what she suspected was his standard campaign of flowers, compliments and invitations – the first two of which she accepted, the third of which, for months, she refused. To begin with, she wasn't even tempted out of curiosity. Her attention lay elsewhere entirely. He pressed her about boyfriends, lovers, and she told him truthfully that there was no one. He would have been astonished, and piqued, to know that his rival was a woman.

Suzannah Rose Murchie's life had been a candle in the wind – only unlike Marilyn she hadn't even had the oxygen of fame to sustain her small flame. The little to come her way had done so after her death when it was too late to bring any comfort. She'd been a sort of gilded outcast – gifted, wilful, uncompromising, chronicling her life and the people in it without, as far as Api could make out from what she'd read, any intention of making money from it. She'd certainly spent the years from her mid-twenties, the period of her greatest artistic energy, on the breadline, living in the houses of various friends, painting pictures for them in lieu of rent. Apparently there were several houses in London with murals and decorated windows signed S R Murchie – or there had been at the time of the 'Jazz Age' exhibition. Api wondered whether they were all still there, or whether they'd been swallowed up in 'restoration' and renovation over the ensuing two decades.

She'd never married and no reference existed to her having numbered the rich and famous among her lovers. She appeared a person of quixotic emotional tastes, with a flair for friendship – so many people had been not just prepared but willing to have her under their roof, living with them for as long as she wanted, and the article had described her 'moving on' rather than being thrown out. Api had formed

the impression of a freemasonry of generous people, whose
linked hands (this was how she imagined it) had provided a
human safety net for their fragile and precarious friend.

The three pictures shown, though admittedly only small,
poorly printed reproductions rendered even fuzzier by the
Xerox machine, were notable for a teasing, narrative quality.
What they seemed to depict was a moment on the brink, or
in the wake, of a huge emotional storm. The lighting, dramatic
and a little lurid, resembled that generated by a change in the
weather. The figures were turned away – in one case only the
curve of the woman's cheek was visible as she closed a door
– but they seemed to Api to tremble with feeling.

There was a fourth picture, a photograph of the artist taken
in 1925. It showed a thin girl with an intense, serious expression, staring out from beneath a straight-brimmed straw hat.
Her hair had been bundled up into the hat, but thick swags
of it framed her face. There was a symmetry between the
horizontal planes of the brim, the level shaded stare and the
wide, thin mouth with its set lips.

But something had happened. Something unexplained,
which had put the candle out. There were no pictures, or none
that anyone knew of, in the last two years of Suzannah's life,
and no record of where she was living. But she was described
as dying 'almost destitute' in London a few days after her
thirtieth birthday.

This had made Api shiver. The thought of a lonely death
was fearful. Especially because when she looked at the picture
of Suzannah Rose Murchie, she felt she was looking at herself.

She hadn't wanted to part with the precious sheets of paper,
and in the end had compromised by ringing Creighton's and
asking Julian whether she might have a copy to keep. Then
she'd sent off the article to Derek with a thrill of superstitious
dread, like a New Guinea tribesman whose soul is canni-
balised by the camera. A few days later he got in touch.

'Api? I wanted to thank you for forwarding Julian's research
on the mysterious SR. It made fascinating reading.'

'I thought so.'

'I have to say I was a bit disappointed in her photograph. I'd expected something Zelda Fitzgerald-like. More glamorous, more poor butterfly.'

Api felt herself relax. He'd seen nothing. 'No,' she agreed, 'she certainly doesn't look like that.'

'I've got the portrait back, by the way. It looks wonderful. The cleaning up's even more impressive now it's *in situ* and I can make the comparison. Shall we tell Xanthe? Then maybe I can coax her up to town and you and she could come round together for a little private view?'

'Yes, why not.' She would rather have gone on her own, but she could see that this suggestion was only fair, and she could scarcely object when the idea of the surprise for her mother had been hers.

'By the way,' added Derek, 'I hope the bill wasn't too horrific. Julian did say he'd keep it down.'

'No, it was fine,' she said. 'Worth every penny.'

Harry agreed to meet up with Linda on the condition they went out to lunch. He had refused to listen to her over the phone.

'Hold it!' he said. 'If this news is good we can make it a celebration and if it's not so good it will be nothing a decent wine can't improve.'

She wasn't so sure, but there was no arguing with him. What's more, they met in the restaurant of the Delancey Metropole overlooking Hyde Park where, with no fuss of any kind, Harry was assured of the perfection he expected. It was not what Linda wanted. She didn't relish laying this unsavoury problem before him in such a loaded context – like a cat bringing a dead bird to his feet.

Since she was committed, however, damage limitation was essential. She wore her most achingly chic green and turquoise silk suit, with her hair up.

The dining room was decorated with a central pillar of

variegated fresh evergreens and ivory candles. A miniature version stood in the centre of each table. Harry was waiting for her – he would have been there ten minutes before the agreed time – with champagne on ice and a tiny Asprey's envelope on her place mat. He was immaculate as ever, but frail inside his dapper suit, and slower getting to his feet.

'Linda, this is a delight. You're a feast for the eye.'

'Harry . . .' These days they touched cheeks. His felt cool, the skin slightly loose. She sat down and picked up the envelope. 'What have you been doing?'

'Absolutely nothing. I look at you and I wonder why I bother, it's gilding the lily. You'll have some of this?'

As the waiter poured champagne she undid her present. It was a tiny flower made of peridots and diamonds, set on two strands of golden wire.

'I'm told you put it in your hair,' he said. 'But what do I know?'

She was aware he would have spent hours selecting it. 'You know exactly what to give me. It's quite lovely. Bless you.'

'Here.' He made a little beckoning gesture with his fingers and she handed it to him. 'Let me.'

She leaned forward and allowed him to clip the flower in place at her temple. He was quick and deft – he'd never attempt such a thing unrehearsed – but she tried not to notice how his hands shook.

She turned her head from side to side. 'How do I look?'

'Perfect. See for yourself, ask them for a mirror.'

'No,' she said. 'I trust you.'

He chuckled. 'Not every ugly old man who was told that by a beautiful woman would take it as a compliment. But we know each other, don't we?'

'Yes,' she said, 'we do. Thank you so much.'

He closed his eyes briefly in acknowledgement. 'And now,' he said, 'you order for us. I trust *you.*'

This was a little game he liked to play. He was not being patronising, but chivalrous. She ordered caviar for them both;

sole *bonne femme* for him (he liked the great, traditional French dishes) and plain grilled for her, with spinach and new potatoes. Harry never waited for the dessert menu; he liked to have the 'campaign planned', so she ordered one helping of homemade coffee ice cream, with an extra spoon. She was unlikely to use the extra spoon, it was his indulgence to provide it. 'It's the role of a lady to help a gentleman with his calories.'

'I shall be happy with the champagne,' she said. 'But if you'd like to change?'

He shook his head. 'I'm not the man I was. I've cut down.'

She raised her glass. 'Whatever your regime, you look wonderful on it.'

For the first time, there was not a flicker of a response. Flannel was to be ignored. Once upon a time Linda would have been cut to the quick by this snubbing of her well-meant flattery, but not now.

'How's Lady Frankel?' she asked. 'It's so long since I saw her.'

'Elizabeth's worried about our boy.'

To disguise her moment of guilty shock, to show she had not for a second been confused, she said: 'I saw Jonathan the other day.'

'You did? How was he?'

'Not to speak to. I'd been walking on Primrose Hill and he was on the other side of the road.' She leaned back as the caviar arrived. 'He was putting a young lady into a taxi.'

'Aah . . .' This single syllable, with its lilting rise and fall, spoke volumes – of understanding, suspicion, fatalism.

When the waiter had gone, she asked lightly, 'Why is your wife worried?'

'The young lady. Was she a girl, with –' he held out his hands at shoulder level – 'hair like this?'

'Yes. Very striking.'

'No beauty.' He frowned down at his caviar as if wondering what it was. 'A fury.'

'You don't like her?'

'We don't know her. Except that she is years younger – too young – and very clever. Jonathan is bewitched.'

'Good for her,' said Linda. 'It won't do him any harm to work a little.'

'Possibly.' He nodded at her plate. 'Eat.'

'I'm going to.'

'She runs a restaurant,' he remarked thoughtfully.

'So obviously competent and hard-working. Harry, I don't know what you're worried about, she sounds a paragon.'

'It's not me that's worried. It's my wife.'

'Of course.'

They both understood the conventions of these conversations. Elizabeth was the one who did the worrying: it was women's work.

He sat back, and gave his plate a little absent-minded push; it was clear he wasn't going to eat. 'So what is it you wanted to tell me?'

Linda pressed her napkin to her mouth. The salty pearls of caviar became hard to swallow. She took a sip of champagne.

'It's about Alan.'

'How was he when you last saw him?'

'Well – he looked very fit and happy. They go outside a lot when the weather's fine.'

'I'm glad to hear it. Fresh air and exercise aren't things I go in very much for myself, but I'm told they're beneficial. Did he behave himself?'

'Yes.' She smiled. 'What he needs is a nice girlfriend.'

'They have –' Harry made a vague twirling gesture – 'social events, don't they?'

'I believe so. I've showed you the programme often,' she reminded him. 'But I don't know if actual fraternisation is encouraged. It would be so difficult to strike a balance between freedom and supervision.'

'Mm . . .' Linda recognised the shutting-down in the face

of too much disobliging detail. She had better get on with it.

'Coralie's been there too,' she said.

'Oh yes?' He snapped off a minute segment of Melba toast and popped it in his mouth.

'I was surprised, as you can imagine. She very rarely visited in the past, and I never saw her there – my going was obviously a good excuse for her not to. But not now'

'I see.'

Linda sat back in her seat. She must be relaxed, assertive. This was not her problem.

'She wants to have Al at home.'

'M-hm.'

'She wants to take him away from Aylmer House and have him living with her at Mizpah. With full-time help, paid for by you.'

There was a silence, during which the waiter orbited their table at a distance and decided against removing their barely touched plates.

'Harry? Did you hear what I said?'

'Of course.'

'My own opinion for what it's worth is that it's a very bad idea. He's not a boy any more, he's a big, strong man—'

'But no danger, surely.'

'No intentional danger, of course. He's too – too locked up in himself to want to do anyone any harm. But he's unpredictable and needs constant looking-out for. He could wander off, or start a fire, or anything. And while Coralie's intentions are obviously good, she has absolutely no idea what she's letting herself in for. It will be terribly unsettling for both of them.'

Harry glanced towards the waiter, and touched the edge of his plate. The waiter advanced immediately.

When their plates had gone, Harry said: 'Has she asked the boy?'

'She has. She asked him in front of me. Naturally he said yes.'

'You don't think he meant it?'

'He meant it, but Harry, he doesn't understand the implications, and neither does she. I really think she ought to discuss it with you.'

He gave a thin smile. 'She'll have to if she wants me to pay for this full-time help.'

Linda could no longer contain her rising exasperation. 'You *have* to talk to one another, for Al's sake. But it would be so much better if you took the initiative. Apart from anything else Coralie needs to understand that you're fully involved.'

Harry made minute adjustments to his place setting, his small, elegant fingers hovering over the silverware like a pianist caressing the keys. When he looked up his face wore a bland, unreadable expression that she recognised all too well.

'But, my dear, I am not involved. I have never wished to be. You know that. Aylmer House has provided care. I have paid the bills. You have kept me informed. A simple, old-fashioned, straightforward arrangement, and one that I must say has suited me perfectly. I haven't the least desire to change it now. If the boy's mother for whatever reason wants him at home again I am fully prepared to pay for any help necessary for peace of mind.'

She wanted to scream at him: *This is one problem you can't just throw money at!* But even had that been possible it was not at this moment the most important thing. She might be powerless to stop the ship going down with all hands, but she could, and must, jump off it.

'Harry, there is something else.' He tilted his head questioningly. 'I no longer feel able to make these visits – to act as your intermediary.'

'You're throwing in the towel.' This was one of those idioms which brought out the foreigner in Harry Frankel: it seemed not to sit comfortably in his mouth.

'I'd prefer to say I've reached a considered decision.'

'Because of what Coralie wants to do.'

She hesitated for less than a second. 'Yes.'

He pursed his lips, sighed. 'I don't blame you. I'm only surprised you continued for so long.'

'I was pleased to help.' What else could she say? Admit that simple vanity was the reason?

'But now it has become just too difficult . . .'

Delicately, expertly, he was manoeuvring her into the position of a person falling at the first fence. She knew that it wasn't important, that it was about him and his ego and not about her, but she couldn't let it pass.

'It's become – inappropriate.'

'*Inappropriate* . . .' He made the word sound like something unsavoury he was poking with a stick. 'Very well.'

Linda knew his modus operandi better than anyone: she should have been able to leave it there, but like many another before her was overcome by the urge to justify herself.

'It's too personal, now. Your son is about to face a huge change in his life – if it's allowed to happen – and not necessarily for the better. I don't know. I'm not an expert, and I'm not one of the family. It must be for you and Coralie to decide. Besides,' she added, throwing in everything she could think of now, 'it isn't fair on Coralie to have me in the picture.'

'Perhaps,' said Harry with affected insouciance, 'perhaps not. Ah, here is our wonderful fish!'

'I'm sorry, Jonathan, I can't,' said Api. 'I'm going to have lunch with a friend.'

'Tell me where he lives, I'll come and pick you up.'

'I don't know how long I'll be.' This was perfectly true, but she knew he would hear only prevarication. His voice on the other end became insistent, what she thought of as his pressure-hose voice.

'That doesn't matter. I can wait.'

'No. No, I don't want you to do that. I want to have Sunday to myself if that's all right.'

'Why don't you want to see me? Who is this friend?'

'I never said I didn't want to see you. I'll ring you when I get home. And the friend is my mother's boyfriend. She's going to be there as well.'

'A Sunday, a family occasion. I suppose I can hardly argue with that.'

'No,' she agreed firmly.

'But the next weekend, our weekend away – you have arranged to take it off?'

'Of course,' she said. 'I'm looking forward to it.'

When the call ended she sat still, as she often did after these conversations, minutely examining her hands, like a ruffled cat that concentrates on washing to regain its composure. But she wasn't unhappy. On the contrary, she felt good at the moment, energetic and in command. She had made a resolution: that the weekend after next she'd tell him her decision. The timing was a self-imposed formality. She'd made up her mind.

Derek's house was in Chelsea. It stood on a corner, on the apex of two Georgian terraces, and the three floors above ground level each had a room with a curved wall with a bay window overlooking the square. Approaching it, Api was reminded of the bridge of an ocean liner. In the first-floor window she could see a Christmas tree with coloured lights. On the door, which was opened by Derek, hung a holly wreath.

'I try,' he said in response to her compliment. 'In my bachelor way.'

'I've done nothing yet,' she confessed, relinquishing her coat.

'The young simply tear round on Christmas Eve, so I'm told. Come on up, your mother's here.'

Xanthe was in the first-floor sitting room, looking at the Sunday papers. Api couldn't get used to this new persona, indulged, benign and indolent instead of detached and inert. The kiss she gave her was more than a little self-conscious, for Derek's benefit as much as anything.

'We were actually having sherry,' he said, 'but I have most other things if you'd prefer?'

She opted for white wine and he went off down the stairs again, declaring it was no trouble, to fetch it from the kitchen. Api sat down on the sofa.

'What a great house.'

'Isn't it? Much cosier than you'd think from the outside. It belonged to his unmarried aunt and she left it to him.'

'Good for auntie.'

'By the way,' said Xanthe, 'that was such a nice thought, getting the picture cleaned up. Especially after we had words about it last time out.'

'Not especially,' said Api. 'It's all very well me banging on about wanting to keep it and look after it but what have I ever done towards its upkeep?'

Xanthe laughed. 'It's only a picture!'

Even now, thought Api, *she has no idea.*

'Derek hasn't shown it to me yet,' went on Xanthe. 'He wanted to wait till you got here.'

Api was about to remark that she'd already seen it, but realised that this might not have been mentioned, and kept quiet.

'Has he shown you the research they did?' she asked instead. 'About the artist?'

'He gave it to me but I haven't had a chance to read it yet. The artist's name didn't mean a thing to me, but that's not saying anything. I took a quick glance at the other pictures. Rather nice, I thought – rather Dutch, those half-lit figures.'

'Did you see the photograph of her?'

'Funny little thing,' said Xanthe. 'Glaring out from under that big hat. But she must have been tougher than she looked to deal with Grandfather.'

Derek returned with the white wine and poured a glass for Api.

'Shall we go and take a look at him in all his scrubbed-up glory?'

The portrait was in the dining room, immediately below where they were sitting. Like the drawing room it was austere but comfortable, the table laid for lunch. Against the dark green wall opposite the window hung John Ashe. Api had half hoped he might seem out of place, but no, he might always have been there above Derek's Adam fireplace, commanding not just this room but the whole square, and London beyond.

To gain a perspective Xanthe went round the dining table and stood between it and the window, arms folded.

'I must say he looks a good bit brighter, though that might be the frame . . . Derek, this is *just* the place for him. All these years he's been needing a really imposing fireplace, don't you think, Api?'

'It's certainly better than the attic.'

'Point taken. But what an improvement. Thank you so much, both of you.'

Derek said: 'I've grown rather fond of him; he's company for me. He can stay here till the call comes. Shall we eat?'

At the five-star Hotel Imperatore in Rome, Jonathan could never have guessed that Api was nervous. Not nervous of him, but of this kind of situation. Until very recently she had had no experience of what might be thought of as good living, except that which she helped dispense at the restaurant. She did not yearn for it, only because in some strange way she felt herself unworthy. She was a small, soiled person who had sunk lower than anyone could possibly imagine; this sort of thing was not for her.

Jonathan had showed her that it could be, and she was learning. If she felt out of place – in a box at the theatre, sitting in the Jag (sometimes with a driver!), meeting his rich, cheerful friends, going to restaurants infinitely more fashionable and expensive than the one where she worked – she covered it up with an air of perfect self-containment. She came to understand that as with clothes, so with one's manner, less was more: it could fool people. She wore black, always, the plainer and smaller the better. She wore her hair either loose in a cloud or in the tightest, sleekest ballerina-bun, twisted with black velvet. She wore make-up that emphasised her pallor, with colour on her lips only; no mascara on her lashes, only a hint of russet-gold eyeshadow. A heavy black watch, tiny gold earrings. The look, cheaply and simply done, achieved elegance through its uncompromising plainness. As for her, she listened intently, spoke little but to the point, laughed only when she thought something genuinely amusing, and didn't fidget. She might not inwardly be calm, but she could be still, and people mistook this stillness for composure. Minimalism was her shield and her defence.

She had met Jonathan's parents only once. They'd both been courteous and charming, but not fooled for an instant. She had been subjected to the practised scrutiny of devoted and discriminating parents. Jonathan was their only son, the apple of their eye and heir to their millions, and she was the latest in a long line of girlfriends. She was quite sure that Lady Frankel knew her dress was from a high-street chain, and that Sir Harry considered Lowell's brash, but that neither of those things bothered them so much as her youth, and Jonathan's infatuation. They didn't dislike her, and were far too polite to show it if they had, but they couldn't understand what was going on, and were suspicious of what they didn't understand. She in her turn liked them, but could not take on what was essentially their problem.

The Hotel Imperatore on the Via Veneto was Italian high style at its most jaw-droppingly sumptuous – a palace of marble the colour of rhubarb fool, glittering cut glass and gold. In this, the last week in December, on the thirty-foot-high ceiling of the immense foyer the crystal chandeliers alternated with even bigger ones fashioned out of evergreen and white roses, each supporting a dozen white tapers. In the reception area stood an eight-foot tree trimmed with red and gold, in the foyer one twice the size, all in white. Both were covered in real candles, each with a tiny shade. The cocktail bar was a bower of waxen roses and gold satin ribbon. A little orchestra played music from *The Nutcracker*.

In the lift on the way up to their rooms there was one other passenger, a woman in a floor-length sable cape with a high, upturned collar. When she got out, Jonathan put his lips to Api's ear.

'I'm going to get you one of those.'

'You mustn't.'

'Why not?'

'It would be a waste of money.'

'I've got it to waste.'

'It's not me.' She looked at him, quite fiercely. 'You know that.'

'But it could be,' he urged. 'It could be if you let it.'

She shook her head. 'No.'

Their suite was at the top of the hotel and on the corner of the building – two double bedrooms on either side of a drawing room on two levels, with a semi-circular balcony. In this respect it reminded Api of Derek's house, like the prow of a ship. The colour scheme was a silvery eau-de-Nil, the style French eighteenth-century, the tone one of muted luxury. Api's bathroom alone was bigger than the living room at her flat.

As soon as the porter had gone, practically bowing his way out of the room with a fistful of notes, Jonathan wrapped her tight in his arms.

'You like?'

'I do.'

'One of the best hotels in the world. That's not one of ours.'

'I believe you.'

'Api.' He kissed her voraciously. 'Api . . .'

'Let me unpack,' she said, 'and have a bath. It's all so wonderful.'

He released her. 'You promise?'

She nodded. 'Promise.'

The bathroom was white marble and gold, like a giant jewel-box. The huge central whirlpool bath was circular, with seats on two sides. An array of frosted glass bottles with gilt stoppers stood by the basin. There were three sizes of white towels as thick as sheepskin, two hooded full-length bathrobes, face flannels and cuddly white towelling slippers. The curved glass panels of the shower were engraved with climbing roses. Standing inside it was like standing in a misty, mysterious garden. As the immense gush of hot water poured over her and the scented foam curled around her feet, Api told herself: *I am as entitled to this as the next person. And now I can have it.*

When she was dry, she used the body lotion and the eau de toilette, and rubbed the luxurious moisturiser into her bare face. She put on her plain white silk shift and brushed her damp hair carefully so that it hung in a long, undulating curtain between her shoulder blades. She looked in the mirror at her virginal self and thought: *This is the outside me, pure and simple, and it's mine to give. What's inside is mine to keep.*

When she stepped back into the living room Jonathan was lying on the blue brocade Louis XV chaise longue, in his towelling robe; bare feet on one arm, head resting on a cushion, head turned sideways to look at the television which was showing football with the sound turned down. She said his name, and the screen went blank. The effect was like a third person leaving the room, a door closing: instant intimacy. He swung his legs down and turned to look at her.

'Api?'

'Here I am.'

She waited, arms at her sides, as he came across to her.

'Oh my God,' he whispered when he was standing close. 'You're like an angel. My own – little – angel –' with each word he dropped a kiss – on her shoulder, her cheek, her forehead, and finally her lips. She stood passive and pliant within his embrace, an offering, and thought: *Two out of three will have to do.*

'Yes,' she said. 'I am yours. That's what I want.'

That night, she held back, knowing that for now it was what excited him. For all these months he'd been in pursuit – let there still be something to pursue. She was turned on herself, more than she'd ever been with Giles, though she knew that a large part of this was narcissism, a relishing of what she had the power to give, and to withhold. That, and the difference between now, and then, brought on a kind of swooning disorientation. The voluptuous luxury of the surroundings, Jonathan's smooth, cherished skin, soft hands and sweet-smelling hair, and her own perfect, fragrant cleanness – it made the past leap up in her head like a filthy, frightening hobgoblin so that she let out a cry—

'You like that?' he whispered. 'Tell me what it is you like . . .'

But she couldn't, and he couldn't wait.

The next day it snowed. They had breakfast in their suite, at the table in the huge window, watching Rome turn grey and white all around them. The drift of the snowflakes made it seem as though they were themselves moving, floating in a glass capsule through the spiralling white.

Jonathan said: 'Now will you let me buy you a fur cloak?'

She didn't let him do that, but when they went out into the cold, muffled streets in the late afternoon she chose a black fur scarf to go over her own narrow coat, and a pair of soft black leather gloves with thick fur cuffs. The scarf stood up around her face like a ruff.

He found the gloves sexy. 'Wear them in bed,' he whispered, 'with nothing else.' The sales lady overheard and sent her a discreet, collusive glance. Out of doors the snowflakes settled on the black fur and turned from diamonds to dewdrops. They snacked on panini in a warm, steamy bar and then walked to a mansion on a hill where the formal gardens looked like a chess-board in the snow, to see the Bernini sculptures.

She'd never heard of them, but he told her: 'My mother brought me to see these when I was twelve, and I was too embarrassed to appreciate them. I had a hard-on the whole time. But next time I was here, I knew why.'

She couldn't believe that a human mind, and hands, could conceive and create such things in marble – the way the flesh of a woman's thigh indented beneath the pressure of a man's hand, the tight mouth and frown of concentration of a youth taking aim, the precise moment when a girl began to turn into a tree, her hair curling into leaves, her arms into sinuous branches, the swirling hem of her dress into roots.

They made love again in the early evening and she thought of the statues, and saw her own white, smooth skin like marble that became warm and plastic beneath Jonathan's hands.

At dinner she wore a high-necked black dress with long sleeves, and her hair loose. When they walked into the hotel dining room she followed the head waiter to their table with her head held high. The place was full of rich and beautiful women but she knew she was looked at. *This is me*, she told herself. *I am doing what I want, and whatever I want I can do.* She would walk in the light, always.

After dinner he took her to a bar that was dark and chic, with a jazz pianist. She was a little light-headed and drank Coke. They brought ice separately in a silver bowl with tongs, like sugarlumps.

'Be careful,' said Jonathan, 'how you do that.'

She smiled at him, the tongs poised. 'Why?'

'Because Coke does vile things to your stomach and may not be much good for diamonds, either.'

The ring nestled among the ice cubes, a tiny asymmetric spray of leaf-shaped stones on a white gold band.

'Oh!' she said. 'Like Daphne. This afternoon.'

'That's what I thought, God knows what I should have done if you hadn't liked her. Here . . .' He put it on her finger. 'No other woman has a ring like that. I had it made for you.'

She spread her hand on the table. 'That was so clever of you. I love it.'

'And me?' he asked. 'What about me?'

She put her hand, the hand with the ring, against his cheek.

His eyes were brown; he would have been a plain man but for those eyes. The lids lowered slightly in response to her touch.

'You,' she said, 'are the man I'm going to marry.'

14

2001 – Bryn, Linda, Api

Bryn stood on the scaffolding in the icy February drizzle with Martin Craig, the contractor, and looked down on what there was of the new Delancey hotel. Since he had been here last, it looked only marginally less like the Western Front. A warlike simile was still apt though: the claggy swamp interspersed with trenches had been replaced by something like a bomb-site, littered with piles of rubble and debris; the half-grown walls looked more like ruins than a building in the making. To add to the effect one or two brisk, opportunist weeds had grown, and gulls, with nothing to disturb them, perched along the top of the scaffolding.

Bryn allowed that his own jaundiced eye might have something to do with it. There was no need for him to be here today, and now he rather wished he hadn't come. Progress was slow; the project was not on schedule. This was not his fault – he had been commissioned for the design only, his responsibility had ended with the acceptance of his final drawings – but it still affected his morale. The whole concept was his, and the delay conveyed an unwelcome foot-dragging about its realisation. It denoted a lack of urgency. This smaller, more uncompromisingly chic hotel was a new departure for Delancey, as well as part of the regeneration of the area. Sir Harry was getting old, the mood was upon him to leave his mark: he wished to be innovative as well as charitable. Always on the qui vive, he'd heard about the Dubai building, the Scimitar, and wanted to be the first to exploit the Mancini cachet over here. He'd given him free rein, and what was the result? This slough of despond.

'What's holding things up?' he asked wearily.

'Delay on materials, usual story.'

'Problem with the local stone?'

'Yeah.' Craig nodded. 'Got to get it elsewhere.'

'So what's the prognosis?'

'Hard to say. I'm in daily contact. Another week before we're up and running?'

'I see.'

Back at ground level, Craig said: 'Sorry we couldn't be more encouraging.'

Bryn felt sure he wasn't in the least sorry. Craig was a cold fish. The delay wasn't down to him: he was the man in daily contact with the suppliers. Bryn was left with the inescapable impression that the fault was his, for having fancy, difficult ideas. Everything would be all right if it wasn't for the architect, went the unspoken agenda. This sensation wasn't entirely new, he often heard a bit of grousing about what was being asked for in the name of aesthetics, but it was usually routine stuff, and predicated on the idea that in the end they were all in it together. In this case, Craig seemed to be dissociating himself: to be saying he'd do what was being required of him, but under duress. He evinced no faith or interest in the project itself. He didn't get it, and he'd never tried to.

The site manager, Geoff Clarke, was a nice bloke however. He was ready with instant coffee when they got back to the office, but Craig declined.

'Got to dash. Good to see you again, let's hope things get moving soon.' And he was off, the wheels of his fresh-off-the-line Range Rover sending up twin arcs of yellow mud as he barrelled away.

'Tinted windows,' remarked Geoff mildly. 'Never seen the point of those.'

'So what do you reckon, Geoff? Is Sir Harry going to see this place finished?'

'No reason why not. Paying the workforce to do nothing's costing him an arm and a leg, but so long as that's not an issue.'

'Not as far as I know. The costings were pretty generous, as I recall; we did allow a contingency cushion for this kind of thing.'

'Tell you what, though, it'll be worth it,' said Geoff. 'It's going to be a real gem if we pull it off.'

Bryn fervently hoped so. Driving home he questioned the wisdom of having acceped the job for Harry in the first place. Working for someone you knew had its drawbacks, and he could never be quite certain what his relationship with the old man was. Sometimes he seemed to be a quasi son-in-law, one of the family. At other times he'd find a distance had opened up, and he was made to feel that he'd been done a favour. He knew he shouldn't be touchy. Harry was an old man, when all was said and done, and the old could be contrary. But it didn't make for a comfortable working relationship. Also, when he'd asked Geoff Clarke if Sir Harry Frankel was going to see the finished job, his agenda had been a selfish one: he didn't relish the prospect of dealing with Jonathan Frankel. Except, of course – he smiled to himself – that Craig would have to deal with him too.

That reminded him that there was the charity lunch to celebrate Delancey Hotels' half-century, and then the damn wedding to be got through in July. The lunch was fine, you knew where you stood with that, and it would at least be generating money for several good causes. But the wedding, dear God! The vast engraved invitation had been standing on their mantelpiece at home for weeks. Generally speaking he enjoyed weddings, but he found it almost impossible to whip up the necessary benevolence towards Frankel *fils*. Plus, this was going to be one of those colossal, no-expense-spared semi-business affairs where, if he read it aright, they'd be stuck on the table equivalent of Room 101 with a collection of stuffed shirts from the Delancey empire with whom he'd be expected to network. He considered himself a sociable fellow, but this wedding looked like hell.

At least Linda would be there, looking wonderful, making

people laugh, oiling the wheels. Not a day went by when he didn't thank God for her. She had redefined the term 'wife', that he had once found so unappealing. He was only surprised (and secretly rather gratified) that she had given up work without, apparently, a backward glance, to look after him and the children. He knew she still helped out Harry from time to time, but now more as an old friend than a former employee.

He rebuked himself for grousing. He was a lucky dog. His house was beautiful, his children apparently happy and smart, his wife quite simply the best. The hotel was a job, and it would get done. There had been nothing the matter with his plans; on the contrary, the whole Delancey board, and especially its chairman, had been delighted with them.

And all of this had to be put in proportion. The Scimitar building was almost finished. The sheikh was ecstatic. It was altogether possible that he'd be set for life.

It was the imminence of the Delancey charity lunch that made Linda do what she'd sworn she would not. She phoned Coralie.

It rang about a dozen times and she was about to give up when Coralie finally answered abruptly.

'Yes?'

'Coralie? It's Linda Reynolds.' She didn't bother using her married name to Coralie, who always affected not to recognise it.

'Yes?'

Linda's heart sank. 'I thought I'd ring and see how you were doing. Both of you,' she added in case Coralie thought she'd forgotten.

'Oh – you know . . . We rub along. Had a few ructions lately, but—'

'Ructions?' Linda's antennae quivered. 'What sort of ructions?'

'Exactly what you'd expect.' Coralie paused. 'I didn't know you were interested.'

'Well I am. Of course I am. I've known you both for years.'

'Because it was your job,' Coralie pointed out. There was some bumping in the background, and a shout. 'Coming! Look, this isn't a good moment.'

'I can tell, but – well – have you got some help?'

'Yes. Of a sort.'

'So you spoke to Harry?'

'No!' Coralie's voice rose so sharply that Linda winced. 'No I bloody didn't, because I couldn't! He wouldn't speak to me, OK? So much for the parents getting together, he doesn't care whether we live or die!'

The line buzzed in Linda's hand. She replaced the handset gingerly, as though it were an unstable device. What was the matter with them? Coralie could be lying, of course, but it hadn't sounded like that. And if she wasn't, then what was Harry playing at? Had he no idea of the potential damage that could be caused? It was almost childish, as if he was trying to show her what happened when people reneged on their responsibilities.

But she had not, she reminded herself, reneged on hers. She had continued to discharge them beyond what was necessary, and given due notice of her intention to step back. She had made this call out of courtesy – out of a sense of *honour*, for goodness' sake – and had been rebuffed. Whatever was happening out there was not her concern.

In the meantime, there was the luncheon at the Delancey Metropole in Park Lane. No fewer than four former PAs were going to be there, as well as the present one, and it was important to Linda not to be one of the herd: to be seen to be something special. Which she was, she knew that. She had bought a bias-cut Jean Muir dress in deep violet, and she planned to wear no jewellery except the peridot flower Harry had given her. She knew there had occasionally been gossip about her and Harry, none of it true, but this was one occasion when she intended to do nothing to discourage it. This mischievous notion helped to revive her spirits, and contributed to her especially warm welcome for

Bryn when he got home from visiting the Bristol site.

'Darling . . .' he said into her hair as she embraced him. 'I've been thinking about you.'

'On site? I bet.'

'No, I have. On the drive home. Wondering what on earth I'd do without you, that sort of thing.'

'Just as well you haven't got to, then.'

They were in the hall and he caught sight of several trainers at the foot of the stairs; it was half-term.

'Where are the kids?'

'Nick's upstairs with Anil on the net, and Sadie's gone to Emily's for the night.'

'That's good. She doesn't have enough fun.'

'I think they're watching the Mel Gibson *Hamlet* and calling it revision.'

'That's fun of a sort.'

They went into the living room, which she had made warm and inviting in shades of lilac and rose. The fire was lit.

Over a glass of wine, she asked with some trepidation about the building. She knew it was late, and that the delay was worrying him. But tonight he was surprisingly bullish.

'It's still well behind schedule, but that's not my responsibility. Or only indirectly, they're waiting for the local stone. The main thing is, it's going to look great. I know it. That's my job, to hang on to the original vision when all about me are disappearing under mud and disorder.'

'Quite right, good for you.'

'I've decided nothing's going to be served by me sinking into the mire as well. I just hope to God it's finished in the old man's lifetime.'

'Oh but surely—' Linda began, and then thought of the last time she'd seen him. 'He's frail, but he's not ill. Anyway he'd never pop off when there's something like that to look forward to.'

Nick and Anil appeared in the doorway. Anil was one of the few local friends who had survived the great divide of

Nick's departure to boarding school, but it had left them with limited social tolerance. There was also the problem that at rising eighteen Nick looked twenty-one to Anil's fifteen.

'Anil's got to go,' said Nick. 'Can I give him a lift home?'

'Not without me you can't,' said Bryn. 'Hi, Anil.'

'Hello, sir.' Bryn sometimes thought the only reason he acknowledged the otherwise Trappist Anil was to elicit this delightful, old-fashioned response.

Nick shifted impatiently. 'Yeah, I know that, rub it in why don't you, but I take the test soon and I need all the practice I can get.'

Anil rubbed his face. Poor chap, thought Bryn, quite happy to return by tube, but caught in a crossfire not of his making.

'Nick, do you mind if we don't, only I've just got in and I'm absolutely buggered.'

Linda got up. 'I will. Anil, are you ready for this?'

'Yes thanks, Mrs Mancini.'

Nick made a 'result!' gesture as they stepped into their trainers. Linda fetched her car keys. Anil poked his head back in.

'Goodnight, sir.'

''Bye, Anil.'

The door closed behind them. Gazing into the fire, Bryn considered his son. There was something frightening about a boy looking like that. So bloody – beautiful, was the only word, though it made him wince just to think it. And with that knowing air . . . He sometimes wondered whether boarding school had been such a good idea, and if girls featured in Nick's life at all. They must do. That they weren't in evidence didn't mean a thing, what were all those two a.m. finishes about if not sex? Bryn had always looked forward to the time when his son would bring home lovely girls to Sunday lunch, with whom he could flirt mildly, but with every passing day such an idyllic and respectable scenario seemed more staggeringly unlikely.

★

The luncheon was on a Monday. The Saturday of the preceding weekend was the last day of half-term, when Nick and Sadie had to be back – Sadie by five, Nick by seven, so the journey was mapped out. Bryn and Linda both went along, but Nick drove most of the way, causing his sister to lean her head back and close her eyes in grim terror. The truth was, Sadie preferred the ordered certainties of school to the excitements of home. She especially liked to be away from her brother, whom she found increasingly disturbing. She could not relax when he was around. Though she adored her parents and had missed them horribly to begin with, some of her happiest times recently had been spent with her Aunt Jocelyn, and Phyllis, in their comfortable flat in Swiss Cottage, where everything was mapped out by long usage, and the atmosphere one of civilised predictability. Nick was content to be back at school for the reason that, catlike, he made himself pretty much at home anywhere.

Now – relegated to the front passenger seat, there was no way he was going in the back – Nick remained in the car while Linda and Bryn saw her in at the door. Even at fifteen she was such a sweet round thing in her school sweatshirt that Bryn couldn't resist lifting her feet off the ground as he hugged her. Sadie shut her eyes, both to hide from her own embarrassment and the sardonic look she knew would be on her brother's face.

''Bye, treasure.' Her father kissed her cheek ardently. 'Remember – you can't buck the system.'

This was some kind of joke; he always said it, and she didn't get it. 'I will.'

''Bye, darling.' Her mother's kiss was more conventional, but still accompanied by a fragrant squeeze. Nobody's mother was as beautiful as Linda, it was nearly as embarrassing as Dad's hugs. 'See you in a couple of weeks.'

'Yes, 'bye, seeya,' said Sadie as she scuttled off.

Nick made no mention of his sister as they pulled out of the school gates. But once they were back on the main road he said:

'That do you're going to on Monday. Will your picture be in the paper?'

Bryn laughed. 'Good grief no, not unless we disgrace ourselves! The place will be stuffed to the gunwales with the rich and famous.'

'You'd better get on with it then,' said Nick.

Just before they arrived, as they were sitting in the queue of black cabs in the Metropole's sliproad, Bryn leaned across and kissed his wife.

'You look absolutely ravishing. There won't be a woman there to touch you.'

'Don't you believe it,' said Linda. 'But thanks anyway, darling.'

The champagne reception was held in something called the Borrowdale Suite, a cavernous room already packed with guests getting merry on the free-flowing bubbly. Bryn's prediction to Nick had been right – a quick first glance revealed two members of the cabinet, several sports stars and a positive constellation of actors, male and female. The announcement of their own names by the toastmaster caused not the tiniest blip in the hubbub of self-congratulatory conversation. But Elizabeth appeared almost at once.

'My *dears* . . . Linda, you look quite lovely. Thank you so much for coming. Come and meet some people.'

The people they met, a former England soccer manager and his wife, were charmingly impressed by Linda's connection.

'You probably know him better than anyone in this room,' said the manager.

Bryn beamed. 'I bet she does, actually!'

Linda chose her words carefully. 'With someone like Sir Harry I think different people know different sides of him. For instance, I've never been exposed to the terrifyingly intolerant tycoon I keep hearing about.'

'Nor us,' said the man. 'He's always been absolutely charming.'

'So which Sir Harry do you think *you* saw?' asked the wife.

She seemed a nice woman but Linda sensed the glitter of female curiosity.

'Oh, you know, the offstage one – a bit more relaxed, sometimes tired, sometimes down in the mouth. But always polite and proper.'

The manager chuckled. 'Proper – there's a word you don't hear often these days. An old-fashioned word.'

'He's an old-fashioned man,' said Linda.

Consulting the seating plan in the ballroom, she did a quick calculation. There were twenty-one round tables of eight, the top table being in the centre at the far end of the room. Each of the former PAs was sitting at a separate table in the middle band, around the equator as it were – perfectly respectable positioning, not elevated to Olympian heights but certainly not below the salt. She was pleased to see that she herself was on the centre table, directly facing Harry. She knew it was childish, evidence that she couldn't bear to let go, but after the long and chilly silence since their last meeting, and the dismaying conversation with Coralie, she took this as a sign. She had not been excommunicated.

Bryn had looked for Jonathan Frankel on the top table, but then saw that of course, for courtesy's sake, the three members of the immediate family were spread out – Lady Frankel hosting the table to the right and her son the one to the left. Linda was able to point out a fair number of the shining ones who shared these tables: cousins, nephews and nieces and one or two old friends and business sparring partners.

'Which is the fiancée?' he asked.

'I don't think she's here . . . I saw her once and I'd definitely recognise her again.'

'She will turn up, though,' said Bryn. 'Surely?'

Api, standing by her father's bedside, thought how ironic it was that she would have welcomed almost any excuse not to attend the Frankel luncheon – any but this.

Charles, wired to monitors, lay in a single-bedded room in the High Dependency Unit. According to Gilda, who had already spoken to the doctor, they had run something called the Glasgow Coma Scale on him and discovered that despite a massive and sudden stroke – the result this time of a blood clot – the brain stem was not damaged and he could, in theory, recover consciousness. He didn't look as if he would bother.

It was very quiet. In the distance the last of the morning's Hoovers hummed. Api heard the brisk whisper of a nurse's uniform and the muted squelch of her crêpe soles as she hurried along the corridor outside. The rattle of a trolley, voices in the sluice.

Gilda entered backwards, carrying two cups of coffee, having shouldered the door open.

'There you go. Couldn't remember about sugar.' Api shook her head. 'Sorry I was ages. I couldn't face the machine stuff. I went to the café downstairs.'

'Thanks.'

'Mind if I sit?'

'Sure.'

Gilda sank down on the single black plastic chair. Api wondered if she herself looked as exhausted as that. For the first time, her striking, energetic sister appeared too old for her clothes. Gilda's haggard face was a measure of the situation. She felt a snake of fear slither in her stomach.

For something to say she asked: 'When does Mum get here?'

Gilda yawned mightily. 'One thirty at Liverpool Street. I told her to get a cab.'

'What about the others?'

'I left a message for Judith, and I spoke to Martin. He said he couldn't get away immediately but to keep him posted. God knows where Saul is, he doesn't run to an answering machine and I must have tried six times.'

A nurse came in, bright and practical. The nurses here still wore an old-fashioned cap, a fan of crisp white linen like a bird's crest, that gave them a jaunty air.

'How's he doing?' she asked rhetorically. 'Let's have a look.'

Api leaned on the windowsill. The two of them watched through the steam from their coffee cups as she performed a series of quick checks on patient and monitors. Api couldn't help thinking: *She's so pretty, he'd love this if he was awake.*

When the nurse finished, she said: 'Good.' Which meant nothing except 'I've finished.'

'Is there a smoking room anywhere?' asked Gilda.

The nurse smiled ruefully. 'Not any more. You have to go outside. There's usually a good few others out there, me included.'

'OK.'

Api stood up. 'How is he really?' she asked.

'He's very poorly, but he's stable at the moment.'

'How poorly?' she persisted. 'Is he going to die?'

'The doctor'll be here soon, have a word with him.'

'Give us your opinion, though.'

'Mm . . .' The nurse returned to the bedside and gazed down. Smoothed Charles's hair absent-mindedly with her hand. 'He's peaceful. Still with us. Not fighting particularly, but not struggling either.'

When she'd left the room Gilda put down her coffee cup, rested her head on the back of the chair and closed her eyes. In less than a minute her breathing grew heavy and slow as she fell asleep.

Api went over to the bed. In this situation 'peaceful' was a weasel word. The dead were said to look peaceful. Perhaps what she took for peacefulness merely denoted the passivity of the sick, emphasised by the wires and tubes that monitored, drained and pumped. But he also appeared – she studied him closely – dignified. Awake, his face was always mobile, in a constant state of adjustment, trying to persuade you of something, or to present a moving target. The calm of unconsciousness ironed out the wrinkles and restored some of his lost boyishness, but also lent him an air of wisdom.

She smiled. Wise, calm, dignified: the very last way you'd

describe the normal Charles, the father she might not see or hear again. She laid her fingertips on the back of his hand. Who might never play again. This time it had been a massive stroke. It had only happened today, in the small hours of the morning. The orchestra was due for rehearsals in Bath this evening, so Owen would probably have told them by now, but there hadn't been time for any cards, or flowers or messages.

Api realised that, in his idiosyncratic way, her father had been one of the few people who had begun to understand her. He had at least accepted that she *couldn't* be fully understood. She sat down on the edge of the bed. The prevailing attitude towards him in the house when she was growing up had been the one they picked up from Xanthe – detachment. It didn't much matter what Charles did, because he didn't much matter. She had always thought her mother lazy but now, suddenly, she saw that she might have been wicked.

She went over to Gilda and gave her wrist a little shake.

'Mmm? What?'

'Gilda, I'm going to make a phone call.'

'OK, OK . . .' Gilda twisted sideways in the chair and closed her eyes again.

Bryn saw Jonathan Frankel take a mobile from his pocket, answer it, and replace it. Unbelievable, that a man could have a mobile about his person, and switched on, at this kind of occasion. Less than a minute later he got up, making what appeared to be the most perfunctory of excuses, and left the room. Bryn's wasn't a censorious nature, he had neither the time nor the inclination to sit in judgement on his fellow man, but he considered Frankel obnoxious. On a day when all these people were gathered to celebrate the huge achievements of the father, the son couldn't resist a show of importance. He caught Linda's eye, and she lifted one shoulder as if to say: What can you do?

★

'How is he?' asked Jonathan.

'We haven't seen the doctor again yet. He's just lying there – we don't know.'

'I feel all wrong being here when you're going through this.'

'No, you mustn't feel that,' she said, 'you're exactly where you should be, we both are. I'm so sorry to ring you.'

'I'm glad you did. I want you to call me about anything – at any time. Now Api, obviously I have to get back, but is there anything I can do?'

'Nothing. We can't, and you certainly can't.'

'I mean in the way of getting your father the best possible care. Anything he needs, that might be of any assistance, however small, can be done, you know. At once.'

'I'll let you know, but I think he's in good hands. He always used to say . . .' She stalled, choking on tears.

'Api? Api, I'm coming over there.'

'No, no, don't. He always used to say the NHS would leave your hip decaying for years while they searched for the right piece of paper, but drag you back from the jaws of death in seconds.'

Jonathan didn't laugh. 'He's got a point there. Look—'

'There's just one other thing I wanted to say.'

'What's that?'

'Never think you don't matter.'

'What?' He was baffled, impatient. He added sharply: 'I don't think that.'

'Good,' she said.

'I'll call the minute this is over. If anything happens before then, let me know right away.'

'I will.'

'And remember if there's anything that needs paying for, it can be. Find out. Money's nothing. 'Bye.'

Xanthe's first instinct had been to ring Derek and ask him to meet her, but in the end she hadn't. It might look odd, rushing to her ex-husband's bedside. She told herself she was doing it for her daughters – for the family.

There had been remarkably few occasions in her life when she'd really put herself out. She was not someone who saw any particular virtue in making an effort, for its own sake. If there was an easy route she'd always taken it. Since the advent of Derek it had come as a revelation to her that the small exertions required by personal vanity – hairdos, manicures, the buying of clothes – could actually be quite pleasant. But on the train into London today she was conscious of doing something she did not want to do, for reasons she did not fully understand. She would have given anything to be at home, her peace undisturbed, her lover safely bestowed in town, her family going about their business elsewhere. This gathering at Charles's bedside seemed an occasion calculated to require of her what she was least qualified and most disinclined to give. That was another reason she didn't want Derek there: he would see her emotional inadequacies. She suspected that he would not in the least mind her going to see Charles, would probably take it as further evidence of her selfless nature and wide sympathies, and she did not want him to be disappointed in her.

But here she was, doing her duty. She did not quite believe the girls, who were prone to make a drama out of a crisis: it would be completely out of character for Charles to die. In her scenario he just went on and on into a chirpy, lecherous and mildly disgraceful old age, while she soared upward with Derek, day by day in every way getting better and better. No, he wouldn't die. She knew a stroke was a stroke and not actually attention-seeking behaviour, but she was sure he was milking it for all it was worth. The girls, pale and anxious at his bedside . . . the (probably female) doctor bending low over him . . . all those nurses gliding about . . .

By the time she got in the taxi she had mentally mapped out a day for herself: an hour or so at the hospital, then back into town to buy a suit for Api's wedding (she had never owned a suit; the purchasing of one had become symbolic of her metamorphosis) and *then* she would call Derek, and go to dinner with him, allowing him over the course of the evening to coax from her the affecting story of her mercy dash.

Gilda was just finishing a Marlboro Light by the pick-up point when she saw her mother getting out of the taxi. Her first thought was: *Here we go*, and her second: *She looks well.*
    She let Xanthe reach the entrance before joining her.
    'Hello, Mum.'
    'Gilda – you weren't waiting for me, were you?'
    Gilda shook her head. 'Having a fag.'
    'How is he?'
    'Doctor's due back any minute, then we'll know properly. But not good.'
    'He'll rally, I bet. One thing you can definitely say of your father, he likes life.'
    'A bit too much.' They reached the lift and Gilda pushed the button. 'Honestly. Wait till you see him.'

On the way up, Xanthe sneaked a glance at Gilda. She looked absolutely God-awful. Xanthe did hope her daughter's appearance wasn't a measure of Charles's condition. She had a feeling everything was simply going to implode, and there was the wedding coming up which no one would want to attend.

The doctor (a man) was there when they arrived. Api, who looked a great deal better than Gilda, introduced him as Mr O'Dell.
    'Mrs Durrance, how do you do.' The vowels were slightly clipped – South African or Zimbabwean – and his manner soft.
    'I'm actually the former Mrs Durrance,' said Xanthe. 'But we've remained on friendly terms.'
    'I know, your daughter has explained.'
    'And this is my older daughter, Gilda.'

'Hello, Gilda. I understand you're a big family.' The phrase sounded so Enid Blyton, it didn't convey the right impression.

'Five children, all grown up now,' said Xanthe. 'Now – what can you tell us?'

'Nothing terribly encouraging, I'm afraid. I'd put the chances at fifty-fifty. There isn't a lot more we can do, everything's down to him. He could turn round and come back, we see it all the time. I'm sure it helps that you're here.'

'But he doesn't know that, does he?'

'Not consciously of course. But I've seen PVS patients come round after more than a year with memories of things that were said, and faces, things that imprinted themselves on the subconscious.'

'But . . .' Xanthe tried to turn her expression of consternation into one of thoughtful concern. 'We're not talking a year here, surely?'

'Heavens no, I'd expect him to wake up, if he's going to, some time today.'

'And if he doesn't?'

'Then he could be fading as we speak.'

Gilda began to weep. She sank down on the chair with her head on her knees, her shoulders shaking with sobs. Xanthe perched awkwardly on the wooden arm and patted her back.

Api, arms folded, asked: 'Which is more likely, in your view?'

'He's already gone thirteen hours without regaining consciousness, and experience suggests that the longer that goes on the smaller the chance of recovery after a major stroke.'

'And if he does recover, will he be all right?'

'There's bound to be impairment in speech and motor function. There's always some disability.'

Xanthe feared that Api might have caught the fleeting look of stark terror on her face. Gilda's sobs continued unchecked. Mr O'Dell left, with the promise that he'd be back very shortly.

Xanthe got up and went to the side of the bed. Api was

perched on the windowsill, watching her. This made her even more self-conscious than she already was. For a second there she had thought: *Please let him go! Charles dribbling in a wheel-chair is more than I could stand!* Those thoughts must not be allowed to leak through. She felt as though her face were in an iron mask. But he looked so serene, so *grown-up* somehow, that her fears receded. This wasn't Charles as she knew him. He had moved on.

'By the time he was my age,' said Jonathan, 'my father had achieved more than most men do in a lifetime. And now he's lapping me!'

There was amiable laughter. The luncheon had reached the speeches stage. People had turned their chairs to face the top tables. Ties were loosened and cigars lit. The eyelids of one or two of the older guests were already growing heavy. There were three speeches listed on the menu: the toast to Sir Harry by his son, reply by Sir Harry and a toast to Delancey Hotels by a well-known and respected comedian of the ruffled-shirt and charity-golf variety.

Linda knew her husband disliked Jonathan, but she didn't think him so bad. He faced the classic difficulties of the son-in-waiting, and Harry was notoriously tenacious of power, as well as a poor delegator. Jonathan had too much money and not enough to do – a problem which, while she realised many men would have given their right arm for it, remained a problem nonetheless. And he was making a good job of the speech, striking the right note and achieving a balance between the affection due to a father and the recognition of the public figure. Admittedly, present company defined the term 'captive audience'. They'd paid a hundred pounds a head for the privilege of accepting the invitation and were simply delighted to be part of the great, the good and the prosperous who were able to do so, and count themselves among the friends of the Frankel family.

'. . . so I ask you all to rise,' said Jonathan, 'and drink the health of your dear friend, my father, and a wonderful man – Sir Harry Frankel!'

There was a soft roar of chairs being pushed back.

'Sir Harry . . . Harry . . . Sir Harry . . .'

As they sat down Bryn put his lips to Linda's ear. 'At least he kept it short.'

'Ssh.'

She watched Harry get to his feet. He tailored his movements these days to minimise any appearance of decrepitude. So he rose deliberately rather than slowly, adjusted his cuffs with finger and thumb, looked around him with obvious delight.

'Honoured guests,' he began. 'You didn't come all this way at vast expense to listen to *me* . . .'

Xanthe sat down on the only chair in the room. She was suddenly tired, not by the journey she'd undertaken to get here, or even by the emotional exercise, but by the uncertainty. She had no idea how long she would need to remain here. She had brought an overnight bag, but whether she would stay in a hotel, or with Derek or even, God forbid, in the hospital, she didn't know.

She turned to Api. 'Have you spoken to the others?'

Gilda, wiping her eyes with a tissue, said: 'I did. Martin said to keep him posted, he could come down tonight if necessary. Judith's got a message, but I couldn't raise Saul. I ought to go and try again.'

'Can't you use your mobile?' asked Xanthe.

'Mum – this is a hospital, it fucks up the technology. There's a payphone on a trolley thing up here, but it's always taken. Otherwise there are phones in the plaza.'

Api said, 'It's my turn, I'll go.'

'Do you want change?'

'I'll use a card.'

Xanthe put out a hand to her as she left the room, but she appeared not to notice.

★

It was a relief to Api to be out of there. Xanthe had tried to catch her hand but she had just pretended not to see.

She didn't bother looking for the ward phone, but set off along the corridor for the lift. She wanted to escape and the plaza with its cafés, shops and crowds would do just fine. She shared the lift with an old man in a wheelchair being pushed by a porter. From a frame over the wheelchair hung a bag of fluid. The old man was skeletally thin, his skin a waxen yellow, the lines around his bird-mouth grey. But when he caught her looking at him he smiled, and his false teeth looked incongruously large and perfect in his shrunken little face. The porter was an almost indecently robust-looking man in his forties, in a lumberjack shirt and desert boots. When the lift door opened on their floor, he said, 'Here we go, mate.' Api thought of Giles.

Down in the plaza she found four payphones positioned around a central pillar in the seating area. All four were in use so she took a seat and consulted the back of her small diary for phone numbers. Martin had home and office lines and a mobile, with voicemail on all three. Judith had home and office, and an answering machine at home. Saul had only one phone and worked at home. At three o'clock in the afternoon he was as likely to be there as anywhere. After what seemed hours of unnecessary conversation, one of the phones came free. If there was a queue, she ignored it, darted in and dialled Saul's number.

Astonishingly, he answered on the second ring.

'Yeh-ello?'

'Saul, it's Api.'

'How's it going?'

'Fine. Saul, it's about Dad. He's had a stroke.'

'He hasn't, has he?'

She closed her eyes. 'Yes, and it's not good. Gilda and I are here, and Mum, and we just saw the doctor. He said it's fifty-fifty.'

There was a pause. 'You're joking.'

'No, Saul. Gilda tried to call you earlier.'

'Sorry.'

'That's all right, but you know – if you want to be here—'

'When he goes, you mean?'

Momentarily choked, she nodded.

'Api?'

'That is what I meant.'

'OK, thanks for letting me know. You'd better tell me where you are.'

Next she called Judith, and got Ruth.

'Api, we got your message. I'm so sorry. Do you think Judith should come down?'

'Only if she wants to. There's nothing anyone can do.'

'So it's pretty serious.'

'Yes. But I wouldn't want to drag Judith into London . . .'

'Tell you what, we'll have a talk about it, and if she wants to I'll come up with her.'

'Thanks, Ruth.'

She gave her the address of the hospital and called Martin, on his office line.

'This is the voicemail of Martin Durrance. I'm sorry I'm away from my desk at the moment but please leave your name, telephone number and any message and I'll get back to you soon. Thanks.'

'Martin,' she said, 'it's Api. This is to tell you that the doctor says it's fifty-fifty for Dad, and he's not wildly optimistic, so you might want to come down. Don't call my mobile. You could ring the hospital for news, he's on Albery Ward. See you.'

When she rang her brother's mobile, he answered right away. She could tell from the background noise that he was driving.

'Martin, is this safe?'

'As houses, I'm on the M6 heading in your direction. What gives?'

'It's about fifty-fifty.'

'Holy shit. OK, look, I've really got to see this guy in Wolverhampton, but I'll explain the situation, keep it short, and then be on my way. Is Mum there?'

'Yes.'

'Bearing up?'

She wanted to say 'of course'. 'Yes.'

'Right, thanks for calling. 'Bye.'

Api stepped out of the stall to make way for a woman with reddened eyes. She wondered how many life-and-death situations were being enacted under this roof right at this moment. Hundreds, probably. The cast of some of them were down here now, eating pitta wraps, buying teddy bears, reading papers, reviewing changed lives, as well as making emotional phone calls. Her father was part of that now. From that small bed in the small room all those floors and corridors away, fine invisible threads spread out like a spider's web to the other members of the family.

She glanced at her watch again: twenty past three. At the Metropole they'd be into the speeches; there was no point in calling Jonathan. She hadn't even asked the doctor if there was something, some miracle-cure that only money could buy, but it seemed to be too late for that.

The way back to the ward seemed longer, uphill. As she approached Charles's room the door was open and she could see the back views of two nurses and the doctor.

It was fortunate that the comedian – who'd achieved national-treasure status – had lost none of his old powers, because he delivered a stand-up routine lasting nearly half an hour. The audience's hilarity was genuine and Linda saw that Harry for once had his guard down and was laughing uncontrollably. Elizabeth had come to sit near him, and they leaned their heads together, helpless with mirth. It was nice to see.

When at last it was time to leave, Bryn said: 'That was a nice occasion, very well done. You have to hand it to the old boy, he's inspired enormous affection.'

'He has,' agreed Linda. 'Plenty of enemies too, but one has to assume they weren't here today.'

'If you want to get in the queue for a personal goodbye, go ahead. I'll wait for you in the lobby.'

Linda hesitated. She would have liked to, if only to set aside the awkwardness of their last meeting but the Frankels were barely visible among a small crowd of well-wishers.

'No,' she said, 'I won't bother. They're swamped.'

'We shall see them again,' he reminded her as they left the ballroom, 'at the wedding.'

She was waiting to retrieve her coat from the cloakroom when Jonathan Frankel came up to her.

'Linda – I know you're about to go, but Dad particularly wanted to have a word with you before you left.'

'Oh – well – of course I'd like to.'

'He spotted you heading off and sent me.' He turned to Bryn. 'That OK with you? Just a few minutes?'

'Sure, I'll be waiting downstairs.' He held out his arm for her coat. 'No rush. Give him my best.'

Back in the ballroom the Frankels had retreated to easy chairs in the corner. Half a dozen other people, mostly family, were with them. The hotel staff were beginning discreetly to clear the tables.

Jonathan presented Linda. 'Here you are. I caught her.'

'Linda . . .' Harry attempted to get up, but the adrenalin had ebbed now, and she stepped forward to stop him.

'Don't get up, please.'

Elizabeth rose. 'You sit here, my dear. I'm going to collect my flowers and find a cup of tea. Will anyone join me?'

She moved off, the others, including Jonathan, taking the hint and following in her wake. Linda sat down next to Harry. There was a pink flush on his cheekbones and one of his legs was trembling slightly.

'You're wearing my favour,' he remarked.

She touched the flower. 'Of course.'

'You look lovely as ever. Best in the room.'

She laughed. 'Hardly! But thank you so much, Harry – we were only saying what a splendid—'

'I'm afraid I haven't taken Coralie's calls.'

'I know.'

'You do?'

'I spoke to her, just to see how they were getting on.'

'But Linda, I thought you were laying down your burden.'

'It was a courtesy, that's all.'

His mouth tightened. 'Far more than she deserves. She's become a menace. I will not be pressured and harassed.'

'No, of course not.' Linda kept her voice even. 'What about Al, though?'

'If it gets too much for her she'll send him back to the –' he flapped his hand – 'the home. Sooner rather than later, I should think. I'm not going to abandon them, I shall make it my business to know what's going on.'

She wanted to ask, *But how, if I'm not there?* 'Good.'

'Don't go calling her again, will you?'

'Not if you don't want me to.'

'I don't.'

'Then no, I won't.'

He adjusted his position, lips pressed tight with discomfort. 'You're coming to the wedding, aren't you?'

'Try and stop us.'

'She's a strange one, the girl he's marrying – I told you. No beauty. No chatterbox, either. Still, these things don't matter so long as it works. She has him on a lead. Extraordinary.'

'Sounds like love!' said Linda gaily.

They were left alone with Charles. It was obviously considered the right thing to do, to give the relatives a few minutes to say their farewells and make their peace. That was a strange phrase, thought Api: by definition the only person at peace after a death was the dead person himself.

Nothing had happened, apparently. Gilda and Xanthe had

been talking, and hadn't even known. When the nurse came in to do her regular check, she told them. 'I'm so sorry, he's gone,' is what she'd said.

None of them cried. Gilda had already done her weeping; she looked exhausted and washed-out. Api was numb. Xanthe's expression was fearful.

She sat down heavily, glancing from one face to another in utter distraction.

'What am I going to do? What on earth am I going to do?'

Api looked at her, hard. 'Mum, you were separated. You have Derek.'

'But that's not the same!' wailed Xanthe, in a voice Api had never heard before. 'He doesn't know me like your father did. Who will understand me now that Charlie's gone?'

15

2001 – Api

Api went to look at the house in Hardwicke Row because she knew she should; and because Jonathan wanted her to. The truth was, she didn't much mind where they lived. They were going to start off in Jonathan's luxuriously large warehouse loft apartment in Wapping, and she would have been perfectly happy to stay there. Jonathan had pointed out that they ought to start afresh somewhere new, in a place that was theirs as opposed to his, but it wouldn't have bothered her at all. She had always been transient, had never put down roots anywhere, even in the house where she grew up which she had left without a backward glance.

She knew that most women would have given their right arm to be in her situation – marrying a man so rich that he could cash-buy a beautiful house in the heart of London and given the job of choosing it herself – but she remained indifferent. It was as if all her energy and determination had gone into the decision to marry Jonathan, to change her life, and now there was none left over to deal with the practical consequences of that decision.

She tried, for Jonathan's sake, to express interest and enthusiasm. They had already been to look at five or six places, some of them so grand she failed to imagine herself living there at all. It was not only their size, for she had been brought up in a large house, but the level of *haut décor*. The concepts, the notions, the elaborate and immaculate decorations and attention to detail. The sheer quantity of possessions. She herself possessed very little, which was the way she liked it. And the Wapping loft was bachelor-minimalist. How would they fill an enormous place? When Jonathan rather impatiently pointed out that she could go shopping, she was filled with dread.

Once, standing in the 'magnificent 40 x 20 ft double-aspect drawing room with many original period features' on the first floor of a mansion in Holland Park, Jonathan had clasped her round the waist from behind and said, as he squeezed her tight:

'Look at this – think of the fun you could have with it!' But she was unable to think of it as fun, just as a huge and intimidating responsibility. She wouldn't have known where to begin. The current owners had gone for a look not unlike the hotel on the Via Veneto: luxurious silver, grey and blue, with many beautiful Georgian pieces and some tastefully blended modern ones. She had a horrible feeling they were standing on a silk carpet.

'I quite like this,' she ventured. 'The way it is now. It suits the house.'

She felt him laugh, his chest bumping against her back. 'Yes, Api, but they'll be taking it with them.'

'Anyway,' she went on, as if he hadn't spoken, 'we'd have to live with it a bit to know what we wanted.'

'Er – no.' He released her, and turned immediately into the other Jonathan, brisk and overbearing. 'You and I will not be living with builders and decorators. We decide; they do; we move in. That's the order of play.'

'Just strip it back, paint it white and leave it empty, then,' she said. 'If it was good enough for you in Wapping it's good enough for me.'

That had made him laugh. 'I suppose it'd be a talking point . . .'

Anyway, they hadn't gone for that one in the end: the garden was north-facing, no good for evening parties, he said. She thought: Oh God, parties! but then remembered they would be catered.

The Hardwicke Row house was in Highgate. Jonathan had

already seen it during the horrible week of Charles's funeral. Since then a previous offer had fallen through and the vendors were anxious to sell, so there was some time pressure. He was sorry he couldn't accompany her this time, but he was down in Bristol checking on the progress of the new hotel. Api didn't mind; she was pleased to be going to look at a place without feeling that her reactions would be monitored.

The weather had changed in the last couple of days, and given blue sky and sparkling sunshine. It was only the end of March, so as everyone kept saying there could yet be snow, but at least this brightness was like evidence of good faith: the season would turn soon. She was ambushed by sadness on the way up, and had to turn the car into a side street so that she could weep. Her tears were for her father and for herself; for all of them, really, and the mess they'd made of things in the past. But, she reminded herself as she continued on her way, there would be no more mess. She had taken charge of her life, and from now on it would function properly. She would see to it. She would walk in the light.

Hardwicke Row itself was wonderfully pretty, a parade of immaculate Georgian red-brick, with white paintwork, iron railings, flights of steps and trees just beginning to show a dazzle of spring green. The houses, though fine and large, were not as intimidatingly palatial as the others they'd looked at. She could only think that their Jane Austen elegance must have compensated for that in Jonathan's eyes. 'Go and check it out,' he'd said. 'I think you'll like it.'

This time he was right. Number 5 Hardwicke House was at the centre of the terrace, double-fronted and a little more imposing than its neighbours. The owners, Adrian and Ben, were a charming gay couple in their early sixties who treated her more like an honoured guest than a prospective buyer. When she arrived at a quarter to twelve, *prosecco* and cheese straws awaited her in the ground-floor living room and it was perfectly clear that this was to be no ordinary house-view.

'Of course we've already met your fiancé,' said Adrian. 'And he said you weren't able to come with him for family reasons.'

'My father had just died. I was helping my mother sort out the funeral.'

'Oh dear, I am sorry. This must be a difficult time to be looking at houses. You've got such a lot on your mind.'

'Yes,' she said. 'But with getting married, there's lots to look forward to.' She realised that though she had said this, or something like it, many times over recent months, this was the first time it had felt smooth and real, like a sweet in her mouth.

Ben, who looked the younger of the two, said: 'Absolutely. We've been together twenty-five years. Highly recommended.'

'That's marvellous,' she said and knowing she must be practical, added: 'Could I ask why you're moving?'

'Of course you can. We haven't been driven out by plague, infestation, subsidence or the neighbours from hell, we just want to be in the country. Also, my mother's still alive, believe it or not, ninety-three and still self-propelled, but she lives in Chichester, so we've been looking in the neighbouring villages. With some success, fingers crossed.'

'What about round here?' She looked out of the window at the raised flagstone pavement opposite and the row of trees, each slim polished trunk surrounded by a railing. 'Tell me what it's like.'

'Heaven,' said Adrian. 'We used to be in Islington and we adored it, but fifteen years ago we spent a Sunday up here, saw the board up, knocked on the door –'

'Rather cheekily now I look back on it!'

– 'and that was it, love at first sight, and it's only got better. The house is a dream, as you will see, the garden is – well actually I shall shed a tear when we say goodbye to the garden, because it's my pride and joy – and the area has everything you could possibly want.'

'Including,' said Ben, 'the people, who are lovely. There's privacy, we're all terribly English, no borrowing cups of sugar or anything, but there are some nice parties, we all know each other and when our cat Mort was run over people couldn't have been sweeter. No "it's only a cat" attitude, they understood we were heartbroken.'

Adrian took up the song. 'And although this street and the next one are a bit of a heritage enclave, no one's precious, about it. Plus, you've got the Heath, you've got great pubs and restaurants. Are we overdoing this?'

'No,' said Api, laughing. 'Can I look round now?'

'Ben will do the honours. Let me charge your glass.'

It was simple, really. Here, at last, was a house she could imagine living in. The rooms were ample and elegantly proportioned, but not vast. Adrian and Ben lived as she would want to do, comfortably and with an eye to good things but not showily. Warm dark colours made the house welcoming, but the long windows made it bright. Books, more than she had seen elsewhere, were everywhere, and from the basement kitchen/dining room a French window opened on to the garden.

'But it's big!' she exclaimed as they went out. 'I never guessed it would be this size!'

'About ninety foot long,' Ben told her, 'but we've set it out like this in different areas so that it seems larger. South-west facing, too, so you can sip your sundowners out here till nearly ten o'clock on a fine summer's evening.'

She wandered up the garden and Ben, a good salesman and a shrewd judge of character, didn't accompany her. From the sunken patio, steps led up to a section like a room, surrounded with greenery, from which an archway gave on to a sunny lawn, spiked with crocuses. At the end was an old-fashioned rose arbour with two secluded seats. High brick walls clad with climbing plants provided complete privacy.

Returning after a few minutes she said truthfully: 'I love it.'

'Well,' said Ben. 'That makes two of you. Your fiancé was quite smitten, but most importantly he thought you'd like it.'

'I do. I really do.'

'And if you're happy, he's happy.' Ben gave her his sweet smile. 'Sensible man.'

After about another half an hour she left. They offered lunch, but now she needed to be alone with her thoughts and to take a walk around the area. It was quarter past one, and had become quite warm; the red brick of Hardwicke Row positively glowed, or maybe that was what was meant by rose-tinted spectacles. She realised that she had asked very few pertinent questions, that her whole response had been governed by the atmosphere and appearance of the place, but Jonathan would have done all that. She knew that if she let him know right away how she felt about the house, it could be theirs.

She went down to the end of the street, where you could walk through to the next terrace. There was no vehicle access though, so there would be no through traffic. As she turned to go back up to the village and find something to eat she saw the name of the road: Crompton Terrace. It rang a bell, and she paused, trying to think where she'd come across it. This wasn't a part of town she was familiar with; she must have read it somewhere, in the paper perhaps? Nothing came to her.

She left a message on Jonathan's mobile.

'I love it, I really do. Can we live there? I'm sure dozens of other people must be after it, so we have to be quick! Speak this evening, yes?'

It was only when she was halfway across town to a dress fitting that she remembered where and when she'd seen the name Crompton Terrace, and when she did, she almost ran a red light.

Suzannah Rose Murchie had stayed in a house there. And her painting was on one of the bedroom walls.

She'd have skipped the dress fitting, but the dressmaker's flat in Bloomsbury was en route to her flat. And there wasn't that

long to go. After Charles's death Elizabeth had written a lovely
letter, saying that she mustn't worry for an instant about the
wedding, which could be postponed until she felt ready. But
in the end they chose to stay with the original date, as being
'what Charles would have wanted'. Api wasn't quite sure
about that. Her father, always vain, might well rather have
liked the idea of things being shifted on his account. But
there it was.

She couldn't concentrate. Though she loved the dress, it
was at the halfway stage and still had pins and lumpy edges.
The dressmaker, Mrs Kronski, had been recommended to her
by Elizabeth, who was also paying, Api didn't like to think
how much. It was one of the many things that Xanthe had
been exercised about.

'How can I possibly compete?' she'd wailed. 'I feel so
useless!'

Api had assured her that a generous Harrods voucher and
the portrait of John Ashe were more than enough, and that
anyway it wasn't a competition. In fact, the picture was the
most important thing. When her mother had asked her what
she wanted it had been all she asked for, but that hadn't gone
down a storm either.

'I can manage a little more than that!' Xanthe protested.

'Mum, we don't need anything. And as far as I'm concerned
that will be the best present of all – out of everything, I promise
you.'

Xanthe was only partly mollified. 'Anyway, you shall have
something else as well,' she said.

The dress was satin, the dark silver-grey of a black pearl,
straight, long-sleeved and high-necked with a sculpted fish-
tail train. Elizabeth had offered her the pearl and diamond
headdress she'd worn on her own wedding day, and when she
saw it she'd accepted gracefully. It was exquisite, the jewels
fashioned into a little spray of roses to hold in place her token
veil, a shimmer of silver cobweb lace that would fall down her
back like a narrow waterfall into the pool of her train.

To Mrs Kronski, it was just another job.

'Don't get any thinner, dear,' she said, from her position on the ground at Api's hem. 'I can only make adjustments up to two days before the wedding. Still,' she added, clambering heavily to her feet, 'it makes my job easier, a figure like yours.'

Back at her flat, Api found the envelope containing Creighton's notes, kicked off her shoes and curled up on the sofa, running her eye quickly over the pages to find what she wanted. Yes! There it was. 'In the summer of 1928, just over a year before her death, Suzannah Murchie spent some months at the Highgate home of the gallery owner Christopher Jarvis and his wife. The striking mural in the bedroom she occupied at 7 Crompton Terrace has been preserved . . .'

But this, she reminded herself, was written in the sixties. There was no guarantee that the mural was still there today, but if it was she would find it. And if there remained the tiniest shred of doubt about the suitability of the house in Hardwicke Row, this dispelled it utterly.

Linda knew that the quickest way to jeopardise her special place in Harry's affections would be to flout his instructions. She had never done so as his employee, and would even less as his friend. But that did not stop her ringing Aylmer House.

She asked to speak to George, who professed himself delighted to hear from her.

'We miss your visits,' he said. 'How is Al, do you know?'

'I think that question's answered mine,' she said. 'He's still with his mother, I take it.'

'I believe so. We've heard nothing.'

'I wonder,' she said, 'have you had any other enquiries about him, since he left?'

'No . . . no. It was only you that came, and much less frequently his mother. Sir Harry used to call from time to time but we haven't heard from him. We did send her home with all the relevant information about medication, prescriptions and so on. I made a follow-up call a week after he left, and she said it was going fine. We have to assume that's still the case.'

Linda took his point, but assumed no such thing.

Bryn approached the meeting with Jonathan Frankel with the gravest misgivings. Whatever his reservations about Harry, you at least knew where you were – he employed you to do your job and expected that you would do it well. He did not intervene. But Bryn had no idea how this would go, or even what it was all about. He had been summoned, that was the only word for it.

You could tell the difference just from their offices. Sir Harry's was a large opulent room with dark walls, imposing pictures and comfortable leather furniture and books – even if as Bryn suspected they were bought by the yard – which gave it the feel of the library in some grand old Oxbridge college. There was no desk as such, just a large leather-topped table with some photographs, a telephone, an inkwell and blotter the administrative hub of a man who no longer had to concern himself with administration.

His son's office was two floors lower down, and half as big again: black and white, spare, the furniture so attenuated that you felt you might cut yourself, acres of uncurtained smoked glass and a desk that was less furniture than statement – about four metres (Bryn estimated) of gleaming white moulded plastic, curved like a boomerang, with a high-backed *Mastermind* chair in black leather. The whole place screamed: 'Crap cut here.'

According to the time of day, Harry offered coffee, tea, sherry or Scotch. On the slate table in Frankel Junior's office stood a large bottle of mineral water and two tumblers. It didn't bode well. He declined the water.

'Thanks for coming in,' said Frankel. 'I wanted a word with you about the Bristol site.'

'Yes, I was down there a few weeks ago.'

'I was there yesterday. Nothing's happening.'

'They're waiting on the special stone order.'

'So I gather. That's what I wanted to discuss.'

Bryn waited. He sensed this was a situation in which the less said the better. Frankel had called the meeting, it was Frankel's beef, and he himself was not responsible for the progress of the building.

'I can't tell you how much I detest seeing a project bogged down like that. Not only because it's costing Delancey money with every second, but because it's terrible publicity. There's our board up, trumpeting the new hotel, saying how sensational it's going to be, and what do people see? A building site with no building going on. A quagmire, actually. It doesn't look good. I'm extremely unhappy about it.'

Bryn noted the 'I' – did this mean Harry was no longer part of the equation?

'I'm sorry,' he said mildly, 'but I don't really see what I can do.'

'It's the specialist materials that are causing the problem.'

'I know that, but it's an aggravation that goes with the territory when you're trying to do something different.'

'Could we not use something else?'

Bryn had foreseen something of the sort, but he still bristled. 'You could, but it would be so much better if you didn't.'

'Why? I'm positive the same effect could be achieved with a similar stone, and we'd save thousands – hundreds of thousands – by getting the place up on schedule.'

A little voice in Bryn's head told him that this was why he'd never taken on this type of project before, and why he should never have done so now.

'The hotel was always going to be expensive,' he said. 'It's something new and exciting. That's what your father was after and he was delighted with the plans.'

'He'd be far from overjoyed with the mess I saw down in Bristol,' said Jonathan icily. 'I decided to keep it from him for the time being. He's not as strong as he was, he doesn't need the worry.'

'I spoke to him after I was there last,' Bryn pointed out. 'I told him things were temporarily held up. He accepted it was part of the process.'

'What I want,' said Jonathan as though he hadn't spoken, 'is to get new materials on site, get the men on double time and finish the job. The plans were fine,' he added, 'but this is hard-think time.'

Bryn couldn't remember when he'd last felt so angry. 'The plans were a little more than fine,' he said quietly. 'They were spectacular. You're going to have something completely unique and beautiful, to rival any of the great hotels in this country. High concept and high quality mean high cost.'

'We'll keep the concept.' Frankel's choice of words made it sound like a done deal. 'But execute it differently.'

'You mean you'll compromise.'

'We'll be practical.'

'Have you talked about this to your father?'

'Sir Harry's handed this one over to me. He'll agree.'

If I stay another second, Bryn thought, *I'll punch his smug face.*

He stood up. 'I'm handing over to you, too. I don't need this. Excuse me.' At the door, knowing he was being melo-dramatic, he turned. 'And next time you're expanding, find another architect.'

'Don't worry,' said Linda when he told her that evening. 'Sod the lot of them. Who needs them? Once the wedding's out of the way we can let them all go.'

'Oh God!' he groaned. 'I'd forgotten about the bloody wedding!'

The Frankels' wedding present to their son and his new bride was the refurbishment of the house in Hardwicke Row. Api would have moved into it as it was, but in the end she and Jonathan agreed to have it redecorated in the existing rich colour scheme of crimson, cobalt and jade green, with Turkish rugs on the floor and big, comfortable furniture. Api's confidence took wing. She knew how she wanted the house to look and had the money to make it happen. She discovered the heady pleasure of buying beautiful things, the power and the sense of freedom to be derived from seeing something wonderful and saying at once: 'I'll have that.'

When Gilda saw the house she was, to use her own word, gobsmacked.

'Api, Jeez . . . ! I hope you know how lucky you are.'

'Yes, I do. I really do.'

'It's magic. I thought it might be – you know – big and posh but alien, not something I'd envy you. But this, wow! Need a live-in housekeeper?'

Api laughed. 'A team of Filipinos at the very least.'

'Joking or not joking?'

'Joking. I mean, can you see it?'

'I don't know . . .' They were sitting on the seats in the rose arbour, looking back at the house. Suddenly Gilda leaned across and pressed her hands to Api's cheeks, making her lips pout. 'Little Api! My weird little sister! Who'da thunk it? When I remember all that shit you went through.'

Api pulled her hands away. 'Gilda, no! Don't go there.'

'I'm sorry. It's just that it's like a fairy story, it really is.' Gilda's eyes narrowed. 'In every respect, I hope.'

Api ignored this, but Gilda had always been tenacious. 'Is it?'

'What?'

'Is he your prince?'

'Yes.'

'OK, don't confide in me.' Gilda rummaged in her bag. 'What do you think I'll do, stand up and expose you before your wedding guests?'

'Don't be silly. Jonathan's great.'

Gilda lit a cigarette. 'Can you hear yourself? Take it from me, those are not the words of a woman in love.'

'Get off my case, Gilda,' said Api. 'My feelings are my business.'

'And his, remember.'

Api rose. 'I'm getting cold, let's go in.'

After Gilda had gone she sat on the window seat of the big ground-floor room, with her back against the side, and her arms wrapped round her legs. The wedding was only two weeks away. There were white flowers growing around the trunks of the trees opposite, their heads nodding through the curved black railings. The house was still, and empty. A faint smell of paint lingered; the decorators had started on the top floor. The smell, and the empty walls with the ghostly marks of pictures and mirrors, reminded her of why this was all meant to be – why, no matter what the quality of her feelings for Jonathan, she belonged in this place. And it was he, after all, who'd brought her here. The disparate threads of her life were all coming together. John Ashe would hang on the wall over the stairs, there, opposite the door. And just down the road was the house where Suzannah had lived: Suzannah Rose Murchie, her double.

Not for the first time, when she left the house she walked down the slope into Crompton Terrace and stopped outside number 7. She had never seen any signs of life when she'd been before, but on this occasion the front door opened and an elderly woman came out, with a Great Dane on a lead. She smiled at Api.

'Good afternoon, isn't it gorgeous?'

'Yes – good afternoon – I wonder, could I ask you something?'

'You may,' corrected the woman in a not unpleasant schoolmistressy way.

'Do you live here, at number seven?'

'I do.'

'Please don't think me rude, only we're moving in up the road in Hardwicke Row.'

'Lucky girl.'

'And I'm interested in the artist Suzannah Rose Murchie.'

'Ah – the mural lady.'

Api's heart pounded. 'Yes. I've got a picture by her.'

'My dear, *we* have yards and yards.' The woman laughed agreeably. 'If you're genuinely interested you must come and look some time.'

'I'd absolutely love to.'

'Won't ask you in now because we've set off and it's not fair on the brute,' said the woman. 'But come any time outside office hours and I'll show you.'

'Thank you, I'll take you up on that.'

The woman held out her hand. 'Daphne Gates. I'm in the book, initial only.'

'Api Durrance – but when I move in I'll be Api Frankel.'

'Congratulations!' Daphne moved off. 'I'll see you soon.'

Api was going to Jonathan's that night. She had left the car outside her flat and it was scarcely worth making the detour to fetch it, so she went down by tube. The midsummer evenings were light and for this reason she didn't hesitate to use the underpass that ran beneath the dual carriageway by the warehouses.

She passed a woman and a couple coming out in the opposite direction, but once in the underpass she could hear only her own footsteps. The walls were a yellowish brick. A yellow brick road . . . This notion was so in keeping with her high spirits she took advantage of the solitude to do a little tap dance, the beat of her shoes picked up by the walls so that the sound was like that of not one but two people dancing. She hummed, a tune her father used to play on the fiddle, 'Phil the Fluter's Ball'.

It was as she stopped dancing and humming that she heard the guitar music – very faint, really no more than a tangle of random notes. She stood there listening, a little out of breath, and more than a little embarrassed in case the musician had picked up on her silliness. She was a few yards short of the T-junction, where the two flights of steps took you north or southward on the opposite pavement; there must be a busker

near the stairs somewhere. When she'd gone only a little further
a shadow slouched across the wall opposite – the shadow of
an animal, made huge by the wall lights that were perma-
nently on. When the dog itself appeared it was not huge, but
squat and strong. It walked slowly to the centre of the underpass and stood there staring, as if deliberately blocking her
way. Api wasn't afraid of dogs, and this one looked old; she
kept walking.

The second she reached the junction several things
happened. She recognised China, who turned and began to
follow, and she saw Dodge, leaning on the wall with his old
black coat at his feet, playing the guitar. The case lay open
on the floor. The shock of seeing him was intensified by the
suspicion that he'd known where she was – otherwise why
would he be playing here, in this deserted and unpromising
place? Had he followed her? And how long for?

Api had seen him first. For a split second she had the advantage, but was petrified, unable to move. The dog waddled
slowly past her. Equally unhurriedly, Dodge looked up. Their
eyes met. He continued to play, and to stare. She was paralysed. Had he planned this? Had every moment of every day
since her escape been leading up to this moment, and all her
efforts been for nothing? His presence seemed to have sucked
the oxygen from the atmosphere, she could scarcely breathe
for fear.

A couple of young men came clattering down the south
stairway. Api knew that she must get out, but could not bear
to turn her back on Dodge. She walked straight towards him,
banking on her judgement that she would pass him at the
same time as the men, that they would be between her and
him. Her mouth felt sticky, her heartbeat boomed in her ears.
Keep walking, she told herself. Keep – walking. Now she was
level with Dodge, and yes, thank God, the men were too, for
that instant their intervening presence afforded her protection. One of them threw a coin which landed with a chink in
the guitar case. The dog was sitting on the black coat. She

reached the steps and ran up. When she was almost at the top, she heard him say, softly but distinctly:

'Hello, Api. Where've you been all this time?'

She ran like the wind up the rest of the steps, then doubled back on herself, half panting half sobbing, ricocheting off a woman on the pavement, with no time or breath for an apology. At Jonathan's block she leaned frantically on the bell, staring over her shoulder, sure that at any moment she would see first the stunted, staring dog and then the long shadow of Dodge, slipping across the walls towards her . . .

'It's me! It's me – open up *quickly!*'

In the big, silent lift she didn't so much as glance in the mirror, for fear of what she might see. When the doors slid back on the fourth floor Jonathan was waiting in the open doorway of the apartment. She ran past him, and right across the great white, clean space to the wall of glass that over-looked the river, to where she could run no further. He closed the door and came over to her, turning her into his embrace.

'Api – what's up? What on earth's the matter?'

She couldn't speak, shook her head violently against his shoulder. He pushed her back from him a little way and tried to ease her face up to look at him. When he couldn't, his small store of patience began to run out.

'Api, for Christ's sake! Has something happened?'

She shook her head again, and found her voice. 'No . . .'

'Then would you mind telling me what all this is about? Here, come and sit down.' He led her to a chair and she slumped into it, her legs buckling under her. 'I'll get you a drink.'

He put a tumbler into her hands with a shot of whisky in the bottom, and when she grimaced said: 'I know, I know – treat it like medicine.'

She managed to swallow a couple of mouthfuls and he pulled up a chair in front of her and sat leaning forward. His irritability was curiously comforting: it helped put Dodge in his place.

He took the glass off her, put it on the floor and clasped her hands. 'Now then – what? Do I need to call the police?'

'No. I'm sorry—'

'Don't apologise, explain.'

'I got a fright, that's all.'

'That much I gathered. It must have been a helluva one, I've never seen you like this. Look at you.'

Whatever he said, his manner made her feel she should be apologising, but she resisted, knowing it would annoy him. Instead she took a deep breath. The truth but not the whole truth would have to do.

'I thought I saw someone I used to know when I first came to London, that I used to be terrified of. He was – it's hard to explain – weird. He used to push me around.'

'He hurt you? Because believe me it's easy enough to make him wish he'd never been born.'

'No, no he didn't actually hurt me, or anyone as far as I know. He was just scary.'

'And it was definitely him you saw?'

She knew that she couldn't allow Jonathan to intervene, that to do so would be to let Dodge over the threshold. She said: 'I don't know. I thought it was, but perhaps not. But it brought it all back.'

'All what?' He frowned. He didn't understand, and how could he?

She summoned a weak smile. 'Oh . . . What it was like to be young and poor in London – away from home for the first time. I'd run away, for goodness' sake, I was the original mixed-up kid, and I came into contact with this, this crazy man. It was a strange time all round.'

'OK. I get it – I think. But Api, for God's sake tell me if there's something that's bothering you that I can do something about, yes?'

She nodded, suddenly exhausted. 'I will.'

'Good.' He got up. 'Take that coat off and let's start all over again.'

She shrugged out of the coat and he took it. 'There is something you can do,' she said.

'Tell me.'

'Don't talk about it any more. Please.'

He frowned. 'Very well.'

He was put out, she could tell – by the inconclusiveness of it all, by his inability to help – and went to fetch himself a drink. When he returned, he asked: 'So how did your sister like the house?'

'She wants to be our live-in housekeeper.'

For a moment Jonathan looked genuinely alarmed. 'Pass.'

'No, she loved it.' Api pressed on, telling him how the decorators were doing, when the curtains would be ready, that she had ordered the change-of-address cards – putting distance between herself and the events of half an hour ago. Escaping Dodge.

That night she lay awake, tense and spooked, until the small hours, and then slept only fitfully. During the night, she slipped out of bed several times to look out of the window, sure that every shadow was moving. Once she was positive she saw the dog, standing stock-still on the pavement. For several minutes, until her eyes began to hurt, she stared down, but then decided it must be some inanimate object, a cardboard carton blown by the wind, and went back to bed. Next time she looked, the object had gone but there was no comfort in its disappearance. It must have been China.

The next morning she accepted a lift with Jonathan into the centre of town. He offered to bring the car round from the off-road parking at the side of the building and pick her up at the door, but she said she'd come with him. She did not want to be alone in the street for even a second.

Outside the Delancey building, he asked: 'Will this do? I could get the driver to take you wherever you want.'

She shook her head. 'No, I'll be fine.'

They kissed, and she held his neck tight, reminding herself that he would do anything she asked.

'Sure?' he asked.

She wasn't, so she kissed him instead.

She wasn't due to meet the florist at the church in Belgravia until eleven, but it was a beautiful morning so she set off to walk there. The wedding, by mutual consent, acknowledged the Frankel spending power and was mainly a Frankel affair, but the flowers and the music were the province of the Durrances. No one in the family had inherited Charles's musical gifts, but Xanthe in particular possessed a good knowledge and appreciation of music, and had shown a surprising enthusiasm for the project.

'Your father won't be there to give you away,' she said (Api was to be accompanied up the aisle by Martin), 'but he can be there in the music.' It was almost, Api thought, as though her mother loved her father more now that he was gone. She wasn't shocked by this. When her mother had wailed: 'Who will understand me now?' she could have answered: 'Me. I will.' Charles's legacy was an intangible one: a process of forgiveness was beginning.

Xanthe had come up to London to see the church and help choose the flowers. It was the same day she'd met the Frankels. She'd been tight-lipped and jumpy when Api met her at the station but in the cab after lunch she'd visibly relaxed.

'They're very nice.'

'I told you, Mum. What did you expect?'

'I don't know – brash cash, I suppose. To be patronised – no, to *feel* patronised, which I realise isn't the same thing. But anyway, I didn't.'

The flowers were to be white, blue and lilac with lots of grey-blue and purplish foliage to echo Api's dress. She'd agreed to carry a single white rose, for something to do with her hands; she didn't want a bouquet.

She arrived at the church, in its snug little square, at half past ten. The organist was there, practising, and she sat down in a pew at the back, not exactly listening but letting the music flow over and through her. She had no particular feeling, social, spiritual or cultural, towards churches. They had not figured in the Durrances' life and she did not even know what her parents' religious affiliation was, if they had any. She knew that Jonathan's father was Jewish, but in marriage had chosen Elizabeth, a true daughter of his adopted country. Jonathan had seen a church wedding as a foregone conclusion, for practical, social reasons because it would suit more of the people invited, but a rabbi would be present to say the traditional Jewish wedding blessings, the Sheva B'rachot, at the end of the wedding ceremony There would be two hundred and fifty guests at St Bede's and afterwards at the sumptuous Mayfair mansion hired by Harry for the reception. She knew the Frankels felt they were keeping it small, for her sake, but to her it seemed a fantastic number of people, at least half of whom she wouldn't know.

There had been a church on this site – she knew because the vicar had told them on their first visit – since the fifteenth century, but the present one was largely Victorian, full of elaborate and sentimental decoration. The windows were beautiful though, shedding their long, rainbow beams on the nave. The music stopped, and a minute later the organist appeared, carrying a briefcase, a sweatshirt round his shoulders. He nodded and smiled, and then she heard the clunk of the door closing behind him. She understood the meaning of sanctuary: this was a safe place.

The silence seemed to settle round her, seeping back like water to fill the space left by the organ music. She had felt a little awkward about using this church, with which neither of them had even a geographical connection, but Jonathan had no such scruples: 'They should be glad of the custom,' was his view. Fortunately the vicar turned out to be a smooth, charming man, perfectly suited to one of the smallest and richest parishes in the country. It was hard to believe that many of the local inhabitants were fervent worshippers, but the building testified to their generosity, and to the fees from numerous society weddings.

Because she'd been thinking about him at that very moment, she jumped when she heard the vicar's voice.

'Good morning. Having a recce?'

He was standing in the aisle, resting a hand on the back of her pew: film-star handsome, a man burnished by faith, and a certain justifiable self-satisfaction. Api explained that she was meeting the florist.

'Excellent, make yourselves at home. You're using Mariette, aren't you? Wise choice, she's absolutely first-rate.'

He was an old hand at weddings. To her consternation he sat down next to her at the end of the pew.

'How is Jonathan?'

'He's fine.'

He looked at her intently. 'And you? This can be a stressful time for a bride.'

'It is busy, yes.'

There was a short pause, during which she could still feel him looking at her. She was uncomfortable and would have liked to get up, but could think of no good reason to do so and didn't want to appear rude.

'Forgive me for asking,' he said gently, 'but if there's anything at all you want to talk about, or to tell me, you know you can. It's what I'm here for. To soak up the worries and help address the doubts – if there are any.'

'There aren't.' She sounded snappy, she couldn't help it.

'Splendid,' he said. But he didn't move, and a second later he said: 'Since we both seem to have a moment, perhaps I might say a prayer.'

She was trapped. He closed his eyes, his hands linked loosely between his knees. Hot with embarrassment, she did the same.

'Dear Father in heaven, we ask Your blessing on Apollonia and Jonathan, soon to be married in this place. May they have pleasure in each other and peace in Your love. And we ask You to help us find the calm that comes through knowing You, and the joy of knowing we are Yours. For Jesus Christ's sake, Amen.'

Api muttered 'Amen', unaccountably close to tears. The vicar turned to her, and held out his hand.

'Well, I'll leave you to it.'

'I'm not a Christian, you know,' she blurted out.

'That doesn't matter.' He shook her hand. 'You may not believe in Him, but He believes in you. Have fun with Mariette. I'll see you at the rehearsal if not before.'

As he walked away, Api was trembling.

Bill Makepeace collected the electronic organiser he'd left in the vestry, and went out via the south aisle. The girl was still there: the young bride dressed in black. The sun was streaming through the windows this morning, but its beams didn't fall on her. She sat in a shadow of her own making.

Api spoke to Derek and arranged for the portrait to be delivered on the same day as some other items – two sofas, and the dining table and chairs – were arriving at the house. The decorators had almost finished, but she still made sure that the deliveries would come in the late afternoon, so that they'd be gone when the picture arrived. Jonathan had never seen it, but had been quite happy for it to hang in the position she'd chosen, on the stairs, facing the front door, and the reinforced hooks were in position.

That afternoon, the fine spell broke. Thick clouds turned the day dark at three o'clock, and a scudding wind strafed the streets outside and hurled rain against the windows of Hardwicke House. For the first time Api was aware of draughts. Scurries of cold air slipped around her ankles, and an ill-fitting window on the top landing shuddered as the wind caught it.

When the picture arrived she persuaded the delivery man, by means of tea and a tenner, to hang it in its appointed place. Again there was the unveiling, the removal of the blanket in which it had travelled. Sipping his tea when the job was done, the man took a semi-proprietary interest in his handiwork.

'Blimey. Relative of yours?'

'My great-grandfather.'

'They liked their frames big in those days, didn't they?'

'He was a very rich man.'

'Yeah?' said the man. 'He doesn't look very happy with it. Still, they say the best things are life are free, don't they?'

When he'd left, she closed the door behind him and stood looking up at John Ashe. He hung on the turn of the stairs, and on the first landing there was a window. The angle of the sullen, rainy light from above made it look as though the dark side of the picture were cast into shadow naturally. Ashe might almost have been standing there in person. She remembered the dreams she'd had before she'd escaped from Dodge, the way John Ashe had seemed to be coming down from the attic to seek her out. There was no need for that now. He was here, where he belonged, with her.

She switched on the lights and went down to the kitchen to make a cup of tea. The landlines were in now, and she sat at the table with the directory and looked up a number.

'Daphne Gates?'

'Speaking.'

'Daphne, it's Apollonia Durrance here, we met the other day – I'm moving in up the road in Hardwicke Row?'

'Yes, hello! Do you want to pop down and look at my wall?'

'May I?'

'Do, I've just got back from work and it will give me a lovely excuse to have a second cuppa and put off walking the dog in this atrocious weather.'

'I'll be there in five minutes.'

It was more like three when she presented herself at the door. Daphne Gates opened it accompanied by the Great Dane whose enormous head was on a level with Api's elbow.

'Be ye not afraid, he hasn't the least smattering of aggression. Out of the way, Seth. Come in, pot's still full.'

She led the way to the kitchen at the back. Seth followed, tail wagging, and flopped down on a rug near the stove. The house was smaller than those in Hardwicke Row, narrower and with no basement floor. The garden, visible through the kitchen window, showed a small area of mown lawn – the rest was overgrown.

Out of politeness, Api accepted the cup of tea that Daphne pressed on her, and tried to conceal her impatience. She answered questions about herself, Jonathan, the wedding and the move, and learned that Daphne was a school secretary and long divorced, before asking:

'So who did you buy this house from?'

'Ah. Now. Believe it or not, I was born here.'

'That's amazing. How many people can say that?'

'Obviously I haven't lived here always. My mother was left it by her godfather, a man called Christopher Jarvis, who lived here in the twenties and thirties. He was married but I don't think that women – other than my mother – played a large part in his life. She and my father were here almost twenty years until dad died, and she continued for some years after that. I was an only child and lo! this delightful house was mine. Before that I had an extremely modest flat in Belsize Park. It's a bit daft, really, moving from a small flat to a house and garden at my time of life, but I was called back, d'you know? And it stops me sitting about.'

Hard though it was to imagine Daphne sitting about, that wasn't what caught Api's attention.

'So if your mother was Christopher Jarvis's goddaughter she must have come here sometimes.'

'Oh, frequently, I believe. She was a very pretty girl and this was quite an artistic enclave round about that time. There are two or three blue plaques in this little complex of streets. None for *our* lady of course, she was a bird of passage.'

'Your mother might even have met her, too?'

Daphne raised a finger. 'I think so, and I'll show you why. Come along with me.'

At last. They left the tea and Api followed up the two flights of stairs to the top floor. The house was homely but shabby: loved, but not cosseted.

'This is the one,' said Daphne, opening the door on the right of the landing. 'Go on in, and prepare to be amazed.'

Api entered, and gasped – the room was full of people! At least that was her first impression. The single bed stood against the side wall opposite the window, and the remaining few pieces of furniture, a chair, a small chest of drawers and a narrow wardrobe, were on either side of the door. This left the wall opposite clear, and it was completely covered by Suzannah Murchie's mural.

There must have been upwards of fifty people in it, of both sexes and all ages. Though they were of necessity close together, forming a throng, it was clear that each figure was an individual portrait. A few seemed to be painted as couples, but most were individuals, not relating to the others around them. The effect was overwhelming.

'Good fun, isn't it?' said Daphne. She switched on the light. 'There are forty-seven souls altogether, I've counted. I believe some of them were notables in the artistic world of their day, who came to visit, some were friends and relations of Christopher Jarvis, and others were people Suzannah knew, that she did from memory. No one I recognise I'm ashamed to say, *except* . . .' She stepped forward and tapped the wall. 'This one – Suzannah's self-portrait. Not unlike you, actually. And this one – my mama!'

Api moved closer. You could see now that the painting was swiftly done and impressionistic. The second figure that Daphne had pointed out was a girl who might have been anything from early teens to mid-twenties, with reddish-brown bobbed hair and a smiling, open face, like an illustration from an old-fashioned school story.

'Isn't she jolly?' said Daphne. 'I think she'd have been about nineteen.'

'What was her name?'

'Georgina. Georgina Fullerton in those days, before she was married. Look,' she added, 'I know it backwards, but you'll want to take your time. I'm going to leave you to gaze, and go and get on with things downstairs. Be as long as you like, turn the light out when you leave.'

She withdrew and her footsteps faded away down the stairs. Api heard her voice, two floors below, talking to the dog in the kitchen. Up here it was very quiet but for the rain and yet – it was as if each of those faces, all so different, gave off a signal, a sort of ultrasonic beep that demanded attention. She moved to the left-hand side and began to work her way across. They were young and old, smiling and solemn, some caught in action, like a snapshot, some posed and still.

She paused at the self-portrait. Suzannah showed herself in a blue dress with a large pale collar. No hat, this time; her hair was loose, and her face calm and expressionless. She was the still centre of the painting, gazing out from her crowd of subjects without comment. Letting them speak for themselves.

Api had reached the right-hand side of the wall when she saw him, and felt the familiar thump of recognition. Dark-haired and dark-suited, his left profile towards the artist, his back turned on everyone else.

John Ashe.

16

2001 – Bryn, Api

Judith had been persuaded by her partner, Ruth, that they should attend the wedding. She herself had never been to London, was nervous of going now, and had little or no interest in the occasion itself.

'Api doesn't care if I'm there or not,' she complained. 'She won't even notice.'

'Of course she will,' said Ruth. 'It'll be a big wedding with lots of people she doesn't know very well, and it will be a real support to her to have her whole family there. We must go, Jude. You might even enjoy it.'

Judith shook her head. 'I shan't. I won't know how to talk to anyone. What if they don't sit us together?'

'I'll ask them to. Anyway, they *will*. Nobody splits up couples at weddings.'

The result was, they were going. They'd been shopping, and found a smart dove-grey dress and jacket for Judith and a cherry-red trouser suit for Ruth. Neither of them were hat-people but Ruth had also bought herself a wicked black gros-grain handbag and matching shoes with a little bow on the toe. It was clear to Judith that whatever her own misgivings, her partner had none, and was in fact raring to go. This made her rather grumpy.

'Why don't you go on your own?'

'What?' Ruth's expression was incredulous. 'Now that would be silly. You're the sister of the bride, I'm just tagging along on your coat-tails.'

'You're much better at all this than I am.'

'It's not a competition, Jude. You'll be there to be yourself.'

Judith remained unmollified. About a week before the wedding, Saul rang up.

'I can't say I relish the prospect, I shall be a complete fish out of water . . . But I thought if you guys were going, maybe I could bum a lift.'

'Hang on,' said Judith, 'I'll pass you over.'

'You're joking!' exclaimed Ruth. 'I'm not driving into central London. Train from Ipswich and then we might indulge in a taxi from Liverpool Street.'

'Could I join you then? On a safety-in-numbers basis.'

'Why not? I intend to enjoy myself,' she added pointedly.

'Is Judith not exactly brimming over with enthusiasm either then?'

'You could say that.'

'Let me have a word with her.'

Ruth held out the receiver. 'Back to you.'

'What?' barked Judith ungraciously.

'It's a wedding, we must go in the right spirit.'

'There's no point in pretending – Ruth's making me go.'

'And quite right too. Come on, it'll be a poor show if the family can't turn up and look cheerful for Api's sake. It's only for one day. What's Mum doing?'

'Staying with her boyfriend.' Judith squeezed every last morsel of disparagement from the word, and the following three: 'At a hotel.'

'Good,' said Saul. 'Well, see you under the departures board.'

In addressing the 'and partner' element on his wedding invitation, Martin Durrance had found himself spoilt for choice. In the end, weddings being what they were and because he had a principal role at this one, he decided to go on his own. His heart was still very much his property, and a partner, no matter how glamorous, would cramp his style at what he was prepared to bet would be an occasion overflowing with trust-fund totty. He would have a more amusing time unaccompanied.

Also, in his role as Api's sponsor he was to attend the rehearsal this afternoon, and was being put up at the Delancey Metropole on the nights before and after the wedding, along with their mother and her new bloke. Any of the two or three young ladies he could have taken might not have responded well to what he considered to be the peculiarities of his family. At least Judith and her girlfriend wouldn't be at the hotel, nor Saul as he understood it; they were doing their cheap-day-return thing, which was entirely typical. Gilda was a free agent. He hoped that if she brought someone along, whoever it was would be halfway respectable. Though the alternative might turn out to be amusing.

Martin was wedded to his wheels. His heart lifted as he finally broke free of the M6 contraflow and put his foot down. To his surprise, he felt a sudden and unexpected pang for his father. He'd have loved the show-off aspect of all this, and been good at it, too – the only member of the Durrance family (apart, Martin allowed in all modesty, from himself) who would have more than kept his end up. Still, it had fallen to him to act in Charles's place and he intended to fulfil the role in style.

He still found it astonishing – well-nigh incredible – that Api was marrying this amount of money. Not just comfortable, two-car, second-home, Home-Counties prosperity but serious bucks. An empire, for fuck's sake! He would almost have been less surprised if Gilda had done it, she'd always been a bit of a buccaneer, and had the looks. Instead of which she was still underachieving for Britain – shacking up with a series of sub-Glastonbury no-hopers while she airbrushed models in a studio and waited for the big break in the skies.

Martin lit a cigarette one-handed as he waited for a lane-hog to get out of the way. But Api, fuck a duck, what a turn-up! He didn't believe for one moment that she was in love with this bloke, but he didn't hold that against her. He suspected love was overrated, certainly as a basis for marriage.

What he couldn't get his head round was why Jonathan Frankel wanted to marry Api. Now that *had* to be love – no common-sense reason could possibly account for it. When Martin had gone down to London to meet Api and discuss arrangements he'd been introduced to Frankel, and rather liked him. He was of a type Martin dealt with quite a lot in his work – smart, driven, workaholic, a bit humourless, warmed up with a drink inside him – except that in Frankel's case he barely needed to work at all as he understood it, just sit back, bark a few orders and watch the coffers fill.

Even allowing for Api's new and foxier persona, cool, chic and black-clothed, there was no accounting for it. And anyway who was to say which was cause and which effect? At which point had this guy, absolutely loaded, well trav-elled, worldly, presumably experienced with women, fallen head over heels for funny little Api Durrance from nowhere? He seemed bewitched by her. Mind you, Martin mused as he tossed his cigarette-end out of the window, there had always been something a tad witchy about his sister. Even when she was young, when she was the one who was no trouble, who kept her head down and herself to herself, she'd had the air of a child who knew things no one else could know. Secretive, but not about secrets the rest of them would understand.

Not that they'd exactly been a family who clustered round the table of an evening sharing their experiences of the day. He for one had hardly spoken between the ages of seven and seventeen; it had been his only – and enormously successful – bid for attention. All he'd wanted to do was stay at home and commune with his computer, and his silence had achieved that end. His mother had left him to get on with it, his father had wandered in and out from time to time, expressing his bafflement and admiration, and at eighteen he'd got a lowly job with a computer software company. It had gone on from there. He had never really had a relationship with any of his family (though he might have done, he realised now, with his father). There had been a period of a few months, long after he'd left, when Api had been in some sort of bother in London, fallen in with the wrong crowd etcetera, all quickly sorted out. For years he'd felt, with a mixture of wistfulness and pride, that he'd left them all behind. Until now. When Api, with a single bound and with no effort on her part as far as he could see, was about to become absolutely filthy rich and have a surname that was a household word. Martin wasn't jealous, he was fiercely proud of his self-made status and the distance he'd put between himself and the inadequacies of his upbringing, but he was curious.

Perhaps, he thought, swinging at speed into a service station to fill up, all would be made clear over this weekend. He was looking forward to it.

Like her brother, Gilda suspected Api of not being in love; but, unlike him, she disapproved. Whatever else Gilda was, she was no cynic. She herself was petrified by the mere idea of marriage, and considered that the only possible reason for entering into such an arrangement was 'true' love, whatever that might be. She had experienced the false kind many times, the fool's gold that got you all excited and turned out to be worthless. But she was sure the real thing was out there, in the same way that she was pleased other people believed in God on her behalf.

And another thing: she had not rescued her little sister from that disgusting creep for this. She did not mind that neither Api nor her parents had ever really thanked her for that, it wasn't the Durrance way – but she *did* mind that Api was kidding herself she cared enough about this walking wallet to spend the rest of her life with him. Or worse still that she wasn't even kidding herself, that she was just a shameless, heartless little gold-digger. This Gilda refused to believe.

She was profoundly uncomfortable about going to the

wedding. The invitation specified 'and partner', but there was no persuading Mac.

'You're joking! No chance, no way – oh no!'

'Come on, for my sake.'

'No emotional blackmail, either.'

'It's not. But it's not my bag either and I could do with the moral support.'

Mac wagged a finger. 'It may not be your bag, pet, but it is your sister. You have to show up. But I don't.'

'Please?'

'Tell you what, I'll be right here waiting for you when you come back.'

'Thanks a bunch!'

'My pleasure.'

As Gilda scoured her wardrobe for something to wear, she told herself that everyone seemed to have forgotten Charles. It was only a matter of a few months since he'd died, but they'd all moved on and left him behind as though his death were of no account, just something unfortunate that had happened on the way to this damn wedding. Remembering Xanthe's cry of 'What am I going to do? Who will understand me now?' she'd rung her mother to try and express this feeling. It hadn't been quite the consoling exchange she'd hoped for.

'Do you ever think of Dad?' she'd asked, and realised too late that she might have sounded accusing.

'Of course I do!' Xanthe had replied in a tone both aggrieved and snappish.

'Me too. I wonder if he knew we were all there when he— at the hospital.'

'The doctor said it made a difference, you heard him.'

'Yes, but that was if someone regained consciousness. I hadn't seen Dad for six months when he had the stroke.'

Regaining her equilibrium after a jerky start, Xanthe said soothingly: 'I'm sure he knew.'

'Can I ask you something?'

'It depends.'

'What did you mean when you said, "Who will understand me now?"'

There was a tiny pause. 'I don't remember saying that.'

'Come on, Mum, you must do – just afterwards.'

'I was distraught. So were you, by the way.'

She made it sound like some macabre competition. 'I know,' said Gilda, 'I remember. And I remember you asking who was going to understand you.'

'Well – Charles and I had been together a long time, since we were very young, and I suppose . . .'

'Yes?'

'I suppose I just meant that we all change. We're not the same people at fifty that we were at twenty-five, so . . .'

'But you did love him?' asked Gilda. 'You do miss him, don't you?'

'Gilda!' Xanthe's voice rose dangerously. 'We were divorced. Irretrievable breakdown, irreconcilable differences—'

'Oh bugger that! Did you *ever* love him?'

'Yes, I—'

'And do you miss him?'

'We weren't—'

'Forget it,' said Gilda. 'See you in church.'

She wasn't proud of her handling of this conversation. Xanthe's *cri de coeur* in the hospital had been perfectly natural, as was her justifiable reluctance to analyse it now. Gilda had simply wanted some recognition for her father: the source of this desire was her own guilt at not having kept in touch. But then, she reminded herself, when had Charles ever been a proper meat-and-potatoes father to them? Whatever unspoken arrangement he and Xanthe had between them, they should have seen to it that their children weren't short-changed. She and the rest of her brothers and sisters had all learned emotional laziness and indifference at their parents' knee. But what a shame! she thought now. What a terrible, crying shame! And what a legacy – it was probably the reason that Api was about to walk down the aisle with a man she didn't love, and the reason she herself so passionately wanted her not to.

As far as Saul was concerned Api's marriage (if not the stuffed-shirt wedding) was a Good Thing. In his case marriage to the lady horse-dealer had never been on the cards, but he had been very comfortable and content living at her place until she got engaged to a National Hunt jockey and asked him politely to leave. He had acceded equally politely, only grateful that it had lasted so long. Saul was not a harbourer of grudges, nor did he have any moral qualms about financial one-sidedness: not everyone could be rich, and some rich people liked the power that generosity gave them.

In truth he scarcely knew Api, so he took her decision at face value. This is what she said she wanted to do; that was good enough for him. He hadn't met the bloke, but that was neither here nor there – he wasn't the one marrying him.

As regards his other siblings' partners he was equally relaxed. It was good that Judith had found someone and he quite liked Ruth, whose bossy competence reminded him of the horse-dealer. He didn't envy Martin his portfolio of showy, high-maintenance blondes, but fair play to him. And Gilda, to whom he'd always felt closest, had been round the block a few times as well, though he'd never been able to work out if she was serial dumper or dumpee.

He'd been astonished when their parents had announced they were separating. Well, 'announced' was too strong a word, it was more that the news filtered out. He'd always thought they were thoroughly sorted. Admittedly they didn't spend much time together but plenty of people claimed that was the secret of a happy marriage. When they were together they always seemed to get on well in an opposites-agreeing kind of way. There had never been any rows, or atmospheres that he could recall. Home life had ambled along contentedly enough. If asked, Saul would have said he'd had a pretty happy childhood.

Still, it did make you realise that stuff could be going on unnoticed, like an underground stream that no one was aware of till it broke the surface. His face-value policy was OK but it didn't prepare you for surprises.

Xanthe was sufficiently unsettled by the conversation with Gilda that she allowed it to spill over into her next meeting with Derek. She had never discussed Charles, and certainly never made him out to be the villain of the piece, but neither had she striven officiously to dispel the idea. Derek saw her as a strong woman, wronged but spirited, a mantle she'd been all too happy to assume.

But first Charles's death, now Gilda, had reminded her that it wasn't quite like that. When Derek came out the following weekend, she found herself saying as they sat on the beach in the sunshine:

'I've been thinking quite a lot about Charles recently.'

'You would do,' he replied gently, 'with the wedding coming up and so on. You must miss him.'

Xanthe felt a lump in her throat that for a moment prevented her from speaking. He sensed this and put his hand over hers.

'It's quite all right,' he said. 'Don't upset yourself.'

She swallowed hard. 'The thing is . . . we went back such a long way.'

'Of course. And you had your wonderful family together.'

'You're much too good to me.'

'Nothing's ever too good.' He tried to look into her face, but her head was averted. 'Do talk about it if you'd like to. Not if you don't.'

She shook her head. 'I would in a way. But I don't know what it is I want to say.'

'It doesn't matter. I'm here when you do.'

She heaved a shaky sigh. 'He wasn't a bad person. Charles. He really wasn't.'

'I'm sure.'

'He was good, in lots of ways. Kind, charming, talented – a wonderful musician. If he played away a lot – I mean – in both senses – that was because – because—'

He squeezed her hand. 'Spit it out.'

'Because I let him. You could almost say I encouraged him. I didn't want the same things. He liked to be off on tour with the orchestra, he was a party animal. I wanted to be at home with the children.'

'A thoroughly honourable position if you don't mind my saying so.'

Xanthe could feel herself being sucked back, losing ground in the face of his sturdy sympathy. She braced herself for unaccustomed honesty. 'Yes, but he may have felt – pushed out.'

Derek took her shoulders and turned her, firmly, to face him. 'Look. You did not push him out. You may not have called him back, but that's not the same thing. And anyway –' he raised his voice slightly to quell her protest – 'and *anyway*, you have absolutely nothing to reproach yourself with. Your children testify to that.'

'They're Charles's children, too,' she said.

'As you say, he wasn't a bad person.'

Xanthe felt her face getting out of control, melting, distorting, oozing tears. 'I did love him, you know . . . In the beginning.'

'I know that.'

'And I do miss him. Sort of, you know, knowing he's there – oh Derek, I don't deserve you, I am such a silly cow!' She collapsed on his shoulder, sobbing. All the artifice and careful reconstruction of the past months were washed away, along with her pride. She felt his arms go round her, his hands rubbing her back.

'Ssh, ssh, come on, you are no such thing, and I absolutely adore you and deserving doesn't come into it.'

After a moment she lifted her head and he said: 'I'm afraid I don't have the time-honoured large clean hankie about my person.'

She sniffed and smiled, still crying a little. 'It's OK, I've got a tissue . . .'

'But I do love you, Xanthe. And I'd like to marry you.'

It was just as well she had the tissue, because now she burst into tears all over again.

Three nights before the wedding, Jonathan had had dinner with his father. In keeping with the man-to-man nature of the occasion they dined in the private suite next to Harry's office, the meal catered by the in-house chef: smoked salmon and quail's eggs, fillet of beef, lemon tart; standard dishes, plainly and perfectly prepared. Harry toyed with his, but waved his hand to encourage his son.

'Eat, eat . . .'

'It's all very good.'

Harry grunted. 'Can she cook?'

'The basics.'

'As long as she learns. Food is much more important than sex, you know.'

'It is?'

'In keeping a marriage together.'

Jonathan was used to these unregenerate pronouncements of his father's, intended to provoke as much as advise.

'In that case we'll make sure to hire a good cook.'

With a visible effort, Harry topped up their glasses. 'Tell me about her.'

'The cook?'

'Your Api.'

'She isn't mine, for a start. She's her own woman.'

'She still works in the restaurant?'

'No, but she'll do whatever she wants to do, I'm quite sure of that. Dad, before you ask anything else, may I say something?'

'I was hoping you would.'

'I know you and Mother don't really like Api.'

'Did we ever say that? Did we ever do anything to make

you think that? It has nothing to do with us. If you're happy, we're happy. Simple.'

Jonathan, pushing his pudding plate aside, persisted. 'If it was we wouldn't be having this conversation. I realise Api's different – I didn't expect this to happen either. She came out of left field and surprised me. But I do know she's the woman for me. We can be a good team.'

Harry brushed at an invisible speck on his lapel. 'Are you mad about her?'

'Come on, Dad. You'd be the first to say madness is no basis for marriage.'

'Go on then. Surprise me, now.'

'She's strong. She has no pretensions. And she has reserves. We have a lot to learn about each other.'

Harry made a little clucking sound as he clipped a cigar. 'Ah . . . You think you can make her fit the mould.'

'I wouldn't be so stupid.' Jonathan tried unsuccessfully to keep the exasperation out of his voice. 'But I tell you something – she wants to be *my wife*, more than anything. It means something to her.'

'Money?' murmured Harry, as he drew on the cigar.

'Escape,' said Jonathan. 'She's escaping.'

'Having met the mother, this I can accept . . . And escape, unlike madness, is a good basis for marriage?'

'Not on its own, no. But with goodwill on both sides—'

'Listen to yourself – goodwill!'

'More than that, of course. Much more.'

Harry laid his unused spoon and fork side by side at a distance of two inches. 'But you are on parallel tracks.'

'If you like. Never clashing.'

'Never touching.'

'Oh – we touch.'

'That's not what I meant,' said Harry, affecting prudishness when it suited him. 'I was talking of something else.'

Jonathan sat back. 'All right, your turn. Tell me about you and Mother. The secret of your success.'

There was a long pause. The smoke from his father's cigar curled and wandered in the air between them like all their unspoken thoughts.

'That secret,' he said at last, 'is a secret.'

If Jonathan had hoped to put his father on the back foot he knew he had not succeeded. He did not resent Harry's inter-rogation – the habit of respect, of deference to age and expe-rience, was too deeply ingrained – but this was something he could not expect him to understand. Whatever Harry said, his strong partnership with Elizabeth had nothing to do with romantic madness and everything to do with a powerful and pragmatic mutual regard. Love and loyalty had naturally followed. Success had bred success.

If Jonathan was honest with himself he knew that his initial pursuit of Api had been little more than a reflexive response to rejection: the capricious desire to have what was being with-held. But that had changed with time. This, he had come to realise, was not the usual member of the treat-'em-mean brigade, playing by the rules, stringing him along for the sake of it. When he had described her to Harry as 'her own woman' he had meant something much stranger and more alluring than mere independence, financial or otherwise. She seemed to inhabit her own emotional and psychological microclimate from which, though he himself might be for ever excluded, she surveyed the world in a different way. Jonathan was the first to recognise that he was not naturally intuitive but he knew instinctively that to have Api at his side would be to have gained something not given easily. A prize.

Even he could not fathom her reasons for agreeing to marry him, and he didn't try. He did not wish to understand his future wife, but to harness her mystery. And in doing so to step out from Harry's shadow.

Now that John Ashe was there, Api felt the house was truly hers. It didn't matter what other turns it took, how many strangers passed through its doors, or what her responsibilities would be, none of these things troubled her now that he stood on the stairs, looking down at her comings and goings, presiding over her life. His presence filled the house and gave her confidence. His shadows didn't frighten her – she had shadows too.

She was enchanted, too, by the presence of Suzannah, only a few yards away. Suzannah who looked so much like her, and who had also been under his spell. They were going away for three weeks after the wedding, and would move straight into the house in Hardwicke Row, so she was back and forth most days, letting in workmen, taking delivery of orders – and visiting Daphne.

When she told her about John Ashe, Daphne smacked her hands together with satisfaction.

'The grumpy chap, bottom right! I've often wondered who he was. He doesn't look in the least pleased to be there.'

'Well, he sat for her at some point, I've got the portrait to prove it.'

'Your great-grandfather, you say?'

'On my mother's side.'

'But your mother never met the artist? Too young, I suppose.'

'She certainly never said. No, I'm sure she didn't. I think she knows even less about her and Ashe than I do.'

'Because you're *fascinated*,' said Daphne.

'Yes,' said Api, 'I am.'

The afternoon before the wedding, they had a rehearsal for the principals at St Bede's. Present, besides Bill Makepeace, the rabbi and the organist, were Api and Jonathan, Xanthe, Harry and Elizabeth, Martin, Andy the best man, and a couple of ushers. Saul was to be an usher as well, but as there was never the slightest chance of him coming up before the day he would have to be briefed at the time.

The weather was unseasonably vile. With no heating on at this time of year, the church felt chilly. Rain spattered on the windows, and they needed the lights on. The organist sat wearing his mac. Their voices echoed. In the background Mariette and her team were in and out with stands and boxes, bringing a rush of cold damp air through the west door. Api found it hard to imagine how different everything would be next day. Their small group was lost in this vast, cheerless space. The young rabbi looked tense and nervous – Api couldn't blame him.

Only the vicar was cheerful, veteran of countless weddings and familiar with the collective mood swings contingent upon them.

'Why don't we warm up with a verse or two?' he suggested. 'Clive, run us into "Praise My Soul", could you?'

Api would have shrieked 'No! We can't, there aren't enough of us!' but the organist was off, and right on cue Bill Makepeace was off too, hitting the first note true and loud in a confident baritone. His assurance infected them, and they joined in, sheepishly at first but by the second 'Praise him! Praise him!' they were singing heartily and smiling, amused at themselves for having managed it.

'Excellent!' said Makepeace. 'Imagine what that's going to be like with the church full of people. We'll raise the roof.'

Non-churchgoers to a man, they marked out the service. As Api and Martin waited at the bottom of the aisle for their cue, he said: 'How many did you say were coming?'

'About two hundred and fifty.'

'Nervous?'

'No.'

'You will be.'

'Speak for yourself.'

'These days I do. Remember—'

'Bride and brother!' called Makepeace. 'Off you set!'

'Yes,' whispered Api as they moved forward.

'I was foxing!'

'I know.'

★

When she arrived at his side, Jonathan lifted her hand and kissed it without meeting her eyes. He'd had a haircut which made him look younger, but he also looked tired and pre-occupied: a stranger, suddenly, that she was going to marry. She didn't mind that, so long as no one saw it but her. She smiled and kept hold of his hand for an extra second or two. When she released it, it seemed to drift away from her.

They went through the traditional words of the marriage service, which neither of them had wished to change; or perhaps they had shied away from the complex intimacy of those decisions. Each of them stumbled once or twice. The vicar reminded them that a poor dress rehearsal was provi-dential and provoked a little rustle of sympathetic laughter.

'And now,' he announced, 'the Jane Eyre bit. The chance for a man with a grudge.'

Xanthe was the only one to pick up on this. 'Has it ever happened at one of your weddings?' she asked. 'Someone bursting in with an objection?'

'Never,' said Makepeace, giving her his winsome smile. 'But there's always a first time.'

He read through the sequence rapidly, with no other purpose than to acquaint them with it. But on 'they are to declare it, or forever hold their peace' the church went dark, swiftly and silently as though it had been covered with a giant hand. There was a split second of shock, and then Makepeace said: 'What a time for a power cut. But one thing a church is not short of is candles. Hang on.'

The others began to talk, Martin and the ushers laughed together, but Api and Jonathan stood in silence, waiting, staring at the shadowed altar, and the chandelier above it that swung on its chain in the draught.

In the house in Hardwicke Row the glass in the windows streamed and wavered under the onslaught of the rainstorm. Inside in the uneasy twilight, inanimate objects took on a different character. Chairs were like crouching animals.

Mirrors became opaque. Pictures were like windows – especially the portrait on the stairs, from which John Ashe seemed
to lean forward, and look about him.

'Let there be light!' said the vicar, returning with candles and
matches. He lit the first one and stood it on the shelf of the
choir stalls. 'And lo . . .'

A couple of minutes later the power returned, to a ripple
of applause. Those present concluded that it was a good sign
– after that, tomorrow was bound to go well. They took
heart. The voice of the pale young rabbi as he intoned the
seven blessings was sweet and sonorous, a note that seemed
to resonate below all the rest, like the double bass in an
orchestra.

Rehearsal over, they gathered near the west door, peering
out into the rain, while Makepeace and the rabbi conferred
on the chancel steps. Nobody had brought an umbrella. The
Frankels' driver was waiting, and they offered to drop Api
and Xanthe at the hotel. Martin and Andy braved the elements
for taxis for the rest of them.

Jonathan and Api kissed, briefly. Everyone else talked assid-
uously among themselves, giving the young couple some
privacy, but Api had never felt more watched.

'Au revoir,' she said. 'Sleep well.'

'No worries on that score. I'm blitzed.'

Api said: 'I love you.' It was not as hard as she imagined,
and when she saw the look in his eyes, it was almost possible
to believe it.

'My dearest Api.' His voice became ardent, intense. 'And I
love you.'

He pulled her close and held her tight against his shoulder.
'You and me,' he whispered. 'You and me.'

The next day the weather was no better. A high wind lashed
the tops of the trees along the Bayswater Road, dervishes of
rain swirled through the streets and across the park, the gutters

ran in torrents and the pavements leapt under the onslaught. Many of the crawling cars had headlights on.

The windows of the hotel were tinted, and the insulation perfect. Api, standing in the warmth in her silk pyjamas, might have been watching a film. She could feel nothing, hear nothing of what was happening outside.

All morning she was completely alone in the womblike room. Her dress and veil hung ghostlike on the outside of the wardrobe. The phone rang twice but she didn't answer it. At one o'clock there was a knock on the door. It was Xanthe, elegant in a mulberry lace suit, and carrying a hat of the same colour, decorated with silk roses.

'Do I look all right?'

'You look wonderful.'

'I came to see if there was anything I could do . . . Or just whether you'd like some company?'

'That's kind of you,' said Api, 'but no thanks.'

'But I feel awful leaving you on your own on your wedding day – I mean, a bride should have someone about when she's getting ready, and I thought—'

'I'm fine. And it's me that's leaving.'

'Don't say that!'

'It's true.'

Xanthe fussed unhappily with her suit. 'Martin said he'd rung but you hadn't answered – he'll come and fetch you at two.'

'Fine.'

'I'll see you there then.'

'See you there.' She began to close the door but Xanthe put her hand on it.

'Api – there must be something I can do? I may not have been a very good parent, and this could be my last chance to help in some small way.'

'Honestly,' said Api. 'I can't think of a thing.'

This time she shut the door gently but firmly in her mother's face. It was too late. She had already left.

★

On the morning of the Frankel wedding, as they were getting changed, Bryn confided in Linda.

'I feel a fraud. I shouldn't be going to this thing.'

'Why ever not? They adore you.'

He laughed. 'That's a slight exaggeration, my darling. The old man likes me well enough, for your sake, and Elizabeth's never less than charming, but Jonathan and I lock horns every time we meet.'

'It's only his manner.'

'That's no excuse. The fact is we don't like each other. I suspect he sees me as some sort of interloper, who's wormed his way into his father's affections and got work on the back of it.'

'You're being paranoid.' Linda presented her back so that he could pull up her zip. 'Harry uses charm like a weapon, Jonathan doesn't do charm at all. It's not just you, he's the same with everyone.'

Bryn did up the hook and eye at the top of the zip and kissed her neck briefly to show he was done. 'I dare say. But remember the stand-off over the Bristol project.'

'Forget that.'

'It's way behind schedule.'

'That's not your fault.'

'Perhaps not, but I'm the arty-farty architect who insisted on special materials.'

'Harry commissioned it. If it's what he wanted, I don't see that Jonathan has any say in the matter.'

'Nor me, but he does.' Bryn sat down on the edge of the bed to lace his shoes. 'And I think he's increasingly taking over the reins.'

'Do you know what?' Linda looked over her shoulder at him in the mirror. 'You should let it go. You've done your bit. Harry's delighted. When the pictures of the Scimitar are in circulation you won't even remember this, and Jonathan will be spitting tacks.'

'I expect you're right.' Bryn rose and slipped his jacket off its hanger. 'I still wish we weren't going. On the other hand, that's a terrific hat.'

'Look,' said Linda, 'paparazzi! Nick will be pleased.'

There were certainly three non-official photographers hanging around outside the church, but they ignored Bryn and Linda.

'Bigger fish to fry. I suppose we shall have to say "groom",' muttered Bryn as an usher approached, 'though God knows it sticks in my craw.'

'Ssh, it's big smile time. Oh, isn't it beautiful . . .'

In the cab on the way to the church, Ruth wouldn't have dreamed on commenting on Saul's appearance, but Judith was never anything less than direct.

'You could have worn something smarter.'

Saul, perched on the flip-seat, glanced down at himself. 'I'm wearing a suit, for God's sake.'

'It's going bald.'

'Just a bit of wear and tear. Api won't mind.'

Judith stared out of the window. Ruth gave Saul an encouraging smile. 'You look fine. No one's going to be looking at us anyway.'

'Ain't that the truth.' He leaned forward and tapped his sister on the knee. 'Hear that? They'll all be gazing at Api.'

Judith twitched her knee away. 'I hate London.'

'Come on, Jude,' said Ruth, 'you've never been before.'

'Because I knew I'd hate it.'

'Well,' said Saul. 'You both look nice anyway. Step we gaily.'

Gilda cut it as fine as she could, and sat at the back of the church, in one of the pews behind the font. She could scarcely believe all this – the rows and rows of shiny people, done up to the nines, the fountains and waterfalls of silvery flowers, the rich roar of the enormous organ – all this was for *Api*? She remembered that Martin was standing in for Charles, but she couldn't see the others and supposed they must be nearer the front. On the way in she'd seen Jonathan, but he hadn't recognised her. He was a cold fish in her view. She just hoped Api knew what she was doing, because he didn't strike Gilda as a man who made allowances for failure, his own or anyone else's.

'Gilda? Gilda!' It was Saul, wearing a yellow rose buttonhole and a worried expression. 'What are you doing back here?'

'Fine thanks, and yourself?'

'You're family – they'll think I'm not doing my job properly.'

'I can't help that, I don't want to sit up there with everyone looking.'

'Judith and Ruth are. I will be.'

'Sorry.'

His eyes narrowed suspiciously. 'You are coming afterwards?'

'Probably. No promises. Anyway I'm here now, so leave me in peace and stop making a spectacle of both of us.'

In the interests of protocol, Derek wanted to go in before Xanthe.

'You're supposed to make an entrance,' he said when she protested. 'You're the mother of the bride.'

'Come in with me at least – we can part company then.'

'Very well. I shall bask in reflected glory.'

'I don't feel very glorious.'

'Never mind,' he said, 'you look it. And don't worry about Api, either. She's going to be fine, and if she's not it certainly won't be your fault. Come on, head high.'

Seeing her mother come in, Gilda felt bad about what had passed between them the other day. She looked great, a really attractive woman for her age, and Derek had more of the air of a bridegroom about him than Jonathan bloody Frankel. Gilda suddenly decided, at that moment, that she would enjoy herself today: she would eat, drink and be merry and make Mac seriously regret he wasn't here.

'Smart bride,' said Martin as they got into the car. 'Nice one.'

She was conscious of him staring at her, but she didn't mind. He wasn't sickeningly needy, like their mother. His curiosity was straightforward nosiness, not some warped attempt to work out what she was thinking.

'I'm looking forward to seeing everyone,' he remarked as the Silver Ghost sat in traffic at Marble Arch. 'Hope they'll all show up.'

'I don't mind if they don't,' she said.

'No . . .' He gazed at her, impressed. 'You really don't, do you?'

'Except Gilda, I want her to be there.'

'She was terribly cut up at the funeral. More than anyone. I was kind of surprised, you know?'

'She was the eldest,' said Api. She couldn't keep the bitterness out of her voice. 'She can remember when they were happy together.'

It was something she'd thought about, often, since Charles had died: Gilda's privileged position as the first-born, the love-child, after whom everything had simply slipped away down-hill with the rest of them, a textbook demonstration of the law of diminishing returns. No wonder Gilda had intervened when she'd been Dodge's prisoner – she was the only one endowed with a sense of family. She stood at the centre, between the tying of the knot and the loose, frayed ends. Api knew what she owed to Gilda, but on a hundred occasions jealousy had shrivelled the thanks in her throat. And now the gratitude had pretty well atrophied.

'Can I say something?' said Martin.

She turned to look at him.

'Congratulations, little sis.' His mocking grin invited her to mock herself. 'And I mean that very sincerely.'

★

Linda, a connoisseur of such things, admired the appearance of the bride's mother. She was a handsome woman,
not elegant, a little wild and wounded-looking, a face gouged
with downward, disappointed lines like Jeanne Moreau.
Linda approved the burgundy lace with its long tunic and
ankle length skirt . . . a bit too much hippyish hair showing
under the hat but on the whole . . . a good eight out of ten,
and in circumstances which only the most exhibitionist
would relish.

Bryn tweaked his cuff back. 'Ten minutes late.'

'Not surprising, it's pouring out there, the traffic must be
terrible.'

'I suppose.'

'Don't fret.' She tapped his knee, and couldn't resist adding:
'Think how much worse it must be for the bridegroom.'

Bill Makepeace was glad that everything was now in order
and ready for the off. He had had a slightly trying morning,
having discovered that no general power cut had occurred
yesterday afternoon, and that consequently the source of the
problem must lie in the system of St Bede's. But having
checked everything himself and called out an electrician at
vast expense, they'd not turned anything up.

Now he watched from the porch as an usher ran out to the
bridal Rolls with an umbrella. How strange, the girl was
wearing a shimmering grey that blended with the summer
rain. And with that cloud of pale hair . . . A ghostly bride.

Like the trouper that he was, Bill buffed up his smile and
stepped forth to meet her.

Hundreds of faces turned towards Api as she walked up the
aisle on Martin's arm. Faces wearing polite, indulgent smiles,
the women's with a glint of assessment and calculation. One
she noticed in particular, a gloriously pretty red-headed
woman in a feathered hat, the warmth of whose smile seemed
completely genuine. Though how could it be, when they didn't

know one another? Never mind, the sweetness of that one stranger's smile was like a blessing.

'You may kiss the bride,' said Bill. He enjoyed this little embellishment, and had found that congregations like this, largely made up of non-churchgoers, enjoyed it too. With the approval of the couple he generally included it, and these days there was quite often a ripple of applause.

This was a standard kiss. Not the full-on Rhett and Scarlett embrace that some couples went in for, nor the slightly sheepish peck on the cheek of the shyer ones; but he did notice one thing. The bride's eyes remained open, gazing through and beyond her new husband's cheek as though looking at someone on the other side.

I've done it, thought Api as Jeremiah Clarke heralded their walk down the aisle. *I've escaped!*

Everyone now was smiling with equal warmth; there was a release of tension and the pleasant anticipation of dinner, drinks and dancing to come. Api looked this way and that, but there were very few faces she recognised. Her family were behind her, in the procession which she and Jonathan headed. Suddenly, she felt capable of anything. She smiled back at the strangers, like a new queen entering her realm.

Two-thirds of the way down the aisle, she saw him. He was standing next to the lovely red-haired woman she'd noticed on the way in. They were together, and his smile, like hers, radiated confident benevolence.

It was the man from the beach. The man who knew about love.

It took only a split second for her to see that he recognised her, but did not instantly remember. Whereas she did more than remember: the image and the experience had never left her. Then she had been neither girl nor woman, lost somewhere between a longing for protection and a desire for something altogether different.

Now, in the space of one step, halfway between the altar and the church door, Api, the new Mrs Frankel on her husband's arm, crossed that no man's land. And realised in a revelatory instant that her triumphant self-determination was a sham, and that she was entering not a safe haven, but an uncharted wilderness.

17

2001 – Bryn, Api

Something happened to Bryn at the Frankel wedding. He recognised it as one of those days when his life acquired a new dimension. There had been other occasions of momentous change, and it may have been a symptom of middle age that he found himself enumerating them: the peace garden, marriage to Linda, the birth of his children . . . Perhaps this was what was meant by 'counting one's blessings'? There were others: his accident; parting from Sally; which, he philosophised, had been blessings in disguise.

The legacy of that dark and rainy wedding day was not a blessing. Rather the opposite, though at the time he would have considered the word 'curse' too strong. Its effects were insidious, and disturbing. Uncertainty entered his life, and loss of control, like an unpredictable but steadily encroaching physical condition that he was powerless to influence. The mark left by the encounter with the girl on the beach was still there, it seemed, and had changed its character.

Looking back, he wondered whether a pattern had been set before that – one of which the girl was a part. The encounter with her had been only a few months after the dog got run over. The summer when the children grew up. Whether her death was symptom or cause Bryn couldn't say and didn't care to investigate, but thenceforth the tenor of family life was different.

Of course they were growing up anyway, but it had taken that horrible event to push them into the next stage, the one where magnetic north was no longer home and parents, but somewhere different, and unexplored. With Flo gone they no longer wanted to spend holidays in Suffolk, and two years later Linda and Bryn had sold the house on the prom. Sadie was happier at school anyway; holidays didn't mean much to her, and the competitive glamour of Barbados beach life or posing on the piste was anathema to her. Nick could occasionally be tempted to ski *en famille*, provided a friend could come along. But in truth it marked the beginning of the end of family holidays.

The fabric of family life grew looser. Linda had helped a friend arrange a silver wedding party, and received so much praise for her efforts that she'd begun to do more of it. Word of mouth spread, and friends of friends started to approach her on a business basis, confident of her flair and her meticulous attention to detail. She was a perfectionist. Friends and, later, clients, knew they were in safe hands. Bryn watched as a new career took off.

There was a general sense of letting-go. He told himself that this was natural – healthy, even. Relationships passed through different phases and they were entering a new one in theirs. A rock-solid relationship could easily withstand a few changes. And soon they would share a new focus.

For years Bryn had wanted to build his own house. All the time spent on other people's projects, putting a shape to other people's dreams, had helped formulate his own. It was an expensive way of acquiring property, but not of achieving perfection. He'd done fantastically well in recent years, largely due to the sheikh and his great glass and gold folly in the desert. If anyone had told him, when he'd been lying in hospital in his twenties with one career in tatters and no other on the horizon, that he was going to become this rich and successful, one of the few in his field to be known by name to the general public, he'd have laughed them to scorn. It would have seemed like a bad joke. Now, he could afford to indulge in self-congratulation.

The house would be his present to himself. The plot of

land on which it would stand was one of the loveliest in England for a domestic dwelling. Indeed it invoked the quintessence of Englishness, with the river softly encircling the rising ground, the trees on either side, the hills in the distance. The rooftops of the town a mile away only added to its magic: a reminder that this was a place set apart. He had taken Linda there one long summer's afternoon; they'd dreamed together as they walked along the river bank. Now the sheikh's money had secured the dream. The land was his; the drawings were on paper. Soon the building would start.

Years before they'd visited a glorious Arts and Crafts house on a lake in Northumberland, and now he aspired to those architectural values – a house traditional in feel but modern in outlook; that made use of its position and aspect, and admitted as much light as possible; and was structurally simple but elegant. Some of the windows would have panels of stained glass. There would be carving around the fireplaces, the finials and window seats. And two terraces, like broad steps, would give on to the open lawns that ran down to the river.

Linda, he sensed, was indulging him. The children – Nick in particular – were less than enthusiastic about leaving London. But this was only an hour and a half from the Smoke, and would encourage them towards independence. Bryn had no intention of running his life to suit them in the way some of his contemporaries did. He loved them, but had no problem letting go. That Nick was lazy came as no surprise, given his looks and cleverness. But no amount of paternal love could blind Bryn to his son's vanity and cunning. He had no fears for Nick, but the same could not be said of Sadie, who had emerged from her beetle-browed, black-clad phase into something different, but equally worrying. She was driven, touchy, obsessive – vulnerable. Would the young man exist who could meet her exacting standards?

Still, the house on the river would be perfect. It would go back to first principles: clean lines, sound materials, attention to detail; no shortcuts, no fudging and no compromise. It would be a good house as well as a beautiful one, a serene and solid marriage of form and function.

Bryn knew he was lucky. Not just in the way of good fortune, but lucky that bad fortune hadn't come his way. If ever complacency threatened, it was salutary to remind himself how nearly things might have gone wrong with the Frankel project. He had chosen to walk out on Jonathan Frankel, taking the justifiable view that changes to his plans were not his responsibility. But he had still been haunted by the possibility of disaster – that safety might be compromised by the slightly inferior materials and the need for speed. But now he had to allow that things were going well, and looking almost as good as he'd hoped. With the opening in sight, congratulations were being heaped upon him and Jonathan, to be fair to him, had so far kept his distance and not so much as hinted at any disagreement.

In the meantime, the Scimitar building had shot Bryn to prominence. It had been one of those jobs which could only possibly come one's way once, and for good reasons. The sky was the limit, in every sense, but the sheikh wanted the job done the day before yesterday. He had explained to Bryn on their first meeting, that he wished him to design a tower that would seem to 'explode out of the desert sand', accompanying this with a dramatic hand gesture that left Bryn in no doubt as to what was envisaged.

It had to make people gasp, to be overwhelmingly the most magnificent and tallest building in the city; and it must shine like the sun, glitter 'as if jewelled'. Work had been fast and furious, but fun. What Bryn gave the sheikh was a soaring, tapering blade of pure white concrete, clad in faceted glass that put the Koh-i-Noor to shame, and picked out in real gold. This orgy of conspicuous expenditure eclipsed anything in Bryn's experience. But he derived a devilish pleasure from creating something so stupendous, so dazzlingly glamorous, and so gloriously, shamelessly *useless*.

That, he still considered, was the measure of riches: they could be squandered on nothing more than self-proclamation. Of course the building was to contain the sheikh's office, if you could call it that. It also had dining suites, a ballroom, a leisure complex, a floor-to-apex atrium down which a waterfall flowed and over which exotic finches fluttered in a glass aviary, and a private cinema. Other than the numerous maids who cleaned these sumptuous spaces every day, the only people to pass through its doors regularly were the sheikh's sons, who used it for parties. It was purely and simply a monument to unimaginable wealth.

But the desert folly in all its gorgeous, vaunting vulgarity had put Bryn himself beyond the reach of money worries, and enabled him to begin the house on the river.

Another, darker reason fuelled Bryn's desire to build the house, apart from the realisation of a dream. He needed to be further from London, which had become haunted.

The moment when he'd seen her face, as she walked down the aisle with her new husband, was like someone placing their finger on the epicentre of a bruise. He experienced the echo of that first startling sensation. But he couldn't remember where, or when, he'd experienced it. Somewhere he had seen that face, but the hair, the clothes, the context and the expression – especially the expression – differed so much that he was confused.

And then, a moment after the young bride's eyes passed over him, everything came rushing back, and the small, unfocused pain flared a sharp stab of memory. He was half dizzy with it, so that when Linda turned to him and said: 'They both look wonderfully happy,' he didn't know what she meant. He hadn't seen the same thing.

'Do they?'

'Yes!' She nudged him. 'Don't be curmudgeonly, Bryn, it doesn't suit you.'

★

In the reception line, Jonathan introduced them.

'I don't believe you've met Api, my wife. Api, this is Linda and Bryn Mancini. Linda used to work for my father.'

Bastard! thought Bryn, putting Linda in her place like that. But now Api's hand was in his. It was hot and dry, almost feverish, when she looked so cool.

'Are you sure we haven't met before?' he asked. 'I seem to recognise you.'

'I don't think so,' she said. 'But you never know, we might have seen each other somewhere. Anyway, it's lovely that you could come . . .'

She had deflected his question and was already turning to the next person, but he knew that he hadn't really needed to ask. She not only remembered him, but had never forgotten.

Throughout the evening he found himself seeking her out with his eyes, watching her. It was easy during dinner when she was on the top table, but when dinner gave way to dancing she was lost among the guests. Twice, though, she was suddenly there, visible, and looking back at him before her eyes flicked away, and the second time it all came back to him. She was dancing with her brother, the young man who'd given her away. She had removed her veil and the jewelled rose that held it, and as she spun beneath her partner's arm her hair floated round her pale face and there! He was taken back to the grey, booming beach, Sadie's sobs, the cold surf dragging at their ankles – and catching a stranger looking at them, a strange girl with wild hair and a white face and that – that *glare* of something that was not quite envy, nor anger, nor despair, but a mixture of all three: a fierce, greedy longing.

That fury on the beach was today's fairy bride.

After dinner the newlyweds worked the room, Jonathan setting off in one direction and the girl in the other. Jonathan reached their table first.

'Thank you all so much for coming. I hope you're having a good time?'

They all confirmed, some more enthusiastically than others, that they had. Linda added: 'We were saying, your parents are both looking wonderful, Jonathan – they must be delighted.'

'I believe they are. They love Api, of course.'

'Naturally, she's a lovely girl.'

'And a very strong young woman,' said Jonathan in his humourless way. Bryn couldn't look at him without wanting to punch him in the teeth.

'She'd need to be to take on the Frankels . . .' commented a wag, putting the exchange safely back intowedding-banter territory, and Jonathan moved on amid well-meaning chortles.

Linda touched Bryn's hand, and murmured in his ear: 'Look at it this way, you never have to speak to him again.'

'If I ever have to it'll be too soon!'

'That'll do, here comes the bride.'

The men rose as Api approached. One of them offered her his seat and she took it. Bryn, sitting opposite, couldn't avoid looking at her without appearing rude. There was talk about the ceremony, her dress, the honeymoon, the house where they'd be living. Her voice was a little husky but low and clear; in church it had actually been easier to hear than Frankel's staccato rumble. Yes, she said, she'd probably go back to work, but not for a few months, not till they were settled in the house and she'd got used to everything . . . Harry and Elizabeth were fantastic . . . yes, there were lots of members of her family here, should she point them out?

Bryn listened to the words, but heard something else: something audible only to him. When she rose to leave she sent a smile round the table as she went, and as it passed over him he felt again that butterfly-brush of recognition. But why, then, had neither of them been able to say it? Say: Yes, that's it, we met each other on the beach at Aldeburgh on that stormy Sunday morning, how extraordinary . . . And then he remembered why: the moment it had happened it had become a secret.

The invitation had said that Mr and Mrs Frankel would leave at eleven thirty: guests' carriages at midnight. But by eleven Bryn was ready to go. The event for which he had braced himself with glum stoicism had turned into something unimaginably different. Circumstances which had been, if disobliging, at least predictable, had proved tumultuous and moved beyond his control. It was as if in the recent past he'd picked up a strange virus which had lain dormant, till now: a virus new to science, exposing him to threats and symptoms which he couldn't predict.

In the taxi on the way home, Linda cocked her head to look into his face.

'Hello? Anyone there?'

'Sorry, darling. Was I a party pooper?'

'You were fine, considering.'

'I can't pretend I'm not glad it's over.'

'Tell me something . . .' Linda's voice had a musing tone which he'd come to mistrust. When she mused, she was at her most perceptive. 'When had you met Api before?'

It was his opportunity to banish the secret, but he didn't take it. 'I don't know.'

'She was the maître d' at Lowell's. Maybe it was there.'

'Maybe . . . I don't know the place offhand, but perhaps some business lunch or other. I seem to have seen her face somewhere.'

'Like me,' said Linda. 'Only I know where it was. I saw her with Jonathan once, near Primrose Hill, but of course I didn't realise then that she was anything more than a casual acquaintance. She made an impression on me though.' She glanced at him. 'As she clearly did on you.'

'Not that much of an impression,' he said, adding for good measure: 'And anyway, as you rightly pointed out, with a bit of luck we need never see them again.'

*

Several months passed before the invitation arrived. *Mr and Mrs Bryn Mancini – Jonathan and Api Frankel – At home – Thursday December 15th – Drinks 6.30–8.30 – RSVP 5 Hardwicke Row N6.*

'Why on earth are they inviting us?' said Bryn, though he knew perfectly well why.

'Perhaps she took to us at the wedding, or took to you, anyway. No, I can't imagine, but it's nice of them.'

'Frankel doesn't do nice.'

'Anyway, here's what I suggest,' said Linda soothingly. 'We accept, and on the night in question you manifest a diplomatic illness or an urgent last-minute meeting and I'll go on my own.'

'That's hardly fair.'

'But I *want* to go, and you don't. I'm dying to see the house, and there are bound to be tons of well-heeled people there who want their parties to look fabulous. This is the easiest way.'

It was the easiest way, but not as Linda meant it. Bryn had his own reasons for not wanting to socialise with the Frankels, and was unequivocally glad that he no longer had to do business with Jonathan who had little respect for employees, past or present, and had even less time for him since the success of the Scimitar.

But this did not prevent him, during the intervening period, wondering what it would be like to be there.

On a Friday about two weeks before the party he was in Leeds at one of the few 'Whither British design?' conferences he still attended. At Linda's insistence he had arranged to visit his mother for the night on the way back, but there was still time to kill on the return journey so he made a detour of some thirty miles to take a look at the Pals' Memorial now it had bedded in. He didn't tell Sam this time, he wanted to take things at his own pace and without the need for anything but dispassionate professionalism.

He should have known that such objectivity would be out

of the question. The town, the situation, the very nature of the memorial didn't allow for it, and he was proud of that. It was what he'd striven to achieve. The moment he got out of the car the atmosphere of the place caught him by the throat. It was a little later in the year than when he'd last been, with Nick, to the Remembrance Day service: a cold afternoon, with the blue sky swept clear by the glacial wind endemic to these northern hills.

His first impression was that the place looked splendid: radical, dignified, permanent. He'd wanted the tower to echo the grand old chimneys of the industrial revolution as well as having a dignity and grandeur of its own. And it did, it really did. He began by walking round the perimeter of the site, looking at it from all angles. As he did so he reflected that of the two towers that had marked the past few years of his working life, it was this solemn grey stone monument, not the sheikh's glittering extravaganza, which inhabited his heart and his imagination.

When he'd circled it once he walked across the grass to take a closer look. Perhaps it was inevitable that he should now notice some less attractive details. The scattering of litter, the occasional evidence of unconscientious dog-walking, the bare patches where the area had been used for playing football. At least football was a local obsession, and the lads whom this place commemorated would certainly have played wherever there was space enough to do it in those streets Sam had showed him. It was important not to be precious about such things.

He reached the tower and went inside. It was an area twelve foot in diameter. There were the names engraved on the wall – he'd wanted them to look as if the owners had carved them there – and the simple round plinth with the safe containing the book of remembrance, the words of the poet, and on which stood the smooth, slate dish where a flame could be lit for special dates and services. He had held out against any sort of electric light, and it took a moment for his eyes to adjust.

When they did he felt a swoop of disappointment. The place had been used by local kids as the equivalent of a bus shelter. On the floor lay used matches, a couple of messy roaches and rather more fag ends, a lager bottle and a used French letter. His face creased with disgust; he swept them against the wall just inside the door, using the outside of his shoe. He sat down, deflated, on the stone bench which ran round the wall. Was it wrong, to object to this? There had been no vandalism that he could see; perhaps this evidence of fairly normal youthful activity was no worse than the ad hoc football pitch outside. But there was a smell, too, they'd peed in here as well as the rest. What was worse, no one had stopped them. Weren't there older people to take these kids to task, to make them clear up after themselves, to exercise a bit of natural authority? God, he thought, *I'm* getting old. Drink, dope and sex scares had swept Nick's school at fairly regular intervals, so how much harder must it be to police such things in a neighbourhood like this? The tower was private, secluded – perfect, in fact, for whatever use the kids wanted to put it to. What was the answer? Security lights, alarms? It was unthinkable, the last thing he'd envisaged. He wondered whether he should tell Sam, but decided against it. If he didn't know it would enrage and upset him, and if he did it might be perceived as an accusation.

He got to his feet heavily. As he did so he noticed the crack in the floor. It ran from just in front of where he'd been sitting, behind the central plinth in a southerly direction. He pressed hard with his foot: there was no give. Suddenly prickling with professional anxiety, the young intruders forgotten, he followed the crack to the point where it joined the wall, made a rough calculation as to its position, and went outside.

He could see nothing, but he could feel it. With both hands pressed to the wall he could detect the merest suggestion of a swelling, scarcely more than a tension like a three-month pregnancy. Standing back, he could see nothing – could almost convince himself it was his nervous imagination. But the moment he was in contact again there was no denying the evidence of his hands.

He couldn't believe it. Subsidence. With all the care that had been taken, the time, attention and hard-earned money that had been lavished on this labour of loyalty and respect, how was it possible? The engineer, a man he himself had recommended as one of the best in his field, had been here for days, testing the soil, sinking boreholes, running the most rigorous tests, in the knowledge that an area like this could well contain small unlicensed individual excavations from a hundred years ago. Bryn's head swam, and he had to lean back against the tower with his hands on his knees for a moment until his vision returned to normal. Everything had been done by the book. Neither engineer nor surveyor's researches had thrown up anything inauspicious. This had been a clear, sound site, and perfectly suited to its purpose.

When he straightened up, still a little shaky, two teenage girls in jeans and denim jackets were walking across the grass about thirty yards away. He could tell by their manner, the averted head of the one closest to him, that they'd been watching and were talking about him. When they were just passed they bent double, clutching one another, in fits of unkind laughter, doubtless thinking him drunk. Bryn forgave them. They had no idea that they had just been in danger of their lives.

Once they'd gone, he collected himself and inspected the tower once more. This time he could feel nothing, and could make out no discernible curvature. Obsessively he went inside, and traced the path of the crack again. He had exaggerated its length, he found; it stopped short of the wall. When he stamped on it there was no give. He came back out and repeated the exercise a third time, moving his hands like a mime artist up and down and across the icy flank of the tower. Nothing. Maybe, he allowed himself to think, he had been wrong.

Instead of going back round the ring road he went through

the centre of town and pulled over outside the town hall. Somewhere inside that preposterous concrete monstrosity there was the file – now doubtless a computer spreadsheet – containing all the original details of the survey, the minutes of the planning meetings, and of the pre-planning, when the tower had been no more than a lowly agenda item and he himself known to no one. It was ironic that even the obnoxious former mayor, Chapman, was probably taking credit for having hired the architect responsible for the Scimitar building. If he went in now, Bryn was by no means sure to whom he should speak. Apart from Sam, who might very well have retired. And what would he say – that he had felt uneasy about a single crack whose extent he had misjudged, and a slight, perhaps imaginary, distortion of the wall? At the same time if he had even the most nebulous doubts about the building he should surely mention them to someone.

A horn blasted, reminding him that he was occupying a set-down point, and he raised a hand in acknowledgement and pulled away. He'd ring Sam when he got back, get a name, and write suggesting a meeting.

His anxiety lessened during the course of the journey, and was further dispelled by a surprisingly jolly evening at his mother's – she was increasingly frail, but still vivacious and mercifully independent – with Alison and Malcolm, after which he was a little too pissed to get back in the car. He slept unusually heavily and left after breakfast, by which time the tower and its putative problems seemed a great deal smaller, as if viewed through the wrong end of a telescope. By the time he arrived home he had recalibrated his state of mind to the extent that he was rebuking himself for an uncharacteristic attack of the vapours. He would have been unlikely to mention it to Linda, even had she been in.

It was unusual for him to have the house completely to himself, and he relished it. He loved his home in a way that he was beginning to realise was out of the ordinary. Even now when they were thinking of moving on he liked the look of it, what he and Linda had done with it. But far more importantly he loved the atmosphere, the sense of peace and safety, which they would take with them wherever they were. He carried with him two distinct impressions of home from childhood: the fraught, edgy, unpredictable place that it had been when his father was there, when hostility and tears waited always just below the surface. And the blessed calm and content once he had gone, when he, his mother and sister had done as they pleased. Linda had recreated that for him: she knew him so well, him and what she chose to call his Libran love of peace and harmony, order and beauty. He wasn't sure about any astrological root; surely every sane person wanted those things. He did however recognise in himself a strong need for emotional tranquillity, and a distaste for confrontation that might be construed as a desire for peace at any price.

This train of thought led him to Sally, who had remained gently at the very back of his mind over the years. Now there, he thought, was a situation so like his own upbringing that he had needed to do nothing more than take his place in it. He wondered if he'd treated Sally as badly as Mary said. After all, she had been happy too. They had enjoyed three years of affection, intimacy and contentment which was more than some people had in a lifetime. His children were now older than her daughters had been when they met. He tried to picture himself on his own, and with the children around, and could scarcely imagine how hard that would be. Sally had done so much, worked so hard, been the boss at home, and yet managed to remain warm and welcoming. She'd be nearly sixty now. At least one of the girls might be married, or an investment banker, or both. Sally herself might be married. He found himself thinking that it would be a wicked waste if she were still single. The weasel sentiment that she'd make some lucky man a wonderful wife slipped into his mind and he banished it. That was to salve his own conscience by diminishing her. Sally was worth more than that.

Once or twice over the years since their parting he'd considered getting in touch, out of a sense of friendship and, yes, responsibility, just to find out how she was, but had never done so. He was torn between doing the spontaneous thing, the thing he wanted to do, and the prospect of perpetrating some gross emotional solecism. Sally herself, he was sure, would have taken any such action in the right spirit, but the girls were a more unstable proposition altogether and it might have caused upset where the very opposite was intended.

His eye flicked over the invitations on the mantelpiece – carol services at the children's schools, three Christmas bashes, a black-tie dinner party which he knew would be dull beyond belief, a couple of business do's and the Frankels. Linda was right: just because that strange girl had invited them didn't mean he had to go. It was extraordinary the way an atmosphere of deceit had crept into his marriage when no deceit had been perpetrated, or only by default. He had only not told Linda about the girl on the beach because he wasn't sure what to say. Such a tiny, unimportant thing to have such a profound effect. Thinking about her, he could almost feel the girl looking at him now. If he looked up quickly he might see her – pale face, wild hair, light eyes – beyond his own reflection in the mirror, and then he'd turn and there'd be no one there.

His skin shrank into goose-flesh. Here, in his home, his sanctuary. There was something his mother used to say: 'Don't let the witch over your doorstep.' He was in danger of doing that. Api was no witch, but she was mysterious. She thought about him, intently, as he thought of her. He might not, yet, have let her over the doorstep, but he had made the far greater mistake of letting her into his head. And the invitation was a message that said he had been in hers.

There had really never been any question of Linda's leaving well alone as far as Coralie was concerned. She had long ago been entrusted with keeping the secret, and the habit was now ingrained. She hadn't been often – this was her third visit since the lunch with Harry, though each time she promised herself it would be the last,

If the visits were a penance, she was aware that they were a penance closely allied to pride of the worst sort. Officious do-gooding came perilously close to self-aggrandisement. The possibility that her deception, and consequently Harry's, might be found out was both awful and thrilling. It was not something she would wish on any of them, which was why she came to Mizpah, braved the awfulness to do chores and buy little treats – and lied that it was on Harry's behalf.

It *was* awful, there was no denying it. The modus vivendi that Coralie and Al had established only worked in the sense that neither of them had the will or sense to change it. The house was squalid (the cleaning lady having left the day Al arrived), the garden was overgrown, the windows dirty and the place smelt. Neither Coralie nor her son were themselves clean, in clothing or in person. The television was always on in the living room, and commercial radio played ceaselessly in the kitchen. Al actually slept in the living room, his bed was in there and very often he was in his pyjamas – stained and improperly fastened – in the middle of the day when Linda came. Linda had seen to it that there was a latch on the doors of the kitchen, Coralie's own bedroom, the bathroom and the upstairs lavatory. She had also at her own expense found a replacement cleaner made of sterner stuff than the first. It turned out that Harry was still paying a slightly reduced amount to Aylmer House for one of their outside carers to come in for an hour a day to help with shopping, bath Al if necessary and supervise his medication, which stood in a miniature chest of drawers in the dry-goods cupboard. Linda always asked Coralie whether the carer came regularly, and the answer was always 'Yes, for what it's worth.' She herself had met the girl and she seemed nice enough, no slouch and agreeably unshockable.

'I've seen worse,' was her reply to Linda's question.

'You don't think there's any – danger, to either of them, in this set-up?'

'Oh no. No, no! They're right as rain. They won't get photographed for *Hello!* but they're rubbing along fine.'

Linda hoped so. She had nothing with which to compare the situation. The only reason she called when she was on her way was not for their benefit, but hers – to give Coralie a chance to rally round a bit, make sure they were both dressed and so on.

On this particular Monday, she rang from the car just after she left, and Al picked up the phone. She could hear the television braying and jangling in the background.

'Al! Al, it's Linda!' She found herself speaking too loudly, as if he were deaf.

'What do you want?'

'I'm coming to see you.'

'I'm busy.'

'Is your mother there? Can I speak to her?'

'She's in the toilet.'

'Will you tell her I'm coming to see you?'

'Yes.'

It was hard to recall the exhilaration which had once accompanied this drive out of London, to visit Al at Aylmer House. The good thing she was doing back then, the role that had so flattered her vanity, had turned into this mire of deceit. And it was vanity that had sucked her back in when she had extricated herself. She was deceiving everyone, including herself, but she was too far in now to retreat.

Since she had started doing the party decor in a more serious way there was no difficulty in finding a reason to be out of town for the day, and anyway Bryn had always been relaxed and uncurious about what she got up to. He liked her fully independent life, though he'd have been shocked by what today held in store for her.

★

Even if the cleaner had just been, there was always a lot to do. A pattern of sorts had evolved. On the way into town Linda would stop at the bank and pay a cheque into Coralie's account. After she arrived, she and Coralie made a shopping list, and then when everyone was ready – which could take some time – she drove the three of them to the out-of-town supermarket to stock up. This was when she fully appreciated the difficulties of the situation. Al would orbit them as they patrolled the aisles, taking things off the shelves that they didn't need, addressing strangers, making loud remarks and occasionally adjusting his clothing with unnecessary rigour to the alarm of other female shoppers. It was a process to which Coralie was inured, but Linda still found it an ordeal. Misleadingly, Al didn't look especially strange; he'd retained his dark good looks, so his behaviour came as more of a shock. Somewhat treacherously she tried to make it clear from her own manner that she was the outsider, the helper-out, and left Coralie to deal with Al while she piled stuff into the trolley.

There was a café near the supermarket exit, and the lure of a hot, reviving caffeine-hit was always too much for Linda. Once in there Al would embark on a second breakfast of historic proportions, and Coralie would have hot chocolate with a squirt of cream and a slice of cake on the side. It was an oasis of relative calm in spite of Al's messy way with a fried egg. Then it was back to load the car, and return to the house for what generally amounted to three hours of intensive cleaning and tidying.

On this occasion Coralie appeared to have made some effort prior to Linda's arrival. The place was reasonably tidy, in that you could walk from A to B unimpeded, and the washing machine was going round. But this turned out not to be as good a sign as Linda had hoped. Coralie was in a mutinous mood.

The rumblings began during the list-making process, while Al watched *Richard and Judy* in the other room.

'So how are the happy couple?'

Linda kept her voice light. 'Fine as far as I know.'

'We read all about the wedding in the paper.'

'That was some time ago, Coralie.' Linda took the lids off successive storage jars, checking the contents. 'We haven't seen them since then.'

'But you and your husband were there.'

'Yes. You've asked me that before, I told you.'

'Not that I expect or want to be invited to these things. I suppose it'll be the patter of tiny feet in no time.'

'Do we want cheese, or is there loads in here?' Linda opened the fridge to reveal an array of uncovered leftovers and half-full packets well past their use-by date. 'Does Al still like that liver sausage?'

'He's not fussy. He likes the yoghurts with the hundreds and thousands.'

'What about bathroom stuff?'

'Wouldn't know, can't remember.' Coralie was beginning to talk like her son. She patted out a rhythm on the kitchen table with her palms. 'You don't have to do this, you know.'

'I like to. Harry wants to know you're all right.'

'Then he could come himself.'

'Coralie, we've been over this so many times. This is what you wanted. All this – having Al here and so on. You can't have it both ways – make it harder for yourself and then suddenly decide you want Harry to be more involved. He can't be, we're all too far down the line for that.'

'What's all this "we"?' asked Coralie. 'The only "we" is me and my son. And in case you hadn't noticed we're doing fine.'

'You are,' said Linda. 'You absolutely are. I didn't expect—'

Too late she saw the purple flush rise in Coralie's cheeks. 'No, you didn't, did you? You thought we weren't up to it.'

'Not at all. Not many people would be. It's a huge responsibility to take on. I'm full of admiration.'

'Full of shit,' declared Coralie, rising to her feet. 'Has anyone ever told you you're a patronising, meddling cow?'

'There's no need—'

'Allow me to be the first!'

Linda found herself entertaining the distinct possibility that Coralie might be nearly as mad as her son and a great deal more dangerous. She sat still and spoke as quietly as she could, so as not to raise the temperature any further.

'Coralie, you've got this completely wrong. Harry only wants to help and you're quite right, I'm just the gofer. I didn't for an instant mean to imply that I have any real part in your difficulties.'

'Ah!' Coralie wagged a finger. 'Ah! I never said *that*. I never said you weren't part of our *difficulties*. You most certainly are. You always have to be in there, don't you? On the case, putting yourself about, you love it. Well I don't love it, not any more. I've had it up to here. I want you to get back into your car, and take your money and your poxy Marigolds with you, and clear off!'

'Coralie—'

'Now!'

'I really think we should calm down—'

'Do you?' Coralie came round the table, Linda rose hastily and blocked her advance with the chair. 'Do you now? Well I don't give a stuff what you think, you are *not part of this family!*'

'Very well, I'll go,' said Linda, as calmly as she could manage. Al had appeared in the kitchen doorway, alerted by his mother's raised voice. Beyond him Richard and Judy's agony aunt purveyed her homely wisdom to an empty room.

'Could you be quiet,' he said.

Linda was suddenly frightened, caught in a pincer movement between these two large and unpredictable people who now seemed to have formed an unholy alliance.

'Excuse me, Al,' she said, smiling pleasantly, her legs trembling. 'I'm going now.'

Bryn and Jim met for lunch at the Prince of Jaipur near the Post Office Tower. It was an old haunt of theirs. These days they only got together a couple of times a year and it was generally for a curry, which was both a shared passion and cheap enough to take account of the disparity in their circumstances. Without either of them saying as much, both men realised as the years went by that theirs was a true and solid friendship: they could say as much or as little as they liked, time and altered fortunes made no difference, they were easy with one another. The friendship could be picked up and put down without ill feeling: however long it was neglected for it always revived on contact. Most of Bryn's friends from the old days had fallen away, but Jim was a constant.

He was waiting at their usual table in the middle left-hand alcove when Bryn arrived. As was customary, they got in beers and ordered their food before embarking on any conversation.

When the Cobras arrived, Jim asked: 'To what do I owe this pleasure? Bored out of your skull or something?'

'I was at a bit of a loose end. Linda's gone off somewhere, so naturally I thought of you.'

'Anyway, glad you did. And how is the beautiful Linda?'

'Doing beautiful parties for people, it's going really well. Victoria?'

Jim made a hand movement like a plane taking off. 'I could stay at home and write my novel if I wanted to.'

'Why don't you?'

'Because I know perfectly well that I'd do fuck all if I was at home. I don't know how you guys do it.'

'I have a studio, I treat it like an office.'

'Yes, but come on, it still takes a will of iron.'

'The tyranny of the deadline helps. Plus in my line of work as well as a big powerful client there are hundreds of jobs riding on what I come up with. People's livelihoods depend on it. A bit of pressure's a great taskmaster.'

'Good point. Nobody wants my novel yet. Best to stick with the day job.' Jim paused as the poppadoms arrived with the usual quartet of dips. 'A great tradition – the white one, the orange one, the raw onions and the one no one ever has.'

'Lime pickle, I like it.'

They helped themselves in silence. After a moment Bryn said: 'Actually I'm thinking of retiring.'

As so often when he was with Jim, the remark had escaped his lips before the thought had properly formed. But the minute he'd said it he realised it was true.

'Jammy bastard,' said Jim. 'What brought this on?'

'When I say retire—'

'You don't mean to do nothing you mean to pursue your numerous other interests and spend more time with your family, yeah, yeah, yeah.'

'I don't know what, to be honest. All of the above, I suppose. And whatever presents itself. But the truth is I don't actually need to work.'

'No, I think I hoisted that in when I saw that fucking great skyscraper in the business section . . . Why is mango chutney hairy?' Jim balanced a large chunk on a shard of poppadom. 'Won't you be bored shitless? I mean I wouldn't, but you never know.'

'I don't think so.' Jim's mouth opened to receive the tottering mouthful. 'I'm building a house of my own.'

'A word of advice.' Jim's voice took on a note of friendly sarcasm. 'Make sure you tell Linda.'

'I have.' Bryn stopped. It was a joke, of course, but he couldn't quite bring himself to laugh.

'Get out, go on!'

Linda was leaving anyway. There was no need for Coralie to manhandle her. The fact that she did so advertised just how badly she wanted to – any excuse, was what her rough gestures said. Mercifully, Al was so surprised he got out of the way and didn't join in as he might easily have done. Linda had almost reached the door when Coralie gave her a push that jolted her forward and then while she was still off balance another, harder one that sent her flying. The point of her shoulder slammed into the wall; it felt as if every bone in her chest was being compressed. Winded, she gasped and held up her hand to ward Coralie off, but all she did now was open the door wide and stand next to it, puffed up with rage.

'Go on, go!'

Aware only of Coralie's enormous, threatening presence and Al standing goggle-eyed in the background, Linda left. She was shaking with shock and hardly able to breathe but she tried to maintain her dignity and walk as upright as she could. Getting into the car was agony. She let out a whimper which she hoped they couldn't hear. They were watching her from the doorway; the word 'Mizpah' stood out mockingly against the white paint above their heads.

It took her twice as long as usual to get home. She ached all over and was sure she might have cracked a collarbone or a rib, or both. She prepared a story for Bryn – the car was unmarked and she didn't want to leave herself open to accusations of not wearing a seat belt, so it had to be a fall. A path had been icy, that would do.

But when she got back at about four he wasn't there. She was almost weeping now with exhaustion, pain and a sort of relief that she didn't have to tell one more lie immediately, on top of all the others. The Christmas tree had arrived and was standing propped up at the bottom of the area steps. She hobbled upstairs and ran herself a huge hot bath with half a pint of a blue mixture 'Scientifically Proven to Relieve Stress'. Here's a challenge for you, she thought: show us what you're made of.

She lowered herself into the water and lay there. Gradually, over the next half an hour, as her aching bones eased slightly she grew calmer. She had been told to go, in no uncertain terms, and she had done so. She would deal with whatever happened – if anything did – when the time came. In the meantime she had had an unpleasant but not life-threatening fall and would soak up whatever sympathy came her way.

She was in her dressing gown, gingerly pulling on socks, when she heard the front door. It was clear, as Bryn bounded up the stairs and into the bedroom that he was in a buoyant mood. He didn't even notice her wince as he clasped her in his arms.

'It's all going to be all right!' he declared. 'You hear me, woman? It's all going to be fine!'

It was the opposite of what she felt, but it was nice to hear him say it.

Next day, after a sleepless night, Bryn took her to Accident and Emergency: she had broken her collarbone. They X-rayed her and showed her the damage, but said there was nothing they could do except put her arm in a sling for a while to remind her not to do anything rash. The sling turned out to be a particularly hideous loop of pink rubber like something intended, as Bryn said, for internal use. When they got back, with Linda subject to virtual pin-down, he outlined his plans for the country house. It was clear that the project had occupied a great deal more of his thoughts, time and energy than she had realised. He was on a roll.

'It's time for full steam ahead,' he declared. 'I've had it with London, and there's no need for me to accept any commissions except those that take my fancy. You can have a free hand with the interior decoration, it'll be a stunning advertisement for our combined talents. This time next year, my darling, we could be in our kingdom by the river.'

His enthusiasm broke over her in a great wave, swamping her. She was too weak to withstand it. Perhaps, she thought, everything really would be all right.

When the day of the Frankels' party came round, Linda had to admit she didn't feel like going. She was still shaken up and sore, and found sitting in the car uncomfortable. She was also, in a way that was less easy to explain to Bryn, in shock: prone to weepiness and easily tired.

'I must be getting old,' she confessed. 'I'm afraid I can't face it.'

'You had a very nasty accident,' he said, and then, to her

astonishment, added: 'Perhaps I'll go, in that case. To show the flag.'

'Bryn! It's the last thing you want to do.'

'I can tolerate a glass of bubbly at the fellow's expense. And I like the old man.'

'I doubt they'll be there, he's not very mobile these days.'

'Whatever.' Bryn kissed her. 'Maybe my conscience needs salving. I'll see how I feel when this evening comes round. Anyway,' he added, 'you wanted to know what the house was like. I'll be able to tell you.'

He made Linda some supper and left around seven, in order to arrive when things were in full swing and he could set his own pace. He knew he shouldn't be doing this. The decision about the house had made him foolhardy: the realisation that he was in a position to change his life. The Pals' memorial was history, in every sense, it was the future that was important. With a bit of luck this evening would demonstrate how exaggerated had been his response to young Api Frankel. Maybe he had been in the grip of some male menopausal fantasy and was about to dispel it.

He located the street and found somewhere to park less than a hundred metres away. Incredibly, as he walked to the house it was snowing lightly, not lying, but tiny crystalline flakes spiralling through the air, grey in the dark, sparkling in the lamplight.

The moment he saw Hardwicke Row he thought how much Linda would have loved it. It was enchanting. He only hoped Frankel hadn't filled his house with Bauhaus and Jacobsen and smoked glass and white paint. Nothing would have surprised him.

He needn't have worried. The house was gorgeous. It was a great deal grander than it appeared on the outside and full of wonderful jewel colours and rich textures. The restraining hand of taste prevented it from resembling a souk, but it still gave the impression that a millionaire hippy had been given a free hand, and it worked beautifully. An eight-foot Christmas tree stood in the hall, blazing with light. The floors were covered in wonderful ornate rugs. The guests – there seemed to be hundreds – were tanked up and having a wonderful time. Elegant Filipinos in dark red uniforms moved amongst them. The party occupied the whole of the ground floor as far as he could see; it stretched through every doorway and beyond. Bryn helped himself to a glass, moved to the foot of the stairs and took stock.

He couldn't see his host and hostess anywhere. He was sure he'd know if she was nearby – he'd feel that fingerprint on his senses. Now he spotted Jonathan Frankel near the doorway of the largest room, talking to a smart, thin couple who seemed to be leaving.

'Hello. Are you being looked after?'

Her voice came from behind him, on the stairs. He started.

'Yes, thank you. Good evening, lovely party.'

He turned and she leaned forward to exchange a polite social kiss. Again, she looked so cool but her cheek was hot.

'Is your wife here? Linda?'

'Sadly not.' He explained about the fall. 'But she sends her very best and gave me time off for good behaviour.'

She stood next to him as though that was exactly where she wanted to be, as though finding him had been the sole object of her coming downstairs. She wore black taffeta, very tight, short and chic; minute black opals in her ears; sexy black shoes with hourglass heels.

'That's what I was giving myself,' she confided. 'Every so often I have to have a moment alone.'

It struck him as an odd thing to say, confiding in him, a stranger, about her own party and her attitude to it. But to her, of course, he wasn't a stranger. His skin prickled with excitement.

'I can understand that.'

'Can you?' She turned her pale, sagacious Elizabethan look on him. He felt as though he were in a quicksand, where every unintentional movement got him further in, proclaimed something about him that even he didn't understand.

'Yes,' he said. 'Large numbers of people, especially in one's own house, can be very exhausting.'

Apparently satisfied with this she looked away again. There was a moment's silence but she made no move to leave his side. Nor did anyone come up to them – she had the ability to erect an invisible barrier around herself.

'You know about these things,' she said. 'What do you think of my house?'

He caught the 'my', and it made his head spin. 'It's wonderful, what I can see of it. Is everything your choice?'

'Mostly. Jonathan doesn't have all that much time.'

'You have terrific taste. Or at least, your taste accords with mine. And Linda's, interiors are more her thing. She's devastated not to be here.'

'You'll have to bring her another time,' she said, and he detected a slight *froideur*, before she became suddenly more animated. 'Shall I tell you about an amazing coincidence? About this house?'

He remembered how young she was. 'Yes, please.'

'I have a painting of my great-grandfather. I've always had a thing about it and my mother gave it to me when I got married. We never even knew who the artist was until about two years ago. And now it turns out that she – the artist – once lived near here! Only for a few months, she was never anywhere for long, but she did a mural on the wall of her bedroom, and it's still there.'

All this came out in a rush quite unlike her other remarks. Again it was impossible not to believe that she was confiding in him.

'Yes, that is a coincidence. There are forces at work, you see . . . Where is your great-grandfather?'

'Here.' Odd that, he thought. Most people would have said 'There'. She turned and pointed up the stairs behind them. 'I had him cleaned up. What do you think?'

He thought the portrait scary and forbidding, and its frame overblown.

'It's very imposing.'

'He was a millionaire,' she said. 'Richer even than the Frankels for his day.'

'Which was?'

'I think he died in the late 1930s. None of us knows very much about him, really.'

'It shouldn't be hard to find out. He's well within the scope of family records.'

'I wouldn't know where to start.'

Another unheralded suggestion rose to his lips. 'Maybe I could? It would amuse me and I'm not going to be too busy in the near future.'

She began to say 'That would be—' but Jonathan was waving at her from the middle of the hall as the thin couple left, and she concluded: 'Lovely to talk to you, I'd better do my duty.'

Bryn stayed about another half an hour, and spoke to a couple of people who had been at the wedding, including, briefly, Api's sister Gilda, an eccentric beauty with the longest legs he'd ever seen and one too many drinks inside her for discretion.

'I tell you what, Glyn.'

'Bryn.'

'Bryn, sorry. I tell you what, I hope Jonathan realises what he's taken on.'

Bryn laughed. 'What he's taken on? How do you mean? I should have thought it was the other way round.'

'She's been through a hell of a lot,' said Gilda darkly. 'To hell and back, no shit.'

'I'd never have guessed.'

'You wouldn't, no. But I reckon she married him to get away from things, and it won't make any difference.'

'No? All this?' Bryn glanced around. 'She seems to have taken to it like a duck to water.'

'Uh-uh.' Gilda shook her head. 'Api's a changeling. She could do anything.'

A little while after that Bryn left. He had managed to avoid speaking to Jonathan, and Api had disappeared. As he went out of the front door he looked up again at the portrait on the stairs and realised he had omitted to ask the man's name. Though he wouldn't forget his face.

'So?' asked Linda from the sofa. 'How was it?'

'Great house, you'd have loved it.'

'Damn. Did you behave nicely? Will they ask us again?'

'Yes,' he said. 'I think she will.'

18

2001 – Api

It was a relief to Api when her novelty to her husband began to wear off. It put their marriage on a more equal and even footing. She never for a moment thought that the cooling of their relationship signified its end. But it did set her free. If all Jonathan wanted of her was her cooperation, then her feelings were her own to do with as she liked.

It had not taken Gilda's prodding for Api to recognise that she was not in love with Jonathan. Even so, this new level of pragmatism would not have been available to her had she not seen Bryn Mancini again. On her wedding day, the very day on which she was to take charge of a new life and discard the old, the sight of him had reminded her not only of what she lacked – she had come to terms with that – but of how fiercely, madly, she desired it.

The remainder of the day had been a blur. She had somehow got through it, by allowing herself to be carried along. Never had her façade of composure stood her in such good stead. All she could think of was him – where he was, who he spoke to, smiled at and danced with. Her nerve ends hurt with the effort of tracking him in the crowd. She was in pain. Like the little mermaid in the fairy story she danced, smiled and delighted her guests when every step, every breath, was agony.

Their honeymoon had felt like an exile. The ten-hour flight that put thousands of miles between herself and Bryn was torture, a rack that stretched her almost past endurance. But the more pain she was in, the greater her composure. Jonathan would never, ever, know what she was going through. All through the long sunlit weeks on their elliptical blister of sand in the turquoise sea she was calm: she breathed her way through the slow footsteps of the seconds . . . the minutes . . . the hours . . . the interminable, golden days.

Every morning before Jonathan was awake she left their cabin and went to the very end of the boardwalk, where she could sit and gaze down between her dangling feet at the sea creatures that thronged the water between rippled white sand and surface. There were shoals comprising hundreds of tiny fish like flocks of brilliant birds swirling, hovering, gliding and darting, driven by a unifying shared impulse. Sometimes small sharks whipped across like nuclear warheads. Once she saw a huge ray, its ghostly wings beating in slow motion as it passed beneath her; another time a turtle, its unwieldy bulk graceful in submarine flight. She would sit there for an hour or more, ravished by the silence, and the voluptuous colour and grace of the undersea world, until Jonathan came on to the beach for his morning swim and raised an arm to her. On the first few mornings he swam out to her, rupturing her peace with his splashy crawl, fracturing the surface of the water as he bobbed about and shook the drops from his eyes. At those moments she hated him, and she didn't want that. After a few days, when she saw him she would get up and walk purposefully back. By the time he reached the water's edge she'd adjusted to the prospect of their shared day, and would swim to meet him, imagining the water as a kind of wetsuit between her and his amorous morning embrace.

Apart from that hour in the morning, the island, billed as paradise, was purgatory for Api. Its very beauty and isolation made time stand still – one of its great selling points. Jonathan slept and slept, but she barely slept at all. She resisted sleep, feared it almost. So far from everything, what would happen if she never woke, or woke to a different reality where Bryn was no longer?

Her feelings might have been easier to bear had she been able to call them infatuation. But this hard, ineluctable obsession was surely more than that. She was possessed by her longing to possess.

And with the longing for love came hatred. Hand in hand, side by side, in church they'd caught her between them. She might have known from his eyes, his smile, his way with his daughter on the beach, that he would have a lovely wife. Api had no doubt that she was not just beautiful but passionate, loyal, good, deserving of his devotion. She tortured herself with Linda's imagined perfection. She loathed it, wanted it gone. Or if not gone, then spoiled, so that he would no longer adore her.

After their return there had been all kinds of small opportunities for Api to feel in touch with him. Their wedding present to begin with. They had played completely safe, choosing six Waterford whisky tumblers from the list at Harrods. She'd half-hoped that they might have gone off-list, and sent them something individual, perhaps a little idiosyncratic, but why would they? She reminded herself that not he, but the wife, was their connection with the Frankels, and that doubtless she would have been responsible for buying the present.

The thought made her quite nauseous with jealousy. In spite or because of this she laboured long and hard over her thank-you note, in order to strike the right tone. She must be sure to include him, perhaps to mention his work for Delancey – though she knew that for some reason Jonathan didn't like him – and to imply, lightly of course, that there would be future occasions to get to know one another better. All four of them, of course. She was the price that had to be paid.

In the end she had written:

Dear Bryn and Linda, (she put his name first, a small thing but important to her)
Thank you so much for choosing the beautiful crystal glasses. We're absolutely delighted, and shall think of you

whenever we use them. I'm no great drinker, so I hope it
won't be letting the side down if mine contains Diet Coke! We
scarcely had time to talk at the wedding, but I feel I know
you through my new family, and look forward to meeting
and getting to know each other better in the very near future.
I'd certainly welcome your expert opinion on our lovely house
in Highgate for which I've had sole charge – a big responsi-
bility, but an enjoyable one.

Thank you again for your most generous present.

Love, Api Frankel

She read over the final draft several times, concerned that it
sounded too girlish. She had originally put '*with love from us*
both', but had altered that. Was just '*love*' too informal? She
decided not. It was casual, it implied an ongoing friendship.

A little while after that, the wedding photographs arrived.
Oddly, she had almost no photographs of herself over the
years. The Durrances had not gone in for them. There had
been a handful, no more than a dozen, when she was about
five, taken by Charles to use up film after one of his overseas
trips, and consequently all showing her in the same clothes
in the same setting. The garden at home, with her in shorts,
a striped T-shirt and wellington boots, pushing a three-legged
toy buggy containing a Cabbage-patch doll. Its chubby,
currant-eyed face provided a stark contrast to her small pale
one, set in a long-suffering expression.

But here were endless pictures of the new Api. Jonathan
pronounced the album 'not bad' and she was deputed to order
prints and circulate them. But as soon as she could she curled
up on the sofa on her own and pored over the pictures in a
spirit not of vanity but of curiosity, fascinated and a little
shocked. Nothing showed. Not a trace of the battleground
inside her head. Jonathan stared four-square at the camera as
if facing it down, a man well satisfied with his situation. She
seemed tethered to him by gossamer, a thread so fine it might
break at any moment and allow her to float away. She hadn't

realised, either, how thin she was; and it was said you put on half a stone in photographs. She looked – she tilted her head, seeking a metaphor in her mind – like a grey flame, an ecto-plasm. Her eyes in the photographs were bright, but her face remained unsmiling. Later, in the pictures taken of her dancing, there was an occasional smile, but her eyes seemed dull. In the pictures of her on her own she saw Suzannah looking back at her.

There were two of Bryn and his wife. The first was outside the church as they arrived, every inch the red-carpet couple, the must-have guests. Her smile was one of brilliant, prac-tised gaiety; he looked more restrained. Perhaps, Api thought, he hadn't wanted to be there. Perhaps it had been a terrible chore for him. Had that changed, she wondered, when he saw that it was her? Feverishly she looked through the pictures of the reception until she found one of their table, but immedi-ately she wished she hadn't. There they were, this time looking not at the camera but at each other, sharing a private joke, she leaning her forehead on his shoulder, eyes closed in laughter, he looking down, his hand about to touch her hair, pleased that she found whatever it was funny . . .

She tortured herself with these pictures, turning to them constantly so she could look at him, but having to endure her at the same time.

When she took the album to show the senior Frankels, she was careful to position her questions on the subject late, and casually, so as not to arouse suspicion. Harry was out having lunch at his club, which made things a little easier: Elizabeth always gave the impression she liked talking woman-to-woman with her daughter-in-law.

'Tell me a bit more about these two,' said Api. 'Jonathan wasn't very forthcoming.'

'No, well, he and Bryn seem to rub each other up the wrong way, the way men do,' said Elizabeth. 'It's not what you or I would call serious. A clash of egos. They're such *boys*.'

'So that's how you know him, is it – he's a work associate of Jonathan's?'

'I wouldn't put it quite like that. It was Harry who commissioned him to design the hotel in Bristol. No, we got to know him because he married our lovely Linda.'

Api didn't miss a beat. 'And how was that?'

'She was Harry's PA, years ago. For oh, a long, long time. She was his favourite. He used to say she was the sort of girl you could depend on totally to do the right thing at all times. I sometimes wonder if he didn't have a little thing for her, but you know?' Elizabeth touched Api's hand confidingly. 'If he had I wouldn't have worried. I trusted her completely, just as he did. Linda would never have let us down. Never done a thing to hurt us.'

Api smiled. 'She's very attractive. I noticed her in church.'

'It's that colouring,' agreed Elizabeth.

'And does she still do any work for Harry?'

Elizabeth shook her head. 'Not really. I think he sometimes asks her to help out, I don't know . . . They have lunch from time to time for old times' sake. But no. She has a successful business of her own these days.'

Api's skin prickled. 'What sort of business?'

'I think she arranges parties – arranges the way they look – the flowers, the decorations, the colour scheme – she's always been gifted like that.'

'And he's an architect?'

'Yes. Terribly distinguished so I understand though I don't know much about these things. He was responsible for some Middle Eastern thing that made him a lot of money. The work he did for Harry and Jonathan was superb, I don't know why Jonathan's such a grouch, they just seem to put their heads down and—' Elizabeth pressed her fists together, illustrating. 'It's too silly. And he's such a dear, such a lovely man.'

Those were the phrases that rang in Api's ears as she went home. 'A lovely man' . . . 'our lovely Linda'. Love and longing

swelled in her own heart, and were stifled, like a cancer, by
jealousy. She was sure that whatever they shared, she could
trump it. Linda might be beautiful, good and gifted, but she
could not give everything to him in the way that she, Api,
could.

She ordered prints of the photographs in which they
featured, and sent them to the Mancinis, with another little
note. *Thought everyone would like one of themselves in their
wedding best.*

A couple of weeks later a card showing the famous Pre-
Raphaelite Ophelia arrived for her. On it was written simply:
Thank you – reminds us of a lovely wedding – Linda and Bryn.
She had no idea who had written the words, since she didn't
know the handwriting of either.

She tried to find out from Jonathan why he disliked Bryn,
which turned out to be easier than she thought, because directness always worked best with him. It was on one of the rare
evenings when Jonathan was back before eight, and they were
having a drink in the garden.

'Your mother said you don't like Bryn Mancini,' she said.
'Why's that?'

'He's an opportunist.'

'Really? Does he need to be? She said he was a very distinguished architect.'

Jonathan's mouth tightened. 'I wouldn't know about that.
He's made money, and he certainly played the advantage after
he married Linda Reynolds. Dad was dazzled by all that
prizewinning stuff. But he wasn't right for us. The Bristol
hotel was set to go down the pan with millions of pounds
because of his precious ideas. It had to be rescued.'

'It's turned out well, hasn't it?' said Api.

'No thanks to him.'

'Your mother likes him. She likes both of them.'

'My mother likes most people, but then she doesn't have
to do business with them.'

'When I met them at the wedding I liked them too.'

Jonathan smiled without looking at her. 'QED. Linda's out of the same mould. To hear my parents talk you'd think she came somewhere in between Princess Grace and Mother Teresa. She was just another good-looking PA on the make who wormed her way into Dad's affections and made him believe she was indispensable. After all this time she still sees him. I don't know why my mother puts up with it.'

'But there's nothing going on, surely?' asked Api.

'Come on, Api, he's got more sense than that. No, the Marcinis are professional leeches.'

'I'm surprised you wanted them at the wedding.'

'I didn't. But it made the parents happy.'

Api understood. Why wouldn't she? She was uniquely placed to recognise jealousy when she saw it.

Over the months following the wedding her feelings of desolation were replaced by something steelier. Her confidence in her role as the new Mrs Frankel grew as she realised Jonathan trusted her. Whatever else, he was uninterested in domestic and social detail: she could write her own job description. And her marriage would be a job, she decided. She would work hard and be good at it. Her conscience would stay clear. It had been her intention to go back to work as soon as possible, but as time passed the prospect became less attractive. She had money now, and the comfort and freedom it bought. The house in Hardwicke Row was her realm, and she was proud of what she'd done there – everyone who visited was bowled over by it. Jonathan had let the Docklands flat, and they planned to buy an out-of-town property, perhaps in East Anglia, or Gloucestershire.

Api favoured the latter, because she didn't wish to be too close to her mother. But then Xanthe and Derek had gone off and got married, without telling anyone till afterwards, and to everyone's even greater astonishment she had moved into Derek's place in London. The two houses on the coast were to be sold and – the surprises were unending – it was announced that the new Mr and Mrs Powell were looking for a place in France at which to spend weekends and holidays, and to which they would eventually retire. Api felt sad for her father, with whom no plans had ever been made, who had had to find his pleasures elsewhere. But then she reminded herself that he had at least *had* pleasures, while Xanthe carried on her discontented life in the family home. They had reached their accommodation back then; now perhaps Xanthe was due some indulgence.

There was a lot in the Aldeburgh house. Some of it went with Xanthe to London, some into store with France in mind; the rest she left her offspring to dispose of.

'She says we can take anything we want,' Gilda told Api over the phone, 'provided we arrange to have it taken away. And the rest can go to the sale rooms or the dump. Then she wants it to go on the market with vacant possession for a quick sale. She's put me in charge – Api, help!'

Api was happy to oblige. It was late November. She picked a weekend in December and wrote to Martin, Saul and Judith to tell them that she and Gilda would be at the house then, and they could come at any time that suited them over the two days and make their choices – first come, first served; she and Gilda would get rid of the rest.

En route to Suffolk in Api's new black Boxster, Gilda expressed misgivings.

'I have an awful feeling there'll be blood on the carpet.'

'Why? One thing this family isn't, is sentimental about stuff. And to our credit we're not materialistic either. I bet we wind up getting the whole lot piled in a van and taken away.'

'Easy for you to talk,' said Gilda. 'The woman with every-thing.' She glanced at Api. 'If that's what you are?'

'Nobody is. It's a silly thing to say.'

'Still all right with Jonathan?' asked Gilda. And when Api remained silent added: 'You will be so long as no one else comes along.'

Api knew that Gilda was the only person she might have

confided in. But she did not do so, and realised that now she probably never would. She was on her own.

They had forgotten Xanthe's laziness. The house was almost full. Apart from her clothes (and not even all of those), personal possessions, books and perishables, everything was still there. As once before, she had simply sloughed off her old life, stepped out of it and left others to clear up.

'Holy fucking cow!' exclaimed Gilda, dropping her rucksack in the hall. 'Where do we start?'

'By turning on the heating and the hot water, and then going for fish and chips.'

In the interests of getting their strength up they had fish and chips at one of the tables at the back of the shop rather than bringing it back. When they returned, Gilda had formed a plan.

'OK, here's what we do tonight. We put the clothes in bags for the charity shop. We empty drawers and cupboards and anything worth saving we put on the dining-room table to be sorted through. The idea is to get everything visible. The rest we bag up. First thing tomorrow one of us goes for more bin bags and boxes.'

There was a portable stereo in the kitchen and a shelf full of Charles's old CDs in the living room, so they got to work to the accompaniment of Elgar, Brahms and Rachmaninov. By midnight twelve crammed bin bags stood in the hall, the dining table resembled a white-elephant stall, pictures and mirrors were ranged along the walls and those contents of the kitchen cupboards worth preserving were on the kitchen table.

The house had three bedrooms, with a full complement of bedding but no sheets except in Xanthe's room. These they put in the washing machine, to join the contents of the airing cupboard outward bound on the following day. That night the sisters moved one of the other mattresses into Xanthe's room and lay down beneath their uncovered duvets. Api took the one on the floor, but at once she wished she hadn't. The past scurried round and over her like a spider. She began to shiver.

'We never did this, did we,' said Gilda from above. 'Shared a room?'

'No, but then you were the oldest and I was the youngest.'

'I never shared with anyone. None of us did.'

'We had a big house.'

Api heard Gilda prop herself up on her elbow – she was staring down at her in the dark.

'But we wouldn't have done anyway.'

'Perhaps . . . Gilda?'

'Mm?'

'I can't sleep down here. I'll go back on the bed next door.'

'Don't do that!' Gilda turned on the bedside light. 'Hop in here.'

'No.'

'Come on. There's loads of room. Don't worry, I've never harboured impure thoughts about a woman, let alone a sibling. Get *in*!'

Api slipped under the duvet. Gilda put out a hand and rubbed her arm. 'You're frozen. Ap?'

'Don't fuss. It's the floor. I'm the woman with everything, remember? I've gone soft.'

'Hmm. Whatever you say.' They stayed apart, not touching except for Gilda's finger on her arm, softly stroking until the shivering stopped.

'Night, Ap . . .'

'Night.'

A moment later Gilda rolled away, her breathing slow and deep. But Api remained awake until the window began to turn grey.

First to turn up next day was Saul, who made no bones about his need of stuff, to the extent that he'd hired a van to take things away.

'You did say first come, first served?'

'Absolutely,' said Gilda, providing him with red stickers. 'Bear in mind we got here last night. Anything with a yellow dot's mine, but there isn't a lot. A couple of pictures, the stereo and the big wooden chair out of the kitchen.'

Before he could ask, Api said: 'The only thing I wanted was the portrait, and Mum gave it to me.'

'Then here goes.'

Judith and Ruth arrived at midday and laid claim to some kitchen equipment and about half the CDs. They lunched on bought-in sandwiches and beer. It was Judith, naturally, who commented on the haul in Saul's van.

'You've got absolutely loads!'

'I got here early.'

'But where will you put it all? That cottage of yours is tiny.'

Saul flushed slightly. 'Does it matter? I'll find somewhere.'

'I bet you're going to sell it,' said Judith, without any particular edge. Everyone else simultaneously realised that that was precisely his intention, and scrupulously avoided catching each other's eye. There had been no conditions placed on the distribution of the house contents, and to do so now would have been to open a Pandora's box they all preferred to leave closed.

In the afternoon Api left them sorting through the bedlinen and went for a walk. The weather was unseasonally soft, a watery sunlight gleaming on the calm surface of the sea and making the bare arms of the trees shine.

Without having consciously decided to do so she walked along the promenade to his house. It was a large 1920s villa set back from the prom, with a glassed-in verandah at the back overlooking the garden and the sea. She knew that they occasionally let it out or lent it to friends, so it didn't surprise her to see a young woman out on the tussocky winter grass, kicking a ball with a toddler. She might not have said anything, but the woman looked up and caught her eye and smiled.

'Good afternoon.'

Api paused. 'Hello. You're very energetic.'

'Anything for a good night's sleep.'

'Isn't this the Mancinis' house?'

She gave the ball a push with the side of her foot. 'Not as far as I know.'

Api realised she had completely overlooked the obvious. 'I'm so sorry, it must be *yours!*'

'Actually no.' The woman laughed. 'We're borrowing it from friends for a week. But they're not Mancini. Maybe the people before that – the architect?'

'That's it,' said Api. 'I do apologise, I didn't realise they'd moved.'

'Oh, about a couple of years ago, it must be, since our friends bought it. I must say it's wonderful to be able to use it from time to time. It's a lovely house, but then you know that.'

'Yes. Right, well, sorry to have disturbed you. Enjoy the rest of your holiday.'

So they'd gone. And she had missed her opportunity.

She walked back along the beach where she'd first seen him: not that long ago, and yet she'd been a child. In flight from her mother and her own temper. And now both he and her mother had flown. Just when you thought you knew how things were, they changed, and you had to start all over again.

Martin's email to Api had been predictably casual. 'May get there, don't worry if I don't. Can't think of anything I'd be likely to want. Thanks for asking anyway.' However he did show up at about nine o'clock that night, when Saul and his groaning van had already departed. Judith and Ruth had opted to stay, and they'd got in an Indian takeaway and were sitting round the kitchen table.

'Curry, fantastic, wish I'd known. I'd have got here earlier.'

'Take a pew,' said Gilda. 'There's plenty, I'll go and get another chair.'

Martin opened a beer. 'Saul not get here yet?' Api explained that he'd been and gone. 'Pity. I wasn't going to come, but then I thought it isn't often we all see each other, better make the effort.'

'It's good to see you,' said Ruth.

Martin pulled a sardonic face. 'Notice who said that. The one non-sibling present.'

Gilda returned with a bedroom stool and joined them. 'There's a lot of small stuff set out in the dining room, you might find something of sentimental value.'

'Does anyone else find this weird?' asked Martin. 'As though Mum had died?'

Api said: 'In a way she has. The old Mum. She just wants everything got rid of so she can be her new self unencumbered.'

'Is there anything of Dad's?'

'Still quite a lot of CDs.'

'I might take those if nobody wants them. Is this lamb jalfrezi? It's wicked.'

In the morning when Api came down to make some tea, she was surprised to find Martin already up, and dressed, surveying the things spread out on the dining table.

'Junk really . . .' he mused as she came in, 'but it's funny how it brings things back. Remember this?' He picked up a bent brass toasting fork. 'Mum used to make toast by the fire but she never waited till the coal had gone red and the toast was always sooty.'

'She was no cook,' agreed Api.

'Cook? My digestive tract has never recovered. Here's that *babushka* Dad brought back from Moscow. Or what's left of it. Was it you demolished that?'

'Probably.'

'Macramé potholders . . . 'struth! Windchimes . . . table lighter, cigarette box. Did you ever see those before?'

'They were in the drawing room. On the mantelpiece.'

'Anyone would think they used to have parties. Did they ever? In fact, did they have friends?'

'Yes,' said Api. 'They used to go out, sometimes. But they didn't ask people back.'

Martin picked up a small glass paperweight and turned it

over in his hands. 'Do you think she was happy when we were growing up?'

'You were older. What did you think?'

'I thought about me. Myself. It took up all my time. Anyway, you've always been the canny one.'

'I think she was content. She didn't mind Dad always being away. It meant she could take life easy.'

'With all of us . . . Not many women's idea of an easy life. Most of the women I associate with would regard it as something just this side of the salt mines.'

Api picked up a gold powder compact, and wondered if Charles had given it to Xanthe, and if she'd ever used it.

'She didn't work very hard.'

Martin drew his brows together in astonishment. 'I can't believe you said that. We were her life.'

She was taken aback. 'We may have been the only life she had, but that doesn't mean she made any effort.'

'No effort? All the shenanigans with Gilda, and me giving the whole world the silent treatment and having to be taken out of school, not to mention –' he lowered his voice slightly but spoke with even greater emphasis – 'not to mention Judith and all her problems. She must have felt she was never going to get out from under.'

'Saul was no trouble,' said Api. '*I* was no trouble.'

'Saul, I grant you. He at least had the decency to wait till he left home before becoming a layabout. But you kept up the family tradition in the end, running away and shacking up with undesirables. Christ, even Dad got involved.'

'*Only* Dad,' Api corrected him. 'Only Dad got involved. Mum had no idea about anything, she sat at home waiting for things to get sorted out.'

'Well I never . . .' Martin put the paperweight down slowly and carefully, as if replacing an egg in a nesting box. 'I must say I am surprised.'

'Sorry. It's how I remember it.'

He walked away from her and stood looking out of the

window. It was a grey morning with a light rain falling.

'Do you think she's happy now?'

'Yes.'

He turned and his expression was hard. He wasn't going to forgive her. 'Not just "content"?'

'No, I think she's happy. Because she's realised she can make Derek happy.'

He digested this for a moment, and then rubbed his eyes with the heels of his hands. She was taken aback by his shock – that their two experiences had been so different.

'Sorry,' she said again, but hotly. 'I realise how all that sounded.'

He shook his head. 'I don't think you do, Api. I don't think you can.'

'Anyway,' she said, 'if you're so bloody grateful and appreciative you've had a funny way of showing it all these years.'

'I beg your pardon?'

'Swanning off and leaving everyone to it. Making your pile. Let's be honest, the only reason I'm the one who doesn't embarrass you any more is because I got rich. And the only reason you showed up at the wedding was because you smelt the money and thought you might be able to pull.'

There was a short silence, vibrating with insult and offence on both sides. Then Martin walked to the door, saying as he passed:

'I'll be off. There's nothing here I want.'

She heard him run up the stairs two at a time to collect something from the room where he'd slept. But she didn't go into the hall, and the next she saw of him, after the front door slammed, was getting into the car. His outline seemed to shimmer with anger. He didn't look back once.

She thought: *I'm getting more alone by the minute. And the trouble is I don't care. I'm much worse than Xanthe ever was. I drive people away.*

Gilda came into the room, arms folded against the morning chill.

'What happened to the tea? And who's gone out?'

'Kettle's boiled. It was Martin. He had to leave.'

Gilda followed her into the kitchen. 'That was a bit abrupt, he might have said goodbye.'

'Everyone was in bed.'

Gilda sat at the table. 'Did he take anything?'

'No.'

'I see. Well, maybe what he said was true, and he came all this way to see his family.'

They completed the sorting-out during the course of Sunday, and packed as much as they could into bags and boxes leaving curtains and carpets in place. Api, as the only one who hadn't got to work the next day, agreed to stay over and arrange for the disposal of the rest: they'd already booked a van to take stuff to the dump and the sale rooms, it was just a case of seeing it off the premises, alerting the estate agents, and locking up. The For Sale sign would go up as soon as the place was empty. Xanthe and Derek were delaying the sale of Derek's property until they'd found somewhere in France.

Judith and Ruth set off at two in their pin-neat Honda, the boot and back seat filled with their spoils.

'We'll write to Xanthe,' said Ruth. 'This was so kind of her.'

Api smiled and said nothing. She had done enough harm for one day. Mac and a friend came out in the friend's dilapidated Volvo estate to collect Gilda and her things. It had looked a lot, and included a wing-backed armchair, but somehow it all went in, with the friend, Danny, crouched foetally in the back. His heroic discomfort didn't prevent Gilda from bidding Api a fond farewell on the pavement.

'Will you be all right? We're all deserting you.'

'I'll be fine.'

Gilda embraced her, and planted a kiss on her cheek. ''Bye, Ap. Take care of yourself.'

That's what I do, thought Api as she waved them off. *That's what I'm good at. Looking out for number one.*

Once she was alone she could indulge her pain and longing. Sink back into them as the element in which she truly belonged. She didn't wish to be distracted or healed. She embraced them. Gilda was the one who came closest to seeing how things really were, and with her gone Api felt safe once more.

During the morning she watched, calmly, as the house was emptied of its remaining contents. At midday, when everything had gone, she rang Xanthe to declare the job done.

'Did everyone come?' Xanthe wanted to know. 'Did everyone take something?'

Api thought of Martin. 'More or less.'

'Anyway, I'm glad you all saw one another.' Even now, thought Api, her mother was managing obliquely to take credit for something which was the product of her own inertia. She made it sound as though she personally had been responsible for organising an affecting family get-together.

'I'll drop the keys off at the estate agent's.'

'Thanks. That's such a good job done. How was everyone?'

'Pretty good.'

'Derek sends his love by the way.'

'Give him mine. Must go. 'Bye.'

Suddenly, she couldn't wait to leave. She had no feelings about the house; she locked it up without a pang, and dropped off the keys with a light heart.

The day was hers. She had given Jonathan no indication of when she might be back, so she was not expected. The damp weather had given way to bright, cold sunshine. She rejoiced in the seclusion of her car, and the freedom of the open road. Her happiest moments now were when driving – when no one knew where she was, and she could persuade herself that anything was possible.

At the junction with the main road there was a diversion in place, but it didn't bother her. Indeed, when she reached the point where she might have picked up her usual route she decided against it and opted to continue along the coast, and back across country through Essex.

It was one of those days when she felt she could have gone anywhere, done anything, been whatever she wanted. Incredible enough that Apollonia Durrance, the runaway, the no-hoper, the willing victim who had been lower than a dog, should now be Mrs Api Frankel, with a platinum credit card and a Porsche: if she could do that, then surely there was nothing she could not do. Seen from the perspective of the sparkling, empty weekday countryside her life was a thing created by her. If there was something it still lacked, that she wanted most in all the world, then it should be within her grasp.

At one thirty she stopped in a seaside town to stretch her legs and find something to eat. It was a small, plain place with little of the calendar-charm of some of the villages she'd driven through. The pub looked drab and uninviting. But there was a convenience store where she bought a wrapped sandwich and some orange juice, and she decided to get back on the road, drive inland and turn down the first attractive lane she came to for an impromptu picnic.

As she drove slowly out of the town she saw Linda Mancini. She recognised her instantly, but the unexpected sight took a moment to register. At once she pulled over, and even backed up a little way, confident of her invisibility.

The little MG was what she'd seen first. Since becoming the proud owner of a performance car herself she had become sensitised to others, especially in an unlikely context. The car had drawn her eye, and then the door of a terraced house behind it had opened and Linda appeared. She wore jeans, flat boots, a guernsey sweater over a white shirt, and was carrying a jacket – a perfectly smart-casual look for a day in the country. But that was the only predictable factor in her appearance. Her face from which the glorious red hair was pulled back into a ponytail, was white and gaunt, and her manner lacked all its usual composure and *joie de vivre*. She positively stumbled out of the door, glancing over her shoulder as if escaping from something in the house. As she fumbled in her bag for her car keys two figures appeared in the doorway – a wild-haired woman, heavy-set and wearing an expression of stony malevolence, and a tall, blank-faced man. There was something odd about them, something that didn't add up; Api couldn't imagine what their relationship might be to one another, or to Linda, who now clambered into her car, started, stalled, and finally pulled away at speed.

The big woman withdrew, the man peered out of the door after Linda's car and then stepped back jerkily, as though he had been pulled.

The moment this little vignette ended, Api could scarcely believe she'd seen it. The terraced house looked dour and blank. The street was quiet. But then, for a moment, the man's face had appeared in the window, apparently staring directly at her. Unaccountably alarmed, she started up the engine and drove off.

Her alarm was soon replaced by satisfaction. She could not escape the impression that she had been vouchsafed an insight, made a gift of something she did not yet understand but might well, in the fullness of time, be able to use.

19

2002 – Bryn, Linda, Api

As the months went by, the house by the river grew. The bull-dozers and JCBs did their brutal work, cutting and gouging the soft green shoulder of land around which the Eaden ran. The foundations were laid, the bare coppice of scaffolding went up, the walls rose. By the time the building was finished, and work begun on the inside, it was hard to remember what the land had been like before. Even the most grudging towns-people acknowledged that the house blended in with and even enhanced its surroundings. Those who had met its owner were beguiled. He often came down, not just overseeing things but walking by the river, or round the town. It was clear he loved this place; and the people who lived there, seeing it through his eyes, loved it more. They liked the idea of a metropolitan millionaire, bringing his ideas and his wealth to their town. A few knew who he was, and as word of his reputation spread it induced a proprietary pride in the locals. In his field he was first among equals, honoured and admired. And he had chosen this place to build his house.

They were more right than they knew. The house on the river had become a touchstone for Bryn, the symbol of changing fortune. If he could only complete it, and move himself and his family there, he would have escaped his demons and all would be well. Until then he must live with this strange mixture of anxiety and elation, where anything could happen.

He realised that he had contributed, colluded even, in this state of affairs. The evening that he had gone to the Frankels' party on his own he had chosen to take the path that would lead to where he was now. He had elected to deepen the deception begun in Aldeburgh and furthered at the wedding. He had, if not allowed the witch over his doorstep, then voluntarily stepped over hers.

Following the conversation with Api, he had called to thank her for the party, and to ask the name of the man in the portrait.

'I'm so glad you rang,' she said. 'I realised almost at once that you didn't know his name, but I didn't want to bother you.'

'It's no bother,' he assured her. 'I'm intrigued.'

It was true. He set out to find out about John Ashe with an almost feverish enthusiasm – not to assuage any curiosity of his own, but to be able to go back and say: 'Here it is, here's what youre after. This was your great-grandfather.' To make her a gift of his efforts. But to his surprise and frustration his researches drew a complete blank. It was as if the man had never existed, or every trace of his life and work had gone with him to the grave. She had said, with fierce pride, that he had been a millionaire – in those days that would have been doubly exceptional, but all the usual sources, Somerset House, the Public Records Office, revealed nothing. Through it all he would suddenly catch himself worrying at the problem, and ask himself why on earth he was going to all this trouble to find out about the ancestor of a young woman he hardly knew, when none of this was anything she – or any one of her family – could not have done themselves. He even questioned whether she needed or wanted the information at all, or was simply managing him at a distance for reasons of her own. But he had offered to do this, and making the offer had given him a rush of conceited pleasure. He had not told Linda about the search. It had not required any subterfuge; there had simply seemed no point in mentioning it.

At the point of admitting defeat, he rang Api again.

'I'm sorry. He's an elusive fellow.'

'Don't worry, it was kind of you to try. In a way it's the mystery that makes him so fascinating. And there's not much known about the artist, either.'

'The one who lived down the road.'

'For a few months. Her name was Suzannah Rose Murchie. You might be able to find out something by investigating her – but what am I saying!' she laughed. 'This really is not your concern!'

'No, but since I've started.' He had already written the name down, and went over the words several times with his pencil. 'Don't worry, I shan't lose any sleep over it, but I'll keep my eyes open.'

'Thank you. If you would.' She had a formal manner for such a young woman. Listening to her he could see, so clearly, her pale face with its high forehead and floating hair, the face of a Faerie Queen . . .

To break in on his own thoughts, he said: 'I just hope if I do find out anything that it won't spoil the mystery.'

There was a pause and when she spoke he thought she might have been smiling. 'It won't spoil anything.'

It was a curious feature of this period that while he and Linda seemed to be drifting apart, he fell in love with her all over again. Her business was growing exponentially, and much of his time and attention was taken up with the new house. But looking at her across a distance he saw her once again as she had been when he first met her – not as the accomplished wife and mother, whom he'd also adored, but the sparkling, flirtatious, dynamic man's woman who had swept him off his feet all those years ago. He was in awe of her energy, dazzled anew by the high-octane charm now being brought to bear on her customers.

Sometimes it struck him as ironic that she was achieving this new success at a time when neither of them need ever work again. But then he'd tell himself that their increasingly parallel lives were perfectly natural, and even healthy. They had never been the sort of couple to smother one another in a stifling symbiosis, and this new chapter rekindled, in him anyway, the excitement of the *amoureux*.

On an increasingly rare evening in together he said, only half-joking: 'You know I'm quite shy of you these days.'

He was standing in the doorway of her office. She was sitting at the computer, and she laughed without taking her eyes off the screen. 'Come on, Bryn . . .'

'No, it's true.' He came over and put his arms round her, pinioning her own arms. 'Leave that for a moment.'

'I should, shouldn't I?' She wriggled. 'Let me out then.'

She rose, but he sensed her attention was still elsewhere. 'Let's go and sit outside,' he suggested. 'And watch the sun go down.'

She laughed. 'We'll have to be quick!'

'You know what I mean.'

It was only eight thirty and high summer, but the shadows of the two immense trees at the end of the garden were already spilling on to the patio, and soon the more solid one of the house beyond would follow. In town, the last knockings of even the sunniest day came early. On the banks of the Eaden it would be different.

He brought her a glass of wine. 'A sundowner for sundown.'

'I must go easy. I ought to finish that proposal tonight.'

'You'll work better for a break.'

'Some say . . .'

'Just think,' he said. 'When the new house is ready we'll be able to watch the sun set over the horizon.'

She shivered theatrically. 'Don't say that, you make us sound like the folks that live on the hill.'

'That's good, surely.'

'No, it's *old*, Bryn.'

She was laughing, but he could see she meant it. He forced himself to ask: 'I'm not railroading you into this, am I?'

'Certainly not! For one thing you know me better than that – I'm not so easily railroaded. And for another I'm perfectly capable of seeing myself right.'

He felt a premonitory chill. 'How do you mean?'

'I mean that I shall be able to enjoy your – our – beautiful house so long as I have a little place in London to retreat to. A businesswoman's *pied à terre.*'

Bryn, who could think of no reason at all why this wasn't a good idea, was nonetheless shocked.

'Will that be necessary? I mean with the computer, and we shan't be that far out of town, and very central. After all, you're likely to pick up new clients in the country—'

'Bryn!' she interrupted. Her expression was quizzical and amused. 'We aren't necessarily talking rational here. I'm just saying that a little place in London is what I would *like*. It would make life a squeak more convenient, and more enjoyable. It doesn't have to be pricey, I'm very happy to rent some studenty attic.' Her smile hardened a little. 'It's not a problem, is it?'

'I'm not sure . . .' He didn't know how to tell her he was devastated. 'I suppose I imagined that we'd be together at Eadenfield.'

'And we will, a lot of the time. Most of the time.'

'It's not as if you can't come up to London whenever you like. The last thing I want is for you to feel you're tied down. I want this house to provide freedom, like escape –'

'Escape from what?' She looked puzzled.

'Oh, the usual – the Smoke, the rat race, the pressures.'

'If you mean the city and the buzz, I like all those things. The rat race is a horrible expression. It demeans people and their jobs. If such a thing exists, you and I have never been part of it, we've always been lucky enough to do what we liked doing.'

'I agree. And I thought you liked the idea of living in the country.'

'Give me strength!' She shook her head in sudden, violent exasperation, eyes closed. 'Bryn, what is all this? It doesn't suit you to be plaintive and needy. You're doing a fantastic job on the house but it was always your idea. I don't feel this need for – for *escape*. I shall love being there, just not every minute of the time. Life changes. You can't step in the same river twice.'

He was hurt, but mindful of her accusation strove to hide it. 'You're right. And if the place turns out to be a white elephant we can always sell it.'

'We can, but we won't want to. Not if you don't turn your escape into my pressure, hm? And now, Kubla Khan – may I return to my labours?'

She went back upstairs. The shadow of the house beyond the trees crept over the patio, and the light in the study came on. It was a gentle evening, warm and sweet, and he continued to sit there in the dusk. He'd always liked the half-light and the strange, sculptural quality it gave to things. The nymph, at home here as she had been in his bachelor garden, became more visible now the intrusive glare of day had gone. This evening she seemed not coquettish but wistful: her over-the-shoulder glance had something vale-dictory in it. Bryn, unused to anxiety, felt a cat's paw of something close to fear.

In bed that night when he put his arms round his wife he sensed a difference. Not a physical one, there was no holding back, her arms went round him, her open mouth touched his shoulder, his neck, his face, her leg threaded between his so that the soft inside of her thigh cushioned his groin. He ached with love and desire, but her warm accustomed response couldn't conceal the new strangeness that was there.

'I'm sorry.'

'It doesn't matter.' She snuggled against him, no longer passionate but comforting. 'Just so long as you're not losing interest in me.'

'Linda—'

'Joking.'

'I love you.' The well-worn words muffled the desperate importance of what he was saying. 'More than ever, more than I can say.'

'Good.' He heard her getting sleepy. 'That's nice. Me too . . .'

In another moment she'd gone, and he was left alone.

'Since you're a gentleman of leisure these days,' Jim said over the phone, 'I wondered if you'd care to come along and talk to some of our students at the end of Arts Week.'

'Happy to,' said Bryn, 'but will they have the remotest idea who I am? People see the work of architects all the time, every waking hour of their lives, but the vast majority couldn't tell you the name of a single architect, living or dead.'

'We'll publicise you. Put up pictures of the Scimitar, that'll ring a few bells. Anyway the closing lecture is pretty much of a three-line whip, you'll get an audience if only because there's a jolly afterwards.'

'In that case, my pleasure.'

Bryn didn't particularly look foward to the engagement. Jim was an old friend who had never asked a favour before; it would have been churlish to refuse, but students were the audience he liked least. They were either bored from the outset, or seemed to regard architects as among the enemy – fat cats who needed telling. The questions were often sticky. They certainly wouldn't see him as an artist; the only mitigating factor was that he didn't see himself as one either.

A few days later he got a letter from Jim, enclosing a leaflet about Arts Week.

'You'll see from this,' Jim wrote, 'that it's a kind of end-of-year showcase for the arts students. Helps to keep the college on the map and hopefully to gain university status in a year or two, though God knows why that should make any difference but it seems everyone wants to be able to say they have a degree these days. Better a good honest diploma, fairly got, than a faintly bogus degree, I say, but what do I know . . .

'Thursday night's the big night, when you're on. After that there's wine and peanuts in the hall. You can bring Linda along if she wouldn't mind being ogled by a hundred or so lads young enough to be her son . . .'

Linda declined. 'Is that mean of me? Do you mind being thrown to the lions on your own?'

'Not in the least. In fact I'm not sure I'd relish you witnessing my humiliation.'

'Nonsense, you'll be a roaring success. Go get 'em.'

In the event the talk didn't go badly. He made the sensible decision to play it with a very straight bat. Better to come across as a little dull, but with one's air of solid integrity intact, than as a flash bastard playing to the gallery and telling jokes which ran the risk of failure. The assembled company – students, lecturers, parents and public – listened politely and applauded respectfully. Only a few questions followed, the fourth (and inevitably last) of which was the obligatory bouncer.

'How do you feel about competitions?' The speaker was a large, long-haired young man in a combat jacket.

With the talk over, Bryn was a touch demob happy, or he might not have answered so swiftly: 'Pretty good, since that's how I started my career.'

'No reservations about making a fortune out of child murder?'

Bryn cursed himself. He should have seen it coming. There was always some clever-dick who prided himself on having done his homework. To be fair there were a few rumbles of 'Shame' but these were balanced by murmurs of righteous curiosity. From the corner of his eye he could see Jim shifting into winding-up mode, but he knew he must at least attempt an answer. If only, he reminded himself, to say what he wanted to say.

'Right . . . I was pleased then, and am still pleased now, to have been given the opportunity to do something useful with a site which would otherwise have become a demonised no-go area. There was a small amount of prize money which enabled me to make a donation to the Trust. It would certainly be true to say that winning that commission opened up other opportunities, but I'm not going to apologise for that.' He knew at once that he'd struck a false note, and there was another rumble. 'Can I ask,' he said, 'whether you've seen the peace garden yourself?'

'I'm not a ghoul.'

Bryn looked around. 'Has anyone?' Oddly, a few hands went up, like children in class. 'Anyone like to tell me what they thought?'

A woman began speaking, very quietly, realised she couldn't be heard and raised her voice. 'I went to see when I read about it in the paper. I thought it was very effective, but maybe the money could have been put to better use like, I don't know, more intensive policing, better ways of tracing missing youngsters . . .' She tailed off. 'But as a piece of work, it was impressive.'

'Thank you. Actually the prize was a tiny fraction of the money that came in after that horrific case, most of which went into the sort of project you describe. Clearly the house couldn't remain there – who would have lived in it? – and something had to be put in its place. So the answer to your question –' he addressed himself to the man at the back, who had sat down again – 'is that my feelings about competitions of this kind are entirely positive, and while it was certainly helpful to my career to win that one, any good fortune I've enjoyed since then has been down to my own efforts and has in no sense been built on the terrible deaths of those children. On the contrary, I hope the peace garden helped the families and the community to heal and to achieve a degree of closure.'

There was a smattering of applause, a good many po-faced absentions. He couldn't blame them. You pompous-sounding prick, he thought as he sat down, relieved to see that Jim was already stepping into the breach.

'Sorry about that,' Jim said as they headed towards the hall. 'I'm afraid he's something of a professional baiter. He even gave the Poet Laureate a hard time when he was here for our jubilee.'

'In a way it's a valid topic for debate, but it could have been more felicitously put.'

'He doesn't do felicitous.'

'I realise that now.'

'Anyway, you kept your composure remarkably well. I particularly admired your trick of batting a question back at the audience. Ever considered politics?'

'Only in the most unflattering terms.'

The next hour was spent in drinking warm white wine and eating small cold sandwiches while chatting to members of the senior common room, parents, and the more sociable of the students.

'I promise,' said Jim in an aside, 'to take you for curry very soon, but it's my responsibility to show you some of the students' work.'

Bryn clapped his friend on the shoulder. 'Then you must discharge it . . . No, seriously, I'd like that.'

He found the exhibition more interesting than expected. There were the products of various writing workshops, a small recording studio with original compositions being played, fashion design (though Bryn couldn't help feeling that the clothes were more suited to *Blade Runner* than the school run) and art and sociology projects. He paid particular attention to the last, as it was Jim's subject.

'So,' he asked, 'this work contributes towards their degree?'

'Diploma in our case, we're working on it, remember? But yes it does. They have a certain number of required modules and one which is their own choice. Vetted by me, just so they don't all decide to investigate the role of lap-dancing in modern urban society.'

Bryn paused. 'Here's the one that got away.'

'That girl's rather good actually, has a way of looking at things. She wants to make television documentaries, don't they all . . . But good luck to her, they could do with a few like her.'

Bryn opened the folder. 'May I?'

'Feel free, that's the idea. I'll be in another part of the forest, hail me when you're ready to move on.'

The project was entitled 'Unfit for Heroes – the London Underworld Between the Wars'. He could see that Jim was right: its author had flair. As well as an enormous quantity of researched data and statistics concerning everything from organised crime to venereal disease, she had adopted a perspective: that of a young woman living in London seven decades on – and asked the question: what were the social, economic, political and personal factors that might contribute to her becoming the victim of criminal exploitation, as opposed to her equivalent of the 1920s and 1930s? And what had been the influence of the Great War on the men, and some women, who had become the exploiters? He had no idea whether it was good science, but it made lively reading. She had a section on something she sweetly called 'The hero/villain interface' which in spite of the wince-making subtitle put forward a cogent and colourful argument that the very characteristics and experiences which could make a man a hero – opportunism, single-mindedness, a lack of concern for personal safety, a dash of vanity – could just as easily, in different circumstances, create a vicious criminal; and that the extreme conditions of war were precisely calculated to do both.

Absorbed and entertained, he read through the text. This girl had the ability to carry you along with her hypothesis, and to turn her evidence – and her opinions – into a sort of story. Reservations only surfaced when you looked up from the page, and even then the story stayed with you.

She was a natural populist, eager to reinforce her arguments by any means at her disposal: at the back of the folder she had put together four pages of cuttings and photos from the period, in the style of a collage, as if scattered on a desk. Stories of heroism in the trenches blended into images of the returning wounded with nurses in attendance, and then again into news items and court reports of various kinds of vice and villainy, accompanied by more photographs. He skimmed through these as he was meant to do – the intended effect was almost cinematic – occasionally turning the folder to read headlines. Clever, effective . . .

He stopped, his attention tugged by something that had caught his eye a split second earlier. He adjusted the angle of the folder to take a closer look.

The photograph from *The London Crier* of 21 February 1930 was captioned 'Vice king holds court at the Apache Club'. The quality wasn't great, and not improved by copying, but it was still an arresting image. A group of people, three women and a man, stood at a bar. The women were good-looking but overpresented, even allowing for the rather hard hair and make-up of the period. Their stance, attitude, flashing smiles all proclaimed them as women who profited from their appearance: showgirls or prostitutes.

In the centre of the group was a man: unmistakably, the man in the Frankels' portrait. John Ashe, immaculate in white tie and tails. From amongst his strenuously vivacious companions he stared back at the camera with Red Indian-like impassivity. The woman on his right was speaking into his ear, her hand raised to shield her words from the photographer, though her eyes slid teasingly towards the camera. There was no sign that Ashe was flattered or charmed by the presence of the girls. Though they hung about his shoulders there was no reciprocal touch. He stood poised, balanced, ready to walk away the moment the picture was taken. He held neither drink nor cigarette, his hands hung at his sides like the hands of a gunfighter. His eyes were black stones in his pale face. Even allowing for the photograph's poor definition, the left side of his face appeared to be pitted and furrowed with what might have been smallpox scars.

Bryn was about to close the folder when he found Jim standing next to him.

'Good stuff, isn't it?'

'She's very persuasive. Is she here, do you know?'

'Travelling.'

'Do you think she'd mind if I had a copy of this picture? A friend of mine's interested in the place where it was taken.'

'Sure, no problem – I'll get a copy run off and send it round to you.' Jim glanced about. 'Would you like to see more? You're extremely welcome, but I think you've done your bit now if you want to cut along.'

'Then let's go. But thanks,' said Bryn. 'I hope you won't misunderstand me if I say I enjoyed it a great deal more than I expected.'

He was left with the dilemma of what to tell Api. Any pleasure he might have taken in uncovering new information was mitigated by the nature of the information itself. At the party he had had the strong sense that she hero-worshipped her great-grandfather in a way only made possible by the mystery surrounding him. In the end he decided to try and find out a bit more before taking the decision. After all, he reasoned, though he was certain it had been John Ashe in the photograph, there was no concrete identification.

He got back to an empty house and a message from Linda on the answering machine.

'Hi there, welcome home. Hope you wowed the students and that they were suitably appreciative. Darling, I'm going to be late because I've realised I'm in the right neck of the woods to call in on another prospective client, so I'm going to see him early evening. Hope that's OK, it makes time-and-motion sense. I should be back around nine. Don't wait supper. Au revoir.'

Bryn poured a drink and went upstairs. Seated at his desk, he logged on to the web and keyed in the words 'London Crier'.

Linda arrived at Hallem Hall at six on the dot, having first located it and killed a little time parked in a farm gateway down the lane. The house was a jewel of a small manor house, set in a hollow in the surrounding farmland, encircled by a moat on which ducks sculled and preened in the evening sunshine. Every aesthetic and commercial instinct told her that this would turn out a worthwhile extension to her day.

As she crossed the drive from the car the front door opened and a man in jeans, a sweatshirt and stockinged feet greeted her.

'Linda Mancini?'

'Yes, how do you do.'

He gave her hand a brief tug. 'Christopher Sclater, good to meet you. No trouble finding me? Silly question, since you're here.'

'No problem at all, your instructions were perfect.'

'They have to be, or you'd still be orbiting the village, that last bit of lane's not easy . . . Can I offer you a drink?'

'A soft one would be lovely, whatever you've got.'

'Orange juice coming up. Take a pew and I'll be right with you.'

The rumpled English charm of the room, like that of its owner, did nothing to disguise its essential aristocratic elegance. Beneath the open newspaper on the sofa, the piles of books on the floor, the clutch of invitations on the mantelpiece and the tower of eclectic CDs was the sort of pricelessly beautiful old furniture that must surely, she thought, have belonged to the house before this man's occupancy. Accustomed to notice such things she had spotted the hooded eye of a discreet security system as she drove up, and now it was possible to see why.

Sclater returned with the drinks.

'You won't mind if I have a beer? I've been mowing the lawn, of which there is an unfeasible amount.'

'I think you deserve one.'

'That's what I tell myself.' He sat down with a contented sigh. 'I employ an excellent chap from the village to do the complicated gardening, but it seems a waste of his talents and my money to chug back and forth on the mower, so that's

my contribution. I take credit for absolutely nothing except
the somewhat wavy tramlines.'

'So,' said Linda. 'Tell me about the party.'

'My sixtieth birthday. It seems rather self-indulgent but
since I don't have a family to lay such things on for me I
thought I might as well do it myself.'

Without thinking, Linda said: 'I can't believe you're sixty.'

'The job is yours!'

'I'm sorry,' she said, but they were both laughing. Sclater
patted his stomach. 'The trick is to push the wrinkles out from
the inside.'

'That's why they say that past forty women have to choose
between their face and their figure.'

'Is that so? Thank God I'm on this side of the gender divide.
Now look, I was thinking of having about a hundred people
for dinner and dancing in the middle of February. That's as
far as I've got.'

'Let's see . . .' Linda got out her next-year's diary. 'Valentine's
Day is a Friday, but I don't know what you think of that as
a theme.'

'That is my birthday, actually. I was trying to avoid the
inevitable blizzard of hearts.'

'You don't have to be obvious. You could have a colour
scheme – say red and white. Or yellow and white, not everyone
knows that yellow roses are for love, and yellow is wonderfully springlike, it lights a place up.'

'That has possibilities.'

'Fancy dress?'

He shook his head. 'Since childhood my experience of fancy
dress has been that while other people look fantastic, I look
ridiculous and feel uncomfortable.'

'No fancy dress. At your party you must look and feel
tremendous. Black tie? Because if you're not worried about
formality you can extend the colour scheme to the guests, ask
them to come wearing whatever they like, with something in
a particular colour. Black and white with gold or silver is a

good one, easy to achieve, gives people lots of scope and it looks fabulously glamorous en masse.'

'Yes – yes, I can see that. Hang on, perhaps we're doing things the wrong way round, the first question is where. Would a marquee be completely out of the question in February?'

'Certainly not. I have a couple of companies I deal with all the time, and the marquees are designed to withstand anything the weather can throw at them. But your house is so pretty it would be a shame to waste it, you could have drinks in here beforehand and then go through—' She stopped, conscious of getting carried away. 'Now *I'm* doing things the wrong way round. Because I don't know your budget.'

'Limitless,' said Sclater. 'You can't take it with you.'

Bryn switched off the computer an hour later, none the wiser. The website had contained a good deal about the history of the *London Crier*, its proprietors, provenance and political stance (to the right), but references to content were limited to its angle on world events such as the Shackleton expedition, the Armistice, and the General Strike. And two world wars: the paper had folded in 1947.

He tried another tack, and keyed in 'Apache Club, London, 30s'. This produced nothing so he widened the request to 'London nightclubs, 1930s'. Now he was confronted with literally hundreds of sites. The Apache had a substantial entry mentioning its brief flowering from 1922 to 1934, its location in Romilly Street, and its character and clientele: '. . . a raffish small nightclub renowned for the anonymity it granted to the famous. A place where stars, royalty, and artists could mix with ordinary people and the underworld with no staring and no questions asked. Only two things were needed – money and style. The club's owner, "Piggy" Swynton-Brooke, notoriously reserved the right to refuse entry to anyone considered insufficiently interesting. No one was exempt from Piggy's whim of iron. A duchess was once turned away for having put on more weight than was acceptable, on the same night that the hugely fat jazz singer Muriel LeBarre was welcomed with open arms. At its height the Apache was the best-kept secret of London nightlife. But ultimately the feature that had been its greatest strength became its downfall. The rich, the famous and the blue-blooded were no longer prepared to put up with Piggy's alcohol-fuelled rudeness, its popularity waned and it closed, forgotten, only twelve years after opening.'

Bryn downloaded this information, and switched off the machine. He sat gazing out into the darkened garden. It looked as though the 'vice king' tag had been right. John Ashe, millionaire and man of mystery, and object of Api Frankel's hero-worship had been no more than a thumping crook.

Two hours later Linda shook hands with Christopher Sclater.

'We can give you a wonderful party,' she said. 'You have the perfect setting.'

'I'm glad you like it.'

They walked over the drive to her car. 'Has the house always been in your family?'

'Hell, no. I bought it. All my friends thought me completely barmy to buy a listed manor house at my time of life, they forecast alcoholism, madness and a sticky end, but here I am five years later and happier than I've ever been. I like the village and it likes me, because I let them use this place for all manner of junkets and fundraisers.'

'That's very good of you.'

'Isn't it?' He beamed wickedly. 'Does your husband like cricket, by the way?'

The reference to Bryn came as a slight jolt to Linda. 'He doesn't play. Rugby was his game, years ago, but he had an accident that put him out.'

'Poor chap. Still, you can't play rugger for long. Cricket you can, pretty well into your dotage, which I intend to do. I only asked because I have a social match here each year in the summer, and you might like to come.'

'It sounds fun.' She opened the door of the car. 'I'll send a proposal in writing in about a week to ten days. Don't be alarmed by anything I say, it's all up for discussion at this stage.'

'I shan't be in the least alarmed. I enjoyed our meeting.'

He stepped back, as she started the engine, and when she looked in the rearview mirror he was still waving, his arm scything slowly back and forth, as she turned out into the road.

Bryn loved to watch his wife when she came in from these trips, sparkling with self-satisfaction, her movements quick and her manner vivacious. He knew from her kiss that he was getting the overspill from the charm offensive she had launched earlier on others, but he didn't mind that. His evening's researches had left him feeling a little bleak – her return lifted his spirits.

'So how were the clients?' he asked as she heeled off her shoes and curled up her legs on the seat beside her.

'Couldn't be better. They adored the proposal and we're going to go ahead, incorporating one or two ideas they've had as well.'

'Congratulations. And what about the off-chance – the one you made a detour for?'

'Oh, perfectly nice . . . A slightly eccentric but well-to-do bachelor celebrating his sixtieth birthday on Valentine's Day. I think we can do business, so it was worth the trip.'

'I'm glad to hear it.'

'He wanted to know if you played cricket.'

'I hope you told him.'

'I did, but we might get asked anyway, he's that sort of chap.'

Bryn smiled, rubbing his hands through his hair. 'You mean the sort who's developed a crush on you.'

'Heavens, no,' said Linda. 'It wasn't like that at all.'

It was early September, and they'd been back from Italy for just over a week when the phone rang at around midday. He was due to drive down to visit the house, and Linda was in,

so he left her to take the call. It was impossible to deduce,
from the light resonance of her voice two floors below, what
the nature of the call might be, though he didn't think it was
either of the children. After a few minutes she came to the
foot of the stairs and called up:

'Bryn! Bryn?'

'Yup?'

'It's Api Frankel. She called to say that Harry's not well.'

'Oh God. Serious?'

'Hard to say . . . Anyway, she wanted to relay some message
to you from Jonathan, can you pick up?'

His heart sank. 'Sure.'

'Api . . .' he heard Linda say. 'Thank you so much for letting
us know about that, I'll be in touch with them right away. I'll
pass you over to Bryn now.'

Bryn waited for the click. 'Bryn here.'

'I'm sorry to disturb you when I know you must be working.
I shan't keep you.' He heard, beneath the politeness, that hint
of assumed intimacy.

'That's perfectly all right, I'm just engaged in desk-clearance
prior to going away for the night. Look, I'll get the details
from Linda, but I'm sorry Sir Harry's unwell.'

'Yes, I thought the two of you would want to know. He
hasn't been himself for months, but it's official now.'

Bryn let a respectful pause elapse before asking: 'Linda said
there was a message from Jonathan?'

'Oh well . . . no, I think we had crossed wires. It was just
that really.' He didn't believe her and was confident she'd never
intended him to. 'As a matter of interest, did you happen to
come across anything about John Ashe?'

There was no harm, he told himself, in revealing a little of
what he'd discovered.

'I've been keeping my eyes open. And I did find a picture
of him, quite by accident, but it doesn't tell us anything. I'm
pretty certain it was him – in a nightclub in the thirties
surrounded by gorgeous girls.'

She laughed, gratified. 'Brilliant!'

'Evidently a popular fellow. Nothing more concrete I'm afraid. But perhaps you won't be too disappointed. The mystery remains intact. Enhanced, if anything.'

'Yes.'

He sensed her reluctance to end the call. 'Well, Api, I'd better press on if I'm to get out of town in reasonable time. Did you want another word with Linda?'

'No.'

'If I should come across anything else about Ashe I'll let you know.'

'Thank you. You must come and have dinner some time. So I can meet Linda.'

'We'd like that. Give our best to Sir Harry, and Lady Frankel, if you see them before we do.'

'I will.'

''Bye now.'

'Goodbye.'

He rang off and sat still. He could hear Linda moving about down below, but could see Api, sitting like him, thinking of him. What he wanted was for Linda to come upstairs and rescue him, pull him out of this unhealthy, lonely reverie. But in a moment she called out that she was going, and would see him tomorrow night, and then the front door closed behind her. He was in a quicksand, but when he struggled and waved his arms she simply waved back, unable to see that he was trapped.

Api went to visit her parents-in-law on her own because to go with Jonathan at the moment was simply too difficult for everyone. Charles's death was still fresh in her memory; she recalled only too well the emotional complexities of it all, like a hedge of thorns around the stark fact of their loss. Even so she found Jonathan's anger incomprehensible. He seemed to see his father's illness as a conspiracy against him which, having finally been exposed, now presented a set of problems

which it was his sole responsibility to solve. Why had a diagnosis not been sought sooner? Why hadn't he himself been
told at once? Why wasn't every potential treatment being more
thoroughly explored? Why was everyone so apathetic in the
face of cancer, when the world was full of people who had
overcome it and gone on to lead healthy and fulfilled lives?

In vain did Elizabeth explain that diagnosis had been late
because in a man of Harry's age the symptoms were mild –
and that Harry was not so much resigned to his fate as in a
dignified accommodation with it. Jonathan's father would, she
pointed out gently, rather live out what was left of his life in
the places and circumstances he knew best and where he could
perform a useful function and enjoy himself, than be shunted
about from pillar to post in search of a procedure which could
at best buy him only a small extra parcel of time.

'He's always been a fit man!' Jonathan protested furiously.
'It's nothing short of shameful to give in so easily!'

The more agitated her son became the calmer and more
emollient was Elizabeth's manner. 'You're saying he should be
ashamed?'

'We all should. He could have years of productive life ahead
of him.'

'Jonathan, your father's in his eighties.'

'So it's all right for him to give up, on himself and the rest
of us?'

'It isn't like that, you're being too hard on him.'

'Really? It seems to me I'm the only person who wants him
to recover.'

Api, who had witnessed this particular exchange, didn't
know how Elizabeth had prevented herself from either
bursting into tears or scratching her son's face. Instead she
displayed a near saintly restraint, and an unwavering and
generous patience.

And in the middle of it all Harry – increasingly frail but
never less than immaculate – continued to be himself. On
good days he still went into his office for a couple of hours

in the morning. He took calls, he lunched (though usually at home or in the boardroom, since he found restaurants exhausting), he expressed increasingly sharp opinions, he followed the racing on television and he placed extravagant bets. Api saw that Jonathan never inflicted his outbursts on Harry. In fact to watch the two of them together you would have been hard-pressed to know that anything out of the ordinary was going on. Father and son preserved the man-to-man proprieties of their relationship. They discussed, in descending order of importance, business, sport and current affairs. Matters of life and death were taken as read.

Api knew Jonathan was hurting but found herself at a loss to know how to ease the largely unacknowledged pain. Over the past couple of years she believed that she had acquired a sense of how things worked in the delicately balanced triangle that was the Frankel family. Harry was the man from nowhere who had created an empire and who had nothing to prove. Jonathan by contrast, carrying the only son's full burden of indulgence and expectation, had much to prove daily and lacking his father's flair could do so only by working three times as hard. Harry was oblivious to his travails; Elizabeth stood between them, supporting the whole fragile structure.

It was now that Api took her courage in both hands and stepped into the role of daughter. Here, she sensed, was a situation in which she could have an influence, produce an effect that would benefit them all. She sleepwalked her way through all the duties of wife, except this one. Bryn, she thought, who knew all about the labour of love, would be proud of her.

She arrived at the Frankels' house in the late afternoon, which she knew to be a good time for Harry, who would have taken a rest after the morning's exertions. She did not have a key, and Jonathan's was with him, so she rang and waited. The housekeeper answered the door.

'Mrs Frankel, come in now.'

'Is everyone in, Lucia?'

'In? Oh yes. Oh yes, yes . . .' Lucia's manner was one of dignified melancholy at the best of times; now it would have suited the role of undertaker's mute. She rolled her eyes. 'Upstairs.'

'I'll go on up, shall I?'

'Yes, yes, Mrs Frankel, you go . . .' Lucia retreated, shaking her head.

As Api went up the stairs she could hear voices. The door of the smaller, first-floor sitting room with its view of the garden was open and now she could see her father-in-law in the apricot velvet *bergère* chair, sitting near the window. His legs rested on a footstool, his expression was amused and attentive. He was dressed in what was for him a relaxed manner, that of some grand old actor-manager of the twenties, with a short satin dressing gown and silk scarf over smart grey trousers. But the skin of his face was like parchment. As she crossed the landing he spotted her, and raised a hand, which he then let fall as though its weight were too much for him.

She heard Elizabeth say, 'Who's this coming?' and then her mother-in-law appeared in the doorway. 'Api! My dear, this is nice. We were just having some tea.'

Api kissed first Elizabeth, then Harry. As she sat down she saw that the other visitor, sitting on the floor in jeans and a white sweater, was Linda Mancini.

Jealousy flooded her stomach, her head – her mouth, she could taste it, bitter and hot. She must have managed to say something polite, for Linda said: 'Hello, Api!' and then: 'Time I wasn't here.'

'No, Linda, you mustn't go,' said Elizabeth, genuinely disappointed.

'Yes I must.' Linda got to her feet, dusting the seat of her jeans. She wore narrow tan boots with a cowboy heel. 'Api's here now.'

'Come over here . . .' Harry raised his arms, making little beckoning movements with both hands. He was so thin he looked like a puppet. When Linda leaned over to kiss him goodbye he tapped the back of her shoulder. 'Sail Away in the two thirty at Newmarket, hm?'

'I'll remember. Is that one of yours?'

He slapped the side of his face. 'I never back mine, it's bad luck.'

Linda slung her bag over her shoulder. ''Bye Elizabeth – no don't come down. I'll tell Lucia to bring up another cup, shall I? 'Bye, Api, sorry to rush off like this, but . . .' She gave her a collusive look as if to say they shouldn't tire the invalid. She touched Api's cheek with her own and added in a low voice, 'It was good of you to ring, thanks.'

As she went, Harry's eyes followed her, and Elizabeth's indulgent smile lingered as though she, and not Api, were the daughter they'd never had. Api was almost nauseous with loathing. But then she remembered what she had seen, and thought, *You have a secret, and very soon I shall find out what it is. Your life won't be your own. And it will be the beginning of the end of everyone loving you.*

The house, when Bryn got down there, was coming on well. Now that the roof was on he could feel the interior proportions which until now had been shrunk and distorted by their surroundings. He took in the prospect from the river-facing windows, around which they planned eventually to install deep window seats. On the south side were two wide, shallow terraces – Linda had plans for an old-fashioned rose garden – and then an expanse of greensward, smooth but not too manicured, would stretch to the river bank. There would be a boathouse or shelter down there, somewhere you could sit in peace and watch the river flow by. He had come to realise, as the house progressed, how important seclusion, a sense of being sequestered from the world, was to him. More so than to Linda, who it seemed could not be happy without her London *pied à terre*. He was concerned lest this desire for escape was a sign of timidity, the onset of old age.

When he had checked the progress of the work and gone through a list of snags and necessary decisions with the contractor, he went for a walk around the perimeter of his parcel of land; his kingdom. It had cost him an arm and a leg, but would have been worth it at twice what he'd paid. The peaceful satisfaction to be gleaned from simply knowing that it was his was beyond price.

He had done some research into the history of the little town and discovered that its shape and focus had shifted over the centuries. At one time, when proximity to water had been vital, the central line of what had then been a thriving large village had extended along the river, into the shoulder of land he now owned. The remains of the mediaeval manor were still visible in the shape of a wooded mound beside the road beyond his gate. As late as the First World War, apparently, there had been one or two cottages near the river, and the tumbled stones of an ancient bridge formed a promontory on which anglers sat peaceably for hours on end at weekends. This too pleased Bryn. His house was no brash newcomer, but an echo of what had been, a re-creation of times past before the town had withdrawn and huddled round its commercial interests, turning its back on the river.

He reached the river bank and paused, fascinated as always by the different strands of flowing water: the still depths beneath the bank's overhang, the swift bustle over gravel and streaming weed like mermaid's hair, and the sudden bubbling, racing tumble in those places where the current was unaccountably strong. For most of the river was calm, gliding smoothly along the path it had taken for centuries. Bryn supposed that, centuries on, his piece of land would be worn away, and there would remain no more than a small outcrop, a bumpy vantage point for future anglers. He liked that: he'd be a small part of the town's history then, and its geography too, in collusion with the river.

A pair of swans with two grown cygnets in tow rounded the bend from the west, heading back towards their nest in the reed bed up river, near the town. Bryn stood still to watch them. Registering his presence, the cob sailed on to the inside track, wings raised in a feathery arch above his back. The pen and her young, secure in the cob's protection, sculled gently on the far side.

The cob approached to within a few metres of Bryn and paused, wings still lifted. Bryn looked at him, feeling admiration for his beauty and respect for his pride and courage. The swans would be his neighbours; he hoped that in time the cob would recognise him and learn that he was not a threat but a friend and ally.

They regarded one another. Something about the swan's intense, black stare, and the impassive confidence with which it gazed from its own element into his, reminded Bryn of something, or someone . . . He shook his head.

It was only when he began to walk once more, and the swan powered on to rejoin its family, that it came to him – the black eyes with their implacable challenge were like the eyes of John Ashe.

20

2003 – Api, Linda, Bryn

Spying, Api found, gave you a sense of power. Not real power, because in her case she had no way – yet – of exercising it. The spying, like masturbation, was a solitary, secret vice, guilty and intensely pleasurable.

She discovered also that it was easy. Jonathan was not interested in how she spent her time provided the house and diary were kept in order and the requisite number of social engagements fulfilled, home and away. More importantly people were not wary, and only saw what they expected to see. Watching Linda being thrown out of that house had shown her that. You could be right there in front of someone, on their doorstep, but they wouldn't notice you. She realised that it would take only one small mistake to change all this and sensitise her subject to the situation. So she was never foolhardy: she judged to a nicety what she could get away with.

As a result she now knew where the Mancinis lived, what they did, and how they spent their time. She knew when they came and went – or what the most usual patterns were, because they weren't creatures of habit or routine. She recognised their children, their cleaning lady, and some of their friends. She knew which local shops and restaurants they patronised. Apart from the forest-green MG in which she had seen Linda drive away that day she knew that these days Bryn drove an Audi A6 estate. She had downloaded most of the information on his website and had been to see the Children's Peace Garden and the Pals' Memorial. Both of these had made her cry as if her heart would break. How could one person have so much love and still retain the space in his head and his heart to do work like this? To imagine it, and then to make it happen? She was awed – crushed – by such emotional capacity. The Peace Garden in particular made her feel sick with humiliation. She remembered, just, the reports in the papers about what had happened here, people talking about it with horror and sheer disbelief. Now it seemed to her that she could so easily have been one of those lost children. Bryn would never guess from having met her just how horrible, how revolting and frightening, that episode in her past had been. And if he were ever to find out, he would be repelled. The children commemorated here were innocents. They had not colluded in their fate. Whereas if not for Gilda she might have become something terrible and inhuman. The sort of creature for whom Bryn would never have created such beauty. She hated the lost children for their martyrdom; envied them the irreproachable sanctity of death.

Api had no friends now, and rarely saw members of her own family. She did not count as friends those people with whom she and Jonathan socialised – they were part of her job as wife, a duty she discharged efficiently, and just well enough to maintain credibility. But all her emotional energy was reserved for Bryn. She lived for that moment each day when she was alone, and could pick up the threads of her real, inner life.

She had discovered one thing that threw her into turmoil. Bryn was building a house for himself and his family, in the country. She'd followed him; she'd seen it. One Sunday when Jonathan was away she'd driven down on her own and walked along the nearby river. It had been a day of soft rain and the outline of the house was smudged, hiding from her. There was no one on site and she would have gone right up there and stood inside it, but suddenly she encountered wire across the path and a sign hanging at a crazy angle which read: PRIVATE. THIS PROPERTY IS PROTECTED BY ADVANCED SECURITY SYSTEMS. TRESPASSERS WILL BE IDENTIFIED AND PROSECUTED.

Identified and prosecuted . . . She was stricken. It was as if he'd read her mind and knew her intention. But then she told herself it wasn't him, it was just a form of words, a system he'd bought to protect what was his. He couldn't know that she too was his, completely. She stood there for minutes, peering through the rain. Two swans – a couple, presumably, since they mated for life – rested motionless on the stippled surface of the river, watching her.

'Do you have to go?' asked Bryn.

'No, I don't have to, but I want to.'

It was what she'd said before, about the flat in London. It was somehow impossible to argue with such a simple statement. A reasoned answer might have elicited an equally reasoned response.

He tried a different tack, asking playfully: 'Can I come?'

'Bryn. It's business. I'm only invited on a watching brief. And as a thank you. I don't suppose I shall stay till the end.'

All he heard was the word 'suppose'. 'You look very nice,' he said.

'Thank you. The theme's black, white and glitter.'

'I'm jealous.'

She laughed; she didn't believe him. 'Good.'

'Please don't go.'

'Don't be a spoilsport, darling.' She said this in the tone of a woman whose good humour, let alone whose sport, his pathetic complaints stood no chance of spoiling. 'This is work, remember?'

'Nice work.'

'Yes, very, and profitable too – think of all the well-heeled potential customers I'll be drinking fizz with.'

'I shall be thinking of little else.' He picked up the paper. 'Lucky bastards.'

Linda dropped a kiss on his cheek. 'If it makes any difference I consider myself fortunate to have a husband who can still get jealous.'

'Go on. Have fun. Say happy birthday to Sclater for me.'

★

Sadie, at the top of the stairs, watched her mother leave. She was so beautiful, in her black dress with silver embroidery twining down from bodice to hem like ivy wrapping itself round her. And she looked so young, shrugging on her fur-collared coat, bobbing to look in the hall mirror, swirling out of the door . . . At seventeen Sadie knew she would never look like that, and she feared she would never feel like that, either.

She went downstairs and across the hall where her mother's scent still hung in the air, the intoxicating essence of glamour. Her father sat in the drawing room, looking at the paper. He had no drink and there was no music on. The fire wasn't lit. It struck Sadie that she wasn't the only one without a date on Valentine's night.

'What's for supper?' she asked.

'I think there's one of Mum's fish pies ready to throw in the microwave.' He glanced at his watch. 'Is it time?'

'Not really, I'm not bothered.' She sat down, and her father folded the paper, and his arms, and smiled at her.

'Why don't we put the fish pie in the fridge and go out?'

She looked at him warily. 'And do what?'

He gestured expansively. 'London lies before us. The theatre, the cinema, the Italian restaurant up the road – perm any two from three.'

'OK.'

'Which?'

'Cinema and Italian?'

'Good choice. I suggest we put our coats on, go up to the picture palace and see whatever's about to start and is suitably cheesy.'

Walking up the road, eyes watering in the cold wind, Sadie knew that many of her friends would consider it majorly sad to be going to the cinema with your father on Valentine's night. And perhaps it was, but that wasn't how she felt. It was *great* to be with him. She felt safe, happy – and attractive. With her mother she could feel the first two, but the third was simply impossible and no matter how often she told herself it didn't matter, it mattered enough. Her father saw her in a way her mother didn't. She felt that they were allies, against what she couldn't say, and that the alliance had grown stronger in the last year or so.

Also her father was anything but sad, and if he was alone on Valentine's night that was almost enough to make it cool.

At the multiplex, cheesy wasn't a problem. It was wall-to-wall cheese. Bryn said he was in the mood to rediscover his inner child so they opted for computer-animated farm animals and *really* enjoyed it. At Da Bruno he was hailed like a long-lost son; in spite of not having booked on this night of all nights, a table was miraculously found.

'Right,' he said, 'no messing! We're going to go for it, starting with a bottle of something red and hearty.'

Sadie didn't usually drink wine. Out with her friends she stuck to spirits and mixers as they did. But her father in this mood was hard to resist.

'You know,' he said over the *spaghetti alle vongole*, 'there's no girl I'd rather be out with tonight.'

'What about Mum?'

'I said girl. Your mother is a grown woman.'

'Where is she, anyway?'

'At one of her do's. Some chap's sixtieth birthday bash that she's designed.'

'Didn't you want to go?'

'I wasn't invited.'

'Aren't you pissed off about it?'

'No – because a) it's only business. And b) look what it got me – a night out with my beautiful, clever daughter.'

Sadie blushed. 'Steady on, Dad.'

'It's true. I miss you.'

'But I'm here,' she pointed out.

'I miss being *with* you. Remember Aldeburgh when we were all there together? I actually used to think, "This is happiness." I was happy and I knew it.'

'Clap your hands.'

'What?'

'If you're happy and you know it, clap your hands.'

'But how often can you say you actually know you're happy?' persisted Bryn. 'Happiness usually goes by on the nod. If we're lucky, it's our default condition . . .'

Sadie discerned then the distant, haunted expression that her father sometimes wore these days, as though he could see something the rest of them couldn't. Whenever she caught that expression her whole world lurched.

'When can we go and see the house again?' she asked.

'Any time!' He switched back to the here and now. 'It's nearly ready. We'll be able to move in in the spring. Looking forward to it?'

'Pretty much . . . I wish it wasn't so far from London.'

She felt him studying her, glancing from one eye to another as though reading her. 'If it's any consolation your mother's keeping a place in town, which will presumably have a floor, so you won't be entirely cut off from civilisation.'

This remark was intended to be encouraging, but Sadie took something else entirely from the information.

'Why's she doing that? Won't she be living with us?'

'Of course she will, but she wants to keep a base in London to work from.'

'Dad.' Sadie felt the horribly familiar, sour taste of worry rise up into her mouth. 'Is everything OK – with you and Mum?'

'Of course it is!' He laughed and put out a hand to cup her cheek, rocking her head gently. 'We have a full life, that's all. No slip-sliding away into rural retirement. You wouldn't want us any different, would you?'

'No,' said Sadie. But in her mind hovered the image of her mother – wondrously glamorous, beautifully dressed and gorgeously scented – off to attend some distant party, on her own. She wanted to cry.

Pudding time,' said her father. 'Chocolate tart and pistachio ice cream, it is.'

Nick Mancini reckoned he knew the signs. Or could interpret the signs in the light of others' experience. At least three of his mates at university had recently been through the bust-up of their parents. In one case, apparently, there had been someone else, but overall the lads agreed that the oldies simply wanted to move on. They got the family off their hands and suddenly looked at each other and thought, 'What?' and decided to call it a day. There was a bit of acting-out for propriety's sake but that was what it amounted to. They'd all been told fifty was the new thirty and off they went like the clappers to pastures new.

Nick was unsentimental – not bothered, frankly. He thought it pretty extreme of his father to build a fucking great house in the country, like some mad weaver-bird engaged in a courtship ritual; and it was pretty cool of his mother to hang on to a base in London so there would still be somewhere to crash. But if the fertiliser struck the air-conditioning he could face the prospect with equanimity. He couldn't picture his parents engaging in a hate-fest, it wouldn't be their style. Whatever happened would be civilised, the aftermath amicable, and – a consideration no student could afford to sniff at – the hand-out rate would double overnight.

He was ready, and said as much to Dervla Kennedy, two years his senior, law-scholar and lay *extraordinaire* after a particularly gymnastic screwing session in her flat off the Cowley Road.

'I've got so used to the idea it'll be weird if it doesn't happen. I hope they don't let me down.'

'Jesus, Nick! It's you that's weird. If my parents split up I'd die.'

'Gender difference. I bet my sister feels like that, not that I've discussed it with her.'

'Anyway,' said Dervla, relieving him of the spliff and taking a drag, 'it hasn't happened and I'm going to pray it never does, even if that does spoil your fun.'

'Fine,' said Nick. 'You do that. I'll let you know.'

The phone rang at ten o'clock, when Api was running herself a bath. She knew the moment she heard Jonathan's voice what he was going to say.

'Dad's gone. About fifteen minutes ago.'

'Jonathan, I'm so sorry. What can I do?'

'Nothing for the moment. I'll stay the night with Mother.'

'How is she?'

'Doing well, considering, but it hasn't hit her yet. Your company could be invaluable tomorrow while I do the bloody awful admin.'

'Of course.'

'And if you could make some phone calls – tell your family and any friends you think should know. You do appreciate the funeral will be Jewish – tomorrow or the next day? It was the one thing he stipulated, to go out as he came in.'

'I understand.'

'And then I suppose we'll have to have a memorial service—' His voice snagged and broke off.

'Jonathan?'

'So I'll see you tomorrow,' he said curtly. 'Early as you can make it.'

'I'll be there. Please give my love to Elizabeth.'

'Will do. She's one of the old school, she'll come through with flying colours.'

'And you?'

'I'm fine. It's not as if it was unexpected, he's been determined to bail out for ages.'

She heard the bitterness. 'Perhaps it's for the best then.'

'That's the received wisdom. Night, Api.'

'Goodnight. I'm so sorry,' she said again.

As they talked, scarcely realising what she was doing, she'd walked down the stairs, and now stood holding the handset, looking up at the portrait of John Ashe.

Her heart was cantering. All she could think was: *There will be a funeral, and then a memorial service – and I'm bound to see him!*

By eleven she had told, or left messages for, the members of her family. Then, light-headed with adrenalin, she left the house, got into her car, and headed south.

When they got back, Sadie said: 'Light's flashing, there's a message.' She knew who it would be. 'I'm going to bed.'

'Night, darling. I enjoyed this evening.'

'Me too. Thanks.'

She couldn't bear to give or receive a kiss; she needed to be up in her room, with the door closed, before he picked up the message.

Linda's voice was matter-of-fact and businesslike; there were no party sounds in the background: 'Bryn, I'm going to stay over. It's getting late and I've had a couple of drinks so it seems sensible to join the house party – I can apparently be squeezed into some housemaid's cupboard or other. By the way it was a great success and I've dished out my card right left and centre so it has been worth it! I'll hit the road the minute I wake up in the morning and be back in time for breakfast. Hope the fish pie was all right. Night-night the two of you, sleep tight.'

Bryn digested this and pressed the 'Delete' button. He had just poured himself a large Bushmills when someone knocked on the front door. He paused, glass in hand, in the hall. Who would knock rather than ring the bell? There was something intimate, conspiratorial even, about the sound – someone had seen the light, knew he was here, but didn't want to disturb whoever might be upstairs . . .

He put his glass down and went to open the door.

This was a moment, Api knew, when nothing would serve her like the truth.

'I apologise,' she said, 'for turning up at this hour, but I was driving past your door and thought I might as well tell you in person . . .'

'Please,' he said, 'come in, come in out of the cold.'

She stepped into the warmth and he closed the door after her.

'What is it?' he asked. Then, seeing her face: 'I was having a nightcap, would you like one?'

'I never do, but thanks, I will.'

'Go in, sit down, I'll bring it.'

He disappeared into the back of the house. There seemed to be no one else here, but as she removed her coat and hung it on the banister she thought she heard a sound at the top of the stairs – had she come back? Was she here too? But the face she glimpsed was that of a teenage girl, his daughter.

She said 'Hi' but the girl was gone almost as soon as she appeared.

He brought her drink into the drawing room. 'There. Tell me. Sir Harry?'

She nodded. The tears she had not shed till now stung her eyes.

'What a damn shame. Api, I am so, so sorry. When did this happen?'

'Earlier this evening. Jonathan's over there, I've just been making phone calls, letting people know. I went out for a drive, it sounds silly, but I realised I was near your house, and you've been friends of his for years . . .'

'You do me too much honour. Linda has, but she's not here, she's away for the night. She's going to be devastated. When's the funeral?'

'Tomorrow or the next day.'

'So soon?'

'It's the Jewish way. He wanted that.'

'Of course.'

'And there'll be a memorial service in a few weeks.'

'We shall certainly be there. Poor Lady Frankel. But she

has Jonathan, and you, and he was very much loved. She won't be short of support.'

'Jonathan says she's incredible. Holding up really well. I suppose she's been prepared for some time . . .' She swiped at the tears with her fingers.

He got up from his chair and sat next to her. His big hand, when he laid it on hers, was warm. 'And what about you, my dear?' he asked. 'Apart from losing one hell of a father-in-law, I suppose there must be all sorts of implications for you and Jonathan.'

'I expect there will be – I haven't really thought about it.'

'You'll be fine. One day at a time. Tell me what happened. Linda said he was pretty good last time she saw him – I think you were there too – she said he was more or less himself. Gave her a racing tip. She should have taken him more seriously, she only won a fiver on an each-way bet. Anyway, tell me.'

Api did as he asked her. Spoke the words that meant nothing. 'He died in his sleep. Jonathan thinks he turned his face to the wall, but I don't think it was like that, more that he was handing over the reins in a dignified manner.'

'Very well put. You must say that to Elizabeth.'

As he said this he moved his hand gently on hers – to comfort her, but it felt like the most sensuous of caresses. She removed her hand and put down her barely touched glass. The whisky, his touch, his proximity lit her up, turned her on, like a torch.

On fire, but purposefully and slowly, she dipped her head and lifted his hand to her lips. Her hair shielded her face. She kissed his hand repeatedly, laid her cheek on it with eyes closed, kissed it again, tasting her own tears on his skin, buried her mouth in his palm, breathing his name . . . She did not want to see his face, to know what he might be thinking. She would allow neither thought, nor reaction, nor past nor future to intrude on this moment of exquisitely secret closeness.

★

Bryn looked down. He could not see his own hand, enveloped as it was by her cloud of fine, silver-brown ringlets. But he could feel her small mouth, hot and damp, and the smear of her tears. Her breath bloomed in his hand, he felt the petal-touch of his whispered name. For seconds he was transfixed, spellbound by her sensuality, which seemed both imperious and self-abasing.

Profoundly disturbed, he put out his hand to touch her. But the instant his fingers brushed the tendrils of her hair, the spell was broken. She sat up, releasing his hand, and their eyes met with that familiar visceral shock of recognition. Though her cheeks were still wet, there was neither shame nor embarrassment in her expression: nor any emotion that he could have put a name to.

'Api . . .?'

'I must go.' Her voice was light and even.

He saw that, for now at least, it was over. Her manner warned that nothing should be mentioned. She had allowed him a brief glimpse of her feelings, and just as swiftly concealed them. Already he could scarcely believe it had happened and he was sure that was what she had intended.

She rose. 'I should never have disturbed you so late.'

'Not at all. I'm so glad you felt able to . . .' He stumbled like a sleepwalker through the polite responses; felt suddenly that he must speak his wife's name, like a talisman. 'I'll tell Linda and I know she'll be in touch.'

She walked silently into the hall and he followed. 'Will you be all right?'

'Yes.'

He eased her coat over her shoulders, and she turned to face him. She stood still as a statue, arms at her sides, but her eyes closed briefly as he kissed her on either cheek.

'Goodnight, Api. Drive carefully and try to sleep well. I'm sure we'll see you very soon.'

'Thank you,' she said. 'Goodnight.'

★

Sarah Harrison

Api walked to her car, knowing that he was watching her. She felt her power, like a flame's – hot and brilliant. She looked back only when she was drawing away. And of course, he was still there.

As she sped, too fast, through the flashing night-time streets she was vouchsafed an insight: that – sometimes – there was strength in surrender.

Bryn's last view of her was her pale face turned towards him and her hand raised in farewell as the car pulled away. He could still feel, almost taste, that hot skin against his lips. When he closed the door, he was trembling.

'Who was that?' asked Sadie from the top of the stairs.

'Api Frankel – she's the daughter-in-law of Sir Harry Frankel, that Mum used to work for. Mum and I went to their wedding, remember?'

'Sort of. What was she doing here?'

'Sir Harry died earlier this evening. The poor girl's a bit knocked for six, she was passing and I think she wanted a bit of TLC.'

'He wasn't her father,' Sadie pointed out brusquely.

'True, but these things are always a shock. And since the Frankels are a sort of dynasty, her husband moves up a notch as a result of this. It's a lot to take on board.'

Sadie turned to go back to her room. 'Poor thing, my heart bleeds.'

Bryn let her go. He was exhausted. In spite of the hour, he would have liked to call Linda; but she'd not left a number, and her mobile was switched off. Then it occurred to him that Sclater's number was bound to be somewhere among the papers on her desk, or on her laptop.

He went upstairs to Linda's office in the small back bedroom on the first floor. Sadie's door was closed and he could hear music on the other side of it, blanking him and his goings-on. They had had such a nice evening, it had been such a comfort . . . but now suspicion had slipped its thin blade between them and prised them apart. And though he himself had done nothing he felt guilty, flayed by her suspicion.

He went into Linda's office and turned on the light. She was a tidy, organised worker and the room felt curiously peaceful – there were flowers on the windowsill, a mirror with a decorative enamelled frame on the wall, a calendar with amusing photographs of dogs, that Sadie had given her last Christmas. This calendar was reserved for social events and family anniversaries. A sparsely functional two-year planner had Party Peace functions marked in black felt-tip. He saw that 'Sclater 60th' had been crossed off, and was unaccountably relieved. He breathed deeply, to calm himself and to inhale these connections to Linda.

She had an electronic organiser, but he couldn't find it: she must have taken that with her. He riffled through the pile of mail in her wicker correspondence tray and found a letter with Sclater's name, address and email across the top, with Linda's pencilled 'dealt-with' tick next to it.

He sat down with the letter in front of him, and lifted the handset.

Christopher gasped, and bucked violently. As Linda came up for air she was thrown to one side, slick with sweat, his fluid trickling from the corner of her mouth.

After a moment his groping hand found her hair. He curled his fingers in it and coaxed her upwards so that their lips met in a blind kiss that was clumsy from the aftershock.

'I can taste me . . .' he whispered.

'You haven't lived till you've tasted it.'

'I thought –' his mouth found hers again, biting a little at her lower lip – 'I thought I'd lived. But apparently not.'

'Happy birthday.'

'It has been.'

'And thank you for showing me what the far side of sixty looks like.'

He moved her head from side to side. 'What does it look like?'

She gathered him into her hand, took his nipple between her teeth. 'The promised land,' she whispered.

Bryn's eye travelled down the page.

'. . . thanks largely to your efforts it promises to be a memorable evening. I've no idea what the protocol is on these occasions, but I feel we've become friends, and I'd like to invite you to the party. Not, I hasten to add, as some sort of unpaid consultant for the evening, but as my honoured guest . . .'

There was a bit more, confirming various details of the evening, and the letter ended: 'So I *very* much hope to see you on the 14th. Love, C.'

Slowly and quietly, Bryn replaced the handset.

Linda sat with her head in her hands, weeping. Mourning, thought Bryn – keening. He was shocked by the strength of her grief.

'Darling, darling . . . come on. I gather it was very peaceful, there was no big crisis. He just slipped away. As we'd all want to do when the time comes.'

'But I didn't *know*,' she moaned. 'I wasn't *here*!'

'It would have made no difference. And actually I considered calling you in spite of the hour, but thought better of it. I didn't want to spoil an occasion, when there was nothing you could do.' There must be times, surely, he thought, when along with the babies and the drunks, God protects liars.

Face still covered, she shook her head dumbly. Sadie appeared in the doorway.

'I'm going to my computer course.'

'Breakfast?' he asked.

'I'm OK, I'll get something there.' She eyed her mother warily. 'See you later.'

'Sure. 'Bye, love.' He waited till the front door closed and sat down next to Linda. 'Look, I'll make some coffee. Then why don't you ring and talk to Elizabeth? I bet she'd like to hear from you.'

There was another shake of the head. She seemed utterly broken. 'I should never have stayed the night.'

'You did right, especially if you'd had a drink.' He had to say it: 'This isn't like you.'

She sat back with a sigh, massaging her tearstained face with party-manicured hands.

She was wearing the long black evening dress – at least she hadn't gone prepared to stay – with her coat still over the top. Though he didn't like himself for it, he found her vulnerability captivating. There had been scarcely a glimpse of it since the time, long before their marriage, when she had talked about her brother. She was always so gallant, so invincible and sure. He could have forgiven her anything. Now maybe she would cling to him, they could both cling to the mast, not drown, find safe haven.

'Coffee,' he said.

When he gave it to her she looked up into his face for the first time. 'Thanks, Bryn. I don't deserve you.'

'You do, because it doesn't take much. Sugar. Drink up.'

After the coffee she got up and splashed her face with water from the kitchen tap. Without her vivid make-up she had a true redhead's pale colouring, and he was briefly reminded of Api.

'I'm going to take your advice,' she said. 'And call Lady Frankel.'

'Go ahead. And then you can have a hot bath.'

She put her arms round his neck. They had always been a perfect fit, and as the years had gone by that hadn't changed; he was a little heavier, she a little lighter than they had been, so they accommodated one another like pieces of a jigsaw. He breathed her in – the coffee, the scent that clung to her evening dress, and another, on her hair, which he chose not to identify.

She took the phone into the drawing room. Out of respect

for her privacy, and for the protocol and hierarchy of grief, he pushed the door to as he went upstairs to run her a bath.

Api picked up the phone. She had stationed herself near to it while Jonathan made some business calls on his mobile, rescheduling the next two days' meetings.

'Is that Api? Api, it's Linda Mancini here. I realise you must have a million things to think of, but I was so—' Her voice broke and Api didn't catch the next word. '. . . to hear about Harry.'

The sincerity of her grief made Api's gorge rise. But she had rank, not to mention geography, on her side. She kept her own voice sweetly, soothingly authoritative.

'Yes, it's horrible. No matter how much you've prepared yourself for something, the reality still comes as an awful shock. But he died very peacefully, there was no dramatic last-minute deterioration or anything, he just drifted away in his sleep.'

'Poor Harry . . .' There was no attempt on Linda's part to hide the tears in her voice. 'I find it so hard to imagine him drifting anywhere. He was such a force of nature.'

'He'd been ill for ages, though,' said Api. 'He'd changed,' she added, in case Linda – an outsider – might not have noticed.

'I suppose . . . though I was surprised at how much himself he seemed the last time I saw him – I think you were there too.'

'He could always put on a brave face.'

There was a brief silence before Linda asked: 'When's the funeral?'

'Ten o'clock the day after tomorrow.' She gave Linda the address of the synagogue in North London. 'But there will be a memorial service in a few weeks' time.'

'We shall come to that, of course, but I'd like to be at the funeral. Api – is there the slightest chance of a word with Elizabeth?'

Api, aware that she might be overheard this end, chose her words carefully. 'I'm afraid not. She's being absolutely marvellous, but well – right now's not a good moment.'

'I understand. Please will you give her my very best love and tell her how much I'm thinking of her? And Bryn, too.'

'Yes, of course.'

'I'll see you soon. And Api, thanks for all you're doing.'

How dare she? thought Api when she'd put the phone down. How dare she patronise me like that, treat me as if I'm some sort of hired help?

She found Elizabeth sitting at the dining-room table looking at photographs, some in albums, some loose. She was composed, and smartly dressed in a cashmere jumper and checked skirt, but she seemed to have become less substantial overnight, as though grief were wearing her away.

'Who was that on the phone?' she asked, her eyes still scanning the photos.

'Linda Mancini.'

Elizabeth looked up. 'Linda? I'd like to have talked to her.'

'She had to dash, but they sent you all their love. I gave them the news last night,' she added pointedly, 'but she was away.'

'She's so busy with this new business of hers . . . Did you tell her about the funeral?'

'Yes.'

'I'm sure she'll come if she can.'

'Yes,' said Api. 'I'm sure she will.'

Linda lay in the hot, scented water Bryn had run for her. A second cup of coffee stood on one corner of the bath. The elegant black-rubber-clad radio that he had bought for her for this purpose stood on the other. Vaughan Williams' 'The Lark Ascending' mingled with the fragrant steam. Her eyes were closed, but her stomach was knotted with tension.

Among all the important tasks contingent upon Harry's death, there was one outstanding, which only she could perform.

After her bath she put on jeans, boots, a sweater and jacket, tied her hair back and ran down the stairs, brisk and businesslike.

★

Bryn emerged from his studio and followed her.

'A transformation! Feeling better?'

'Yes, and I've got a meeting.'

'Best thing.' He watched as she did her usual little bob at the hall mirror. 'How was Elizabeth?'

'She couldn't come to the phone. But I spoke to Api, she said she was doing all right – what you'd expect really.'

'When's the funeral?'

'Tomorrow morning. I shall go – all the more reason why I must make this meeting today.'

'I'll pass on that one if I may. I didn't know the old boy well enough.'

'Whatever. 'Bye, Bryn.' She made a kissing mouth in his direction. 'See you later.'

''Bye,' he said. 'Take care.'

The door closed behind her. The moment's vulnerability was over. She was moving away from him again, carrying with her everything that she knew.

She could have telephoned, but it seemed to her that would have been cowardly and inappropriate. Harry had gone, and she was the sole repository of his secret. The responsibility of which he had, to all intents and purposes, relieved her, had reverted to her on his death.

Linda thought that never till now had she known what it was to be alone. Because of what had happened last night she had even forfeited the right to tell Bryn. She could offer no excuse, even to herself. She had gone to bed with Christopher Sclater willingly, lustfully, even calculatingly. For the past several months she had basked in his flattery and attention. With Bryn undergoing some mid-life crisis, increasingly preoccupied, obsessed with the new house, hardly ever in town, she had blossomed in the warmth of another man's admiration. She had been such a good wife for so long – she knew many women who took it for granted that there would be lapses, flings, affairs, along the way. Women who claimed that a long marriage depended on such things for its survival. She had never believed them. She and Bryn were different. But now she had discovered that was not the case. For her, anyway: Bryn's very uxoriousness had made her restless.

She never for a moment doubted that the fault was all hers. Bryn's only crime was to love her too much. As for Christopher, he was a free agent, he had done nothing wrong. Though she had never said it in so many words, she had implied by her behaviour that she too was free, that her marriage was not a constraint, that there was an understanding . . . A lie of the heart, to go with all the others.

And had it been worth it? At the time, yes – oh, yes! The wonderful strangeness of a new body, a different touch, an unexplored mind and imagination. When she'd used the words 'promised land' they had been no mere flattery or flirtation. All this pleasure and discovery was hers to command. She had lost none of her powers. She could see now what those other women meant, for the experience left her feelings for Bryn unchanged. She would love him more, not less, she told herself, because of this. The house on the river would be a palace because of the beauty she would bring to it. Their marriage would be stirred, not shaken. Her elation as she drove home that early morning, still wearing her unfeasibly expensive new evening dress, knew no bounds. She was a woman at the top of her game and on top of the world.

Classic hubris, she now saw. And vintage Harry, to time his departure so precisely, to keep control from beyond the grave. That odd, fey girl – that *child* who knew nothing – had prevented her from talking to Elizabeth. If Elizabeth herself had answered the phone she, Linda, could have drawn some comfort from the genuine warmth and esteem in which she was held by the Frankels. Instead of which she had been brushed off. Left, as it were, to get on with it.

When she arrived outside the house she determined to allow herself no time to waver. Body language was important: speed, directness, confidence. She parked right outside, took the two steps in one, and rang the bell. A curtain twitched, but it must have been Coralie, for almost simultaneously the door was opened by Al.

'Hi.'

'Hello, Al,' she said, stepping straight in. 'Is your mother around?'

'I'm here. What do you want?'

Linda walked past Coralie into the stuffy living room. The television flickered among the clutter.

'Can we switch that off, please? I've got something important to tell you.'

'Al, turn it off . . .' Coralie's stare remained fixed on her as she spoke. 'What are you doing here anyway? I told you not to come back. You're not wanted.'

'I heard all that. But I thought you should know that Harry died last night.'

Coralie sat down slowly.

'Who died?' asked Al.

'A friend of your mother's,' said Linda. 'He was quite old.' She turned back to Coralie. 'I didn't want you to find out about it from the newspaper.'

'Well, you've told us now.' The voice was a whisper.

'I'm sure he'll have made some sort of provision for you. He's been ill for a long time.'

She moved towards Coralie, but her gesture of concern came a fraction too late. The other woman's arm shot out, hand raised. 'No.'

'Coralie, I'm sorry. There wasn't any easy way to—'

'You think all I care about is the money. You're wrong. I wanted a little respect.'

Respect has to be earned. Linda thought it, but bit it back. 'I understand.'

'No you don't. You don't understand a thing. You just love coming out here and being the big I Am.'

'That's not true. How can you think that after last time? I genuinely wanted to be the person to tell you.'

'I bet you did.'

'Because I do respect you, Coralie. I didn't think you'd manage – you and Al on your own, but you've proved me wrong. You've had a raw deal all round. I don't know that I'd have coped so well.'

She held her breath. She had told so many lies, both of commission and omission, that a few more wouldn't hurt and might even do some good. But she was still surprised when Coralie's expression softened, and she said: 'Thank you.'

'And I apologise if in the past I've given offence. Perhaps you can accept that I've been in a difficult position, too.'

'Yes.'

Al stood staring from one to the other. 'Can we have tea?'

'Yes,' said Coralie. 'Why don't you go and put the kettle on.'

When he'd left the room, she added: 'When's the funeral?'

'Tomorrow, but—'

'Don't worry, I wasn't thinking of going.'

'I promise I'll keep in touch,' said Linda. 'Look, I shan't stay. I've said what I came to say.'

Coralie got up. At the front door she paused with her hand on the latch and said, as if to herself: 'What will become of us?'

'You'll be fine,' said Linda. 'Trust me.' Back in the car, she thought, if ever there had been an empty exhortation, that was it.

21

2003 – Api

The memorial service for Harry Frankel was set for early May. As well as those of friends and relations it appeared in the diaries of people as disparate as the Home Secretary and the head housekeeper of the Delancey Avon. Others included members of the rock band Override, the curators of two top London galleries, a clutch of celebrity chefs, leaders of the Jewish community, half a dozen well-known entertainers, representatives of the England football team, a brace of theatrical dames, the directors of several charities, and countless distinguished individuals from every walk of life, as well as over a hundred less distinguished, but loyal and devoted employees and associates.

The late date for the service had been Jonathan's decision for sound business reasons. He wanted his takeover as the head of Delancey to have been effected in as smooth and as low-profile a way as possible, before any high-profile celebration of his father's life took place.

Only now did Api see and appreciate the strength of her parents-in-law's marriage. Even allowing for the differences between father and son, she could see that Elizabeth, herself a strong character, had had to carve out a role for herself in Harry's life, as well as establish one of her own, independent of him. There had never been the slightest doubt that they were a team, the powerful bond between whom was evident to everyone without needing to be publicly expressed. And to Api at least it was clear that Elizabeth, not Harry, was mainly responsible for the maintenance of this bond.

It was love, of course, that made this possible, a prerequisite not available to Api. The fierce emotional energy she had put into the relationship with Jonathan – the determination to make a success of this new chapter of her life – had been diverted on her wedding day. She sleepwalked through her marriage, and if Jonathan noticed his wife's emotional absence, he didn't show it. To her relief, he had allowed himself almost no outward display of grief over his father's death. His voice on the telephone had wavered briefly that first night, and had done so perhaps twice since. Api had caught him on a few occasions with a bleak, empty look in his eyes but to her enormous relief he had never seemed to require anything of her but her practical support, which she was willing to give. Increasingly he spent his time at the office, sometimes staying overnight in the newly-appointed amenity room. When they were together the atmosphere was calm and businesslike. She often thought that they had what many people would have called 'an understanding' – except that neither of them fully understood the other. Certainly Jonathan could never have understood her: the extent of her other life, both internal and external, the energy she expended on it, had to remain an entirely closed book.

Api had been grateful for the Jewish rituals of death, which had taken over and absolved her from too much involvement: the calm intervention of the Chevra Kadisha, the burial society, which had prepared Harry for his funeral; the swift simplicity of the funeral and its earthy acceptance of the body as a mere shell, to be returned as quickly as possible to the ground; the informal period of *shiva* which meant that for the week following the funeral Elizabeth was rarely alone. Api kept her counsel.

Fortunately, Jonathan was so busy that he was even less curious than usual. There were however two people with whom she felt vulnerable. One was her mother-in-law. Elizabeth had a finely tuned intuition and a store of common sense about human nature based on long experience. She was accustomed to observe the way people dealt with her husband, and had played a largely unacknowledged part in smoothing the path to innumerable deals and agreements over the years. She may have known neither the strength nor the subject of Api's obsession but she came close to recognising something in her character which might make her a liability to her own son.

She never behaved with less than cheerful affection towards her daughter-in-law. But once or twice exchanges had occurred which left Api feeling she had been warned.

There had been an instance just as they were about to leave for the funeral that February morning, on a day of grey and bitter cold. Four cars waited in the road outside. A group of eight family members stood waiting in the hall. Elizabeth, Jonathan and Api were still upstairs. From the first, Elizabeth had been adamant that she wished to travel to the synagogue on her own. Jonathan was equally determined that he should ride with his mother. Even now, he continued to argue for this.

'You should have someone with you, Mother. You don't know how it's going to affect you.'

'I believe I do. That's the reason I'd like to be alone for a little while.'

'I shan't intrude.'

'I know that. It's not personal. I appreciate everything you've done, my dear, but this is my wish.'

'But think how it will look!'

'I do,' said Elizabeth. 'I think that it will look better if you travel with your wife.'

'Very well.' Jonathan turned and went downstairs. Api made to follow him.

'Oh, Api . . .' Elizabeth's voice was quiet as she detained her, her manner unhurried. 'My dear, you can calm him down, I hope.'

'I'll try.'

'He has a lot on his mind. So much to deal with. He can't get things into proportion. He needs some managing just now.'

Api was struck by the use of the word 'managing'. 'I don't know if I'm much good at that.'

'But you are . . .' Elizabeth picked up her gloves and put them on carefully. She looked particularly smart and soignée on this sad morning; she had always been one to put on a good show. 'You must be, or you would never have married my son. Now then.' She smiled. 'Let's go down and do what we have to do.'

Api followed her down the stairs. The implication had been so slight, so ambiguous, and yet she knew it had been there. A wealth of understanding underlay those few words: an appreciation of the difficulties of being married to a driven and secretive man; and of the qualities Api had brought to that marriage.

Just before reaching the bend in the stairs Elizabeth paused and looked back at her. 'I know we can depend on you,' she said.

The other person who, less surprisingly, remained on her case was Gilda, who had decided long ago that she did not trust Api to know what was best for her, and who made a point of breaching her sister's self-imposed isolation whenever possible.

It was Gilda, of all people, who having turned up un-invited at Hardwicke Row and found her sister in, and alone, asked:

'So are you going to have babies?'

'I've no idea.'

'What, no plans at all? And you married to a nice Jewish boy?'

'What's that got to do with anything?'

'They're big on family. And his mother must be dying to be a grandmother, especially now.'

'We haven't discussed it.'

'Weird,' said Gilda.

Api felt angry, and frightened, but pushed the feelings back down. 'There's nothing weird about it. There's no pressure, she's very discreet. And Jonathan and I are in no hurry.'

'I bet he'd love it. It might make all the difference.'

'What's that supposed to mean?'

'You know, warm things up a bit between you.'

'They don't need warming up,' snapped Api. 'We're fine.'

'Whatever you say,' said Gilda.

Jonathan did want children, Api knew that, but for what she construed to be dynastic, rather than emotional, reasons. If there had ever been a time when she herself had countenanced the idea, as part of the natural order of things, it was long since gone. On the face of it, they waited to see what would happen, knowing there was plenty of time in hand. Secretly, she took the pill. A baby would be the end of everything. Her time, her energy, her whole future, would be consumed by it. She would never, never, allow it to happen.

After the funeral, the family, Api among them, had followed tradition and passed between the two rows of non-family mourners as they spoke the words of condolence: 'May God comfort you among all the mourners of Zion and Jerusalem.' Linda had been at the end of the row, her red hair almost hidden beneath a broad-brimmed black hat. As the fifty or so mourners dispersed to their cars, Api sought her out.

'Linda, are you going to come back for the meal?'

'I won't, thank you. This is a family occasion.'

'I'm sure Elizabeth sees you as family,' said Api. She took a fierce, masochistic delight in uttering these platitudes from her position of power, now Harry was gone.

'It's sweet of you to say so, but no. I'll call round soon, though, to see her. She's incredible, such dignity. I didn't see a single tear.'

'She's very private.'

'And very strong.' Linda turned away; Api could not be sure whether or not she had said goodbye. There was always the sense of her having had the last word . . . Yet again, the encounter had been unsatisfactory.

More and more, her focus fell on Linda, the obstacle in her path, the object of Bryn's devotion. The mere thought of it – of them – sickened and consumed her. Somewhere at the back of her mind was the notion that real love meant caring more for the happiness of the person loved than for one's own. But, she told herself, *she* could make Bryn happy, given the chance. She could spoil, protect, support and cherish him, she could dedicate herself to him in a way that Linda could never do – if only the way were clear. This was no fantasy to Api, but an achievable aim. And her marriage might be the platform from which she could achieve it.

When Jonathan told her there could be no holiday this year, for the time being at least, her heart leapt. 'Don't worry,' she said, kissing his cheek. 'I understand. I shall be perfectly happy. I've got plenty to get on with.'

It was strange, thought Bryn, the way you didn't really imagine that people whom you had once known well had a life without you. Intellectually you knew that they would be ageing, changing, forming friendships, perhaps falling in love, losing family members and gaining others, but emotionally they were like insects trapped, motionless, in the amber of memory.

And then, to see someone before they saw you always carried the half-guilty thrill of spying, no matter how innocuous the activity they were engaged in. You wanted to prolong the moment, to continue to watch, and assess – because for that moment you owned them, without their knowing it, and ownership conferred power.

He saw the familiar profile in the unlikely setting of Krypton, a champagne bar off Romilly Street where he was due to meet Nick and a friend. The bar, their choice – he'd never heard of it before, and was pretty certain he'd never come again – was in a long basement. The bar staff were beautiful and bored, the prices astronomical, the decor screamingly camp and the clientele might in another age have been described as *jeunesse dorée*, though in this one the gilding had more to do with cash than class.

Bryn, easing himself on to a bar stool covered in puce shag pile, wished he had had the good sense to be late. Very late, since Nick and the girl – Diane? Debbie? – were bound to be even later. It was a long time since he had felt so out of place. It wasn't something that happened to him often these days; he reckoned that as he got older he could expand or contract to fill any given psychological space.

At midday on a Wednesday the place wasn't full. There were a couple of groups of twenty-somethings, and half a dozen people at the bar. His eye was bound to be drawn by the one other person of his own age, sitting at the opposite end from him, unconcernedly doing the crossword, glasses perched on nose. He allowed himself the luxury of observing unobserved. No change, he thought, it might have been yesterday . . . Except that when others didn't change it forced upon you the acceptance of changes in yourself.

After a minute he picked up his glass and walked along the bar.

'Hello, Sally.'

She looked up. There was a split second's confusion before she removed her glasses and opened her arms.

'Bryn! I don't believe it!'

She felt as warm and familiar as ever, the safe haven she had always been. The years had done their healing, the easiness of their relationship was restored. He was ridiculously happy to see her. He pulled up another Day-glo stool and sat next to her.

'I'm meeting my son here,' he said. 'What's your excuse?'

'The same. Well, Amy. She's married now, with a baby, and this is one of her precious days off in town. We go from here to Chinatown for dim sum, and then do a matinée or shops, her call.'

'You're a grandmother!'

'I'm afraid so . . .' She smiled, a mixture of self-deprecation and pride.

'Good for you. You look great on it.'

'Thank you.'

'And Mary?'

'No babies there. She's an accountant; one of her clients is a theatrical impresario which is where we get our matinée tickets. This place is her choice, she's joining us for a drink.' Another smile, this time reassuring. 'But don't worry, neither of them is due till half past.'

Bryn glanced around. With this meeting, the air in the room had changed. He hadn't known how tense he was until he relaxed. His body felt de-magnetised, his mind calm as a millpond. With Sally here he could face even the prospect of Mary with equanimity.

'I hope she's forgiven me,' he said.

'Of course she has. She was young and she thought the world of you. It had nothing to do with you and me – it was just jealousy. She might be a little embarrassed to find you here, that's all.'

'I'm relieved to hear it, she's scary when roused. And how are you?'

'Married, actually.'

'You are? Congratulations, that's absolutely bloody marvellous. Who's the lucky man?' The formulae came to his rescue, tumbling from his lips while his brain stalled.

'He's called Peter, we met three years ago, he's quite a bit older than me and absolutely lovely . . . I couldn't be happier.'

Bryn put his arm round her and kissed her cheek. 'It's wonderful news. I hope the girls are pleased.'

'Yes.' She pulled her brows together in a droll frown. 'Yes, I really believe they are. You know, as long as old Mum's happy . . .'

'Which you are.'

'Which I am.' She looked as if she might have been about to say something else, but didn't, and he came to her rescue.

'More champagne. Why don't I buy a bottle for you and the girls? To celebrate and for old times' sake?'

'God, Bryn, you mustn't!' She lowered her voice. 'It's daylight robbery in here. This is only *sparkling* and it cost a week's wages.'

'Nonsense, think of it as the wedding present I never gave you, I insist. Excuse me.' He ordered a bottle and turned back to her. 'This is so great, Sally. I've missed you.'

'And how's married life with you?' she said, gently but pointedly.

'Marvellous.' Even to Bryn, his voice sounded over-emphatic. 'My two are more or less grown-up, though I sincerely hope neither of them is about to make me into a grandfather just yet.'

'Go on, you'd love it.'

'I'm still old-fashioned enough to want wedding bells first. Or at least a decent period of respectable cohabitation.'

'Dream on, old friend.'

His first impression was that she hadn't changed, but he saw now that had been false. Her style – her hair, her clothes, her minimal make-up, even her manner, was absolutely the same. But this continuity created laboratory conditions in which to see how much she had aged. Her slightly flyaway medium-length hair with its two swept-back wings at the side was grey, the under-maintained highlights almost grown out. Her unpainted nails showed signs of gardening. The lines around her eyes, nose and mouth had deepened. She had put on a little weight and her smart kept-for-best black trousers, black jumper and grey jacket were a fraction too tight – she probably didn't wear them often enough to realise. He was prepared to bet that a safety pin featured in there somewhere. She looked what she was: a nice, generous-spirited hard-working wife and grandmother whose energies were focused on people other than herself. Also (and it shocked him to think this) she had become androgynous. Lovely as ever, nice as ever, a pleasure to hug – but no longer emitting even the smallest batsqueak of sex appeal. Sally was undergoing the steady, remorseless female metamorphosis into invisibility.

To push aside these unwelcome thoughts, he asked: 'Are you still working?'

'Only part-time. I go in two days a week, three during holiday times when they're pushed. Peter's retired, but he keeps very busy as a tour-guide, and I don't want to be home alone all the time.'

'You made yourself indispensable.'

'I don't know about that!' she laughed. The champagne arrived and Bryn approved the cork. 'This is so extravagant of you.'

'We deserve it!'

Five minutes later Nick and his friend – Dervla, that was it – arrived. Bryn introduced them, and said: 'Right, we'll leave you to it. But do give my love to the girls.'

'What girls?' asked Nick as they went to a table. 'Who was that?'

'An old friend,' he explained. 'Last time I saw her, her daughters were teenagers. Now one is a mother of two and the other's an accountant.'

'Not exactly rebels, then.'

Bryn thought about this. 'Not exactly, no.' He turned to the girl, a black-haired, blue-eyed, white-faced beauty with 'trouble' written all over her. 'It's nice to meet you, Dervla. I can't say I've heard a lot about you because he doesn't tell us anything, but maybe you can put that right.'

She took out cigarettes and lit one without, he noticed, offering them round. 'What would you like to know?'

'Whatever you care to tell me.'

She cast Nick a 'get-him' look. 'Grand . . .'

Not long after this Amy and Mary arrived, together. They had once been rather alike, but no more. Amy was pretty, rounded, slightly distraite, a younger clone of her mother. Mary was beautiful as ever and sleekly immaculate, the very model of a modern number-cruncher. Sally poured champagne, and nodded towards him, explaining. They smiled, and raised their glasses.

That was it. Good old Bryn. A blast from the past.

Dervla, he now knew, came from County Cork, had three sisters and four brothers, and was reading law. When he asked her what she wanted to do, she'd replied with a crisp, upward inflection: 'Make a pile?'

He couldn't get used to this way they had of making state-ments sound like questions, and had said, 'You think you will?'

'I know it.'

'She will,' said Nick, lounging back with his arms along the back of the sofa as if he were her agent. 'Take it from me.'

Sally and the girls left first, and made a detour to say goodbye. Bryn rose and effected quick introductions. Mary and Amy were more forthcoming than Nick and Dervla.

'What an incredible coincidence,' said Amy, smiling and poised, utterly grown-up. 'You and Mum sitting at opposite ends of the bar.'

'In all the joints, in all the world . . .' agreed Bryn. Only Sally got it. 'Tell me,' he asked, quickly and quietly, 'are you and – are you both at the same address?'

She shook her head. 'We're in Tunbridge Wells.'

'Great,' he said, oddly appalled. 'Well, maybe we'll . . .'

'You never know,' she agreed. But they did know.

As they left, Nick's eyes followed Mary. Dervla poked him with the toe of her boot.

'Put your eyeballs back in, Mancini, she's too posh for you.'

'You're not wrong,' said Nick. 'Just as well I prefer rough trade.'

'And too old.'

'Oh, I don't know.'

Dervla made no comment, but Bryn caught her mouthing: 'Fuck off.' The exchange seemed entirely amiable.

'How do you know about this place?' he asked.

Nick indicated Dervla. 'She's the drinking consultant.'

'I came here with some friends one night. It was mental.'

He glanced around. 'I can see that it might be . . . And the name? Wasn't there some programme in the eighties?' He realised they wouldn't remember. 'I suppose some image consultant dreamed it up.'

'Not really,' said Dervla. 'It was a crypt.'

'What, there was a church here?' He was charmed, incredulous.

'Sure, I asked the manager.' She said this as though it provided incontrovertible proof. 'When they were doing the searches they found there was a little church here centuries ago – well, it might not have been on this very spot, but near enough, and this would have been the crypt. Mad, isn't it?'

'And sad,' he reflected.

'Do you think so? I don't know. Cities have to change. I wouldn't want to be still living in some hell-hole made entirely out of wood.'

He was bound to agree with her on this, and decided against trying to explain that that wasn't quite what he'd meant. It was too complicated, too nuanced. A function, he reflected wistfully, of getting older.

'Where shall we go for lunch then?' asked Nick, in the expansive manner of someone who might be paying. Bryn suggested that they decide while he went to the gents'. Even this made him feel like some incontinent old fart, though damn it all he'd been here for forty minutes before them.

The cloakrooms were at the end of the obligatory narrow, dark corridor. When he'd emerged and was returning down this corridor he noticed that what he'd thought was a framed poster on the wall was actually a collection of cuttings. Dervla was right. The church, St Botolph's, got a mention, and there was even one of those beautifully drawn spidery plans of the area, dated 1703, showing individual buildings in 'Hob Lane', including a church which looked in about the right position.

But it was the more recent history of the building, rendered in elaborate faux-historical calligraphy, which caught his eye. It appeared to have been, at various times, a jeweller's shop,

a pawnbroker's, a deli and vegetarian café and – this was it –
in the 1930s 'a period as a notoriously exclusive – and just
plain notorious – drinking club, the Apache, noted for its
exotic clientele, whose iron discretion guaranteed privacy for
all, from crowned heads to killers'. No pictures from that
period were displayed, though there was one of the building's
frontage with the pawnbroker's sign outside, and another of
it bearing the words 'Get Fresh', relating to the delicatessen.
But of course, there would have been nothing to show the
entrance during the time of the club. You had to know.

Nick opened the swing door at the end and stood holding
it.

'You all right?'

'I'm not a complete geriatric. I was looking at this.' He
tapped the glass. 'Your young lady was right, it was a church.'

'She's always right,' said Nick.

'What's she like?' asked Linda.

'Good-looking, sharp-tongued, doesn't give a damn.'

'Perfect for our Nick, then. I'm sorry I couldn't be there,
I'd like to have met her. Is he coming back any time?'

'He didn't favour me with the information. I should think
so – he's bound to want maintenance sooner or later. He
seemed fine though. They ate a quite phenomenal amount at
the Parnassus.'

They were in bed. Linda, in a white satin nightshirt, had a
book open; Bryn, in the buff, was lying with his hands linked
behind his head. Unusually, he did not feel amorous, but he
did want to take her attention away from the book, the latest
novel by a comedian-turned-author whom he had never liked
and who (somewhat queasily, in Bryn's view) took a line that
was more stridently feminist than the feminists.

'An extraordinary coincidence,' he said. 'I was sitting in that
place, feeling completely Jurassic, and who do you think I
saw?'

'I don't know.' She glanced at him briefly. 'Jim?'

'No. Do you remember the first – no, second – time we met, I was with the daughter of an old friend?'

'Your current lady friend, I always supposed.'

'You were right. And there she was. At the other end of the bar.'

Linda put the book down. 'Did you go and say hello?'

'Of course.'

'And? Was she pleased to see you?'

'I think so. We both were, she's a very nice woman.'

Linda closed the book. 'Don't make her sound too exciting, will you?'

'She is nice, though. You'd like her.'

'Bryn!' Linda's tone was teasing, but he detected an edge. 'Don't you know that there is nothing, absolutely nothing, half as irritating to a woman as being told she would probably like another woman that her husband once shagged?'

'I just meant,' he said emolliently, 'that it's impossible not to.'

'She sounds a paragon.'

'I wouldn't say that. She has two grown-up daughters and she's a grandmother.'

'What did Nick and Dervla make of this brief encounter?'

'It was nothing like that. He ogled the older daughter and got a kick in the shins for his pains.'

Now there was a laugh in Linda's voice. 'Really? I must shake Dervla by the hand some time.'

'The point *is*,' said Bryn, laying his hand on Linda's satin-covered arm. 'The point is – do you want to hear what the point of this story is?'

'Might as well.'

'Listen properly then.'

She slipped down and lay facing him. He stroked her hair back off her cheek. 'The point is it made me realise all over again how wonderful you are. And what a lucky bastard I am.'

She put up her hand and covered his. 'Bryn . . .'

'And how I never want to lose you.'

She closed her eyes, gave her head a little shake. He wasn't quite sure what she meant, but had to be content with that, because next thing she rolled away from him, kissing his palm as it slipped over her face.

'Goodnight.'

'Goodnight, my darling,' he whispered. 'I love you.'

Soon, Linda slept. But Bryn remained awake for some time, composing in his head the letter that he would write to Api Frankel.

It gradually dawned on Api that the memorial service might mark the beginning of the end of the Mancinis' association with the Frankels. After this final farewell to Harry, what need would there be for them to be invited to functions? Linda might maintain a friendship with Elizabeth for a while, but how long could that last alongside Jonathan's antipathy for Bryn?

She began to panic, and grow careless. The essentially businesslike nature of their relationship meant she and Jonathan rarely rowed, but now came an occasion – only two weeks before the service – when she came close to pushing things too far.

Delancey were sponsoring a major exhibition of twentieth-century American art. It was considered a coup on Jonathan's part that he had secured the deal which accorded perfectly with the hotels' changing image. The name which twenty years ago had been synonymous with a certain bland, large-scale reliability and unthreatening comfort was rapidly becoming identified with *recherché*, elegant, smaller hotels, individually styled, the first of which had been the Delancey Avon. The exhibition's preview on a Thursday night was an opportunity for the Delancey board, and Jonathan in particular, to do some corporate entertaining on a grand scale. There was to be champagne and hot-and-cold canapés from six thirty to nine at the gallery, followed by dinner for a dozen carefully selected shining ones in a private room at the Connaught.

Api was dreading it. Not for its own sake – she had learned what was required of her on these occasions, and could turn in an entirely unexceptionable performance – but because of the hours and hours it consumed. Hours when she might have been thinking of Bryn, watching him, working out what to do. Sometimes when she was standing at some dull drinks party or in a box watching a sporting event in which she had no interest whatever, she could have wept for loneliness. What was *he* doing while she endured this? Laughing, loving, doing work he enjoyed among people he loved and who loved him. The contrast between them, the gulf that yawned between his life and hers, would overwhelm her with a pain so fierce that she would have to absent herself. Occasionally she vomited, and that added to her self-loathing. It would have been unbearable, except that she could endure anything for him; until she had decided how they could be together.

She had enough sense of self-preservation to know that attending the American Artists' launch was essential. A few days beforehand Jonathan gave her a guest list comprising over a hundred names. Those attending dinner afterwards were starred.

'You can't be expected to remember all of them,' he said, 'but you might be able to commit the shortlist to memory.'

'I'll try.'

He touched her hair lightly. 'Feel free to look as beautiful as you like, won't you?'

The small, tender gesture was rare as a rose in the desert these days. It reminded her that he wanted a baby. She tried not to flinch. She knew he was telling her that money was no object. It never was, and she never spent enough of it to satisfy his ego. She thought: *Just when I think he's tired of me, that none of it matters any more, he does this! What does he think is going on between us?*

'Don't worry,' she said, 'I know what to do. Now let me look at this . . .'

She curled up in her chair, and he returned to his. It was

unusual for them both to be in in the evening, and strangeness hung heavy between them. The rhythm of their married
life was one of brief moments of intimacy – sex – interspersed
with days of hectic separation when they often didn't communicate. A situation that suited Api perfectly.

There was music playing, but Jonathan was restless. She
kept her eyes on the page as he opened a book and closed it;
did the same with the paper; turned on the television with the
sound down and surfed the channels – and was finally rescued
by the phone, which he took out of the room. She could hear
him wandering about, and then she glanced up and saw that
he'd gone out in the garden, and was gazing up at the evening
sky, turning round on the spot as he talked business. She
wondered which he could see – the blue-grey spring sky
wearing its sprinkling of early stars, or the face of whoever it
was he was talking to. Which was real?

She returned to the guest list and suddenly there it was:
Mr and Mrs Bryn Mancini. They were invited! They would
be there! She would see him and she would, as instructed,
look wonderful. The whole tenor of the evening changed in
an instant, the strangeness and heaviness lifted. Her husband
had given her the perfect present.

Still, she was careful, when he re-entered the room, not to
give too much away.

'There's quite a few there that I know,' she said. 'I'm looking
forward to it.'

'Good.'

'Would long be over the top?'

'Certainly not. You're the hostess, you set the tone. Anyway
you're never over the top. You're the most naturally elegant
woman I know.'

She smiled. 'What about your mother?'

'She's smart, certainly. Not always elegant.'

'And Linda Mancini?'

He frowned, but he was smiling too. 'Why on earth do you
mention her?'

'I just saw their name on the list.'

'Mm. I felt that the nature of the occasion demanded he be there. Credit where credit's due, for my father's sake if nothing else. With a bit of luck it'll be the last time.'

'The memorial service,' she reminded him.

'That's different.'

Api's heart was thumping, but she looked back at the list. Someone else, quick, someone else. 'And you've got Paul and Rosemary Davies, I like them . . .'

Five minutes later she asked: 'And have all these accepted?'

'Mostly. There are one or two who haven't replied yet.'

She couldn't bring herself to ask.

It was therefore a shock when on the day of the launch Jonathan gave her the revised list and the Mancinis' names were not on it. She was devastated. Her hands and face went cold, she was faint with disappointment.

'Oh,' she said lightly, her throat stinging with tears, 'I see Bryn Mancini thought better of it.'

'Yes, thank God. They were coming but they backed out. Now that honour's satisfied I think we can safely drop them.'

Jonathan left early to supervise arrangements. She could have gone with him but said she needed more time. He should go with the driver, she'd order a taxi. In her room she looked at the dress – a black lamé sheath with a high neck and cutaway bodice, the back bare to the base of the spine. A drop-dead dress which she would now gladly have burned.

She could not go. She stood in front of the mirror and tried to imagine what the next day would be like. What would Jonathan say? Or do? And what would be her answer? She would have to say that she'd been taken ill. It was true! She was sick. Her skin was parchment white, her bones were prominent, her eyes shadowed. She was not herself. People had breakdowns all the time, she had had a lot to contend with. It didn't have to be a physical illness, it could be the truth – she had gone to pieces. Jonathan would be sorry for her, worried to death, a doctor would be called; she knew exactly how to behave, she had been there. She knew what it was to be a lost soul.

She put on jeans and a roll-neck sweater and went down-stairs, turning off lights as she went. The rich, colourful beauty of the house which had once given her so much pleasure and confidence did not interest her now; she wanted only to douse it, to slough it off and leave it.

As so often she paused to look up at the portrait of John Ashe. The street lamps had come on and the picture was just touched by the pale glow through the fanlight above the door. She could see his face very clearly, even the fine red line on his cheek which the encroaching shadow failed to cover. Tonight of all nights he looked benign, gazing down at her from a height, giving his blessing to her and her enterprise.

When she closed the door behind her she was perfectly calm.

The Audi was not there, though the MG was. Api drove up and down the street a couple of times to check that he wasn't parked further away, but there was no sign. When she returned to the house and pulled over in her usual place, a tradesman's entrance twenty metres away, only the hall light was on. She wondered if she'd missed something, but Linda's car was still there. She waited.

It was a full two hours before anything happened. She didn't play the radio, or listen to music, she was too scared of missing something. It became cold. Once or twice she turned on the engine to get the benefit of the heater, but the sound disturbed her concentration and she switched it off again. Only once did she think of what might be going on at the gallery, and that was with a sort of dreamlike dissociation: she recognised, but did not feel, the connection.

When something did happen, it was unexpected. A four-wheel-drive car came slowly down the road towards her, the beam from its headlights washing over her for a second as she sat there. It pulled up further along, about the same distance from the Mancinis' house as she was herself. She watched it idly in her wing mirror. The lights went off. A moment elapsed. Linda Mancini got out. She wore a poncho, with trousers and flat boots. Standing in the road she glanced at the house, and then back at the driver of the car, saying something. She leaned forward. A man's head came to meet hers. They kissed.

Api's heart stopped.

This was no social kiss. The angle of the heads, the lingering contact, the way the man's hand cupped Linda's head, and trailed unwillingly from her as she stepped back revealed desire and a reluctance to depart in every movement.

She held her breath. She had been right to come! Whatever price she paid it would be worth it. Her patience was rewarded.

The big car sat silent and dark as Linda walked across to the house and unlocked the door. She opened it, looked back for a second, and went in. The car remained parked. Api could imagine its driver – his luxurious melancholy, his guilt, his longing – she knew how that felt. After a full minute he drove slowly away. He did not turn on his headlights until he was almost at the corner.

Api's breathing now came in a rush, and her heart raced. All her energy returned; she was elated. Nothing was too much for her.

She left a message with the gallery as she drove back. At home she raced up the stairs, putting up her hand to touch John Ashe as she passed. Twenty minutes later she was in a taxi heading for the Connaught. She knew that she had never looked better.

Jonathan, in contrast, looked terrible – white-faced, furious and sick with worry. He rose the minute he saw her and came to meet her at the door, his back to the rest of the room.

'What in God's name's been going on?' His voice was a ferocious whisper. 'What have you been doing? Where have you been? I rang – I rang the house, your mobile – it's unforgivable to put me through this, and treat our guests in this way.'

'I'm sorry, Jonathan.' Like him she spoke softly but intensely, her hand on his chest, her eyes looking into his. 'I wasn't at all well and I couldn't get to the phone.'

'What do you mean?'

'Not now. I'll tell you later. I am so, so sorry, but there was nothing I could do, and I'm here now.'

'Thank God. Thank *God*. You have no idea. You look stunning by the way. Come, I need a drink.'

He stepped aside and she walked to her place, smiling brilliantly, fully recovered for all to see.

Weirdly, Bryn could see the Pals' Memorial from the lay-by where he stopped to call home. It looked dramatic, just visible between the sunset afterglow and the dull orange aura of the northern town. He had done the decent thing, expressed his concerns, left them to get on with it. There was no hint, in its stubbornly upward-pointing silhouette, of the potential trouble it harboured.

He frowned. She was out, or not picking up for some reason. His own voice on the answerphone explained that Bryn and Linda couldn't get to the phone right now, but if he left a message and the time he'd called, they . . . He pressed the button. No point.

He started up the engine, and took one more look at the tower, which was disappearing as the sky around it faded into darkness. He hadn't seen Sam this trip, thank God. Tomorrow morning early the signs would go up and the temporary fencing would be unrolled around the brow of the hill.

DANGER. UNSAFE BUILDING. KEEP OUT.

The evening had gone well, and the little drama surrounding Api had if anything enhanced it slightly. She was very young, and looked so frail . . . It was hardly surprising in view of all that had happened . . . The mood over dinner was sympathetic to her and her husband.

But Jonathan required an explanation. With the driver in front they spoke very little on the way home. When they got back he walked into the drawing room and turned to face her in the manner of some Victorian paterfamilias preparing to chastise a recalcitrant younger son.

'So what happened?'

'I told you – I wasn't well.'

'You don't look ill.'

'Some afflictions are nothing to do with illness,' she said. The words just slipped out of her. She heard them spoken before she had entertained the thought.

'What?'

'I mean, some things are natural. It's a shame, but it shows there's nothing wrong.' She smiled wistfully. Jonathan came over to her and she laid her forehead on his shoulder. 'I'm sorry, but it happens. You win some, you lose some. And this one, we lost.'

'You were *pregnant?*' She nodded against his shoulder. His arms went round her. 'And what – what are you saying?'

'I miscarried. No –' she heard his gasp and put her fingers over his mouth – 'no, it's all right. It was nothing, really. Nothing I couldn't deal with but it was a shock, and I felt faint.'

'And you came!' He hugged her tightly. 'You came to that damn dinner party! You let me speak to you like that!'

'It wasn't the time,' she said calmly. It was like a prayer. She stepped back and looked into his face. 'Not the time to talk about it. And not the time for our baby. Not yet.'

In bed that night she couldn't sleep.

Her time was coming. And soon.

As if in endorsement of this, the next morning she received a letter from Bryn, with two extra printed sheets enclosed. She read the letter once quickly, then again, more slowly, trying to interpret it to her advantage. Its tone was warm and confidential. It began 'Dear Api' and concluded 'Yours, Bryn'. She must be content with that. For the time being, it was enough that he had written.

On the subject of John Ashe he was clearly being sensitive
to her feelings. 'This is all I've been able to come up with,
I'm afraid. I don't think we should take the picture caption
too seriously, but it all points to him having been a bit of a
rogue, don't you think? And if one has a mysterious millionaire in the family I reckon he might as well be an eccentric
one! If you want to visit the site of the Apache Club it's now
a bar called the Krypton, in Romilly Street. A long, long time
ago it was a church, which makes it all rather weird and
wonderful. If I say that you might know it, that's a comment
on your youth, not your taste, by the way. You'll see what I
mean when you go there . . .'

With Bryn's voice, as it were, in her ears, she studied the
photograph, and the printed sheet. Her small, sour trickle of
disappointment was shortlived. There was a poetic justice in
Bryn being the one to tell her this. In a way she had known
for some time that John Ashe was the dark, and Bryn the
light, towards which she was making her way. This made it
all the more vital that she get there. But everything was working
out. She was coming closer.

Elizabeth had stipulated a humanist service in memory of her
husband. He had been an unorthodox man in every sense of
the word: urbane, international, open-minded. Everybody, of
any religious persuasion or none, should feel included.

Consequently it was to be held in the ballroom of the
Delancey Metropole, in which they had celebrated his fifty
years in the business. After the ceremony drinks would be
served in the Park Suite with its stunning view over the trees
towards the Albert Hall. Harry would have wanted people
to have a good time. The danger was that the event would
be too similar to its predecessor, so the services of a humanist
preacher, a nice woman with the air of a strict-but-fair
headmistress, had been engaged to steer the tone in the right
direction. There were meditations rather than prayers, a
selection of readings and poems that Harry had liked, chosen

by Elizabeth and read by friends and family, and memories of the man from a variety of people from his son to the head chef of this, the oldest and grandest of the Delancey hotels.

One of the readers was Linda Mancini. Api found that she didn't mind. For the first time in years she was perfectly in control of herself, the situation and those around her. She was incredibly, wondrously thin. Her appetite had deserted her. Jonathan was worried in case the severe weight loss had been a contributory factor in her miscarrying, and his anxiety was her best protection. Often, these past days, she was aware of his gaze on her, she would look up to find him watching her, and she'd smile at him. She could afford to. For the moment he was treating her like a Dresden doll, now of all times, when she was at her most invincibly powerful. She was no longer lonely, but on her own.

Linda read 'Fear no more the heat of the sun'. When it came to the line 'Golden lads and girls all must/As chimney sweepers, come to dust' her voice faltered for a moment and the room held its breath. Not Api, who continued to gaze up at her calmly. Afterwards she watched Linda return to her place and sit down next to Bryn. She saw him slip a hand – reassuring, loving – over hers, but she seemed tense and didn't look at him. Api smiled to herself.

Bravely, Elizabeth read too, a passage from Primo Levi. She didn't have Linda's expressive voice, but her status and the plainness of her delivery were almost more moving. It was the only time that Jonathan cleared his throat and swiped his nose with a handkerchief.

At the end they sang 'Land of Hope and Glory', because Harry had adored England, the country that had welcomed, restored and exalted him beyond his wildest dreams, with a passion. The ballroom could have seen nothing like it. Everyone sang their hearts out for his sake and by the end almost everyone had shed a tear or two.

Beyond the ballroom the hotel had come almost to a

standstill – no non-resident trade was being taken for twenty-four hours, and the staff and many of the guests stood in the adjoining corridors and rooms. After the final triumphant 'Make thee mightier yet!' the human machine eased back into action. Two of the older staff stood at the door to direct people to the lifts and stairs that would take them to the Park Suite on the tenth floor.

Elizabeth, accompanied by Jonathan, went upstairs first so that she could greet everyone. Api hung back a little, talking to one or two other people, moving imperceptibly towards the Mancinis. Jonathan glanced over his shoulder as he went, to check she was all right, and she gave him a little nod of reassurance.

In the end she was almost the last to leave the room, and found herself next to Bryn in the doorway.

'Api – hello,' he said, placing his hands on her shoulders and kissing her on both cheeks. 'What an absolutely wonderful occasion. Compared to many people here I scarcely knew Harry, but I could tell this was perfect. He'd have been in his element.'

'I think so. Elizabeth put a lot of time into choosing everything. And everyone read beautifully . . . Where is Linda?' she enquired casually.

He looked round, shrugged, smiled. 'She saw someone she knew. Probably already up there, she was longing to speak to Elizabeth.'

The way he spoke about her . . . Little did he know, thought Api. But nothing could dent her confidence this morning. Standing next to him felt completely right. All too soon his sunny confidence and charm, his innocent trust, were going to be shattered; and she would be there to help him.

She laid her hand on his arm and he at once touched it sympathetically, his attention entirely hers.

'Not really the time and place, I know,' he said, 'but I was sorry to be the bearer of rather disobliging news about your great-grandfather.'

'It doesn't matter,' she replied. 'I'm grateful to you for going to all that trouble. And anyway –' she waved a hand – 'he's history.'

'It's still a fine portrait.'

'Yes,' she said. Her heart pounded in her chest, affecting her breathing. 'I'd better go. I'll see you upstairs.'

'Of course.'

Outside in the corridor she turned left, away from the lifts, to the ladies' cloakroom. It was as she reached the door of the cloakroom that she saw them, standing a little way down the stairs. Two strange people, oddly familiar and yet out of place. Linda was with them.

'Linda!' she said. 'I was looking for you. Your reading—'

Linda turned. Api had seen her look like that only once before, strained and colourless.

'I'm sorry,' she said, 'I can't talk now.'

But it was too late for that, thought Api. Suddenly she knew where she'd seen these strange people. She went down the stairs. 'Hello, I'm Api Frankel. Are you coming up for some champagne?'

'Yes,' said the woman, 'we certainly are.'

Api and the woman shook hands while the man stared. 'I didn't catch your names,' said Api, smiling. Next to her Linda was white. Paralysed.

'That's because we weren't introduced,' said the woman pointedly. 'I'm Coralie March, an old friend of Sir Harry Frankel's, and this is my son, Alan Frankel.'

Linda said, 'Coralie, please—' but Api interrupted her.

'So you're family? How dreadful that I didn't recognise you.'

'You wouldn't have,' said Coralie grimly. 'We're the Frankels' best-kept secret.'

'Well, it's lovely that you're here now. Come on up.'

'No!' Linda's voice was sharp. Api felt soft and sweet as honey. Everything was falling into place around her.

'Why ever not?' she asked innocently. She didn't know the

answer yet but Linda's distress was enough to tell her she was on the right track.

Coralie looked from one to the other. 'She hasn't told you yet, has she?'

'Told me what?'

'I haven't told anyone,' said Linda. 'And now is not the time. Coralie, please go. You're doing this for all the wrong reasons.'

The man spoke, for the first time: 'I'm hungry, is there lunch?'

Api picked up on a certain childishness in his voice and manner. 'There certainly is, Alan. Or at least lots of delicious nibbles. So why don't we stop standing around here and go and make the most of them? Elizabeth will want to see you.'

'No,' said Linda. 'She won't. Api, please stay out of what doesn't concern you.'

'But it does concern her!' Coralie was flushed, her eyes bright. 'She's family too. Unlike you.'

'I accept that. Api.' Linda turned to her. 'Al is Harry's son. Elizabeth doesn't know about him. There really is no reason why she should, for the time being. The best thing for everyone would be if we called a taxi for them and Coralie took Al home.'

'But that's mediaeval!' cried Api. 'And you're telling me that *you* knew, why was that?'

'She was the go-between,' supplied Coralie. 'Harry's messenger girl. I used not to mind, but I do now. It's been too long and we deserve acceptance.'

'Of *course* you do,' said Api. 'But –' she used her power lightly, played it perfectly – 'I agree with Linda, perhaps this isn't the best time.'

She had wrong-footed everyone.

'What I suggest,' she went on, 'is that I talk to Elizabeth and we can arrange a meeting at some time when we're all a little less wound up.'

'That's it!' Coralie pushed between them and headed up

the stairs. 'We're going. Come on, Al – come and meet your family!'

Linda caught her wrist. 'Coralie, I beg of you—'

'Let go of me!' Coralie tore free so violently that Linda staggered back on to the banister. 'Try and stop me and I'll kill you!'

Bryn appeared at the top of the stairs as the two of them stormed past.

'There you are,' he said. 'Who was that?'

Api touched Linda's shoulder. 'Are you all right? Good. I'll leave you to explain as you know all about it.'

She gave Bryn a rueful look as she went by. *Families!* it said. *What can you do?*

She took the stairs to the third floor to avoid going up in the same lift as them. In the Park Suite the guests, mellow on champagne and memories, seemed to float on the tops of the trees in their tremulous early summer green. As she entered the room she was conscious of a reaction spreading from the centre, like the ripples from a jumping fish, that stopped her just inside the door.

'What is it?' she whispered to the man next to her. 'What's going on?'

'Uninvited guests, I believe,' he whispered back. 'Of the most unwelcome kind.'

'Oh no!' she breathed. 'How awful. Excuse me . . .'

She made her way to the middle of the room. When people saw who she was they stepped aside to let her through. Their expressions said that they did not envy her.

A little tableau had formed. Elizabeth, with Jonathan at her side, stood facing Coralie, with Al just behind her, like duellists accompanied by their seconds. As Api arrived Jonathan's eyes darted her way for an instant.

'. . . a lot to talk about,' Elizabeth was saying. 'Shall we go into another room? Jonathan will arrange for some refreshments. Api, come with us, why don't you?'

She shook her head.

The last words she heard were: 'Where's Linda? She should join us.'

Scalded by humiliation, Api left the room, brushing past the Mancinis in the doorway. Linda's face was bruised with shock, but Bryn's arm was round her shoulders. Neither of them noticed Api as she fled.

22

2003 – Api, Bryn, Linda

Api returned to the house alone. It seemed to swallow her. A great, gaudy rotten mouth opening, closing, consuming. She could not so much as look at John Ashe. In a day of shame, her misplaced obsession was just one more shame that she could not bear.

She sat down on the stairs, hunched over her knees, turning her back on the darkness of the portrait. All the buoyancy and lightness of the morning had evaporated. Her body felt cramped, as though a drawstring threaded through every joint had been pulled tight. She was in pain, and could find no relief.

It was precious little comfort that she had been spared Jonathan's disapproval because of yet another of her inspired lies. Since the day of her supposed miscarriage he had been less demanding, less dictatorial, more inclined to make allowances.

The phone rang now. She knew it would be him.

'Hello?'

'Api, how are you?'

'I'm going to lie down.'

'Good.' There was a pause. 'We're in shock here. As you can imagine.'

'Yes.'

'To be honest I can't get my head round it. The extent of the deception. Years and years of it.'

'Terrible,' she agreed. She was exhausted, but added: 'And Linda knew.'

'I suppose her chief loyalty was to my father.' Why was he

being so reasonable? 'Our father, I must now say. She was completely compromised.'

She was silent, and he said: 'Api?'

'I'm still here.'

'Mother is quite extraordinary. Somehow we got through it. She was like a queen.'

The simile was striking. It was unlike him to use fanciful language.

'I must go,' she said. 'I must go and lie down.'

'Yes, do that. At some stage – well, I won't bother you with it now, but very soon some kind of accommodation will have to be reached with these people. They won't go quietly.'

She put the phone down and returned to her place on the stairs. Why should they go quietly? she wondered. Why should they go at all? And why should Linda, the so-smug keeper of the secret, who had lied for all these years, be so easily forgiven?

But Linda had done even worse than that. She was a liar and a cheat who had betrayed her husband. And that, surely, would be much harder to forgive.

Gradually, slowly, a little warmth returned to Api's cold, aching limbs. Bent over like an old woman she went slowly up the stairs and lay down on the dark red satin of the bed. She didn't sleep.

Nick had told Sadie, without sparing her feelings, that of course it was likely their parents would split up. It was practically traditional. There would be a period when Dad was mostly at the new house and Mum mainly in London, and then it would be official: they would no longer be together.

This accorded so completely with Sadie's worst fears that she flew immediately to her parents' defence.

'No they won't! They won't! They've got a really good marriage, they love each other, it's not going to happen.'

'Want to bet?'

She hated her brother like this, cool, clever and patronising. 'You sound almost as if you want it to.'

'Just being realistic, that's all. Dad's no saint. He was boozing with some old flame when we met him in town the other day.'

'You're so fucking pleased with yourself—'

'Language!'

She'd left it there, because she needed to get back to her room before bursting into tears. Her mother she could almost accept . . . she was so flirtatious, such a man's woman, she was bound to revel in other men's attention, it didn't mean anything anyway. But her father – no, it wasn't possible. It couldn't be. Please God, she prayed through her sobs, don't let Nick be right!

He'd gone off travelling now, for three months, but the seed had been sown, and she had very little peace of mind. It was true that her parents were seldom in the house together these days, and neither of them seemed particularly happy. Her mother had lost weight and was looking especially beautiful, but as if she were burning up on the inside, rather than glowing in that special way for Dad. She came and went a lot. Sadie had neither seen nor heard anything suspicious, but that was because she hadn't looked or listened. She didn't choose to. To be 'realistic', as Nick put it, could all too easily make it real.

Sadie felt that she was living her life with held breath.

The day that Bryn and Linda went off to the memorial service was a good day. They left together, looking handsome and happy. All morning as she worked on her computer coursework Sadie warmed herself on the thought of them there, side by side. Out of harm's way. Perhaps, she thought, this would be the start of a more settled period. They were due to move to the new house, which was brilliant, really amazing, in a few weeks' time, and there was a big party planned for the end of the summer when Nick got back. You didn't have a new house, and a party, and all those things if you were intending to separate, did you? To begin with she hadn't been keen on the move to the country but she had adjusted. After all, she'd be able to stay in town with Mum from time to time, and keep an eye on things. She could help them hold it together.

At around two o'clock she heard them get back. It was weird – the front door closed, and it was definitely both of them, but they weren't talking to one another. They went into the living room. Nobody called hello. She wondered if they knew she was in, but having left it for a minute she felt awkward about calling down herself. What were they thinking? Maybe they were talking in whispers? Or one of them was upset?

Sadie closed her bedroom door very, very carefully so that it didn't make a sound. So that they'd think it was shut all the time and she couldn't have heard them come in.

The good day had slithered away. Uncertainty was back.

'I'm lost.' Bryn leaned his elbows on the mantelpiece, head in hands. 'Lost.'

'It's not so strange, really,' said Linda, her voice fluttery with nerves. 'Harry was tough. Hard, in lots of ways. He liked things the way he liked them. He never forgave himself for that one slip-up—'

'Slip-up?' Bryn turned to look at her. She flinched. 'You call that a slip-up? A grown man and his mother kept hidden, covered up, for years on end? It's off the scale.'

'They were perfectly happy until quite recently. Coralie wasn't bothered. She had a nice lazy life and enough money, and Al was safely out of the way being looked after.'

'I forget how much you know about all this. It was your little secret of course, wasn't it, yours and Harry's?'

'It was Harry's secret. I kept an eye on things for him. I enjoyed the responsibility to begin with, when I was young. But then it became a nightmare. Especially over the past couple of years when Al's been living with his mother instead of at Aylmer House.'

'You never thought to tell me? A trouble shared, and so on.' He sounded so bitter and dejected, so unlike himself. It shocked her to think she had done this to him.

'I did think about it, often. But I didn't want you carrying the burden as well. There was no point in two of us having a bad conscience.'

'Linda, Linda!' He shook his head. 'Didn't it occur to you we might have worked something out together?'

'What?' She threw up her hands and sank down on the sofa, back bent and legs splayed, ugly and crumpled. 'What exactly could we have done? Told Elizabeth, when Harry was still alive? Told *Jonathan*? It doesn't bear thinking about. And besides—' She stopped.

'Besides what?'

'Nothing. There was just nothing I could do. The whole thing had gone too far. I was stuck with it. And then when Harry died there was only me who knew. Can you imagine how that felt?'

'Yes.' He sat down next to her. 'I think I can. And I still say it would have been better if you'd confided in me.' He put his arm round her shoulders but she turned her head away. 'Who the hell am I to judge you? You must know I'd never do that. I know how loyal you were to the old boy, and he plainly thought the world of you. You did what you had to do. It must have been hell.'

'It was.' She nodded. 'It sure was.'

'Tell me,' he said. 'Tell me honestly. Is this what it's all been about recently? The rushing about, the nights away – needing to keep a place in town?'

For a moment she said nothing. He held her close, feeling her shoulders heave and tighten beneath his arm as she tried to stifle weeping.

'Mm? Is it?' He waited. 'Darling?'

She turned towards him and he was surprised to find she had kept control: there were no tears.

'Yes,' she said. 'You're right. It was, it was that.'

Over the ensuing days Api reminded herself constantly that she had known nothing. That she, the new arrival in the

Frankel family, was innocent, entitled to be shocked and to keep silent. There was one thing however that she felt it entirely appropriate for her to do. She should speak to the Mancinis.

She arrived in the early afternoon. The Audi was in the street outside, but it was the daughter who opened the door to her. In the hall beyond boxes stood stacked against the wall.

'They're not in at the moment,' she said. 'Do you want to leave them a message?'

'No – no, it's all right, I'll come back another time. When will they be around?'

'This evening I think. They're at the new house.'

'Oh?' Api was taken aback; she hadn't realised it would be so soon. 'You're moving?'

'In two weeks.' The girl grimaced in the direction of the boxes. 'It's chaos.'

From somewhere she found a bright, sympathetic smile, asked the expected question. 'Where are you going?'

The girl told her the name of the town. 'But it's out in the country.'

'I see – well, all the more reason why I must catch up with your parents before they go.'

'Mum's keeping a place in town.'

Yes, thought Api, she would be. 'That sounds like a good idea.'

'Look,' said the girl, 'd'you fancy a coffee?'

'Thanks, why not.' Api went in and the girl closed the door.

'I'm Sadie by the way.'

'Api Frankel, hi.'

'Oh yes, didn't they . . . I'm sorry, didn't your father die?'

'My father-in-law. Your parents came to his memorial service.'

'Sorry, anyway.'

Api shrugged.

Sadie made two mugs of instant and led the way into the garden. 'OK for you out here?'

'It's lovely.'

They sat down on a green-painted park bench. Api realised that she was closer in age to Sadie than to her parents. She thought: *I'm here, sitting with his daughter, like one of the family.*

'You came round one evening before, didn't you?' asked Sadie. 'When Dad was here.'

'That's right.' Api remembered the face at the top of the stairs. 'That was when Harry – my father-in-law – died. It had been a long, long day. I wanted to tell your parents in person, but as well as that I think I needed a bit of comfort.' She smiled ruefully. 'Your dad's good at that.'

'Tell me about it.' Sadie rolled her eyes up. 'He's the biggest soft touch.'

Api sipped her coffee. 'This is so pretty . . . Who does the garden?'

'Oh, that's Mum. Actually they have a bit of help these days because she's so busy. She does party planning,' she added with some pride, and then: 'I like your bag.'

'Prada,' said Api, handing it over so she could look at it.

'Wow . . .' She turned it over in her hands, admiring it. 'It's really cool.'

'So what are you doing at the moment?'

'A computer course in the mornings. And shifts at the burger bar.'

'And then what?'

'The course finishes next week, and I'll get an office job. I don't mind what, as long as it's a proper one. I want to earn some real money of my own.'

'How old are you?'

'Seventeen.'

'Good for you,' said Api. 'I was like that. I couldn't wait to get away.'

'It's not that exactly,' said Sadie. 'It's not that I want to be away from them, my parents are great. But I want to be independent, you know? To be in charge of my own stuff.'

'I understand. You have a brother, is that right?'

'Nick. He's in South-East Asia at the moment, thank God.'

'You don't get on.'

'He's not bad really. I suppose. But he's such a cynic. About relationships, marriage . . . everything.'

Api took her cue. 'I'd have thought it was quite hard to be cynical about marriage with your parents.'

'Yeah, well . . .' Sadie looked away. Api sensed a moment when leaving well alone would yield results. 'They're not together as much as they used to be.'

'They're both so busy,' offered Api.

'Mum is. Dad's been concentrating on the new house. So she's off in one direction and he's off in another. I don't see the point.'

'Don't worry.' Api rose, preparing to make the definitive comment in her role of bird of passage. Sadie didn't know her, she could be who she liked, play the woman of the world, accustomed to shoot from the hip. 'Your mother's frightfully glamorous. One thing I have learned is that an affair doesn't have to be fatal. Some people are high maintenance – they need more of everything. I bet your dad knows that. It'll be nothing a little sophistication can't deal with. I must go. Thanks for the coffee.'

She was sure she had said just enough. Even so, she was on the doorstep before Sadie asked in a small crushed voice: 'Do you think my mum is having an affair, then?'

'Of course not! What do I know, anyway? And don't pay any attention to gossip, you never know when you'll hear something you don't like. But don't consign their marriage to the scrapheap if she is – it's not the end of the world.'

'No.' Sadie looked utterly unconvinced.

''Bye now, it was really nice to meet you.'

''Bye.'

'Good luck with the plans.'

'Thanks.'

The door closed, slowly.

The moment she'd closed the door Sadie leaned against it for support. Her head swam. A great hot swelling of tears blocked her throat. Oh God, Nick was right! It was true, it must be. That woman had known something – perhaps the whole world knew! It was probably common knowledge, accepted, a given thing. And she seemed so assured, as if she had inside information. She'd called on Dad when he was alone in the evening . . . she needed to redress the balance . . . What had she said? '. . . nothing a little sophistication can't deal with' – what the fuck was that supposed to mean?

Sadie had no sophistication. She couldn't deal with it.

Elizabeth looked tired, but seemed genuinely pleased to see her daughter-in-law.

'Harry always believed there was a practical solution to everthing,' she said. 'And I'm trying to take that attitude. But it means there's a lot to do.'

'It must have been awful,' said Api. 'Finding out about it like that, in front of all those people. You were incredible.'

Elizabeth smoothed the rings back on her long fingers. They'd become a little loose since Harry's death. 'The truth is, Api, that it wasn't so very much of a surprise.'

Api gazed at her. 'How do you mean?'

'I mean that I've always been prepared for something of the sort. Harry and I weren't either of us innocents when we met, and he always loved interesting women. That one was *certainly* interesting . . .' She allowed herself the merest glint of justifiable malice. 'So no, I wasn't that shocked.'

Api reminded herself again of her own innocence, before saying: 'But the fact that other people knew, that must have been horrible . . .'

'Linda? I don't blame her, the poor girl was in a difficult position.'

Api felt the sick, sour anger boiling up again. Poor girl? What did it take, she wondered, for Linda to be considered guilty of anything? She took a risk.

'That's not how Jonathan feels. He's terribly hurt. And furious.'

Elizabeth frowned. 'It's only natural. He's going to need a lot of understanding, isn't he, a lot of cherishing . . . And he's not an easy one to understand or to cherish. Don't let yourself be pushed away, will you?'

'I'll try.'

'In the meantime, what can I say?' She gave an elegant, one-shouldered shrug. 'The worst is over. The solicitor and the accountant are coming up with a scheme. Money, thank God, is not an issue.'

'I just hope I'd be as serene as you if anything like this ever happened to me.'

'I'm old, my dear. I shan't say wise, because which of us is? But you see a lot in a long lifetime. I've been lucky – a wonderful husband, a devoted son –' she checked for a second before going on – 'now you. I've never wanted for anything. If this – this other part of Harry's family needs help, then help they shall have.' She crossed her legs and leaned towards Api, changing both mood and subject. 'And how are you, Api? Looking after yourself, I hope, after that horrid business.'

'Yes. There's no need to add me to your list of worries.'

'Because if there's one thing I do still dream of, it's grand-children.'

Api couldn't answer, but Elizabeth seemed to interpret her shrinking silence as youthful embarrassment.

'No, that was naughty of me, I always promised myself I wouldn't say that kind of thing, forget it was ever mentioned. Tell me, how is newly married life suiting your mother? She sent me such a nice letter after Harry died.'

'It was good of you to call on Mother,' said Jonathan over supper in the garden. 'She was pleased to see you.'

'It's the least I can do. Not that she seems to need help – she's doing brilliantly.'

'Somebody has to.' His voice was cold. 'I scarcely trust myself to think about it.'

'Then don't.'

'But there they are!' he exclaimed. 'There they *were* – bursting in on my father's memorial service, with no tact, or taste, or even decency, that awful ill-kempt woman and her wretched lump of a son!'

'Your father's son,' she reminded him. 'He's not to blame for who he is.'

'Don't you start preaching at me, Api. If it had been any woman but my mother on the receiving end of that, and on that occasion, she'd have gone off the scale, and she'd have been entitled to. No one would have blamed her. If it had been left to me I'd have had them both hauled off the premises.'

'Just as well you didn't, it would have been in all the papers and you'd have come out of it badly. We owe Elizabeth a lot.'

'Indeed we do.'

'She seems to have it all under control.'

'Oh, they'll be paid off if that's what you mean. That's what they were after.'

Api continued, coolly: 'And she bears no grudge towards Linda Mancini which speaking as a woman I find even more surprising.'

'I don't. But you know what I think. I've put up with those two up till now, for my father's sake, but they're no longer welcome.'

'I'm sure that he – Bryn – knew nothing about it.'

'Don't you believe it,' said Jonathan. 'He'll have known, one way or the other. Marriage is full of those sorts of understandings.'

Linda had rehearsed the scene in which she ended her affair many, many times over recent days. She had told herself that it was like giving up anything that was wonderful but non-essential. It was unpleasant, but it could be done. There would be a period of pain and sadness, the withdrawal symptoms, and then gradually, a day at a time, the appetite would sicken and so die. She knew it to be so; she had been through the process so many times before she had married Bryn.

She had visited her parents for no other reason than to be in their company, use them as a touchstone. But she reckoned without her mother's sensitive emotional antennae. The moment they were alone together she asked: 'Is everything all right, darling? You're a little wan.'

'I needed to lose a bit.'

'Well you've succeeded. You look very svelte, time to stop . . . How's Bryn?'

'He's fine. Very busy, we both are, what with moving, and work – it all seems too much sometimes.'

'Could you let some of it go? Take things a bit easier? You've made such a success of this business but you're a one-woman show. You could put it on hold for a while, surely?'

'Being self-employed cuts both ways, Mum. If I'm not doing it, no one else is either. I don't want to lose work.'

'No, I can see that, I suppose. But you and Bryn need some time to yourselves. What about Sadie, has she finished the course?'

'Nearly. But you know Sadie, we don't worry about her, she's so conscientious she puts the rest of us to shame.'

'We had a postcard from Nick,' said her mother. 'In Phuket. He seems to be enjoying himself.'

Linda smiled. 'It's his great talent. My worry is that he'll turn out to be the biggest success this family never had.'

'What does it matter so long as he's happy . . .' Her mother gazed at her. Linda felt the gaze, but declined to return it.

'Something I've realised, over the years,' her mother went on reflectively, 'is that it really is true what they say about it being more blessed to give. One's so much happier concerning oneself with someone else's happiness. The rewards are greater, I find.'

Linda took this message to heart. She knew it to be true. She felt the truth of it in her parents' house, with all its sweet, understated certainties. It had given her the strength to do what had to be done.

But she had reckoned without the strength of Christopher's reaction. They stood in the garden, surrounded by the fragrant disorder of old-fashioned roses, while the complexities of their situation cut them to ribbons.

'No – no, Linda, please. Don't do this!'

'I have to, Chris. You must understand. Please don't make it more difficult than it already is.'

'But I *don't* understand!' He was so easygoing, so good-natured, it appalled her to see his face contorted with anger and confusion. 'How can you speak to me as if I'm just some kind of troublemaker, when for the past months so much of my happiness has been bound up with you? I will not be ticked off your list.'

'That's not what I'm doing,' she explained levelly. 'I've been happy too, but I'm starting to feel guilty.'

'You should have thought of that when you practically threw yourself at me . . . No, no!' He clapped his hands to his face. 'Linda, I'm sorry . . .'

'Don't be.' She rode the punch. 'I did, I know I did. But that was then. The fact is, circumstances change. A lot's happened recently to make me appreciate my marriage, and my husband. I love him, I don't want to lose him.' She spoke calmly, simply. She couldn't allow herself to be deflected, though every sentence was inflicting pain on someone she knew didn't deserve it. Tomorrow, she thought, this will be done. And no matter what suffering I've caused, we shall start to recover. We will get over it.

Christopher said: 'You don't have to lose him. Did I ever ask you for more than you could give? For a lifelong romantic I'd say I've been pretty bloody pragmatic! And you were – what's the phrase? – up for it. It was no mere fling, not for me. We're friends, aren't we, as well as lovers? Real friends, soulmates? That's what I thought.'

She couldn't answer him. Couldn't say that yes, they were

friends – friends who had great sex, but soulmates? If she had a soulmate, it was Bryn, with whom she was still connected by the past, by their children, by an imperfect love – and by the thinnest cobweb of lies.

Christopher absorbed her silence like a blow.

'Very well. I see. They do say an affair's always one-sided, don't they, and it appears I'm on the wrong end of the see-saw.'

'Please,' she said brokenly, knowing she sounded pathetic, 'don't think too badly of me. You don't know what's been going on in my life.'

'No, I don't have that advantage. But whatever's happening it means last in, first out, as far as I'm concerned.'

'Christopher . . .'

'Don't let's prolong this. I only hope that now you know your own mind.'

Again, she couldn't answer. That expression 'to know your own mind' had a fresh meaning for her. She had always been so sure of who she was, where she was going, what her thoughts and feelings were. She'd been in charge of the game. But now that certainty was gone. No, she did not know her own mind – let alone her heart, which seemed no longer to be the strong and stable engine it had once been, and had become a pitiful thing on which neither she nor anyone else could rely.

Christopher accompanied her to her car, and held the door for her. He looked stricken, quite ill with misery: his face mottled, great bruise-coloured pouches under his eyes. The knowledge of how simply, in physical terms, she could have eased his sickness, was torture. It was uppermost in her mind when he said:

'I am going to ask one thing of you, Linda.'

'Of course.'

'Don't say never. Allow the future to be whatever it's going to be.'

'Very well. But—'

'That's all. Now go. Go.'

He turned and walked away from her, trudging over the gravel into the house. The door often stood open in the summer, and he didn't close it now but simply disappeared into the cool, dark interior.

On the drive home she felt spaced-out, dangerously so. Sections of the journey were lost to her; she was not conscious of having made decisions about speed, or route. But as she drew near to home, the pull of the familiar brought her back to herself, at least enough for her to spend a few minutes after she'd parked in repairing her face and regaining her composure. She was weak and tired. It was hard to say where sadness ended and relief began. But she had done it.

The house was quiet when she entered it. Echoey, because so much was packed up. It was one o'clock, so Sadie would be due home from her course at any moment. She called Bryn's name into the still, summer emptiness. His answering call came from the garden. When she went through she was surprised to find both him and Sadie out there.

'Hello, you two.' She kissed Bryn. 'Leave you alone for five minutes and you're skiving.'

'Where've you been?' asked Sadie.

'Clients. The wretched people will keep having parties.' Linda kissed Sadie. The second or two that their faces met provided shelter from her daughter's glare. But when she drew back it was still there.

'Have you had something to eat?' she asked. 'Or were you waiting for me?'

'We were waiting for you,' said Sadie.

Linda looked at Bryn, who hadn't spoken once. 'Why don't we all go out? We could walk up to the Marquis, sit in the garden there –'

'You only just got here!' Sadie's voice was sharp and plaintive, on the brink of tears. Bryn looked at the ground. Slowly, Linda sat down.

'What's the matter?'

Bryn said: 'Sadie's worried about you.'

She looked from one to the other. 'Why?'

There was a stifling, clamorous silence. Bryn glanced at their daughter. 'Sadie?'

Sadie's face was flushed, swollen with unshed tears. 'Why does it have to be me, when you think exactly the same thing?'

'But I don't.'

'You do, Dad, you're pretending. You're in denial!'

'What? For God's sake, somebody tell me,' said Linda. Her heart went into free fall. For the second time that day she thought: *It's only words, and soon they'll be said and it will be over.*

'You and Dad are going to split up!' howled Sadie. 'Because *you're* having an affair, and the only person who seems to give a shit is me!'

She dropped her head into her hands, sobbing. All Linda could think was: *They do know. They found out. How ironic that they decided to confront me today, of all days.*

It was in her power to give them all, at last, the freedom of the truth.

'I give a— I care,' she said, looking over their daughter's head at Bryn. 'A lot. I didn't know my own mind, but I do now.'

She saw the shock behind his eyes, like an earth tremor.

'It's over,' she said. 'Because I wanted it to be. Because I want to be here, with you.'

'Do you still love me?' he said over Sadie's sobbing head, so quietly that she had to read his lips.

'Yes. Always.'

'So what did we do wrong?'

Sadie exploded, burst up between them like a hot spring. '*You* didn't do anything wrong, Dad! *She* did! How can you sit there and let her do whatever she wants? It's common knowledge, like that woman said, she just has to do it, she has to have people telling her how great she is, she's like a bloody junkie!'

'That's enough, Sadie.' Bryn got up and tried to put his arms round his daughter but she wrenched away and ran into the house.

There followed one of those thuds of intimate silence, hedged in and intensified by the summer outdoor noises – bees, birdsong, a mower . . . the heedlessness of traffic and voices in a neighbouring garden.

As if he didn't know what else to do with his unwanted embrace, Bryn put his hands in his pockets.

He said: 'It's going to take her a while to get over this.'

'Yes.'

'But not as long as us.'

She looked up at him. 'We will get over it, though, won't we?'

'I hope so . . .'

'Bryn! Please, we *must*. We're doing it now, aren't we?'

He let out a little groan. 'You keep asking me for reassurance. Call me old-fashioned, but shouldn't it be the other way round?'

'I'm sorry.'

'I'm not stupid, and I've loved you too much for too long not to know when something's happening. But it was stupendously naive of me to suppose that by not prying and letting you get on with it I'd keep you. Jesus, the arrogance!'

'But you have kept me,' she whispered. 'I'm here. I'm back.'

'Thanks, my darling.' His voice was thin as a blade. 'I appreciate it.'

She closed her eyes, trying to block it all out, to begin again, but the effect was the opposite. As one closes one's eyes for a kiss, to concentrate the senses, so the darkness brought back a phrase from a few minutes ago, like an echo.

'What did she mean, Sadie, "like that woman said"? What woman?'

'Api Frankel came round when we were out the other day.'

'And – what –' she was bemused – 'they talked about us?'

'Only in general terms as I understand it. Sadie's been

worried about us for ages, Nick's been twitting her about us being all washed up.'

'I didn't know that!'

'Neither did I or I'd have put a stop to it.'

'How dare he?'

'Because he can, I expect. He's manipulative and his sister's a soft target. Anyway, she says she and Api embarked on this rather inappropriate conversation, and on the face of it Api was trying to cheer her up – saying what if someone *was* having an affair? It wasn't the end of the world, that kind of thing.'

'The insinuating little bitch!'

'I really don't think it was intended to be anything more than woman-to-woman stuff.'

'Sadie is not a woman.'

'No, and Api's very young. She probably enjoyed playing the sophisticate to our daughter's ingénue. It's all perfectly understandable in context, but unfortunately it accorded with what Sadie already believed. And,' he lowered his voice. 'Let's not overlook the fact that she was right.'

'So the two of you pooled your grievances and sat here waiting for me to get back so you could throw them all at me.'

'Not exactly.'

'Sorry.' There was nothing she could say that didn't end up hurting both of them. 'As long as you understand – both of you, but especially you – that I'm here because I want to be. I couldn't feel any more dreadful than I do, especially as you need never have known. It really could have been just one of those things.'

She could hear how that sounded and wished she could have taken it back, but when he spoke his voice was only infinitely weary.

'And it will be, my darling. It will be – but not this week.'

23

2003 – Api

Unable to effect changes in other people's lives, Api made changes in her own.

She became even thinner: exquisitely, eerily thin. Her light body made her light-headed, high on her own power. She burned bright with a super-energy, like the fragile filaments of a hundred-watt bulb. She had her hair cut short so that it lay close to her skull like the pelt of an animal. And like a wild animal her senses were sharpened to a point – the smallest experience was heightened and intensified.

She was not dispirited, but galvanised by her failures. She felt cleansed by them, free to start afresh with no complications in her way. She allowed herself to be carried like a dry leaf on the current of other people's concern. Jonathan and Elizabeth were gentle and wary with her, uncertain how to treat her. They blamed the miscarriage (in which she had almost come to believe herself) for the mental disturbance of which her exaggerated weight loss was a symptom. Their uncertainty was her protection. She discovered in herself a preternatural intuition; she could almost read their minds, and play them to her own advantage.

Linda Mancini might not have been discredited with the Frankels. But Api fancied she had said enough to the girl, his daughter, to give her an uncomfortable time. The last thing she wanted was to hurt Bryn, but if hurting him was the price she had to pay for his attention, then it would have been worth it. Very soon she would show him what he meant to her. She would change his life. Other people were muddled, their motives and intentions confused, but she was like a hawk, far,

far above them, minutely focused on her objective. She was flying, and no one could touch her.

All day, on the day that he moved, she was there. She witnessed, with a thrill of anticipation, the dismantling of the house and with it his old life: his unconscious collusion in her plan. She saw him drive off ahead of the lorry, with his daughter. And a couple of hours later Linda, on her own, locking the front door for the last time and hurrying to her own car, overcome by sentimental feelings as he, of course, had not been.

When they'd all gone Api got out and walked over to the house. Already, emptiness had settled over it like a dust sheet. It had forgotten the Mancinis; it waited for its new owner with the undiscriminating blankness of a tart turning tricks.

It would have been madness to follow them to the new house, and Api was not mad. Whatever she did these days it was perfectly and instinctively calculated. She walked a high-wire without a net, but because her eyes were fixed on the other side she was sure-footed as a cat.

Instead she went home, where Jonathan was waiting for her. She could sense at once that he had planned to be there, possibly altered arrangements to do so. That he had been talking about her to his mother.

'Come and sit down,' he said. She allowed herself to be led to a chair and pushed gently down into it, though she was not resisting.

'Api,' he said. 'I want to talk to you, and I don't want you to be angry or upset about anything I'm going to say.'

'I won't be,' she said, but it was as if he hadn't heard her. She wanted to tell him that this was not going to be diffi-cult, that he could relax, that she would do whatever he suggested . . .

'. . . you're not yourself,' he was saying. That was so not true it was almost funny. He was so, so wrong. There was nothing spare, nothing false, nothing extra – just her, and what she wanted. 'I think you need a rest – a proper rest. And perhaps to see a doctor, not because you're ill, exactly, but to check that you're as well as you could be.'

'All right,' she said.

'You're too thin,' he insisted, as if she had raised an objection. 'You look amazing, but there's too little of you. Look at you.' He put his fingers round her wrist and moved them back and forth like a loose bracelet. 'You're disappearing.'

She smiled. Now he put up his hands and laid them on either side of her head. He was so rarely like this, it was as though he were under a spell: her spell.

'A little elf,' he said, frowning. She knew that he was afraid, but only she knew with what good reason.

'Do you like my hair?' she asked, passive as a statue between his hands.

'I do . . . yes, I do. Anyway, it doesn't matter what I think, it's yours to do what you like with.'

'I felt like a change.'

'That's fine, I don't care about that.' A more familiar note of impatience crept in. 'But I want you to look after yourself. We don't want anything like this to happen again. Will you see a doctor, please? For me. Make sure there's no reason why you lost the baby, and whether there's anything you can do to prevent it happening again.'

'I will,' she said.

'Thank you.' He kissed her forehead as if she were a child. His eyes closed as he did so, so he could not see that hers, counter-intuitively, remained wide open. Then he got up and went to pour himself a drink. 'Would you like one?'

She shook her head. 'No thanks.'

'I need it. I've been concerned about you,' he said. 'And so has my mother.'

'Elizabeth has much bigger things to worry about.'

'She's very fond of you. You're as much part of the family as anyone.'

No, she thought, *I'm not. I'm not a part of your family at all*

*and I never have been. I'm not part of any family. I'm what I
choose to be.*

'That's all I've ever wanted,' she said.

'So can I make an appointment with Spranger for you?'

'No need,' she said. 'I'll do it.'

He gave her a half-comical suspicious look. 'Can I trust
you?'

She didn't answer, which prompted him to say, apologeti-
cally: 'Of course I can.'

There was no need to fight anyone to get where she wanted.
On the contrary, she had only to do as she was asked. She
had never been more biddable. She made an appointment
with Spranger and went to see him at his consulting rooms
in Cavendish Street. He was a large, voluble, rumpled man,
avuncular but astute, who had been the Frankel family doctor
for nearly twenty years.

'So, Mrs Frankel, you'd like the rule run over you, is that
right? Complete service and oil change.'

'I am absolutely fine,' she explained, 'but I had an early
miscarriage a little while ago and I promised my husband I'd
have a check-up.'

'Jonathan's quite right,' said Spranger. 'These things aren't
at all uncommon, and nothing to worry about in themselves,
but it's as well to eliminate anything that might be trouble-
some. May I say something? You look underweight to me. A
lot of young women are, these days, but it's something that
needs to be watched. Being too thin won't cause miscarriage
but if it's the symptom of an underlying condition it could
reduce your chances of becoming pregnant again soon.'

'I see.'

'You gave your samples to the nurse? Right. Here's what
we're going to do.'

It was comforting to be in the hands of these calm, conscientious strangers. She was weighed, measured, questioned,
her hearing and sight tested, mildly rebuked for not having

had either a cervical smear or mammogram – and these matters put in hand – and told to return in a week for a second consultation.

When she did so, Spranger was all smiles.

'Your weight is well below what's acceptable for a woman of your height and build,' he said. 'But I imagine that will change fairly soon, because I'm delighted to say that you're pregnant.'

The shock bloomed softly into a quiet satisfaction. She'd failed to renew her prescription for the pill, but since her 'miscarriage' they'd had sex only twice, and this had happened! It was all part of the pattern, the steady current that was carrying her forward.

'. . . need to build up some resources,' Spranger was saying. 'Have you experienced any nausea?'

'No.'

'Extreme tiredness? Tenderness in the breasts?'

'No, nothing.'

'Many women don't, but it's very early days and you might yet develop one or more of the usual symptoms. After that, you'll probably find that you never felt better. Still, I'd like to see you again in a month's time and check that all's well. If you're worried about anything at all between now and then get in touch and come in right away.'

As she was leaving, he asked: 'I take it you'll be telling Jonathan the happy news?'

'Not just yet,' she said. 'After what happened I think I'll keep it to myself until I know everything's going to plan.'

'Fair enough.' His eyes rested on her shrewdly. 'It shall be our secret for the time being. How is your mother-in-law doing?'

'She's amazing.'

'I imagine she's going to be absolutely delighted about this. Just what she needs.'

'Yes.'

'Goodbye, Apollonia – may I call you that?'

'Api will do.'

'Api, then. And I shall look forward to seeing you – a bit more of you, if you can manage it – in around four weeks' time.'

In the car she flipped down the mirror and stared raptly at her reflection. It was astonishing, thrilling, that the face and body with which she was so familiar had become something separate, with a life and energy of its own, no longer a servant but a powerful ally.

'How did you get on with Spranger?' asked Jonathan. 'I hope you were honest with him.'

'It wouldn't have mattered if I wasn't. He has the technology. He knows all there is to know about me,' she said.

'And – what? He's given you a clean bill of health?'

'He ticked me off about my weight.'

'Now perhaps you'll believe it.'

'I'm going back in a month and before then I've promised to try and put some on.'

'You must. But your general health, he says it's good? There's no reason for you to have lost the baby?'

'None at all. It's quite common.'

'It may well be, but I don't want it happening to us again if it can possibly be avoided.'

'Don't worry,' she said. She kissed her fingers and laid the kiss against his mouth, as she had seen done in films. 'It won't.'

Over the next few weeks, before her return visit to Spranger, Api went about her business. She soothed Jonathan by seeming to eat a little more, and some mornings she lay in bed for longer. She made a conscious effort to regulate her activities, so that her days at least appeared to be governed by routine. It was surprising how easily his fears were allayed, now that she had, as he saw it, put herself in Spranger's charge. For a man so driven, so unforgiving and lacking in patience in his business dealings, he had an unshakeable faith in the professions.

She invited Elizabeth to lunch at Hardwicke Row, along

with her own mother, and Daphne. It was a beautiful day and they ate in the garden. It was odd, but gratifying, how simple it was to keep people happy. Whole lives – years, decades – could be managed in this way, she realised. Like the secluded city garden in which they now sat, perfect privacy could be maintained with very little effort while all around normal life continued undisturbed. What a pity, that she had not made this discovery sooner, instead of now, when it would be of no further use to her.

The three older women behaved as if they knew each other better than was in fact the case – it was part of their polite-ness to her. They wanted this to be a pleasant, amiable occa-sion for her sake, though Api was pretty sure that Xanthe, whom she had not seen for months, was too bound up in her own new marriage and imminent move to have noticed anything different about her daughter.

This turned out not to be entirely true. When Api left the table to organise more coffee Xanthe followed her into the house.

'Api, I want to ask you something.'

'Yes?'

'You're not against me marrying Derek, are you?'

Api had to laugh. How to say that she could not have cared less? 'Where did you get that idea?'

'It's so long since we saw you. You seem to have been avoiding us. And before you know it we'll be off to France . . . I just wanted to reassure myself that no one was harbouring any resentment.'

'I can't speak for the others, but I'm really pleased for you.'

Xanthe's face, which had been tight with anxiety, blossomed with relief. 'I realise it must be hard, for all of you, but—'

'I said I'm delighted, Mum. And as far as I know the others are too.'

'We must be sure not to lose touch,' said Xanthe. Api refrained from pointing out that it was she who had extended today's invitation. What did it matter?

When it was time to leave, Daphne took Xanthe down the road to see the Suzannah Murchie mural. Elizabeth waited in the hall for a moment.

'That was so nice, my dear, thank you. Lovely to see your mother again.'

'It was my pleasure.'

'And Jonathan told me you've been to see Mervyn Spranger. I'm so pleased. It's as well to get checked up after a thing like that, for one's peace of mind.'

'He said I was A1.'

'That's splendid. And you're off to the Maldives again in a few weeks . . .'

'What?'

'Oh dear, have I spoken out of turn?' Elizabeth looked genuinely upset. 'How very, very silly of me, it was obviously meant to be a surprise.'

'No.' Api was horrified. 'No, I'm sure that's wrong. We're not going away until the autumn, Jonathan's too busy.'

'Wait and see.' Elizabeth patted her arm. 'Wait and see, hm? But if it should turn out you're being whisked off to the sunshine don't give me away, will you?'

'When? When did he say we were going?'

'I can't remember, it doesn't matter . . . Don't worry, he won't spring it on you without any warning, I've trained him better than that. After all, a lady needs time to get her holiday wardrobe assembled!'

Api closed the door. Instinctively, she looked up to face John Ashe, but found no comfort: only the flat, dark surface of canvas and paint. Panic made her vision dance and her heart race. She pressed her fists over her eyes and drew deep, quivering breaths. This need not be a problem, she told herself. It was a deadline, that was all. Elizabeth had mentioned 'a few weeks' – that would mean three at least, until after she had seen the doctor again.

Plenty of time to do what had to be done.

★

She drove twice more to the house by the river. Already it was bedding into its surroundings, looking as if it belonged. There were signs of the family's occupancy: the cars outside, someone – not Linda – working in the garden, open windows. A driving-school car arrived to pick up the girl for a lesson.

On the second occasion that she was there, she saw Bryn. He was walking across the town's marketplace – empty on a Thursday – with long, brisk strides. When he reached the other side he paused to speak to someone; talked animatedly, touched the man's shoulder, threw his head back at one point and laughed. Already, he knew people, and had made friends. At one time Api might have felt jealous, but not now. She was glad. She felt vindicated, that she had known all along what these new people were only just finding out: Bryn Mancini was a good man, a lovely man, a man in whose warm, bright aura you wanted to be. Soon, she thought, all of that warmth and brightness will be for me. I will be all that he thinks about.

She went into the coaching inn and asked to book a room on the date she had decided upon, but the girl behind the desk shook her head ruefully after consulting her computer screen.

'I'm sorry, madam, we've got a big block booking that night. A lot of guests attending a private party outside town and staying here before and after.'

'It doesn't matter. Can you recommend anywhere else?'

'Let's see . . .' The girl got up and consulted a hotel guide. 'There's a couple of places but I need to check the numbers for you.'

The angle of the unattended screen was not so great that Api couldn't read the single word 'Mancini' running down the right-hand column. She took the sheet of hotel notepaper with names and telephone numbers on it, thanked her and left.

So he was having a party. But of course he had been unable to invite her because of Jonathan and their foolish stand-off.

She'd walked by the river several times now, and was getting to know it. Where it skirted the town, its banks picked up the town's characteristics. Near the church and the community centre it was smartened up, with picnic tables, a tarmacked path and a spanking new footbridge with white rails. Then there was the quarter-mile or so behind the industrial area, some of it fairly respectable, the rest little more than waste ground. This was the part that interested Api. It was private, neglected, there were wooden pallets stacked against a wall, and litter everywhere because this was where kids came to get away from prying eyes: to get fucked, or high, or just wasted. The water below the bank was clogged with a mixture of rubbish and loose vegetation. The centre of the river flowed on steadily, south-westward, but where it lapped the messy bank here it seemed almost stagnant. She found a plank with some white paint on it, part of a broken PRIVATE PROPERTY sign, and threw it with as much strength as she could into the river. At once it began to drift downstream, circling lazily.

She watched until it was out of sight and returned to the car. She drove to the last place where it was possible to park before the road turned away from the river, and ran down the path between the fields, with Bryn's house to her right. There was an angler sitting on the bank, and she stopped running, not wanting to attract his attention. He looked up and gave her a nod. She walked along to where the fence was and found that there was now a stile there, and the intimidating notice had been replaced with a smaller, more civil one, which read: FOR THE NEXT HALF-MILE YOU WILL BE ON PRIVATE LAND. PLEASE ENJOY YOUR WALK BUT STICK TO THE FOOTPATH. This made her smile. The first time they'd met he'd said that to her: 'Enjoy your walk.' It was as though he was speaking to her personally again.

She didn't like to climb over, but sat down on the step. She didn't have to wait long before the plank appeared, idling down the surface of the water. She found a stone near her feet and threw it, trying to sink the plank, but the angler called out:

'Oy Miss – don't throw stones! It disturbs the fish!'

'Sorry.'

'And there's swans!'

'I'm so sorry.'

Exposed and mortified, her secrecy breached, she began the walk back to the car. The plank continued on its way.

Bryn told himself that bricks and mortar could not work miracles, yet he persisted in the quixotic hope that they might. After all, he had seen with his own eyes just what those dry, hard materials could do, the shift they could create in the surrounding air, the tremor in the minds of those who saw them.

The trouble with the Pals' Memorial proved this. It wasn't just the building that would have to be dismantled, but people's memories, hopes and perceptions for which that building had become a repository. He felt it keenly. Twice he had been back to see the tower, shrouded now in scaffolding, neglected on its sea of unkempt grass while committees argued and accusations were hurled, and it seemed to him that the whole town was drabber, sadder – that it had lost something not only from its past and its pride, but its hope for the future.

So yes, the house *could*, if it turned out right, be the answer. And almost the moment they moved, he convinced himself that it would be. The house in London had been a happy home for most of their married life, but now it was as though they'd been in a poorly lit, cramped place where it was hard to breathe or move, and had emerged, blinking, into a bright open space where they could gulp the fresh air. The secrets, complications and imperfections of their lives did not disappear, but they retreated and became manageable. There came a morning, not long after the move, when Bryn woke up, looked at Linda sleeping gently beside him and thought: *We're free.*

He remembered every interview he'd ever heard with refugees who had escaped tyranny and repression to live in

Britain, and how fervently they spoke of freedom being in the very air – how no one who had not experienced the lack of it could truly appreciate what freedom was. Now, he was vouchsafed a glimpse of what that must be like: the sense of pressure lifted, of infinite horizons untrammelled by anxiety.

He turned on to his side and eased Linda into his embrace, stroking and cradling her. The familiarity of her body was enchanting to him. Her arms slipped round him, her mouth opened beneath his though she was barely awake. This sublime intimacy of marriage, its hotline to pleasure and under-standing, was something no other man could take from him. It was his, and he would do anything and everything in his power to hold on to it.

Mervyn Spranger told Api that though her weight was still well below the ideal, it had increased slightly and she was essentially well. It would be quite safe now, he said, to tell her husband, who having endured the anxiety surely deserved to enjoy the good news. She agreed, and said that she would. Spranger asked whether she and Jonathan would be taking a holiday, to which she replied, honestly, that she did not know. But when she got home, Jonathan told her they would be flying out to their honeymoon island in ten days' time. She had prepared herself for this; she was ready for him and expressed her delight.

That night they had sex and he was at his most ardent, but she was approaching the last stage of her plan and acquiesced with peaceful indifference.

A couple of days later she took a taxi to Covent Garden – even now she wasn't going to expose the Porsche to the predations of the locals – and went into the Ironmonger's Arms. At midday it was quiet, except for a few old men, or men who looked old, making their drinks last. She went up to the bar and asked for Karen.

'Who?' asked the girl.

'Karen – she used to be the bar manager here a few years ago.'

'Sorry, there's no Karen here. Bar staff move on all the time.'

'Never mind. Do you have champagne?'

'I don't know . . .' The girl's expression was incredulous. 'Champagne?'

'Yes – a bottle.'

'I'll go and find out.'

After consultation with the new manager a bottle was found, brought, and opened. Conscious of her small but rapt audience Api carried it to a table in the corner, poured herself a glass and sipped it. She was glad Karen wasn't here. Nobody knew her. Her anonymity was intact. The few people present might remember her, and talk about her, and never make the connection.

She drank half a glass of the champagne, and left the rest on the table for whoever wanted it. Then she walked out without a backward glance.

On the pavement outside sat a beggar with a dog. He mumbled something and rolled his eyes up at her. Api didn't look down, but took a twenty-pound note from her purse, screwed it up like a sweetpaper and threw it down on to the man's filthy coat.

On the day of the Mancinis' party she was careful that her departure from home was entirely unremarkable. Jonathan was out of the house early and due to spend the next two nights at the office, because he had work to finish before they went away. She told him that she would be out for most of the day, shopping, and said she'd call him that evening.

When the house was quiet and the housekeeper busy down in the basement kitchen, she put on her wedding dress. Once she had left the house she was going finally to enact the process she had mentally rehearsed a hundred times. Secrecy was no longer an issue. She wanted there to be a story. She wanted people to talk. *I saw her . . . She was wearing . . . No, there was nothing . . . I wish now that I'd . . .* She wished to be remembered, for her story to be told, for complete strangers to add their fleeting memories of her as time went by. Her only fear was of being stopped, or prevented.

She had written her letter to Bryn one evening about a week before. She had not laboured over it, it had poured from her like a melody sung on a single breath. Now it was in its envelope with his name on the front, and the envelope was sealed in a plastic travel-document wallet, the one she would have taken on holiday.

On the stairs she paused to look up at the portrait of John Ashe. She was free of him now, as she was free of Xanthe, of Dodge, of Jonathan . . . His image held neither power nor mystery, his gaze was flat. Detail had receded, she could see only dark slabs of paint cast into relief by the window on the half-landing. She remembered how as a child she had linked him in her mind with Harry Lime, how she had played that old record to poor, nervous Lisa up in the attic, wrapping them both up in her fantasy of seductive, black-hearted glamour. Now it turned out John Ashe had been no more than a crook with a pock-marked face. She wondered what Jonathan would do with him. Contact her mother probably. Derek would urge her to take the portrait back, but she wouldn't want it, and she would win.

She noticed that the picture was hanging very slightly crooked; perhaps someone had brushed it as they went past. Holding the bottom corners of the frame lightly between her fingers, she adjusted it and stood back.

She smiled. Who was the strong one now?

Derek met Julian in the bar at Julian's club, a newish place off Piccadilly that affected an air of grandeur and exclusivity while actually catering for anyone who could afford the astronomical subscription. Dark panelling, mountainous chandeliers and distressed leather sofas were offset by a state-of-the-art swimming pool and gym and a menu devised by one of the city's media-feted *über*chefs.

Julian seemed more than usually shiny and self-satisfied. As they took delivery of their drinks at a corner table, Derek could scarcely fail to notice the gossipy gleam in his friend's eye, and took his cue accordingly.

'So what's new in the world of fine art?'

Julian beamed. 'Oh the usual – bitching, cheating, smuggling, double-dealing . . . It's dirty work, as you know.'

'Just as well there are men of probity like you then, to keep it from disappearing altogether in a mire of its own making.'

Julian chuckled and held his glass of malt aloft, turning it, and scrutinising it through narrowed eyes as if it were a rare Etruscan vase. 'I have however discovered a little something that might interest you. Or more to the point might interest your little stepdaughter.'

Derek wasn't used to the term and it took him a moment to realise that Julian was referring to Api. 'You've found out something new about the portrait?'

'I have. Though whether you pass on the information is entirely up to you.'

'Well, of course.' Derek was beginning to be irritated by Julian's air of smug containment. 'Fire away.'

'Simply put,' said Julian, taking a sip, 'he did her in.'

'Ashe? Did who in?'

'The artist. Suzannah Rose Murchie. At least that was the general supposition, the *on dit* among those in a position to have a view at the time.'

Derek frowned, astonished. 'But that's extraordinary. How do you know? Where did you find this out?'

'A strange coincidence – or perhaps it's simply that once one is aware of something one is sensitised to references one might not otherwise pick up. Sarah was checking through some positively antediluvian files on an unrelated matter and she found a copy of an internal memo about the sale of a Murchie painting about forty years ago.' Julian sipped again, for effect rather than refreshment. 'The memo said that while Murchie at that time wasn't all that fashionable, something might be made of the then widely held belief that one of Suzannah Rose's subjects – our Mr Ashe – had also been her Svengali, and that his power and influence over the poor girl eventually led to her self-destruction.'

Julian set down his glass and steepled his fingers, awaiting a response.

'So not exactly murder, then,' said Derek drily.

'No, no, far more interesting!'

'I suppose.'

'As a humble tradesperson I can certainly see the advantages to the vendor,' pointed out Julian. 'The best commercial move an artist can make is to be doomed.'

'I thought,' said Derek, 'that the best move was to die young.'

'Very well, second-best. And she did that, too. Anyway.' Julian sounded slightly miffed. 'I thought you'd be interested.'

'I am. It's a good story.'

'I never made any greater claims for it.'

'No.'

Julian raised his finger to the waiter. 'Let's have the other half . . . Same again please. So will you tell the owners?'

'No.'

'He was their relation, after all. Your wife's grandfather, the girl's—'

'I realise that, Julian.'

'So it's their story too, in a way.'

Derek had had a long day. All at once he felt tired and dispirited by this conversation. 'Not a very nice one.'

'Damn right!' Julian snorted. 'You don't think your stepdaughter might, well, be at the very least – amused?'

Derek thought of Api Frankel. 'No,' he said flatly. 'No, I don't.'

Api walked out of the house with nothing to cover her dress. She took with her only what she needed, she was unencumbered. It was a perfect day. There was no one in the street, but as she started the car Daphne emerged with her dog, and waved. She waved back, and drove away. She had already chosen the music for this journey, the cello concerto that had been her father's favourite. The car seemed to hover sweetly just above the road. Few other people were going her way; driving was pure pleasure. Everything was so simple. She felt a detached affection for the speck of life inside her – it was her sole companion on this journey.

When she reached the town she drove down to the bottom of a cul-de-sac behind a warehouse. It was parking for commercial vehicles only, but that didn't matter since she would not be returning to the car. She made no attempt at concealment; people were unobservant, and conservative – they saw what they expected to see, and were disposed to find a rational explanation for anything unusual.

She had done her research carefully. This part of the river bank was scruffy and unused and there was no footpath to her left – the river slid round the stained concrete rampart of the warehouse like a castle moat – so she was unlikely to be seen from that side. To her right there was the beginnings of a path, but it was several hundred metres round a long bend before the path was tarmacked. Discarded wooden pallets and plastic sacks lay in an untidy heap along with empty jerry cans, an old cooker, split tyres, an eviscerated mattress and all kinds of other refuse. The edge of the water was clogged with more of the stuff, as well as broken branches, and mats of loose vegetation.

She experienced a moment's anxiety that what she had so clearly pictured might not work – that the pallet would be too heavy, that she wouldn't be able to get it into the water, let alone get on to it herself. But though it was hard work, everything went smoothly. It didn't matter what happened to the dress – it was oddly liberating to allow it to get wet, dirty, torn. By the time she had arranged things to her satisfaction she was hot. Her hair was damp. The dress felt like a second skin, clinging with perspiration.

She sat down on the edge of the bank, close to her handiwork, and took the pills. She had brought two bottles of Evian,
and it was more than enough. While she was taking them a
couple came down the alleyway with a collie on an extending
lead. It darted towards her before they could reel it in.

'Sorry!' they called.

'That's all right – good dog . . . What a lovely morning!'

'Isn't it!' they agreed, and continued on their way.

When they were out of sight she climbed carefully on to
her home-made raft, and took the remainder of the pills. Now
she was feeling slow and detached, her eyelids were drooping,
but she was weightless, too. She dragged the plastic sack over
her, and then more and more of the twigs and branches which
were bound together with hanks of slimy weed.

She grew heavy, then weightless. Her last conscious movement was to push herself away from the bank . . . once . . .
twice . . . Oh, would she never be free? A third time, and the
raft slipped its tangled moorings and drifted towards the
middle of the stream.

24

Bryn

'What's she done?' whispered Linda. 'What has she *done*?'

'I don't know.' He held out his hand to her and helped her up. 'But we mustn't let her do it to us, too.'

He bent down and removed the plastic wallet from Api's folded arms. Already it required a slight tug to release it, and the movement set the raft bobbing. Linda moaned.

'What is that?'

'It's a letter, but we're not going to read it.' He removed the envelope and tore it systematically into small pieces, which he threw back into the water, like confetti, or ashes. 'We're going to let it go. Let it all go.'

In the tall, dry dusty weeds that grew around the base of the tower the girl spread her legs. Bindweed had crawled up the scaffolding, making a screen. They had privacy. It had always been a good place to come, and now it was mad.

It was hot today, and they were hot, too. Gagging for it. He entered her with a grunt and went at it like a train. She lifted up her hips and locked her ankles around his back, gripping him tight with her strong, fat calves. She wanted to beat him to it, or best of all for them both to explode together, but they were a selfish pair of lovers, each hell-bent on their own pleasure. His breathing grew more and more rapid and she knew it was too late, that it was going to be all over. But – fucking hell! the earth was moving, the scaffolding above was slipping and swaying all over the place, this was mental—

The boy shouted in triumph, and a spatter of small stones

fell on his back, and on the face of the girl whose wide, terrified eyes could see what he could not.

There was a distant shout from the direction of the house. Linda looked over her shoulder.

'It's Sadie. They're wondering where we are. Bryn – what shall we do?'

'This.'

He leaned over and pulled the raft close to the bank, moving it to where the willow branches provided a protective arbour. Heavily, painfully, he straightened up. Linda was shaking violently and he put his arms round her.

'We're going to look after her,' he said. 'It's time somebody did.'

Gazing over Linda's head he saw Sadie beginning to walk towards them. In a swift, out-of-body vision he was reminded of another occasion when it was his own daughter he had been rescuing and protecting and a strange, lost girl who had watched with angry longing.

Behind them the Eaden slipped sweetly by. On its surface, the torn letter lay scattered, odd words floating away on its shredded paper petals.

Never . . .   *life . . .*

love . . .

yours . . .

Goodbye . . .